PAST
DUE

PETER SWAN

outskirtspress
DENVER, COLORADO

Outskirts Press, Inc.
http://www.outskirtspress.com

ISBN: 978-1-4787-0237-5

Outskirts Press and the "OP" logo are trademarks belonging to Outskirts Press, Inc.

PRINTED IN THE UNITED STATES OF AMERICA

For my loving family: Joyce, Kimberly, Matthew, Channing

ONE

Their contest had been hard-fought, as always. They had each won a game and the tie-breaker had been complete with blazing serves and thundering overheads. Don Turley had finally won 24-22. They sat on the floor with their backs to the side wall as they cooled down. Vincent Langlow spoke first when they had caught their breath. "You really nailed me with that last shot, Ben."

Nobody but Vince called him Ben, and then, only when they were alone. That name went back a long way. They had been good friends and racquetball rivals for over twenty years. "Well, you left me no choice. You give a man that front left corner, what's a guy to do?"

"Yeah, I know. It was another close one, but next time, you're mine!" Langlow looked at the ceiling and smiled. "The years have been good to us, haven't they, Ben?"

Turley seemed deep in thought, brow furrowed over his safety glasses, then roused himself to answer, "They sure have. We've come a long way, worked hard, and now they say we're 'pillars of the community'."

Langlow laughed, "Well, good, strong posts, at least."

1

They stood up and stretched as they walked to the miniature door in the thick-glass rear wall of the racquetball court. There was something else that Langlow wanted to say, but Turley seemed distracted and hurried through the door. "You staying for your usual sauna?" Langlow asked.

"Yeah. I know that's not your thing, but it kind of takes the stiffness away for me."

The moment for intimate conversation had passed and they took the elevator to the men's locker room two floors above. Langlow stowed his gear in his locker and entered a shower stall. Minutes later, he dressed and waved goodbye to his friend as he passed the window in the sauna door. Langlow had been troubled by the contents of the small package delivered the day before by UPS. He had wanted to talk with Ben about the small object he found inside. There was no explanatory documentation, but the simple imprint on the object's top surface carried a unique message. Despite his vigorous play, Ben had been preoccupied, almost uneasy. Langlow wondered if Ben had received a similar object. By common agreement, there were some subjects they never discussed. Yet, he wished that he had mentioned the package. He decided that, at their game next week, he would talk it over with Ben.

Langlow nodded to several acquaintances as he made his way past one of the Multnomah Athletic Club's several juice bars. The club's parking garage was just across the street and connected by an aerial walkway so Vince had not bothered to wear his topcoat.

As he crossed the walkway, his uneasiness gave way to contentment as he reflected on his marriage to Debra following the death of his first wife. He had been so fortunate to have found such a loving helpmate and wife. The loss of Marilyn had been devastating and for many months he could not get past his depression and grief. Then his respect for Langlow Enterprise's chief accountant had turned into friendship and, ultimately, into a deep love. Fate had given him another chance for happiness. Langlow reached the concrete and brick shell of the garage still deep in thought and took the stairway down to the third floor where he had parked the Lexus. He was turning toward his car when a man wearing a day pack stepped out from behind an SUV. In the dim light, he thought the man had one arm behind his back and it almost looked to Langlow as if he were seeing Richard Nixon.

The man approached and asked, "Mr. Langlow?"

"Yes?" said Langlow and then stopped as he realized why the man resembled Richard Nixon. He was wearing a rubber Nixon mask.

Before Langlow could react further, the man's right hand came into view and he fired a stun-gun. Instantly, Langlow was immobilized. At first there was excruciating pain, then paralyzing numbness everywhere in his body, and then he passed out and crumpled to the concrete like a limp doll. The garage was mostly empty, but the man in the mask could not know when some other club member might enter the area. He worked with practiced swiftness. He yanked quick-ties from his pocket, removed the stun-gun darts, and rolled Langlow over onto his stomach. In seconds, he bound his victim's ankles and wrists. He reached into the day pack he had carried into the garage, pulled out duct tape, and covered Langlow's mouth. He was sweating under the mask from his effort and tension. He felt in Langlow's pocket for the car keys. Those in hand, he grabbed his victim under the arms and dragged him the remaining ten feet to the Lexus. The masked man opened the rear doors and boosted Langlow onto the floor in the back seat. He pulled a light-weight blanket from the day pack and covered the motionless body. No one else had entered the third floor of the garage as he started the engine and drove the Lexus down to ground level. Having taken off the mask and looking completely unconcerned, the driver glanced in the direction of the two attendants. They were conversing animatedly and did not even look his way. He swung the Lexis out of the garage and onto the streets of Portland.

They crossed the Willamette River on the Hawthorne Bridge and were heading south on McLoughlin Boulevard when he heard Langlow stirring. He had anticipated this development in his planning and had previously cruised the neighborhood looking for a quiet back street. Now he turned off on Milwaukie Avenue and took Bybee Street west to Sellwood Boulevard. Residents were returning to their homes after work, but in places there were no homes and almost no street lights on the southbound side of the street where the high bluff over the river was too steep to build houses. Langlow's captor pulled over to stop on the shoulder in one of those places. He switched off the engine and reached into the day pack. He pulled out a hypodermic syringe and climbed into the back seat. He pulled Langlow's pants down over his bottom and injected the ketamine. A car turned into a driveway two hundred feet down the street and the kidnapper slid down in the seat. By the time the commuter had entered his house, Langlow had stopped moving and had fallen into an anesthetic coma. The man who called himself Taylor started the engine and merged into the last of the evening commuter traffic on Milwaukie. He had calculated the time to reach the packing plant would be just under an hour.

He encountered only a few cars on the narrow county road as they left the suburbs and headed into the rolling countryside. Through the darkness, Taylor could make out some hayfields and one farm house. The more open land gave way to third-growth evergreen forests punctuated by the occasional cabin. He cleared a rise and saw the meadow ahead. He turned off the pavement onto a dirt road that climbed a gentle rise to a long, dark building. He stopped the Lexus at the far end of the building beside a rusted steel door. Taylor keyed a padlock open and raised the overhead door. With the Lexus out of sight inside the building, he relocked the door from the inside and used a flashlight to enter the next room. Taylor located the generator and started it with a sure pull on the cord. The engine coughed, then caught and he flipped a switch for the interior lights. He pulled Langlow's limp body from the car and, using a hand truck, transported him through a heavy door into the room that had formerly been an oversize walk-in freezer.

Taylor had studied Langlow's habits and movements in the preceding weeks. He knew of the meetings at the athletic club late on Monday afternoons for some kind of a game. He observed that, when the two men finished, Langlow always left first and that Turley came out about half an hour later.

Taylor had made several modifications to the old freezer room. In the ceiling he had added a powerful strobe light. On a side wall, he had bolted a ring to which he had welded a length of light-weight chain. Now, he wrapped the chain tightly around his captive's waist and padlocked the links together. Then he replaced the quick-ties around Langlow's ankles with a longer version that would allow him to hobble a short distance. Taylor had carefully measured the chain to be sure that his prisoner would not be able to reach either the door or the far wall. Finally, he slit Langlow's pants from crotch to the rear beltline and placed an empty pail on the floor. The man was still unconscious from the injection and would probably remain so for another half-hour, Taylor calculated.

Taylor poured water into a dog's drinking bowl and dropped a few Chicken McNuggets onto a wooden platter. He set the bowl and platter on the floor where Langlow could reach them. He switched off the light and closed the heavy door behind him.

TWO

I eased the car down the gentle slope toward the gate, McDaniel's house finally vanishing from my rear-vision mirror. It was quite a place: a Frank Lloyd Wright knock-off in layered fieldstone set off by an acre of manicured lawn. White, railed fences separated the pastures from the lawn. A corner of the modern barn was just visible behind the house. A more substantial low brick wall bordered the property along the road. I stopped my car where the electric eye would cause McDaniel's heavy ornamental gate to swing open. Through the gate, I eased the Acura back onto Pete's Mountain Road and glanced at the checks on the seat beside me. I reread the figure on the top check and grinned in satisfaction. A cool ten thousand! We had never negotiated for a finder's fee and I had only asked for my hourly rate plus expenses. McDaniels had simply called the extra bucks a bonus for a job well done. It must be nice to be rich enough to be generous when you are satisfied with the outcome.

Wade McDaniels had sold his company that manufactured an ingeniously designed hydraulic valve and was rumored to have received thirty million for it. He retired early and moved to the northern Willamette Valley in Oregon to become a gentleman rancher. He said he had picked me, Rick Conwright, out of the yellow pages because my name was familiar from my stories in the newspaper. So be it. I was enough of a rookie in the private investigator racket that any avenue to connecting with new clients was fine with me.

My job for McDaniels involved finding a prize bull that had been … well, bullnapped, I guess you could say. The bullnappers had been both stupid and unlucky and I had hit a long shot. And Julio's young men had played a big role as well.

McDaniels' ranch manager had been hauling the bull to a stud farm when the thieves stopped him on a back road. They wore ski-masks and had subdued the manager, blindfolded him, and smashed his cell phone all within seconds. They cut the wires to his sparkplugs, then unhitched the trailer and rehitched it to their truck. Their bad luck was having one of the trailer's tires go flat. The trailer had no on-board spare so they had to crawl their way to a rural gas station. There, they were able to buy a recap, but an observant employee noticed the unusual vanity plate on their truck. The legend on the plate, "ARCANA", the name for the picture cards in a Tarot deck, was memorable. I came around the next day asking if, by chance, anyone had seen a truck towing a cattle trailer pass the day before. I was told the story of the flat tire and the weird license plate. From there, the police were able to get the truck owner's name. McDaniels wanted to have the police bring him in for questioning, but I thought we might have a better chance of finding the bull still in the vicinity if we held back a few hours. The guy lived in an apartment so the animal was obviously not at his residence. That's where my buddy, Julio, came in. He owns a messenger service and he agreed to have two of his "boys" tail the truck owner the following day. It worked perfectly and he led them right to the small farm where the thieves were holding McDaniels' prize bull. The police raided the farm, made some arrests and, shortly, the bull was returned to its rightful owner. The animal seemed none the worse for wear, McDaniels was delighted to be able to continue with his hobby, and I could bank a very decent profit for the month.

All in all, I've had a pretty good year-and-a-half since the paper let me go. Some folks say our lives have cycles just like the weather and the stock market. If that's so, two years ago was certainly a major trough in the cycles of my life. Justine had ended our marriage of twelve years telling me she could no longer put up with my long hours at the paper and my obsession with the Darmsfeld story. Funny, that's pretty much how the publisher put it, too. I had been an investigative reporter on the Oregonian staff for the last ten years and had even received a Pulitzer nomination for one of my efforts. But the Darmsfeld story? You could say that was my undoing. I had worked on it for nearly a year. Clifford Darmsfeld was a developer who always seemed to have the inside track on zoning variances, property tax deferrals, and reduced development fees. His projects were highly profitable, but were sometimes politically sensitive. Yet he always got his way. The more I dug, the more convinced I became that he was buying off some members of the planning agencies in the area and exerting undue influence on other public officials. My opening pieces were well received by the readers, but drew immediate legal threats from Darmsfeld. The City Editor started heavily redlining my Darmsfeld stories from then on. I uncovered enough new stuff to have one partial breakthrough a few months later, but, after that, it seemed all my leads dried up. And the paper became much less willing to have its lawyers support my public records requests which were inevitably resisted by the local officials.

Well, you get the picture. Maybe I *was* starting to be obsessed with exposing Darmsfeld and his cohorts in high places, but that's what an investigative reporter does: digs until he gets to the bottom of things. The paper told me to let it be and to find new subjects to look into. I half-heartedly wrote a few pieces on other topics, but spent most of my time still dredging around into Darmsfeld's activities. I felt certain the son of a bitch was crooked and I could not seem to shake my need to expose and discredit him. After Justine left, I admit I resumed smoking and spent a few too many nights in bars. Then I got the clean-out-your-desk memo and I was off to "explore other opportunities" as they say in the financial section stories.

It didn't take me long to decide what to do next. I had always been good at investigating , but I wanted a break from big-city journalism. I knew the business world fairly well, and knew quite a few attorneys doing commercial litigation and a few more doing criminal work. I thought I could make a living as a private investigator. Justine had filed for divorce and it did not look as though she would be returning to our floating home. There would be no one to object if I outfitted the extra bedroom on the houseboat as an office. But even before I hung out my shingle as a private investigator, my luck changed.

My older brother, Phil, is a stock broker in Seattle. We are not all that close, but we stay in touch. Phil had told me about a promising stock. I was in a what-the-hell frame of mind so I used most of my savings to buy the stock. I guess that's when I started to climb out of that trough. The stock soon rose like an express elevator and I sold out with a four-hundred-fifty percent profit two weeks before it nose-dived. Another player on our city-league volleyball team had been trying to talk me into going in with him to buy a twelve-unit apartment building. It was a building that needed work, but we projected that with some refurbishment it would have a positive cash flow and a good occupancy rate. The price was reasonable and I said I was in. I put in my stock market profits and ten weeks of sweat equity on the refurb and ended up a half owner.

With a fairly stable source of income from the apartments, I felt ready to launch my new career. I got my license, signed up for the yellow pages, and started to spread the word. The business was steadily improving and I was starting to enjoy life again. I even forgot about Darmsfeld and stopped smoking—for the third time. So there I was, driving off with McDaniels' fat check to bank and a second one to turn over to the charitable foundation started by my friend, Julio.

THREE

I had been seeing a lot of television newscaster Angie Richards in the last few months. We had agreed to meet at the Dragon Fish on the ground floor of the beautifully renovated Paramount Hotel in downtown Portland. The restaurant proper is to the left of the hotel lobby while the cocktail lounge is on the right. I took a few seconds' detour to check out the spectacular tropical aquarium on the dinner side. A lionfish drifted lazily above undulating anemones while tetras darted through coral-like structures. The restaurant, with its motif of clean-lined, naturally finished wood tables, soft black accents, and artfully placed orchids, was already filling with diners. I crossed the lobby and spotted Angie seated in the lounge with its bright red wall hangings and a more voluble ambiance. The Chinese food at the Dragon Fish is superb, but we would not have time for dinner.

She waved at me across the room as I approached. "Angie! Good day?"

She rose and gave me a kiss as I reached her table. "Yeah! Busy though. I'm trying to get everything cleared up so I can get away."

I knew she was going to Spokane to spend Thanksgiving with her parents. She had told me that

13

her father was the principal owner of a local construction company up there and I gathered they were quite comfortable, financially. She was devoted to her parents and said she had often spent holidays with her mother and father.

We ordered drinks: a Mohito for her and a Black Russian for me.

"What time are they saying your plane will leave?" I had offered to drive Angie to the airport on Wednesday afternoon, but there had been some uncertainty about the departure time.

"Looks like five-ten. Can you get away by three or three-fifteen?"

"No problem. Have you had that talk with the station manager?" I had seen that she was chafing at the bit to get out of the field and have a seat at the regular evening news desk.

"Not yet. But I'm going to ask for a meeting in December when I get back. He's been letting me cover when someone gets sick, but I don't see him letting me have Alicia's or Marilynn's slot." She repositioned a tiny sauce bowl like a chess pawn and smiled at me. "There's a rumor, though, that Alicia's angling for a San Francisco position. If she gets it, I should move up."

One of the things I like about Angie is her independence. She knows what she wants and she won't take guff from anyone. In fact, she used to be a competitive tennis player in college and she has pretty easily beaten me the few times we have played. On the other hand, she relates well to people in all walks of life. I suppose that's what makes her a good reporter: independence, determination, and a good feel for people. I like those things in a person and maybe she sees some of those things in me. I probably have too damn much determination. I'm working on easing the throttle back a little in that department. As for independence, that is certainly not my attitude when I play as the setter on our volleyball team. But as a journalist and investigator, I have always been at my best when given a free reign. As a husband, I was maybe too independent and too locked in on my job, especially in the later years of my marriage. That awareness has crept into my mind a few times lately as I find myself more and more attracted to Angie. I would not say that Angie and I are a serious couple yet, but we certainly seem to be drifting in that direction.

Each table in the lounge had a candle lamp and ours had never been lighted. I fished my lighter out of my pocket and lit the candle. Angie leaned toward me and the candle glow highlighted her blond hair and silky complexion. "Still carrying the lighter?"

She knew the answer, but I played into her tease. "Yes. I carry it as a symbol of my victory over nicotine. Kind of a totem you know … strengthens my resistance and all that."

"Hey, Rick, if it works for you …. ," she chuckled. "You're going to be at your sister's for Thanksgiving?"

"That's the plan. I'm looking forward to it."

"You're really close to Debra, aren't you?"

"Yeah. Phil is six years older than Deb and he left

our household soon after my mother split the scene. So my father raised Debra and me on the family farm outside a small town in Montana. Debra's a couple of years older than I, but kids bond pretty well when there aren't a lot of close neighbors."

"Didn't you tell me she had married fairly recently?"

"Yes. She did well in college and kind of surprised our father by majoring in Finance. She worked for a big accounting firm for a while, then got a job with Vince's company as an internal auditor and rose to be the Chief Accountant. A few years later, Vince's wife died of cancer. And a couple of years after that, he proposed to Debra. It's her first marriage and she seems really happy."

"That's great. What's her new hubby like?"

"Well, he's not so new anymore. They've been married almost three years. I don't know him real well. I've bumped into him when our volleyball team played in tournaments at the MAC and, of course, we talk a lot when I'm over at their house. He seems like a go-go businessman. He'll talk about the metal-forming industry and about sports and politics, but he's pretty quiet when it comes to talking about himself."

"Hah! Typical captain of industry!"

"Maybe so, but he's sure been good to my sis and he's nice to be around. A real solid guy."

We finished our drinks and Angie slipped her hand into mine and nuzzled my neck. "I'm sorry I don't have time for dinner, Rick. I've still got a lot of work to wrap up at the station. As soon as I'm back, I'll fix dinner for us at my place."

"Sounds like a winner! But I thought that The Assistance League had talked you into being the master of ceremonies for its charity auction as soon as you were back."

"No, that's the *next* weekend."

"Oh, good! So I'll pick you up at your apartment around ten-after-three tomorrow."

As we left the Dragon Fish, neither of us could see over the horizon of future events, but that ride to the airport was not to be.

FOUR

I was under some soft, white fluffy material. It was not snow because I was not cold. In fact, I was very comfortably warm. It wasn't popcorn either. Maybe it was feathers. Yes, feathers from that big-bellied bird that kept chirping from above me. I had rolled over to better consider this little mystery when I realized the bird was the telephone beside my bed. Well, I was half right. I was sleeping under an eiderdown quilt.

I reached for the phone. "Conwright."

I heard the agitated voice of my sister. "Rick, wake up! It's me, Debra!"

"What's the matter? It's just a little after six!"

"Listen, Rick. Vince has never come home!"

"Hold on! You mean last night? He didn't come home?" I was now wide awake.

"Yes," she said. "I'm so worried! He's never done that before and he didn't call."

"When were you expecting him?"

"He was supposed to be home for dinner. He usually plays racquetball on Mondays. I called his secretary at home last night. She said he left around quarter to four and he had 'R-ball' scribbled on his calendar for 4:15."

"He plays at the MAC, right?"

18

"Yes. Rick, I'm scared. I called the police around midnight, but they didn't even sound interested. They asked if I had any reason to suspect foul play. I said 'no', but this can't be good. Even if something came up and Vince had to take a night flight to somewhere, he would've called me. And his secretary would've known."

I sat up and pulled the quilt around my legs as we talked. "Yes, something's wrong here. Did the police refer you to Missing Persons?"

"Yes, but when I called there, they politely took my information and said it was too early to take any action! They said something like ninety percent of the people show up within twenty-four hours."

"Okay. I'll be right over. Hang on, Deb. Whatever it is, it'll turn out alright."

I tugged on my usual jeans and a pullover sweater and ran down the floating dock toward my car. Their house was an immaculate white-washed brick colonial on Tolman Street fronted with now leafless birch trees. It was only blocks from the park-like campus of Reed College and it was also not that far from my houseboat. Debra met me at the door. She was fully dressed and looked as svelte as ever, but wore no makeup and I could tell she had not slept at all.

"I should have called you last night, but I kept thinking he'd come home or call me at any time. I was trying not to panic."

"Don't blame yourself, Deb. Do you have any coffee?"

We went into the kitchen that gleamed with stainless steel and was capped with pots suspended from a rack over the central island. I watched as she ground the beans. I figured I was not likely to calm her down, so I might as well ask some hard questions.

"Nobody has called, have they?"

"No. I told you I haven't heard a thing."

"I understand. I guess I meant something sinister like a ransom demand."

Her faced paled. "No. You don't think ….?"

"No, not really. But we have to cover all the bases if we're going to figure this out. Sis, I've got to ask you a delicate question. How's your marriage been working?"

"Just fine, Rick. No problems at all. We've been very happy. You're wondering if there could be another woman?"

"Sorry. But that sometimes happens. Not even a fight yesterday morning?"

"No, absolutely not. In fact we were planning a winter vacation over breakfast. I've been so happy, Rick. He's a wonderful man: loving, considerate, strong. "

"You know I'm glad to hear that. That's certainly been my sense of Vince also. Were you here all evening?"

"Yes, why?"

"I just wanted to be sure he didn't call in and you missed the call."

"No. Besides, we have voice mail on the phone."

Now I was sharing her worry. "Listen, I'm going to start calling hospitals." Debra had been pouring our coffee and she set the pot down heavily on the granite counter as the color left her face. I wanted her to remain calm, yet I needed her to be realistic and prepared for any unpleasant scenario that we might have to face. "Deb, he could've been in an accident. Or maybe he was mugged and the emergency room people can't tell who he is."

I got out the phone book and started working my way down the listing of hospitals. I included hospitals in the outlying areas and suburbs so it was a good-sized list. Debra was trying to keep her composure, but she was very distraught and uneasy. I figured the mugger-took-the-ID scenario was unlikely, but it seemed like the best face I could put on the disappearance. It was a few minutes before nine by the time I reached the bottom of my list and I had struck out at every hospital. I did not tell Debra, but my next call was to the County Medical Examiner's office. I asked whether they had received any fatalities involving a forty-seven-year-old white male in the last eighteen hours and gave them Vince's name. There was a pause while the clerk checked the records.

"No, Sir. We have no record of such a person. In fact, we have had no Caucasian males at all."

Debra had moved closer and had apparently guessed where I was calling. I shook my head to her and thanked the clerk for his help.

"So we know he's not injured and hasn't had a fatal accident," I said with more conviction than I really felt.

She refilled my coffee cup and slid her chair around

the breakfast table closer to me. A lock of hair fell over the side of her face. "Rick, you've got to help me! You're a private investigator. I want to hire you. I need you to find Vince for me!"

I set my mug down and, unwittingly, slid my chair backward an inch or two. "Deb, I may have found a cow, but I'm not geared up for that. I work mostly for lawyers on civil matters and for companies with commercial disputes or security concerns. You need the police or, if they won't step in, one of those big tracer agencies that run down missing people."

Debra put her head in her hands on the table top and started to weep. "I don't *want* some corporate agency! I want the police to be involved, but we can't wait for that! I said I needed you and I *do.* You're family! You're so good at digging into things. For Vince's sake.... for mine! Please say you'll do this. We'll pay you handsomely. Just say 'yes'!"

It was not the amount of any fee that was holding me back. I simply did not think I could help that much and, being in the family, trying to find my sister's husband could be an impossibly large responsibility. Besides, if this turned out not to be sinister after all, I did not want to be the guy who ripped open Vince's most private life. But then there was my sister, weeping beside me. I guess there are some situations where you just can not say 'no'.

"Okay, Sis. I'll do it. I'll have to move fast. I'll call in help if I need it, but I'll keep complete control and I'll keep you in the picture."

She dried her eyes and gave me a hug. "Thanks, Rick." She half-laughed and half-cried and added, "There'll probably be some silly explanation and everything will be just fine, but I'm just so worried for Vince."

I held her tight and said, "I know, I know. Now I'm going to work. I want to start with Vince's doctor and I'll need your help."

Debra looked up the doctor's phone number. He was with a patient when we called, but I told the receptionist it was very urgent and left Debra's number. Five minutes later, the doctor called back. I introduced myself and explained our situation.

"Doctor McPhail, we're trying to cover every possibility. Was Vince suffering from any fatal disease or any condition that could cause him to black out or have amnesia or take his own life?"

"Mister Conwright, I can't reveal information that is within the doctor-patient privilege. I understand your concern, but doctors just can't divulge that sort of information."

"I have Mrs. Langlow right here beside me, Doctor. I think you have met her socially once or twice. She will give you permission to make those disclosures."

I had my doubts that the doctor would find that acceptable, but we had to know about Vince's health.

"I'm sorry, but even a wife cannot lift that veil of secrecy unless the patient has approved that in writing."

"Come *on*, Doctor! I'm Mrs. Langlow's *brother*. I know you have to take my word for it that Vince is missing, but please try to bend the rule a little. We're desperately worried."

There was a pause and I sensed the doctor had accessed Vince's records. "All right. I'll do this much. I can tell you, confidently, that Vince Langlow was in excellent health. I gave him a thorough physical quite recently and he had absolutely no indications – in my exam or in the lab tests -- of the kind of conditions you raised."

"Thank you, Doctor. I'm glad to hear it and that's really all we needed to know."

The doctor wished us good luck in finding Vince and ended the conversation. I turned to Debra, "Does Vince carry any life insurance?"

"Yes, I believe he does, though I don't know how much or with which companies."

"Would the policies be here in the house?"

"I doubt it. They are most likely in our safe deposit box, but I've never really noticed when I used the box."

"How about copies at home?"

"He has a file cabinet with everything organized by folders. I think I did see one labeled 'insurance' once, but I don't know what would be inside."

We went to check out the folder. There were photocopies of the applications and the binders for two policies. The face amounts were plenty high for my lifestyle, but were probably about right for a person of Vince's means. One policy was for $500,000 with a double indemnity provision for accidental death. The other paid $350,000 with no double indemnity. Debra was the named beneficiary on each policy. I saw nothing unusual or suggestive in these policies although I knew that if Vince had, God forbid, suffered a violent death, his widow-the-beneficiary would have to be a "person of interest".

I left my sister's house and headed for Vince's factory in the suburb of Tualatin. The offices were in a separate two story building surrounded by some attractive landscaping and set slightly apart from the larger mass of the factory. I had called ahead and the Chief Financial Officer had cleared his calendar for me. The CFO, Dick Meadows, was in his mid-fifties and looked well-tailored in a forest-green blazer and tan slacks. His narrow face and graying temples were set off by gold-framed glasses. He led me into an office rich in teak paneling and told me that he had been with Langlow Enterprises for fifteen years.

"I haven't seen Vince since early yesterday afternoon. You say he's gone missing!"

"Yes. And for now, that should remain confidential. As I told you, I'm an investigator hired by the family. I'm also Vince's brother-in-law. What I need you to tell me is whether the company was having any financial problems. Any especially nasty lawsuits, a sudden cash-flow crisis or angry employee problems, any corporate skeletons in the closet, any … things of that nature."

"I have spoken with Debra who vouched for you and confirmed that Vince has disappeared, otherwise I would not feel free to discuss such matters."

Spoken like a true bean counter … I could see the

man was covering his ass and felt the need to verbalize it. Meadows cleared his throat and continued, "I'm glad to say we are facing none of those situations at Langlow Enterprises. We've only had a couple of executives or managers leave the company and those were both excellent staffers who simply received very attractive offers from other companies. The managers and staff all like Vince. And just last year, one of the employees in the factory had a bad fire in his apartment and had no insurance. Vince saw to it that the family got replacement furniture … no loan, nothing, just told them to go shopping and bill the company! I can't imagine anyone working here would be an enemy of Vince."

"What about company finances?"

"Financially, we are having a particularly good year. The company, as you know, is privately owned, but when Debra was working as our Chief Accountant and internal auditor, she insisted on an external audit every year and we've continued that practice. We just passed that audit with flying colors last month."

We continued talking for a few more minutes as Meadows gave me further indications that the company's financial situation and its business relationships were not likely connected to Vince's disappearance. I thanked him and said I might need to return later to personally study the records, but that the information he had given me was enough for now. He walked me to the comfortable, if bland, reception area in front of the executive suite. He spoke softly as he shook my hand.

"Now you have me worried about Vince too. If there's any way you think I can help, I want you to call me. He's been a good boss and a wonderful friend."

I flipped open my cell phone as I drove away. Debra had given me the name of Vince's racquetball buddy and I wanted to see him next. He was probably the last person to have seen Vince. I hoped he was truly Vince's buddy.

FIVE

Vince's usual racquetball partner on Mondays was his long-time friend, Don Turley. Debra told me that he was a principal in West & Turley Commercial Realty. I wanted to reach him directly and avoid their company switchboard, if possible. Debra had found Turley's cell-phone number in a Roledex in her husband's den. Turley answered my call on the third ring and I introduced my-self as Debra's brother. I asked if there was any way I could meet with him in the next half hour and added that it was very urgent and important to Vince and his family. Turley sounded bewildered, but I did not want to tip him as to why I needed to speak with him. I had Debra pick up on a portable phone and, between us, we convinced him to postpone a mid-morning appoint-ment and meet with me at his office.

Thirty-five minutes later, I was riding an elevator to the ninth floor of the Portland Building. I entered the West & Turley office suite through twin walnut doors and gave the receptionist my name. She notified Turley of my arrival and he strode onto the Kermin rug in the anteroom seconds later. I saw a man around six feet in his late forties wearing an expensive mid-gray worsted suit with a burgundy tie. He smiled as he greeted me and I saw teeth so perfect that I wondered if he had

28

had them capped. His brown hair was thinning on top and I was fairly sure he was wearing contact lenses. He moved with the grace of an athlete as he led me down a hallway.

"Mr. Conwright, I'm a little surprised that Vince did not set this up for you, but I am at your disposal."

In his private office, I saw he enjoyed a good view to the north over the downtown. An enlarged and framed aerial photo of the Portland riverfront hung behind his desk. He offered me coffee from a thermos on his credenza and said, "So what is this urgent meeting about, Mr. Conwright?"

I could sense the frustration of a busy man who had been persuaded to change his morning's schedule without being told why it was important to have this meeting. "Mr. Turley, Vince has disappeared."

"He's *disappeared?*" repeated Turley.

"That's right. He never came home last night. We are very concerned. Debra has called the police, but with no evidence of a crime, they are not willing to move on it."

"I just saw him yesterday afternoon! We had our regular racquetball game at the MAC. I can't believe this!"

"We've pretty well ruled out medical emergencies and traffic accidents, so I'm afraid we must take it very seriously. Tell me how he seemed when you played your game."

Turley hesitated for a moment before answering. "We go at it pretty hard in these games so there isn't a lot of conversation while we're playing. Mostly just raggin' on each other, the occasional compliment, groaning at our own mistakes… that sort of thing. But afterwards, we usually chat a little, share little things going on in our lives. This time, Vince seemed a little reticent. Probably had something on his mind, but – if he did – he kept it to himself."

"What was the last moment that you saw him?"

Turley's mouth tightened and he tuned out again for a few seconds. I cleared my throat and he came back to the present. "We said good-bye after our showers. Vince started dressing and I headed for the sauna. Oh,… and he waved at me through the glass window of the sauna door as he walked out."

"So you didn't actually see him leave the building?"

"No. He said he was heading home, but did I see him walk out the door? No."

"Do you know how he was traveling?"

"He didn't say anything about that, but I know he usually drives his own car and parks it in the MAC garage and enters the club using the skywalk. I assume that's how he did it yesterday."

"Does he have a reserved spot in the garage?"

"Yes. We ordinary members don't, but if you're serving on the Board of Directors, there are marked spots you can use. And Vince has been on the Board for the past two years."

"Do you know where those stalls are?"

"If I remember correctly, they are on the third floor close to the stairway."

"Good. Now may I ask what you did after your sauna?"

"I glanced at a magazine in the locker room for a few minutes as I cooled down, then got dressed and left."

"And went where after that?"

Turley scowled at me. "What are you questioning me for? You said you were Debra's brother."

"That is true. I'm also a private investigator and I'm working for the family to try to find Vince."

"So you think I could've had anything to do with Vince's …?" he demanded, his face turning red with anger.

"I don't think anything, Mr. Turley. We can't at this point even imagine what could have happened to Vince. I hope you can understand that I need to learn all I can about Vince's activities, his associates, where all the persons dealing with him were at critical times …"

I studied him as I spoke to see if the anger was an act for my benefit. It had looked genuine, but now I saw a flicker of fear cross his face.

"Alright. I suppose that's the way to do it. You should've told me you were an investigator, though."

"Can you tell me now where you went?" I persisted.

"Yeah, sure. My wife is away visiting her sister for the holiday week, so I went to a movie. It was a film I knew she wouldn't especially care to see, so it seemed like a good time to catch it. I decided to go at the last minute, so I grabbed a hamburger at Henry's and went to the early evening show by myself. I got home around quarter after ten."

"Thanks, I appreciate your laying it out." I was thinking there is no way to verify where he said he was. "Did you use your credit card at Henry's?"

He was irritated again, but spoke calmly. "No. And I saw no one I knew there, if that's what you'll ask next."

"Let's get back to Vince. Do you know if he had any enemies?"

"No. He's a businessman so I suppose he's had some unhappy vendors or customers at some point, but 'enemies'? No. He was well-liked and respected. He's on the Board of Directors of the Boys and Girls Aid Society, the MAC, a local arts group. He volunteers for Rotary projects. I can't imagine anyone wishing him ill."

Turley was hard for me to read. He was uneasy about something, but he acted like any violence against Vincent Langlow was unthinkable.

"Do you have any business or financial relationship with Vince or with Langlow Enterprises?"

I thought there was a second's hesitation before he answered.

"No. Our two businesses don't overlap in any way. And he bought the factory property before I started my own firm."

Now I came to a delicate question, but one that had to be asked and one that an old friend and locker-room buddy might know something about. "How would you say Vince and Debra's marriage was going?"

"Fine. He was very devoted to her. If you're wondering whether there was someone else, I'd be very, very surprised. I think he was truly happy to have married Debra."

"Did you see what Vince was wearing yesterday?"

"Brown slacks, corduroy, I think. A beige crewneck sweater. Shoes, I don't know."

"How about a topcoat?"

"I didn't notice a coat unless he checked it downstairs, but I doubt that."

"Did he say anything to you about stopping anywhere on his way home? Or about seeing anyone before he went home?"

"He didn't say anything like that. I certainly had the impression he was going straight home."

I thanked Turley for his help and said he did not need to see me out. He stood behind his desk and said, "Listen, if there's anything I can do to help you with this thing, I want you to call me. I'll also call Debra right away."

I drove over to the Multnomah Athletic Club. I parked in the garage and walked all the levels to make sure Vince's Lexus was not still there. None of the attendants had seen Vince or his car leave and the club's manager told me there was no video surveillance in the garage. I identified the "directors'" stalls and looked closely at the floor. There, I found an empty can of "Quick Start" that must have rolled up against the low, exterior wall. Although the product was used to start balky engines, I doubted that any of the club members owned cars that needed that kind of help. Then it hit me that the primary ingredient in Quick Start was ether. I pulled my digital camera from my pocket and took a picture of the general area to show the can against the wall. Then I took a close-up to show the printing on the can. I lifted the can by two finger tips and took it to my car where I placed it in a large mailing envelope I had left in the back seat. If this had been used to subdue Vince, I hoped there might be fingerprints on it.

When I entered the main building, I checked with the receptionist in the lobby and learned that she had not seen Vince enter or leave. That was consistent with what Turley had told me about Vince using the skywalk to move directly into and out of the building at the fourth-floor level.

Something about Don Turley's demeanor told me he was holding back on me. I could not figure out what he was keeping to himself, but the feeling was there. He seemed genuine enough in his concern for Vince, but there was an overlay of guilt, or maybe it was fear, hovering in the air as we talked. I reached my car and put the key in the ignition, then paused. I thought, here you go, Rick. You're starting to see a secret or conspiracy behind every bush. This guy's one of the first persons you've interviewed and you're already classifying him as suspicious. Slow down! Help your sister and Vince, but don't get ahead of yourself!

It was time to check in with the police. I called my friend, Detective Paul DeNoli and told him we needed to talk.

SIX

Tuesday, November 21st, 12:30 P.M.

I remembered that I had promised to take Angie Richards to the airport. I hated to back out, but I knew that the first hours and days were critical when trying to locate a missing person. Besides, the safety of a fellow human being was at stake and this was not just anyone, but the husband of my sister. I called Angie's home number.

"Angie, it's Rick. Listen, something very important has come up. I'm on a job and won't be able to drive you out to the airport."

There was a moment's silence. "Well, I guess I can take a cab, Rick, or maybe Bill can drop me off."

She sounded a little put out and I really did not like her suggestion that "Bill" might take her in my place. Bill was undoubtedly Bill Terazinni, one of the producers at the station. We had bumped into him one evening at the Laurelwood Brewpub and my take was that he would like to have more than a professional interest in Angie. "I'm really sorry. I wanted to see you off, Angie."

"What's your important new case?"

She said it pleasantly enough, but there was an edge to her phrasing. "Uh, I really can't say, except that it's very serious and I just can't take any time away from it right now."

She seemed to accept that. "Okay. Good luck. I'll miss you."

"Thanks for understanding. I'll call you at your parents, if you'd like."

She said she would like and gave me their phone number. I felt a little guilty not telling Angie what I was working on, but she was, after all, a news reporter. I could try to explain things to her later when I had a better idea of how this was coming down. For now, I thought both Vince's safety and Debra's privacy were better served by not discussing it with outsiders, even including Angie.

I was back in the car about to call Detective Paul DeNoli and tell him I was on my way when I received two phone calls in quick succession. The first was from my sister.

"Rick, I just remembered something that could be important. One of the charitable boards that Vince serves on is The Broadway Repertory Company board. Some people just call it 'The BRC'. It's been around Portland for almost twenty years, but it's always a bit of a struggle, financially, for these arts groups. Anyway, they're starting to have some pretty serious money problems. Vince is on the budget committee and he has been trying to see how they can cut expenses. About two weeks ago, he told me he feared that their Executive Director may've been embezzling. He said he was going to suggest to the board that they get an immediate outside audit and he asked me which firm I'd recommend. But he said, before he brought his suspicions to the board, he wanted to confront the Executive Director."

"Did he ever do that?"

"I don't know for sure. I think he was trying to set up a meeting, but that's the last he mentioned it to me. Could that man feel threatened enough to do something to Vince?"

I could hear the quiver in her voice. "I suppose that's possible, Deb. What was the man's name?"

"Frank was his first name. I've met him once or twice at fund-raisers for the theater, but I can't remember his last name. I think it was Robson or maybe Rollison ... something like that."

The second phone call was from a woman who introduced herself as Vince's private secretary, Madeline Hosford. She came right to the point.

"Mr. Conwright, when you left our office this morning, I couldn't help but hear that something had happened to Mr. Langlow. Mr. Meadows asked me if I knew anything that could help. I thought of something and he said to call you."

"Thank you. Anything you can tell me could help."

"About three days ago, a man I had not seen before came to see Mr. Langlow. I showed him in and, some minutes later, I could hear shouting through the door. Mr. Langlow never raises his voice, but I could more or less make out the words of the other man. Twice he said, 'there must be some mistake!' and another time 'you can't think that!' And just before he came out, he yelled 'you'll be sorry if you drag my name through the mud!'"

"Do you know whom he was with or whom he represented?"

"No. Mr. Langlow asked me to set up the meeting, but he just gave me a phone number. I don't think I heard a business name."

"Do you remember the man's name?"

"I looked at the appointments list I keep in the computer. It was Frank Ralston."

Fresh on the heels of Debra's call, this sounded like Vince's visitor might have been the theater company's Executive Director. I called Ralston's home and the woman who answered the phone said he was at his place of business.

"I'd like to see him today. Could you tell me where the business is?"

"It's Automotive Parts & Supplies. It's in a small building just south of the corner of Southeast Third and Taylor."

"Is Mr. Ralston also connected with The Broadway Repertory Company?"

"Oh, yes he is," she said with some pride. "He's BRC's Executive Director."

I called Paul DeNoli to postpone our meeting and headed east across the Willamette River on the Morrison Bridge. I found Ralston's business in the lower story of a weathered brick building in a neighborhood of warehouses, wholesalers, and commercial service companies. The massive underpinnings of an elevated portion of the I-5 freeway loomed a block away. Ralston appeared to be the only person inside. The old wood-plank floors were finished with a brown stain and Ralston's metal desk was flanked by a scratched-and-worn, green file cabinet and a small table with a coffee maker. A desk-top computer with a bulky monitor was positioned behind him. Metal shelving filled the rest of the space. I saw a display board of some specialized mechanics' tools and an assortment of water pumps, fan belts, lubricants, fuel additives, and solvents on the shelves. I shoved my business card across his desk and introduced myself. When I told him that Vince was missing, expressions of puzzlement and wariness flickered across his face in rapid succession.

"May I ask when you last saw Mr. Langlow?"

He reached into his shirt pocket for a pack of cigarettes and lit one before answering. "Well, I saw him just a couple of days ago!"

"What was the subject of your meeting?"

"I'm the Executive Director of The Broadway Repertory Company. Vince is on the theater's board of directors. It was about theater business."

"Can you tell me what kind of theater business?"

He frowned. "How can that be important to your investigation?"

I shrugged. "I'm not sure, but at this point, anything I can learn about his engagements or concerns in the last few days may be of help."

He took a deep draw on his cigarette and I thought I saw a slight tic beginning under his left eye. "Well, it was about our budget. We've been losing money recently and with expenses up and contributions staying constant at best, it's a matter of growing concern. We were looking at ways to squeeze out more savings in expenses and even wondering if we would have to shorten the season."

My eye fell on a shelf full of red canisters in the background. They were cans of Quick Start. "Are you a paid officer of the theater?"

"Not really. The theater has been a passion of mine for years. I'm not much of an actor, but I try to support theater however I can. They give me a very small stipend and I have a modest expense account, but, basically, I volunteer my services. Besides, I have this little business to run. If the theater's budget can get healthy again, we would hope to have a real professional doing the job."

I had brought along an enlarged glossy photograph of the face of a deceased person from an insurance case I had worked a few months earlier. I pulled it from its envelope and slid it across the desk to Ralston. "Does this person look familiar to you? Has he ever had business with the theater or interacted with Mr. Langlow?"

He studied it for a few seconds and then handed it back. "No. I don't recognize him at all. I'm sure he's not done any business with the theater; at least not through me."

I took the photo back by holding one corner and slid it back into the envelope. I hoped that I now had some of Ralston's finger prints to compare to any prints the police could find on the Quick Start can.

"And may I ask where you were last Monday from

three o'clock in the afternoon onward?"

The fingers of Raltson's right hand started a quiet tattoo on the top of his desk. "Listen, I'm sorry to hear about Vince's disappearance and certainly hope nothing has happened to him, but I don't have to answer questions like that!"

I gave him my most penetrating gaze. "No. You don't *have* to, but why wouldn't you? An acquaintance, a man important to the theater company you run, has gone missing. Why wouldn't you cooperate by assuring me you were someplace else at the relevant time?"

"Because.... Because it's none of your damn business! Now leave me alone! I can't be of any more help to you."

It was time to take off the gloves. "Mr. Ralston, why were you shouting at Mr. Langlow in his office? Why did you threaten him if he dragged your name 'through the mud'?"

Ralston visibly paled and started to rise behind his desk. I saw the tic again. As a dramatic gesture, he swept his arm in front of him, pointed toward the door, and said, "I've had enough of this! Get out!"

His bravura swipe knocked a small piece of paper off his desk and onto the floor on my side. I saw that it was a debit card transaction slip and I knew he had not noticed it falling off the desk. I pretended to drop my notebook and scooped up the slip as I recovered the notebook.

"You're making a mistake, Ralston. One way or the other, I'll find out what I need to know."

Back in my car, I looked at the slip that had fallen off Ralston's desk. It showed a withdrawal of one hundred dollars almost two weeks ago. I had worked on an embezzlement case for a good-sized local bank last year and the vice president overseeing the investigation had been very appreciative of my services. I hoped he might do me a favor. I crossed back to the west side and drove to the bank's modern, brick and glass, three-story headquarters building on Everett Street. After a fifteen minute wait in the reception area, I was ushered into the Vice President's office by his secretary.

"Mr. Ellison, I appreciate your seeing me on such short notice."

"My pleasure, Rick. What can I do for you?"

I told him the type of case I was working and said that I needed his help regarding some activity on a debit card. He immediately looked uncomfortable, but nodded for me to continue.

"I have a transaction slip." I passed the slip to him. "First, I want to be sure the owner of the card is one Frank Ralston. Second, it will be extremely helpful to know if there was any activity on the card from noon to midnight last Monday. If there was, I would want to know the location of the withdrawal or the charge. If everything checks out, Mr. Ralston will never even know I looked into it."

"And if it doesn't 'check out'?"

"I'm sorry to be so vague. If it doesn't, it is conceivable that I may have to discuss it with the police. Mr. Ellison, I think my missing person has been the victim of foul play and his very life may be in danger. I know giving out such information is probably not 'by the book', but those facts could be critically important to finding the missing man."

He glanced at the slip in his hand. "You are lucky. The card used was from our bank. That means that I could get the information quickly, but it also would make it very delicate to give you information about one of our own clients."

"Sir, as I said, if this goes nowhere, he'll never know I asked about it. If it relates somehow to my investigation, it will still be handled discreetly, but it could have criminal implications."

He sighed and nodded. "Alright. Give me a few minutes." He rotated his chair to the right and his fingers moved nimbly on a computer keyboard.

It was less than five minutes later when he swung his chair back to face me. "You have the right card owner. There was only one transaction: a withdrawal at 4:45 P.M. It was from an ATM at this address ...." He scribbled an address on a piece of paper and handed it to me, "... in Newberg, Oregon."

It took me an hour-and-a-half to reach Newberg. It was a town of eighteen thousand where one could find quiet living, a decent private college, a new hospital, and easy access to the fabulous Pinot Noir vineyards of Oregon. Before I left, I stopped by The Broadway Repertory Company's theater and talked a janitor-handyman into letting me have a program for the current production. Inside the program, I found a picture of Frank Ralston along with photos of other staff and the actors. I cut Ralston's picture out and taped it to a plain piece of paper.

When I arrived at the address Ellison had given me, I saw it was a Best Western motel. I walked into the surprisingly large lobby and looked for a money machine. I finally spotted one in the far corner. I approached the young man behind the desk.

"Hi. I was supposed to meet with a man who came to town last Monday afternoon at his motel. I thought he stood me up. I waited at the Holiday Inn for half an hour. When I asked the desk to call his room, they said he wasn't staying there and never reserved there. He called me from Seattle this morning and said he thought *I* was the one who didn't show. Said our meeting was supposed to be here at this place and that I was mistaken thinking that he was staying at the Holiday Inn. It looks like our failure to get together may have cost me a deal. I just wanted to be sure he really was here. His name was Frank Ralston."

The clerk must have bought my story because he checked the computer without hesitation. "No one stayed here with that name."

"That's strange. Well, he said he was expecting to meet me here. Maybe he just hung out in your lobby." I produced the photo. "Here's his picture. Are you sure he wasn't here?"

He looked at the picture, then looked back at me.

"What are you? A private eye on a divorce case?"

"I am a private investigator, yes. But I'm *not* working a divorce case. It's a missing-person case. Believe me, I'm not in any way involved in any divorce business." I dropped a twenty-dollar bill on the counter. "Would you take another look at that picture?"

He grinned, pocketed the twenty, and said, "Okay. Yeah, the guy was here. He wasn't using the name Ralston, though. They arrived in mid-afternoon. He left and covered the bill after dinner. She left about an hour later."

"So he was with a woman?"

"Yeah. A pretty good looker. It looked to me like they had certain things on their minds, if you take my meaning. He even ordered dinner from room service."

"What time was that?"

"The dinner order? I think he called it in a few minutes before six."

"Was the woman wearing a wedding ring?"

"I'm not sure, but I don't think so. They didn't exactly act like a married couple."

"You said he left after dinner. Can you put the time any more precisely?"

"It was around eight o'clock, maybe a few minutes later."

"Did he use a credit card or pay cash?"

"Cash all the way."

Driving back to Portland, I understood why Ralston had not wanted to tell me his whereabouts on Monday afternoon. Very likely he had been shacking up with a dolly-not-his-wife in Newberg when Vince was grabbed. He may or may not turn out to be an embezzler, I thought, but it did not look as though he was responsible for Vince's disappearance.

Detective Paul DeNoli was waiting for me in the lobby of the massive, white, octagonal prism of a building that is the Justice Center. Since it was six-thirty, I had suggested that I treat him to dinner. Paul called his wife to say we were working on a case and that he would not be home for dinner. I knew Paul liked Chinese food so we walked three blocks through a light, misting rain to August Moon on Clay. I was glad to have our discussion away from the Police Bureau. This was partly because we were friends and partly because I was not sure how I was going to play this with the police. Their resources were surely better than mine and, once engaged, they could cast a wider net. But they also looked to be slow getting on the case and, if there was a chance that Vince was still alive, I knew I had to move fast and all out. And, as I said, I am at my best with total independence. If I was going to help, I did not want to spend time in meetings and I did not want to have to wait for approval from higher up to take action. I am willing to take some risks as a lone operative -- maybe even bend some rules about private property or about representing my true intentions -- to discover crucial facts. I felt that too close an alliance with the cops would inhibit my effectiveness.

Being just two days before the holiday, there were not many diners. I picked a table at the back where we could have the most privacy. Paul settled his stocky body onto a chair and mopped a few raindrops off his bald pate with his handkerchief. Paul and I first met when I was doing a story for the paper about five years ago. He was a second-generation Italian-American who had joined the police force right after his discharge from the Army. After twelve years of service, he was in line for a promotion to detective when the shooting incident that provoked the story occurred.

Paul and his partner had arrived on the scene of a robbery-in-progress at a liquor store. The perps, two minority men, each had a gun and started a gun battle. The first robber emptied his gun in a wild fusillade, but his accomplice – further behind him – kept shooting at Paul and the other officer. As Paul returned the second man's fire, the first man dropped his gun and started to run away. He chose the wrong direction and ran directly into Paul's line of fire. He was fatally wounded by a bullet from Paul's gun. That was the way it was finally sorted out, thanks in large part to my own investigation, but, at the time, it appeared that Paul had fired upon a defenseless man. Various activist groups joined the fray claiming the shooting was a callous, racist act by a sadistic and poorly trained officer. Paul was suspended and his version of what happened was being drowned out in the midst of the political furor. In fact, he would have been legally justified in shooting an escaping felon, thought by Paul to be still armed and dangerous, who had been attempting to kill him a half-minute earlier. But Paul and his police-union attorney feared that Paul would be made a scape-goat. I was not entirely convinced of that, but I *was* able to unearth a witness who could corroborate Paul's statements. A week later, it was called a "good" shooting and Paul was back on duty. Three months later, he got his promotion.

Paul was grateful for my work on the story and we became friends. Paul has a wild side – he belongs to a sky-diving club and enjoys the occasional all-night poker game with his buddies on the force – but when it comes to police work, he's all business. When my new career as a private investigator has swerved into the area of crimes, Paul has been a source of wisdom and experience: tutoring me about the methods and procedures of law enforcement. He also has been helpful by providing information whenever he could without violating Bureau policies. I always show my appreciation with a nice bottle of single-malt Scotch at Christmas time. I could not be sure that DeNoli would be assigned Vince's case, if it came to that, but I at least wanted to have Paul in play as a liaison to the Police Bureau.

"So I hear your brother-in-law is still missing," DeNoli said.

"Yes, it's been nearly twenty-four hours. My sister has hired me to try to find him, but so far, I haven't got any decent leads. Is PPB taking any interest, yet?"

"I'm afraid not, Rick. We've got plenty of crimes

we already know about to try to solve. The higher-ups aren't going to put any homicide people on it, even for a solid citizen like Mr. Langlow, until there is some evidence of a crime. You've ruled out illness and accident? Or that he just took a walk?"

"I've covered those bases and a medical problem or an accident seems very unlikely. I suppose there is a tiny chance of trauma-induced amnesia and I'll check the homeless shelters just in case. He's too stable, too vested in his marriage and his business to just leave town to get away from it all. It can't be that."

"That does seem to leave foul play."

"I'm thinking more and more that it's a kidnapping of some sort, Paul."

"Any ransom notes or calls?"

"Not so far, but he is fairly wealthy so he could be a plausible target. Any chance of getting a phone tap?"

"Same problem. Until the D.A. or the Police Chief takes more of an interest, there won't be any court orders. If he hasn't turned up in another day or so, they may want to get involved … maybe even the FBI would get in the act, especially since we're on the Washington-Oregon border and you can make a reasonable case for interstate transport."

"My sister is quite willing to have a tap. I'll put a recorder on the line, but I can't do real-time tracing from that."

"Do you have any connections at the phone company?"

"As a matter of fact, I do. One of the guys on my

volleyball team is a manager at the local office. I'll talk to him and see if he's willing to risk helping me out."

"I know Mrs. Langlow has plugged into Missing Persons. Any developments there?"

"No. Up to now, all they've done is enter his personal data into their computer."

We had finished our moo goo gai pan and mu shu pork when Paul checked his watch. "I've still got some work to finish tonight. Let me know if there's any information I can help you with. I'll talk to my captain to see if he can spare me or someone else to look at this. I've been working missing persons occasionally in the last six months so I think I can at least get a bulletin out describing his car. You said it was a 400-series Lexus?"

"Yeah, a 2009 metallic green."

"If the captain agrees we can get more actively involved, you'll have to give us what you have so far, even if it has all dead-ended."

"No problem. There is one thing you can do now if you're willing." I reached for a paper bag I had brought along. "I've got a glossy photo print and a can of carburetor spray for quick starting. Could you have a techie check them to see if there are any usable prints? If there are and the prints are the same, I'll give you a name to run through the database to see if they belong to a certain person. Right now, I think this person has a solid alibi, but I'd like to remove any lingering doubt."

"Hmm. Want to hold back the name, huh? Well, that's a little sketchy, but yeah, I can do that for you. "

I handed him the bag with the photo and the can.

"Thanks, Paul! I'll keep in touch."

We had just parted on the sidewalk, when Paul turned back and said, "Rick, have you paid those damn parking tickets yet?"

I don't know why I hate to get parking tickets. It seems like I always have something urgent that I'm working on that takes longer than I had anticipated and the meter maid gets to my car just a couple of minutes before I do. And, yes, there have been a couple of times when I could not find a spot and got caught in a loading zone. Anyway, it ticks me off that the city doesn't have softer-hearted meter maids or a few less restricted parking zones. The result seems to be my major procrastination in paying the fines. I have never planned to stiff the city indefinitely, but it's just not something I am inspired to do in a timely fashion.

"I'll take care of them. It just isn't at the top of my to-do list."

"Yeah, right. But you got to understand. Our homicide captain is not the world's most flexible person. If we're going to try to work together and he checks you out on the PPB data base, you'll get his back up right from the start."

"Sheesh! Okay, I'll square the tickets."

"Do that, pal," said DeNoli with a wave and a grin as he headed back to the Justice Center.

I called Debra on my cell phone to make sure there was nothing new at her end. There was not. I told her I had talked with Meadows and Turley and that Ralston seemed to have an alibi. She had canceled her errands and an appointment and was staying at home. I told her to keep the doors and windows locked. I did not know what had happened or why, but I did not want Debra to be unnecessarily vulnerable. I said I would buy a telephone recording device tomorrow and hook it up to her line.

I had just finished speaking with my sister when I noticed that I had a voice message on my cell. I retrieved the message and what I heard told me what my first order of business would be in the morning.

SEVEN

Nathan Alexander Berriman settled back in the velour chair by the window and chose the Metro and the classified sections of The Oregonian to begin his morning ritual of studying the local news and reading the personals. His last con, in Cincinnati, had netted him enough to live comfortably at the DeLux hotel in downtown Portland for at least a couple of weeks. He had negotiated a weekly rate that included a light breakfast delivered by room service. But his tab was running and, given the lifestyle he craved, his funds would not last much longer. It was time to move on, perhaps to Seattle, unless he could turn up a mark in Portland. Nate, as he was known to his peers, saw nothing of interest on the front page and paused to take a swallow of coffee and a bite of croissant. On page two, his eye fell on a photo of a handsome middle-aged man. The accompanying story was about a prominent businessman who had disappeared. The man, one Vincent Langlow, had left the Multnomah Athletic Club on the preceding Monday afternoon and had never been seen again. His car was missing from the Club's parking garage suggesting that he had driven away of his own volition. But the article stated that those who knew him well thought that it was highly unlikely he would have walked out on a strong marriage and his thriving business. The implication was that he might have been abducted or that he and his vehicle had been car-jacked.

Nate had always considered himself to be a creative con artist, one who could spot opportunities where others failed to see the possibilities in a new situation. He read the article a second time, took a deep draw on his cigarette and leaned back in the chair. He closed his eyes, and thought for several minutes. The man was wealthy and had gone missing. Kidnapping was a plausible explanation. If a ransom demand were made quickly and for a reasonable amount, there was a good chance it would be paid. Nate could see there were several risks. The man might be found dead, before Nate had collected the money. Or, the real kidnapper might have already made a demand. Or, the wife might call in the police who would lay a trap. If he were to attempt it, he would have to move quickly, foresee every contingency, and minimize the risks. He let the cigarette smoke slowly drift out of his mouth. His brown eyes narrowed under auburn brows as he concentrated.

Nate had gained an easy confidence in his ability to project any given persona by acting in high school plays. After graduation, he worked for a bookie laying off bets at the local track. There, he learned a lot about human nature. And, at the track, he met a con man who taught him some of the finer points of the trade. He felt a high when he pulled off his first modest scam and he never looked back. Nate missed out on college, but he possessed a cunning intelligence. He had been reasonably successful as a small-time grifter, but now he wanted a bigger challenge. It was time to move up, to reach the next level: greater challenges and definitely bigger rewards. He had always tried to plan his scams to satisfy the old rule: if the mark does not realize he has been taken, the con artist will never get caught. No one is perfect and, three times over the years, his mark had tumbled to the game. Nate had come under suspicion on those occasions and he had been arrested twice, but charges had been dismissed both times.

Nate well understood that separating a sucker from his money depended on finesse and illusion rather than weapons or violence. Now he would be moving up to a much higher level of risk. Langlow's family would soon know they had been taken, and he had to be extremely careful not to cross the line into the category of bodily-harm crimes that carried much stiffer sentences. The scheme he now considered meant he would have to simulate a kidnapping, but even that would move him closer to that danger zone.

He thought about the problem for another two hours as he tested different scenarios in his mind. He suspected that the victim's home phones would be tapped, so the first problem would be how to deliver the ransom demand. Another critical piece was to have the person delivering the money come alone. And he would have to offer convincing proof that the victim was alive and would be promptly released. He also would have to be sure the money did not come with a hidden transmitter to track him once he took possession. He also needed an iron-clad getaway plan. By early afternoon, he had enough of it planned that he took a sheet of paper from the desk and started making a list of things he would need. Then, it was time to line up an accomplice and gather the needed props and devices.

The partner Nate required would have to be skilled with disguises and make-up. Three nights earlier, he was having a Spanish coffee at Huber's when he ran into an old acquaintance in the game, Howard Despaile. Howie was a good six feet tall and looked somewhat younger than his fifty-five years *and* he was a master at changing his appearance. They had exchanged cell phone numbers and he answered Nate's call on the third ring. They arranged to meet in half an hour at The Elephant delicatessen.

It was after the lunch-hour rush and they were able to find a table away from others. The staff still made sandwiches with their trade-mark exuberance behind the glass-fronted coolers full of cold cuts, cheeses and salads, but the boisterous atmosphere of midday was, by then, somewhat tempered. The two men carried their sandwiches to the table and settled into their chairs with anticipation.

"So, Nate," Howie began, "what's given you this sudden woody?"

"It's a high-risk, high-reward play, Howie."

"It's been slow for me lately. Let's hear it."

"You read about this prominent citizen who's gone missing?"

"Yeah. Saw it in the paper. Langley or something like that?"

"That's the guy, Langlow. It looks a lot like a kidnapping and the man's rich. Suppose we put in a demand for ransom. If we're lucky and we move fast, they deliver the money to us and we're out of town, before they learn otherwise."

"I dunno. A lot of things could go wrong. Have you worked it out?"

"Yeah, I have it pretty much thought through. I need one other person. I'll handle the contacts and collect the money. You would have no greater risk than I and would have a simpler, more passive role. I think our chances of getting the money quickly are best if we can hit them for no more than a hundred K. Our expenses should be low. Of the net, you can take thirty percent. Other than helping me with getting the props and the physical set-up, all you have to do is play the role of a bound and gagged Vincent Langlow.

"Nate, this could get heavy. I'll need forty percent."

"You're good, Howie, but this is my mark and my play. I'll give you a third off the top."

Howie refolded his napkin and scratched his ear, then looked hard at Nate. "I guess that's reasonable enough. Walk me through your plan and let's talk about that 'risk' part."

Nate ran his fingers through his coppery brown hair. "We have to contact the wife without using the phone. We have to make sure whoever brings the money comes alone and that the cops are not waiting in the wings. We have to find a house or a building that's a little bit isolated and that we can get into and have to ourselves for a few hours. Where you come in is we have to convince whoever brings the money that this guy, Langlow is alive and will be released ... the 'you see what you want to see' illusion. And, for sure, we both have to have the time and the means to get away."

"Still sounds like a lot of things have to break our way."

"I won't deny that, but I've thought of ways we can stack the odds in our favor. But we'll have to work fast to have this ready to go by tomorrow tonight."

"Give me the details and I'll decide if I'm in."

Nate showed Howie the list he had made and went to get them each a second bottle of beer. At the end of another half hour's conversation, he had a new partner.

They had agreed to pay cash for everything. Nate bought the tools at a Home Depot. He found a pre-paid cell phone vendor in a shopping mall, and a ski mask at a sporting goods store. At a hardware store, he bought lengths of electrical wire, an outdoor flood-light switched on by a motion-detector, and duct tape. Howie picked up the camping cot and the camp light at a Big 5 Sporting Goods store. A yard goods retail warehouse supplied Howie with several yards of heavy black canvas. Nate stopped at a Radio Shack to purchase the batteries and an inexpensive modem that would serve as the electronics box. They went to a Target to buy an inexpensive bicycle, cross-trainers for each of them, and latex gloves. In the toy department, they found a child's rubber stamp set.

Knowing where to buy the canister turned out to be a little harder. They finally thought of going to a medical supply store. Nate arrived just before it closed for the day. The clerk told Nate that the pressurized gases were in a room at the rear and motioned for Nate to follow him.

"Do you have an account here?" the clerk asked when they entered the room where tanks of various sizes were stowed vertically in cradles.

"No. I think my mother has a regular service, but I'm in town for a visit and I just thought it would be a good idea for her to have a small extra one in the house."

"So you want the fifteen pound size? Or even smaller?" he gestured toward the two sizes.

The pounds meant nothing to Nate, but he saw a size that would work and pointed to it. "That small one there."

"What kind of a regulator does she use?"

Nate vaguely remembered that regulators were attached to scuba diver's tanks, but that was the extent of his knowledge. "To tell you the truth, I didn't check. Isn't there a universal fitting?"

"Well this tank is compatible with almost all regulators. Tell you what. If this doesn't fit, get the specs on what she has and bring it back. We'll get you the correct one."

"Thanks, I should've thought to look."

While Nate was getting the canister, Howie went to a store that sold hi-tech security devices and picked up a "bug detector". This piece of equipment was expensive, but it could locate a microphone or radio transmitter no matter how small or how carefully concealed. It would be of critical importance in reducing their risk.

They got back together at a Burgerville at the Oregon Business Park exit off of I-5 south of Portland where they ordered meals.

"Now we need to find a place," Nate said. "Last week I was thinking of working the earnest-money-on-the-house-under-construction scam and I was looking for locations where developers were still completing houses. I found a neighborhood in a burb called Sherwood where there are many houses being built. Several of them are already framed and have the drywall in. As soon as it's dark, we'll drive out there."

"What about security, hard-wired and otherwise?"

"The houses are at too early a stage for there to be anything operational inside, but there definitely could be a roving patrol. We'll have to see if we can spot one and figure out how often he drives by."

"How do we get inside?" asked Howie, still dubious.

"Some of the places still don't have the windows in or the doors on. So long as the location is not too close to occupied houses, we should be fine."

It was Howie who favored a mask over make-up.

"Tell me again how this mask thing works," said Nate.

"I went to this Halloween party with some mugs I met and their women. One couple came with rubber masks and wigs so that they switched identities. The woman looked like her partner and he looked like her. I thought the masks were fantastic! I asked them who made the masks. They gave me a name of this weird novelty place and, a couple of days later, I went there. I was thinking you never know when a place like that might come in handy in our racket. The guy works from photos and has a pretty slick molding machine. The masks aren't cheap, but he makes them quickly and he's good at it."

"What will we do for the photo?"

"I'll take a digital picture of the newspaper photo. I can enlarge and enhance it on my laptop. We can print it at any drugstore. If there isn't time to do that to-night, I'll do it in the morning and give this novelty guy the picture. We'll have the mask by late afternoon."

"What if he recognizes the guy in the picture from the newspaper?"

"Not likely. The newspaper photo was small and black and white. Besides this guy's is sort of a sleaze-bag. I doubt he'd give a damn."

"Okay. It's dark enough now that we can go case that construction site. After that, we have to print that demand letter. We can get that done at your place. Then we'll take it out to the good Mr. Langlow's house."

It took them nearly forty minutes to drive to the town of Sherwood to the southwest of Portland. Nate drove around the perimeter of the construction area and noted down street names and intersections. Then he drove ten blocks away from the development on a street that intersected with Highway 99. A block short off the highway, he showed Howie the place where they would rendezvous when it was over. They returned to the construction zone and parked on the closest street that had inhabited homes. They walked silently through the building sites, watchful for security patrols, until they found a house that was fully roughed in. There was no door or porch and they climbed an inclined plank to enter. The drywall had already been installed.

"This will be perfect. It's far enough from the completed houses that no one could see or hear us and it has the walls up. Tomorrow night, you'll be in that bedroom there. We'll cut the hole in this wall and attach the bomb on the far wall. We'll only have to blanket two windows."

"So where are you going to picket whoever brings the money?" asked Howie.

"They've already got the street lights functioning. I'll get him to stand by that one half a block to the south. I think I can convince him to let me tape his wrists so he's hugging the light post."

"I like it. I think this has a damn good chance of working!"

Howie lived in a rented a house in Scapoose, twenty miles west of Portland on Highway 30. They worked out the wording of the demand. Wearing the gloves, they used the stamp set to spell out the demand message. That process took them half an hour.

"We sure as hell can't just knock on her door and introduce ourselves. You said we're going to the house, so exactly how *do* we deliver this, Nate?"

"We wait here another thirty minutes so it'll be well after midnight when we get there. Then you keep watch from the car and I'll go around the house until I locate the kitchen. I tape this facing inward on the outside of the kitchen window. She'll see it first thing in the morning and that will leave her enough time to get the money."

"You think she'll come herself?"

"I dunno. I kind of doubt it. If she's willing to play ball, I think she'll send a man friend. That's almost better from our standpoint. She might have ways of communicating with her husband or spotting the imposter that we wouldn't even suspect."

"What if whoever comes doesn't think it's him?"

"Whoever it is will want to believe it's him and we have to create the illusion so there's no doubt! But if she thinks we're faking it, we let her take her marbles and go home. I hate to pass up the dough, but we're staying clear of armed robbery!"

Howie brushed the stubble on his jaw with his hand. "And what if the guy she sends with the money has some trick question to ask me? One that only the real guy would know the answer to? Even with tape over my mouth, he would expect some response."

"I tell him that we had to heavily sedate Langlow to move him around. All you have to do is just moan occasionally and move a little, but don't sound like you're awake enough to react to any questions."

Nate dressed in black and wore the ski mask and the gloves as he left the car. If Howie saw a police patrol or security guard approaching he would call Nate on his cell phone. Nate set his ringer to "vibrate" and crept through some shrubbery toward the Langlow's back yard. He had almost reached the lawn when he tripped over one of the wires supporting a birch sapling. He stumbled forward and pitched into a sawtooth brick border between the lawn and the plantings. A brick lacerated his forearm and he involuntarily gave a low cry of pain. He jumped back into the cover of the shrubs and waited to make sure he had not alerted anyone inside the house. After several minutes, he ventured out on the lawn and approached a likely window on the rear wall. There were Venetian blinds on the inside, but they were not shuttered. Nate cupped his hand over the lens of his flashlight and turned it on for a few seconds. Through the blinds he could see he was looking into the kitchen. He paused, wondering if Langlow's wife would be able to notice and read the note through the blinds. He concluded that, even despite the blinds, that was the best place to position the note. He used masking tape to fasten the demand to the window and hurried back to the street. Tomorrow they would assemble the bomb and rehearse the drama that would have an audience of one and would run for only one night.

EIGHT

Last night's message had been from Dick Meadows, the CFO at Langlow Enterprises. They had, after all, identified an unstable employee with a possible grudge against Vince. When I reached Meadows on the phone early Wednesday morning, he came right to the point.

"Mr. Conwright, you asked me about disgruntled employees yesterday. I told you I could think of no person who would fit that characterization. After we talked, I asked our Human Resources Director, just to be sure. He agreed that our workforce didn't have any malcontents. Then he added as kind of an afterthought, 'not since we got rid of McPherson.' I had completely forgotten about Gerald McPherson! "

"So this is a *former* employee you're talking about?"

"Exactly. He never sued us and I wasn't personally involved with him so he had kind of dropped off my radar screen. But as soon as Bud – he's our HR Director – mentioned his name, I remembered the McPherson saga. He was a malcontent all right! I pulled his file from our archives this morning and saw that his work record was even worse than I had thought. He filed a long series of grievances against his several supervisors ... we had to keep shifting him from one unit to another, because he never seemed to fit in .... he contended that he was being discriminated against because of his age, or his Scotch name. He complained that he couldn't get the shift he wanted because of nepotism when a nephew of a manager in a different department won the shift. He said he lost seniority months when he left the company on an extended sick leave. Then his paranoia seemed to intensify. He told people that his current supervisor was constantly looking over his shoulder and was 'out to get him'. HR had to investigate all of these and not one of them proved to be well founded."

"Then you fired him?"

"No, not then. I'm sure his supervisors wished we could have, but we were playing it by the book. He was certainly not a very productive employee, but he was well past the probationary period when these problems began. You know, with a person like that, most companies will tolerate slightly sub-par work. You start thinking, if he'd put one-fourth the energy he puts into his grievances into his job, we'd be happy to let him stumble along. But it's like he *enjoyed* being a grievant, getting in our faces, pushing the envelope of bad behavior. That kind of thing seemed more important to him than just squeaking by with marginal output."

"So how'd you get rid of him?"

"Well, his supervisor *was* starting to watch him a little more closely because he was getting so cantankerous that fellow workers were beginning to feel threatened. This quickly led to his really hating his supervisor. Then he started dropping hints to others that their supervisor was stealing equipment. This, soon enough, got back to the supervisor. Then an expensive piece of measuring equipment was discovered missing from the tool room. The supervisor had been with us for eleven years and Vince trusted him implicitly. Human Resources and Vince guessed that McPherson was trying to set up the supervisor. All the supervisors had individually-reserved spaces in the parking lot closest to the factory. HR rigged a surveillance camera in a van parked a row behind the supervisor's truck. Sure enough, three days later, the camera caught McPherson opening the canopy of the super's truck and putting the missing piece of equipment inside."

"This guy was Machiavellian!"

"Yes he was. We suspended him with pay, held a brief hearing -- that he boycotted -- and terminated him. Would you believe he filed a Bureau of Labor & Industries complaint over his termination!"

"Nice guy!"

"Yeah. He claimed it wasn't he on the video. That we had an actor that looked like him. That the whole episode was a contrivance to get rid of him."

"The Bureau's hearings officer didn't buy that, did he?"

"No. In fact he didn't mince words in his findings and they fully supported our dismissal as being 'for cause'. But this guy never gave up. Next he filed for unemployment compensation. Vince was so upset that the guy had tried to frame his supervisor that he told our attorney to oppose McPherson's claim. We introduced the BOLI findings in support of our rejection of the compensation claim and we won a quick denial. That was the last we saw of McPherson, but they tell me the guy still sends hate mail occasionally to Bud and to Vince."

"Thanks for calling me with this," I said. "I definitely want to follow up on this guy. Do you have a last address?"

"Yes, but it's now almost four years old. It may not still be good."

The greater Portland metropolitan area lies in three counties: Multnomah, Clackamas, and Washington. I reached for the fat telephone book that covered all three as soon as I ended the call with Meadows. There was no listing for a Gerald, or G., McPherson. I used a reverse directory to get the phone number associated with his last known address. The person who answered my call spoke with a heavy Latino accent. He said his name was Hernandez and that he and his family had rented the house eighteen months ago. He had never heard of a Mr. McPherson. He gave me his landlord's name and number. I thought the accent was genuine and tended to believe that he knew nothing about the former employee of Langlow Enterprises.

When I called the landlord, he remembered McPherson well. He told me he had given the man notice to move out almost three years ago after a big brouhaha about leaving trash in the driveway. He had no idea where McPherson was currently living.

I tried a credit check. His credit rating was unremarkable other than the fact that he appeared to have no active credit cards. I realized that I had forgotten to ask Meadows if McPherson was married. I called him back.

"I neglected to ask you if McPherson had a wife. He either has no phone or has an unlisted number or has left the area. It occurred to me that, if he's married, their phone might be listed under his wife's name."

Meadows told me to hold while he checked the file. "Yes, he is married. The wife's name is Margaret, but our records don't show a phone number either."

I thanked him and went back to the phone book. I found an 'M. McPherson' and punched in the number. A weary voice answered my first question.

"Yes, I'm Margaret McPherson. What do you want?"

I gave her my name and asked if I might speak with her husband.

"Gerald and I were divorced almost two years ago."

"I'm sorry to have bothered you. Could you tell me how to reach him?"

"Why do you want to contact him?"

"I'm a private investigator working a missing person case. We fear the person, if he's still alive, may be in great danger. I'm trying to ..."

"You're saying Gerald is missing?" she interrupted.

"No, it's not Mr. McPherson, but I believe he's been in contact with the missing man and I need to talk to everyone who might have useful information."

"I don't know how to reach Gerald. He's... he's not well. He probably does not have a phone and he seems to move quite often. He calls from time to time and he told me he's living in Aloha now, but that's all I know."

"May I come to your home and just ask you a few more questions about him?"

She was understandably reluctant to have a stranger in her home asking questions, but she finally agreed to meet me at a nearby restaurant. Twenty minutes later, I carried coffee and donuts to the booth where we sat. Margaret McPherson was of medium height and a touch on the plump side. Her graying hair was pulled back in a bun and she wore glasses set in a simple pink frame. She was polite enough though the grim set of her mouth told of discouragement and disappointment.

"You said your ex-husband is not well....? Could he be in a medical facility of some kind?

"My ex-husband is bi-polar." She hesitated and then sighed. "I probably shouldn't have told you that. He was a decent enough man when he took his meds. The problem was that he often failed to take them. He'd say we couldn't afford them or that he was fine and didn't need them. Then he was hard to live with. Either he was terribly needy and depressed ... where I had to support him in every way every minute of the day... or else he was going to run the world, manipulate and control everything, and cursing me if I didn't go along with his schemes."

She twisted her napkin and looked down at the table. I could sense guilt mixed with resentment and frustration. Her outpouring to me seemed a brief catharsis and she straightened her posture and gave me a weak smile.

"Did he abuse you?" It was a very personal question, but I wanted to get a feel for McPherson's behavior and lack of control.

She gave another sigh and with a sad smile said, "No. Not physically, at least."

"Verbally?"

She nodded and was back to twisting the napkin. "He could be very demanding. And harsh, if I didn't do everything he ordered. Just words … words, and looks. I begged him to stay on his medication. Sometimes he'd restart it, sometimes not. I finally just couldn't take it anymore."

Her eyes watered up, but she kept her composure. It was as though she was resigned to how it had worked out and was past weeping. I gestured to the waiter for refills and continued to probe.

"Who is his doctor?"

"Dr. Blaine Lowrey, in Tualatin."

"Would you tell me the name of his medication?"

"Why do you need to know that?"

"Only because I'm trying to think of ways to locate him. With the name of the medicine, I might get a lead from a pharmacy."

She looked intently at me and then shrugged. "I think it was Depakote."

"Thanks for your cooperation. This can not have been easy for you. I have one more question. Did Mr. McPherson ever talk about Vince Langlow?"

Her head jerked up and some of the coffee in her cup sloshed to the table top. "Is he the missing person!"

I did not want to confirm that if I did not have to. "You obviously know the name. What did your ex say about him?"

"Gerald suspected Mr. Langlow of arranging to have him fired. He was very upset with his bosses at Langlow Enterprises. I was never sure what kept going wrong at work. Gerald always had an explanation, a justification for what he'd done or what had caused a problem for him. I could understand what he told me and I tried to be supportive, but I also knew that he could be a very difficult person at times. Gerald would even talk of 'conspiracies' at work to make him look bad or to put him on 'work plans'. I never really believed that Mr. Langlow or Gerald's supervisors were evil, but he was convinced of it." She paused for a few seconds and then looked directly at me. "You don't think he has anything to do with Mr. Langlow's disappearance do you!"

I try never to lie to persons I'm interviewing, at least when they are not among those who could be suspects, but this seemed like an appropriate time to dissemble. "I did not say that Mr. Langlow is the one who has disappeared. The identity of my client must be confidential as I'm sure you can understand. In any case, my investigation has just begun and I can't really say there are any 'persons of interest' at this time. But your ex-husband may have useful information so I can't afford to overlook him."

She probably knew I was being evasive, but my response seemed to ease her concern. I watched her leave the restaurant and then I looked up the phone number for Dr. Lowrey. It was ten minutes before the doctor returned my call and he would not come forth with any useful information, as he too cited the doctor-patient privilege. He probably had an address for McPherson, but he would not even give me that.

My next project was to make a list of pharmacies in the Aloha area. Since I was using the restaurant's table as a desk, I ordered a Reuben sandwich for an early lunch. I ended with five pharmacies on the list and as soon as I finished the Reuben, I drove to the nearest one. It was my third stop, a Walgreen drugstore, where I got some help. I told the young woman behind the order counter that I was a private investigator working on a missing-person case and that we feared the man could be in great jeopardy if we did not find him very quickly. I said I was trying to track down Gerald McPherson and that we knew he had a prescription for Depakote.

"Is it possible he has been filling that prescription here?" I asked.

I could see sudden concern on her face. She might well have been thinking that McPherson was the missing person and that, without his meds, he would be in harm's way. I did not clarify the situation for her.

"Doesn't he have family?"

"He is divorced and seems to have no close relatives. The ex-wife is concerned, but has effectively lost track of him."

That seemed to satisfy her. "Let me check," she said and started keyboarding commands into her computer.

"Yes, he has been a customer here, and I don't see that he's filled any prescription during the last seven weeks."

"Can you tell me his address?"

"I think I remember this man. If I have the right person, he had no phone and didn't want to give us an address at first. We possibly could have gotten it anyway through reimbursement records, but we usually ask the customer for it. I told him it could be important for us to have a way of contacting him in case the drug companies issued any cautions or alerts that might apply to particular medications. That seemed to make sense to him and he relented and gave us his address."

Her story was revealing, but I wanted to get moving. I put my notebook on the counter, opened my pen and looked at her expectantly. She looked uncertain at first, but after a few seconds' hesitation, I could see she was going to read the address to me. An older man in a white coat had been standing nearby in their working area in front of shelves crowded with bottles of bulk compounds. As the young woman started to read the information, he spun toward us and challenged her.

"Julia, what are you *doing?* We don't give out information about our customers!"

"But, Carl, the man is missing! His ex-wife can't locate him and he hasn't refilled his prescription for Depakote. Mr. …" she glanced at my card …" Conwright, here, already knew about the prescription. All he wants is Mr. McPherson's address!"

"He can get a court order, if he has to, but we don't give out anything from our records!"

The young woman had laid the record on the counter when the pharmacist named Carl interrupted us. As she explained the situation, her right thumb swiveled the piece of heavy paper around so that it was facing me. While Carl huffed and puffed about confidentiality, I glanced at the address and committed it to memory.

"I'm disappointed that you won't cooperate, sir. The missing man may well be in jeopardy if I can't locate him quickly." I now had what I needed, but I could not resist lecturing this inflexible jerk. "I'll see about that court order," I added and walked away.

I found McPherson's residence in a run-down, rural pocket on the west side of Aloha. There were aging farmhouses, and modest older homes hidden in groves of trees down private dirt roads. But the area was obviously undergoing gentrification. It was not far from a prestigious private golf club, The Reserve, and, just over a rise, five-thousand-square-foot "estates" sprinkled the rolling hills. McPherson, on the other hand, lived in a shabby duplex with aluminum siding and a lawn that had long ago turned into a field of wild grasses. There was one other home off the entrance road and it was surrounded with four junked cars and a penned goat. The duplex was at the end of the road. I caught the smell of wood smoke drifting from a sheet-metal chimney. The wooden porches, once nicely stained, now showed warped boards and splotches of mold.

I had not thought I needed to pack my gun when I left the houseboat. Now I was starting to wish that I had. I felt my jacket pocket to be sure that the can of mace that I usually carried was still there. It was. For better or worse, it was show time. The doorbell apparently did not work, so I rapped on the door. A man of medium height and slender build opened the door with a stern expression. His hair was unkempt and there was salt-and-pepper stubble on his cheeks. His deeply-set eyes alternately drilled into my own and shifted nervously around the landscape. I introduced myself and asked if I might speak to him for a few minutes. He grunted and, without opening the door further, asked me what it was about. I gave him my pitch about working on a missing person case.

"So how could I help? Who's missing?"

With this man, I saw no point in trying to obscure Vince's disappearance.

"Vince Langlow."

A slight, crafty grin appeared on his face. He stepped back and opened the door.

"Alright. Come in. Tell me about it."

"I'm checking with everyone who has had some interaction, good or bad, with Mr. Langlow just to see if I can piece together what may have happened to him."

"And you think I've had some bad interaction?" he asked almost mockingly.

"I know you've written some nasty letters to him. I know Langlow Enterprises let you go."

"Let me go! What a candy-coated way of putting it! They framed me and then fired my ass!"

"When was the last time you saw Vince Langlow?"

"What? Three or four years ago? I haven't seen the son-of-a-bitch since I worked there. How would I know where he's gone?"

"Aside from those letters you wrote, have you communicated with him in any other way?"

"No! Who really sent you here? Was it the company? You bastards have already ruined my life! My wife has divorced me. I can't get a job. They even fixed it so I couldn't get unemployment. I have to live in a shit-hole like this and apply for food stamps!"

"Listen, Mr. McPherson. I'm *not* working for Langlow Enterprises. The family has retained me to try to find Mr. Langlow. You may not like him, but he could be in serious trouble and I need your help."

"I've told you I know nothing about his where-abouts. I wouldn't be sorry to hear he fell off a ship in the middle of the ocean, but I'm not in any way involved!"

It was time to take the gloves off. "Tell me where you were last Monday afternoon, Mr. McPherson."

"Hah! Why should I tell you that?" He turned and started walking toward the back of the house. "I've got to take a leak. I'll be back."

The man was definitely weird: angry, distrustful, instantly disconnecting and leaving the room. I decided to look around his living room while I was waiting. There were six Reader's Digest Condensed Books on a bookshelf, an ashtray filled with cigarette butts, and a manual typewriter sitting on a sturdy table painted a dark maroon. There were some typed sheets next to the typewriter and I was walking over to look at them when he reentered the room. I turned to face him and found myself looking down the barrel of a shotgun.

NINE

Wednesday, November 22nd, 4:30 P.M.

McPherson was gripping what looked like a single-barrel Remington and, this time, his eyes bored into me with feverish hostility.

"So the company sends you to find me and threaten me with this story that Langlow's been kidnapped or something. That's probably bullshit, but – if it happens to be true -- you're probably here to plant some incriminating evidence in my house! I've had enough! So, Mr. Rick Conwright, we're going to play the game *my* way from now on. Empty your pockets very slowly. If you have a gun, lift it out of your pocket between your forefinger and thumb. If I see you gripping it or swinging it toward me, I'll blow you to bits! The police would just find that an innocent homeowner had protected his property from an armed intruder."

I couldn't believe I fell for that 'going to take a leak' line. I should never have let him leave the room, let alone have turned my back on him. I tried to determine how crazy he was and whether he was likely to pull the trigger. I decided it was best to do as he ordered and see if I could later talk sense into him or else get close enough to disarm him. At six feet and a hundred eighty pounds, I had a good size advantage over him. And I was younger and probably quicker.

The trouble was that he did not have to be any great marksman to kill me with that shotgun. Anything in my general direction from twelve feet away would do the job. He was nutty enough to have killed Vince, I thought, and would not hesitate to add me to the list. I pulled the Mace out of my jacket pocket and put it on an end table followed by my cell phone.

I started to reach into my hip pocket and said, "Look in my wallet. You'll see I'm just what I said I was: a private investigator."

He dismissed my offer with a derisive shake of his head. "You come in here asking where I was on Monday afternoon. You people have framed me once and now you're trying to do it again. Turn around and open that first door on the right in the hall."

He marched me to the hallway. I opened the door. A stairway led down to the basement.

"Go down there! I'll call Langlow Enterprises and tell them I have their hireling. We're going to have an end to their meddling in my life! Now move!"

So much for my trying to talk him down off his manic high. I turned on the second step and tried one more time. "I can help you. Let's talk about your situation … see what I can do to improve things."

"Fuck you, Conwright! I'm going to get in some supplies. This may become a siege, but I hold the cards!"

McPherson slammed the door shut and I heard the deadbolt engage. So I was, at the very least, a hostage. But I felt he was so unstable that he still might decide to kill me. I had very possibly found the person behind

Vince's abduction, but I had to save my own skin before I could help Vince ... if he was still alive. I could hear a car starting outside and figured he had left for his "supplies" whether they were to be more shotgun shells or just food and cigarettes. I did not know how long I had to escape, but it was certainly no more than an hour and probably less.

In the seconds that we stood at the top of the stairs, I could see that the switch for the basement light was in the hallway, not on the stairway wall. So I felt my way down the stairs in smothering blackness. By the time I reached the bottom, my eyes had adjusted somewhat and I could make out four small, dim rectangles that had to be air vents in the foundation. Even though it was getting to be late afternoon on an overcast autumn day, enough of the dusky light filtered in that I could gradually get a sense of my surroundings. The part of the basement I was in had a cement floor. I groped my way to the end of the basement furthest from the stairs. I felt the interior wall with my hands. It was a slippery, sloping wall of compacted earth. There was something of a lighter shade at the top of the slope. I felt a dirt ledge and, two or three feet further back, a cement footing and a low, framed wall covered with gypsum board. I tried to remember how the duplex was laid out and realized that the other unit must be on the other side of that stub wall.

I succeeded in climbing up the slope on my second attempt. I hit my head on a joist and found my hands covered with a dank goo that was half mud and half clay, but I was now positioned beside the wall with a mere two feet of headroom. My guess was that the framing in the wall was structural, but that the wallboard had probably been added later to offer some separation between the low crawl space under one side and the full basement under the other side. I believed there was a chance that there would be an access hatch from the other unit if I could somehow get through the wall and into the crawl space. If I were wrong, I would have to go back down the slope and reenter the basement to search in the near darkness for something with which to defend myself when McPherson came back.

I ran my hands along the length of the wallboard. It had no gaps or weak places. I rolled onto my back and braced my hands on a joist overhead. Then I stomped against the wall. Three stomps and nothing happened. I told myself not to panic. I had made a bad mistake in letting McPherson get the drop on me, but I was damn well going to get out of this hell hole. Three more stomps. I thought I felt a little give with the last one. I caught my breath and braced a little better against the joist. Another thrust and I heard a crunching sound as my heel penetrated the gypsum. Two more mighty stomps and the panel disintegrated to form a central opening with a fringe of dangling fragments. I was relieved to see that when the wall was built they had not bothered to attach wallboard to the other side of the studs.

I tore away the fringe and felt for the studs on either side of the opening I had made. Using them for leverage, I pulled myself through the hole feet first until I could roll over and crawl away from the wall. There were a couple of vents on this side offering the same dim light. I crawled back and forth looking for a hatch. All I could see were the soft billows of insulation tucked between the joists. I moved over to the nearest vent to get enough light to look at my watch. It had been forty minutes since I had entered McPherson's unit and probably a good twenty-five since he had left. I was getting ready to crawl back to the hole and look for something to use as a weapon when I saw a recessed area in the insulation off to my right.

In a matter of seconds I was under the hatch trying to lift it. It must have had something heavy on top of it because, straining mightily, I could only raise it about half an inch. I tried yelling. No response. I rolled onto my back and tried to leg-press the hatch upward. I moved it a little further, but it still would not lift off. I was drenched with sweat as I tried again with my legs. This time, when the hatch was open a crack, I yelled as loud as I could from such a cramped position. No response. I tried that routine again. This time I heard the querulous voice of an elderly man.

"Who are you? Why are you down there?"

"I'm being held hostage by the man in the other unit! Let me out of here and I'll explain!"

I thought that I probably sounded like someone having a bad trip on a hallucinogenic drug and wondered if the old man would dare to cooperate.

"There's a bookcase in this closet over the hatch.

I'm not moving it. I don't want you in my house."

My legs were starting to tremble from the strain of pushing on the hatch. "I mean you no harm. Just let me come up and I'll leave your house immediately. I think you should leave too for your own safety!"

"I'm not going to let you come up. I'm calling the police."

"That's fine. Do it quickly! Have them send someone out here. See if you can get hold of Detective Paul DeNoli. Tell him Rick Conwright is trapped under your house."

I slowed down on the names and said them even more loudly, but he did not seem to be able to process all that. He simply said, "I'm calling 911."

I lay there thinking "Great. Here am I, the intrepid PI, hiding from a nutcase with a shotgun and dependant upon a possibly addled old man to call the cops and get me out of here." I checked my watch again. Almost an hour had passed since I had knocked on McPherson's door. I raised the hatch with my legs and yelled to the old man. "Did you make the call?"

Nothing. And then I heard a car pull up. It seemed too quick for the police to have arrived. That meant it had to be McPherson. I crawled back to the opening I had kicked in the stub wall. As I hurried, I again rammed my head into a joist. The pain this time was intense and when my fingers came away from my head slightly bloody, I knew that I had lacerated my scalp. I kept going. I had to get to a position just this side of the stub wall and close beside the hole. If he discovered I had left the basement, McPherson would have to look through the hole. From his side, I could not be seen. If he attempted to enter the crawl space to search for me, I could attack him as he slithered through the hole.

I heard a door open and saw the light come on. McPherson yelled down the stairs. "Now let them come! You're my wild card, Conwright. What do you say to that?"

When I did not answer, I heard him start down the stairs. "Where are you, you piece of corporate shit?" There was a pause and then, "You sneaky bastard! Tried to bust out did you? You can't go anywhere, Conwright. You're mine!"

My legs were starting to cramp from kneeling in the tight quarters and tensing in readiness to attack. I heard something outside the foundation. A voice said, "This is the place. He said it is the unit on the left."

I could hear McPherson breathing hard as he tried to scale the dirt slope just through the wall from where I knelt. Then, he too must have heard the voices of the police and I heard him running up the stairs and locking the basement door.

I crawled back to the hatch and heard them moving the old man's bookcase away from the hatch. Before they lifted the cover, one of the officers shouted, "Come out with your hands in the air! We are police officers and we have our weapons drawn."

"No problem, officer. I'm unarmed and I'll do as you say."

I heard a grunt and they swung the hatch aside.

I blinked at the brighter light and straightened to a standing position with my hands above my head. The two policemen grabbed me on each side by the belt and boosted me out of the crawl space. They had removed the bookcase and all the clothes from the old man's closet and we all stood there for a few seconds as they sized me up. Then they ordered me to brace against the bedroom wall and patted me down. When they were satisfied that I was unarmed and had studied my identification as a PI, they took me outside to stand beside their black-and-white. I waited under the watchful eye of one officer while the other one radioed in to verify my investigator's license, to check for outstanding warrants, and, I hoped, to get a character reference from DeNoli.

"Okay, Conwright, you seem to check out. Now what in the hell were you doing under this guy's house?"

"Like I tried to tell you when I was climbing out of that hole, I was held hostage by Gerald McPherson who lives in the other unit. I came there on a case to question him about his relationship to a missing man, my client's husband. Detective DeNoli with Portland PB knows about the missing person angle. The man accused me of coming to his house to plant evidence connecting him to the disappearance. That's ironic because he's the only suspect in my book. I just got on to him this morning, so I haven't even had time to tell DeNoli."

"How'd he manage to take you hostage?"

"He let me in, but my questions made him very defensive -- especially the one about where he was when my client's husband was possibly abducted. Then he left the room… said he had to go to the toilet. Stupidly, I turned my back on him to look around the room. The next thing I know he's pointing a shotgun at me and telling me to go down into his basement. Lucky for me, he doesn't splatter me then and there. He apparently had in mind holding me as a hostage while he negotiated with the company owned by the missing man. He's a former employee and very whacked out about being fired. Despite my trying to identify myself as a PI, he was convinced I was working for his old company and was out to get him."

"Jesus! What a screwball!" said the younger of the two officers.

"Well, that's one way of putting it, I suppose. I understand that he's bi-polar and doesn't always take his medication."

"So you think he grabbed your client's husband?"

"Well, he certainly has some strong, if twisted, motives and he has a weapon. He's my only lead at the moment."

"You going to press charges?"

"Hell yes! I don't like being threatened with death and having to crawl through mud to save my life. Besides, I want him in custody so DeNoli can really grill him and check his story."

"Roger that. You're lucky the old man was home and called us."

"That's true. He probably did not think he was doing me a favor, but I want to go back and thank him."

"As soon as you finish that, we're going to evacuate him so we can gain entry to McPherson's side without putting anyone else in jeopardy. We have backup now and they tell me he's still inside. He doesn't seem to have a phone, so we'll use a bullhorn to try to talk him into coming out peacefully."

"I hope to God you're able to do that. I've still got a missing man – who's my brother-in-law, by the way – and we need to know if he's alive and, if so, where he is."

"Understood."

It was true that McPherson was at the top of my list, but he was also the *only* person on that list at the moment. He possibly had sufficient hatred and maybe enough paranoia to act out against Vince, but I could not quite see him being clear-headed enough to plan and execute a snatch of an adult without a trace from downtown Portland. I also had trouble imagining how Vince would have allowed a seedy individual like McPherson, bouncing along toward some manic peak, to get close enough to capture him. Maybe the guy posed as a pan-handler and then whipped out his shot-gun, but it did not feel quite right.

They finally persuaded McPherson to submit peacefully though he was still accusing me of sneaking into his house on a mission to plant incriminating evidence. I spent the late afternoon debriefing the McPherson interlude with Paul DeNoli. He told me he had not yet heard anything from the fingerprint lab on possible prints on the photo and the spray can.

I showered off the mud and sweat as soon as I got home. When I felt less like the creature from the black lagoon, I uncorked a bottle of Beaujolais. Glass in hand, I threw a nice New York steak on the barbecue on the aft deck. I felt entitled to a good meal after my adventure in the crawl space. When my phone chirped just as I finished dinner, it was Paul on the line.

"Rick, your guy McPherson's probably going to be committed as dangerous to himself or others. You'll quite possibly need to testify at the hearing. But the most interesting thing we turned up is that he was starting the last day of a seventy-two-hour hold last Monday. They turned him loose mid-morning on Tuesday. He had made a big scene in a department store and started to get violent so our guys hauled him in to the ER and the doc there signed off on a stay in a psych ward. And you were right that he wasn't on his meds like he should've been. So he was in custody at the Behavioral Health Unit at Good Sam at the time in question and couldn't have been the doer for your brother-in-law."

"I'll be damned. Well, guess that makes for a pretty solid alibi. I'll drop the charges if they get him committed. He gave me a hell of a scare, but the important thing is to get him where he can't harm people every time he loses it."

"Sounds reasonable to me. Hey, the print lab called just before I left the office"

"What news?" I asked.

"Well, the preliminary analysis of the fingerprint

boys is that the prints on the can don't belong to Ralston. And nothing turned up on our database or the fed's IAFIS".

I wasn't up on all the law enforcement acronyms, but I knew DeNoli was referring to the FBI's computerized fingerprint database.

"Well, I didn't figure Ralston for it once I found out where he was at the critical time, so I'm not too surprised."

"Where do you go from here with the Langlow thing?"

"Back to square one, I guess. I'm going to dig up some background on Vince and see if anything catches my eye. In the meantime, please keep pressing to get your Police Bureau involved. I'm more and more convinced there's no benign explanation for Vince's disappearance."

"I hear you. Sorry you had such a shitty afternoon, especially since it led to a dead end. Just another routine day in the life of a private eye, huh Rick?"

I closed the phone and took a last swallow of Beaujolais. I was dog-tired, but now, more than ever, I wanted to check in with my old editor, Max Sobel.

TEN

Thursday, November 23rd, 7:40 A.M.

Debra Langlow had taken a sedative to fall asleep, but had passed a restless night and awoke a little before eight in the morning. The sleep had not refreshed her and her anxiety returned as soon as she stepped out of the shower. She slipped on a jogging suit and went downstairs to start a pot of coffee. She finished grinding the beans and glanced out the kitchen window to check the weather. It was at that moment that she saw the paper on the window and raised the blinds. Looking at the ink-stamped words, Debra sensed what it must be even before she started to read it. The message made her tremble:

"WE HAVE YOUR HUSBAND. BRING $100,000 IN UNMARKED $50 AND $100 BILLS … NO BUGS NO GUNS NO CELL PHONES. DRIVE TO CORNER OF WILLAMETTE AND HALL IN SHERWOOD AT 2345 HOURS TONIGHT. FURTHER INSTRUCTIONS IN CAN AT BASE OF LIGHT POST. COME ALONE. DO NOT CALL POLICE. OUR PEOPLE WILL BE WATCHING SO DO AS WE SAY."

Debra started for the back door, intending to yank the demand off the window and bring it inside. As she neared the door, she slowed, realizing that there might be fingerprints on the paper. She touched only the corners of the tape as she detached the note from the window. Back inside the kitchen, she collapsed in a chair sobbing. Debra let the tears flow and the spasms of fear and grief shake her body until she felt composed enough to think. When her strength returned, she called her brother.

"Rick, I found a note taped to the outside of the kitchen window! They must have put it there during the night. It says they have Vince. They want a hundred thousand dollars. Rick, I'm so afraid! It says I mustn't call in the police. I'll get the …."

"Deb, I'm so sorry. We feared it could be something like this, but we have to stay calm and think how to tilt the odds in our favor. Do they say where you are to take the money?"

"Not exactly. I'm to go to a certain intersection in Sherwood and get some more instructions there. I'll get the money, Rick. That's not important. We can afford it, and I have to get Vince back safely."

"I know, Sis. How long did they give you?"

"I'm supposed to deliver the money tonight just before midnight."

"Okay. The first thing is if any money gets delivered, I'll take it, not you."

"God! Would you, Rick? That's asking so much!"

"Don't worry about it. Do you think you can get

the money together that quickly?"

"Yes. I have joint access to our safe deposit box. We should have at least one hundred thousand dollars in there."

"Are you serious!"

"Yes, I am. Eight or nine months ago, Vince had been doing a lot of reading about the national financial system. He developed this conviction that a lot of the banks were poorly managed, especially at the highest level. I kind of teased him about being paranoid. But once Vince gets a notion, he usually follows up on it. We've gradually been withdrawing cash from our various accounts and stashing it in the box. We even have a few collectable gold coins. Vince called the box our 'catastrophe reserve'. Said his parents did the same thing 'way back when'. We've kind of joked about it, but we do have a small percentage of our assets tucked away in that box."

"But there's the FDIC and whatever it's called that the brokerage houses have for street-name accounts … SPIC or something like that."

"Vince was well aware of that, but he just thought we should have a stash that we could get to immediately with no delays or paperwork. I don't think we would have kept building it up much longer but, the point is, I can get the money."

"Will it be in the right denominations?"

"I think most – maybe all of it –will"

"That stash of yours is a piece of luck. Otherwise, I think the bank would insist on making security reports or bringing in the police, or even refusing to give you that much in currency. I'm coming right over and I want to study that note. Don't touch it; there may be fingerprints on it."

"Yes, I thought of that too. I've handled it very carefully."

So we now knew Vince had been kidnapped and that the people who took him wanted money. Ten minutes later, I was at my sister's doorstep. She took me to the kitchen and showed me the ransom demand. It was ink-stamped on plain white computer paper. It was not particularly artful, but there were no misspellings and it did the job. I wondered if the military time could mean that the kidnappers had been in the service at some time. I thought that using the words "light post" instead of "lamp post" might suggest they were in their forties or younger. But those ideas and two bucks might buy me a cup of coffee and that was about all.

"Deb, the police would mark the bills and they'd probably put some kind of an electronic bug hidden in with the money. They could also put a cordon around the area to stop these guys from getting away. Now that we can prove it was a kidnapping, it would be best to bring in the police."

"No! They said not to do that and not to bug the money! They said they would be watching me the whole time! I can't risk harm to Vince. We'll have to do this on our own!"

My instinct was to let the police handle it, but I looked at the fear and torment in my sister's eyes and could not go against her wishes. "Alright. There's a chemical the law enforcement people use to invisibly mark bills. You can see the marks later under certain wavelengths of light. I'll see if I can get some of that chemical."

The police would have the technology and personnel to increase the odds of catching the kidnappers, but Vince's safety was another matter. I did not know a lot about the psychology of kidnappers, but my sense was that they would prefer to take the ransom and get the hell away. The times when victims were killed were usually when the police launched an attack or when the ransom was not forthcoming and they had to eliminate the one person who could identify them. Those factors made me think that maybe Debra was right in not wanting the police involved.

"I'll have to have proof that Vince is alive and will be released in return for the money. But they're not phoning you and they have divided up the directions for getting to the drop-off point, so we have no way of knowing the answer to that question. They have us at a huge disadvantage!"

"We'll have to trust them!"

"You said the note says 'no guns', but screw that! I'll use an ankle holster. I won't pull the gun so long as Vince is okay and I'm not in any danger."

"Oh, Rick! You're so good to do this! For God's sake, be careful!"

"Believe it! I have an idea about how to make sure Vince is alive. I'm going to hide the money somewhere before I get to the meeting place. Not far away, but out of their sight so they'll have to take me to Vince before I'll tell them where it's hidden."

"But their note said they'd be watching!"

"While you're getting the money together, I'll try to scout the neighborhood. I'll look for a place where I can instantly ditch the money out of anyone's sight. I'll switch to a dummy briefcase so they won't suspect I don't have the money with me. So long as the meeting place isn't a long ways from the lamp post with the next directions, it should work."

Debra said she would go to their bank as soon as it opened. I left her house and hurried back to the houseboat to pick up an old briefcase. I continued to have some misgivings about not calling Paul DeNoli and involving the police, but I was willing to do it alone as the best hope of getting Vince back safely. Not that I was not concerned about my own safety, too. If things went badly, they could force me to show them the money and then cut out without telling me whether Vince was dead or alive. An even worse case would be if they panicked and decided to kill both Vince and myself. I would leave my cell phone in the car, but the Beretta was coming with me.

It was late morning when I reached the housing development in Sherwood. The town had been experiencing explosive growth with housing tracts sprouting up everywhere on its southern, northern, and western reaches. With the slow recovery from the housing bubble, the builders started far fewer spec homes and stopped work on many of those underway as soon as the roof was on. The directions in the ransom note took me to a street corner close to the northern edge of a neighborhood of finished homes. Those homes all appeared to be occupied. But, a block away, I saw several acres of houses that never made it past foundations and sub-floors. A dozen more houses were fully framed out and sheathed. A few had windows and doors installed, but most stared back at me like empty-eyed skulls.

I thought it very unlikely they would be holding Vince in an occupied home. So they were either going to direct me to a more distant place or they were squatting in one of the semi-finished houses. Since there still was *some* daytime activity on the building site, it was more probable they would simply arrive that evening, a little before I did, to collect the money. But … would they bring Vince with them? Could we even believe he was really still alive? I thought about having back up, but it seemed too dangerous to involve my friend Julio and his young crew. This would have to be a solo effort.

Some of the roads in the construction area were paved and had curbs and street lights, but others were simply graded and compacted. The entrances to the site were closed off with sturdy barricades. That gave me an idea. Before I would go to the designated street corner tonight, I would inventory all the cars parked on the streets forming the perimeter of the construction site and on the first blocks of the side streets. It might take an hour or more, but I could record the make and license number of every car. If I could compare the before and after inventories, I would know which cars, if any, had left the area that late at night.

Now I had to hunt for a place to stash the money. I located the lamp post where the tin can would be placed. The odds were good that I would be directed into the construction area. I entered the area at the closest point and looked around. I had with me the good-sized briefcase that I picked up at my place. I had filled it with two reams of computer paper. I walked far enough to be beyond where I reckoned the spill of the streetlight would end. If they were going to have me under surveillance as I came in, I figured it would be from a distance. I believed the darkness would give me enough cover to pull off my sleight of hand.

The road I walked on was unpaved. Between the first and second of the naked foundations, I came to a heap of discarded concrete forms. The heap lay very close to the road and I saw an opening where two of the forms lay against each other making a tiny tent. I gingerly placed the briefcase inside. I backed away to check if it could be seen by a casual passer-by. It could not. Then I practiced a few times to see how quickly I could slide it out and make the switch. It proved to be very doable. I left the briefcase inside the heap. For my last prop, I needed something to appear to trip over. I found a piece of twisted sheet metal and laid it in the street just before the pile of forms.

Nate used his digital camera and Howie's laptop to enlarge the newspaper photo of Langlow and took it to the costume and novelty shop as soon as it opened. A soft gong sounded as Nate opened the door and walked inside. Seconds later, a stocky man with shaggy brown hair and wearing a baggy and somewhat soiled cardigan sweater emerged from a back room. He stared for a second at Nate from behind heavy black-framed glasses before asking,

"What can I do for you?"

"I hear you're really good at making masks and you can make them exactly like real people."

"Yes, I can do that."

"We're setting up a practical joke," Nate said as he laid Langlow's picture on the counter. "Can you capture our friend's face?"

The man stared at the picture for a few seconds. "That shouldn't be a problem," he said. "You don't have a color picture?"

"No. We couldn't arrange a candid picture. We got this from where we work … a company directory photo."

"Well you know. It would've helped with skin tone, exact hair color … that sort of thing."

"Sorry, that's the best we could do. This prank was kind of cooked up on short notice. It has to be as good as you can possibly make it, but it doesn't have to be perfect."

"When do you need it?"

"Today, before you close."

"Okay. I'll have it finished by four. It'll be a full head mask, made of rubber. You want a mouth hole, eye holes? Nose holes you gotta have anyway."

"Eye holes, yeah. The mouth isn't necessary."

"That'll be eighty bucks, up front. This process isn't cheap and it's going to take some of my time. You still want it?"

"Sure. Everybody'll go in on it."

"Okay. Who's it for?" he asked as he filled out an order pad.

"Dave. Dave Thackery."

Nate gave the man four twenties and left the store.

Nate and Howie spent the rest of the day at Howie's house assembling their bomb. Each piece in the assembly had to be attached to a backing of sturdy plywood so the entire mechanism could be positioned vertically and fastened to the wall. The cell phone and the battery were placed on the left with wires connecting each to the electronics box. That box was mounted in the middle of the backing along with the flood light. The cylinder was on the right side. They had painted over all the labels and wording on the cylinder, bled off the oxygen and removed the top fitting. They replaced the top with a stubby, round stopper-like plug that they had painted yellow and predrilled to accept the wiring. Wires ran from the flood light to the electronics box and from that box to the top of the cylinder. The whole assembly was just under two feet high and just over two feet wide. It weighed ten or eleven pounds. They had cut an elongated hole at the top of the plywood to serve as a hand hold so the assembly could be carried by one person. Nate would have to drape it with bath towels when he carried it from the car. He would have the cot in the other hand. Howie would come to the house on the bicycle and would carry the mask, the tools, the rope, and the lantern in a rucksack.

It was nearly three o'clock when they were finally satisfied with their work. They drank a couple of Henry Weinhardt beers and toasted to the success of their con. Nate rose to his feet. It was time to pick up the mask. When he returned, they would have a dress rehearsal and do some last-minute contingency planning.

I called Debra on my way back to Portland. She told me that their box held a little over $96,000 and that the bills were almost entirely hundreds with a few fifties. Back on the houseboat, I cleaned and loaded my Beretta and checked the fit of the holster on my calf.

I went to Debra's in late afternoon. I had stopped at a store featuring security hardware and picked up a bottle of the invisible marking chemical. I used it to mark every twentieth bill. Then we transferred the money into Vince's, newer, briefcase. She said she had been calm as she emptied the safe deposit box, but now I could see that her anxiety was almost overwhelming. I fixed hamburgers for us and tried to steady her.

At nine, it was dark and an overcast sky blocked the moon. I drove to Sherwood and began my survey of parked cars. I cruised the streets slowly, only stopping to write down the car's license numbers and make. At one point, a man walking his dog gave me the once over. I thought it would be better to give him some explanation, however thin, than have him call the police about my suspicious activity. I rolled down the passenger side window.

"Good evening."

"What is it you're doing?"

"I'm doing a survey of used cars. I guess the dealer who hired me is looking for a little competitive edge. The idea is to get a feel for the ages and makes and models of cars in a given area so they can better estimate demand."

"Yeah, and people are starting to buy new cars again." His dog was pulling on the leash, but the man was still studying my face through the darkness.

"During the afternoons, I check parking lots at shopping centers; in the evening, they want me on suburban streets. Personally, I can't believe it's all that useful, but if they're willing to pay for it, I'll sure do the survey."

"How late do you keep at it?"

"Well, I'm a little behind tonight so I'll probably go another half-hour. But I don't like to do it too late … could make people uneasy."

"Yeah. I agree. Well, … good night."

Man and dog passed and vanished in the darkness behind me. There was only one more car on that block. I was surprised at how few cars were parked on the street. By the time I finished the grid I had set out to cover, I had just listed thirty-one cars. Even so, it had taken a little longer than I had estimated. It was already eleven o'clock. I drove back to a commercial street where I had noticed a hamburger place, "Barbie's". It had formica counters with that fake mother-of-pearl look and red vinyl in the booths and on the stools. A young man with a mop of red hair, earrings, and a white apron took my order. I wolfed down a burger and a Coke and reviewed my plan for the last time. When my watch showed eleven-thirty-five, it was time to go. I drove back to Highway 99 and then headed to the designated spot. If anyone were observing my approach, it should look as though I had just arrived from Portland.

Nate had hand-printed directions to reach the house and placed them in an empty tin can that he positioned at the base of the light post. Then he drove to the opposite side of the construction area from where they had ordered Debra to park and left Howie's truck there. Howie mounted the bicycle and pedaled toward the unfinished house.

The first thing Nate and Howie did upon entering the unfinished house was to staple the dark canvas over the two windows in the "bomb room". They wore gloves and the new trainers and worked by flashlight to find the studs and to screw the bomb assembly on the east wall. Then, they used a drill and a box knife to cut a small rectangle from each side of the wallboard in the west wall. They cut and removed the insulation from inside the wall to create a viewing port about a foot-and-a-half off the floor. They unfolded the camping cot and placed it in the middle of the room directly in front of the bomb assembly. They turned the camping lantern on at its lowest setting and placed it on the floor to one side. In the dim light, a person looking through the viewing port from outside the room could make out the cot and the bomb. Howie had left the bicycle out of sight in another room.

They had another fifteen minutes until the money was supposed to arrive. Before they had left the house in Scapoose, Howie had tried on the mask. They were impressed how well it had captured Vince's likeness. The fit was tight and hot and, at first, Howie hyperventilated. But he quickly adjusted his breathing through the nose holes in the mask and the transformation was complete. Now Howie pulled the mask over his head again. The man in the novelty shop had also provided a black, man's wig and Nate used adhesive to attach it to the scalp of the mask. Finally, Nate tore a strip of duct tape and pressed it over the mouth of the mask. Then Howie lay on his side on the cot facing the viewing port. Nate brought a loop of the white cord under the cot and around Howie's legs and taped the cord, untied and out of sight, to the back side of the cot.

He repeated the process with rope around Howie's chest. Nate left the house and went to the nearest light post on the street of unfinished homes to await Debra Langlow or her courier .

ELEVEN

Thursday, November 23rd, 11:45 P.M.

I put my cell phone and my wallet behind the armrest in the back seat. I spotted the can on the curb beside the light post right away. I set the briefcase down and pulled the paper from the can. I was right. They were leading me into the construction zone. It was pretty straight forward. I was to enter at the barricade in front of me, go straight ahead for two blocks then turn left and stop at the second streetlight on the right. I stuffed the directions in my sock and started out. When I got to the pile of forms, I did my best version of a trip-and-sprawl that left me right beside the forms. In less than five seconds, I had swapped the briefcases and had the one with the reams of paper in my hand. I regained my feet, dusted off, and made it to the intersection where I turned left.

I reached the street light and had seen no one. I heard a voice from the shadows behind an industrial dumpster.

"Who are you?"

"Mrs. Langlow sent me."

"You have the money?"

"I got it, but I'll have to know that Langlow's okay … that you'll release him."

A man wearing a black ski mask and gloves,

emerged from behind the dumpster. He had a device in his hand with a small wand. "Lay the briefcase down and wrap your arms around the light post," he ordered.

I could not afford to have him going through the brief case until I saw Vince. "There's no bug. You can check me and the briefcase, but I'm not letting go of it until I see Langlow."

"Have it your way."

He stood at arm's length and ran the wand around the briefcase and all over my body.

"Good. You're clean. Now you're gonna brace on this post at a good angle while I pat you down. Don't get smart or the first one's in your knee and we go from there. We don't want anybody to get hurt here, understand?"

This was not a good turn of events. There was a chance he would miss the gun, and so far he had not produced a gun of his own. I decided to comply. I spread my feet and leaned about three feet into the lamp post, still clutching the briefcase in one hand. He started his pat-down. He almost did not go low enough to catch the holster, but I was not that lucky.

"You have a piece! You're sure looking like the heat to me!"

"No. I do some private work. Langlow's used me a few times. The wife knew about me. I'm just a courier tonight. I need to bring Langlow back. You get the money. That's it."

"Give me your ID, Mr.-I'm-not-a-cop!"

"My wallet's not on me. I'm not stupid."

The man in the mask thought that over for a few seconds. Then he took the gun and ejected the magazine. He hurled the magazine through the darkness and pitched the Beretta into the dumpster. "Alright, Mr. Tricky PI, you get your look at Langlow, but no more fucking with me! We said no guns and you already broke the rule. Follow me!"

We walked half a block to the area of partially built houses. He made me go before him up a plank to enter a house. Then he told me to stop.

"Okay. Here's where you have to pay attention. Real *good* attention, because we're all screwed if you mess up. Your man Langlow is in the next room. We had to drug him up pretty good and tie him so he can't move. The reason he can't move is because we've put a bomb next to him with a motion-detector trigger. He moves or you enter the room and ... bloowie ... end of you both. Like I said, we don't *want* anyone hurt. But we need time to clear out. Once you hand us the money, we're going to picket you to that light post back there for thirty minutes. The guys who are watching you have a cell phone and the set up is rigged like this. An incoming call to the bomb phone deactivates the motion sensor. When it's off, the bomb is harmless. But they don't make that call until thirty minutes after we have the money. And for the first twenty minutes, they're keeping an eye on you at that light post. You try to get to him early, the bomb's still armed. You leave the light post, the call isn't made. You follow directions, we have time to leave the scene and the call is made. You can take your guy home. Is there any part of that you don't understand?"

"I understand, but I still haven't seen Langlow or your bomb."

"Get down and look through that hole. You'll see him."

I figured if I got down on the floor, he could cold-cock me from behind and take the briefcase. I wanted a look, but it seemed like the right time to tell him about *my* ace in the hole. "I'll take a look alright, but you got to know something first. The money isn't in this briefcase. It's in another one in this construction area. I look and see Langlow's alive and unhurt and *then* I tell you where to find the money."

"You fucking weasel! Open that case up right now!"

I shoved it over to him. "You open it."

He undid the clasps and shook out the two reams of paper. "Shit! You think you're so smart! You think we're playing *games* here, Mister?" He was keeping his voice low, but practically shouting at the same time. "You screw with us and your client's life isn't worth a frozen turd! You aren't *telling* me where to find the money. You're going to *take* me to the money. And it better be there —all of it -- or this whole thing is going to get really ugly for you and Mr. Langlow!"

They had been very smart about the handoff, but I thought there was still a fair chance that I could get Vince out of there in one piece. I would have to call in the police bomb squad and I might never get Vince's money back but, at this point, I would settle for a stalemate.

"Alright, I'm okay with that. You'll get your money if Langlow's okay."

"Ease up to that hole and don't move your head or your hands once you're in front of it. Take your look, but keep totally still!"

I crouched down to look through the hole in the wall. The light was poor, but there was Vince: gagged and tied to a cot on which he lay. On the far wall, I saw this contraption with a phone, a flood light, a bomb and a bunch of connecting wires. Jesus! These guys were serious! I had to know if Vince was alive.

"Vince!" Nothing. "Vince, can you hear me!" I thought he moved slightly.

"Uhh …mm"

He was alive. "If you can hear me, nod your head very slowly."

I heard another incoherent sound from Vince and I saw his head move slightly. These guys had planned this very carefully. They had stacked the odds completely on their side. But somehow I thought they meant it when they said they didn't want to kill anybody.

"Okay, I'll take you to the money."

I crawled backwards away from the hole in the wall. Ski mask pointed to the door. I took one last look at Vince, then stood up and walked down the down the sagging plank to the dirt in front of the house. Ski mask followed about six feet behind and I led him to the pile of forms. He pulled a small flashlight from his pocket and gave four flashes in three different directions.

"Just so my friends know where we both are," he said.

"The briefcase is there, under those forms. The money's inside."

He peered at the heap. "You get down on your hands and knees and bring it out. Leave it unopened. Then crawl backwards and leave it in front of me. Then crawl back to the forms."

I did what as I was told, wondering if he would shoot me then and there. I knew he had never shown a gun. I hoped he was not carrying and had left the lethal hardware with his "friends". He ran his wand around the unopened case. Then he opened the case and dumped the packets of bills on the ground and went over them with his wand again. I started to stand up.

"Stay down!"

I stayed on all fours, but looked back to see him counting the packets, checking the top bills and a few in the middle, and thumbing through every fourth or fifth one to be sure all the inside bills were hundreds. I debated trying to rush him while he checked the packets, but the way they had it set up, I would gain nothing by overpowering him. In fact, the watchers might flee without making the call to disable the bomb. And, if he did have a gun, by the time I got to my feet and covered the twenty feet between us, he would surely get off a shot at point blank range. I stayed down.

Almost as though he had read my mind, he said, "Our guy who did the wiring is the only one who knows the right phone number. He didn't tell any of the rest of us. So don't even consider making a move on me. I don't *know* the number to disable it."

He was apparently satisfied that the amount was close to a hundred thousand and that there was no homing device in the briefcase or tucked between the bills.

"Get on your feet. We're going back to that street light."

As we entered the spill of the light he told me to grasp the column with both hands.

"Okay. Here's the last stage of this process. Like I said, you're going to stay right here. The guys with scopes have you perfectly covered." He pulled a roll of inch-and-a-half wide duct tape from his jacket pocket. "I'm going to tape your wrists around the post. You may not like the idea, but look at it this way: you stay here nice and visible in the light while I leave. After some more minutes, the shooters leave. After half an hour, we disable the bomb with the phone call. By then you might have freed yourself. If you haven't, the security patrol will see you when he comes around. This way, you're okay, Langlow's okay, and we're okay. At that point, this little soiree is over. You're never going to get a better offer, mister. Now put your arms on either side of the post!"

I had had a couple of minutes to think as we walked back from where I had stashed the money. I was beginning to have some doubts that they really had three snipers waiting in the darkness to shoot if I moved. For one thing, I never saw any blinking lights to acknowledge ski mask's blinks. Second, if they had a whole squad of snipers and a bomb maker besides ski mask, they would have asked for more than a hundred thousand to make the split worth the risk. On the other hand, this guy did not seem to feel the need to carry or flash a weapon at me and that might suggest he had firepower close at hand. In the end, I still had the feeling that they only wanted the money. The only person who approached me had taken pains to explain how it could end with no one getting hurt. And, by wearing the mask, there was no way I could identify him. I decided to cooperate.

He taped my wrists together on the far side of the post. I did not resist, but I did not cooperate either. As he struggled to align my wrists to make the tape tight, his left sleeve got shoved up. For an instant, I saw a prestige-type wristwatch in the gap between the cuff of his shirt and his glove. I could not make out the brand, but I saw two smaller dials on its face and three letters in relief on the clasp of the watch bracelet. The initials looked like "N A B". I also got a whiff of cigarette breath as he leaned against me. As soon as he finished with me, he punched a number into his cell phone. When it appeared he had the connection, I heard him say, "I have the money. Thirty minutes starting now. Be careful getting to the meet. You can see the drop-off guy where I've picketed him to the street light."

Ski mask closed his phone, picked up the briefcase and ran off to the east.

I considered what to do and the order I had to do it in. I was not about to risk monkeying with the bomb or even entering the room where they had Vince before I knew it was safe. If I waited out the entire thirty minutes, I would return to the house and very carefully look through the hole to make sure Vince was still unharmed. If I somehow got loose sooner, I had to get to the cell phone in my car and call DeNoli and have him bring the bomb squad. But, if I got free early, I would have to figure out how to evade the sniper or snipers. Otherwise, I would never make it to the car. I was able to check my watch when ski mask left and it was then twelve-twenty-eight.

I found that I could almost bring my wrists to my mouth. I tried different contortions until I finally got my teeth on the tape. Ski mask had wrapped it around my wrists three times and it took me several tries before I started a small tear through the two outer layers. Another couple of minutes and I managed a little tear in the undermost layer. A minute after that, I had enlarged the tear in the outer layer, but my eye teeth simply could not reach any further. I tried worrying the tape by scraping it along the vertical grooves in the classic metal shaft of the column. That weakened the bond slightly and I repeated the process. Then I noticed an uncapped bolt connecting the base of the post to the concrete sidewalk. I squatted lower and slid my arms down the shaft. By putting my legs out behind me and lying on my stomach, I brought my wrists all the way down to the base. If I was being watched, the snipers might realize I was attempting to free myself. I had to work fast. I felt for the threads of the bolt and began sawing the tape against the bolt. In less than a minute, the tape gave way.

I continued to feel vulnerable in the direct light. Staying prone, I looked around for a rock. There was a lemon-sized chunk of concrete about ten feet away. I sprang to my feet, picked up the chunk, and hurled it at the light. The globe shattered with an explosive pop and, instantly, I was shielded in darkness. I sprinted behind the nearby dumpster and waited. No shots, no sound of anyone approaching. I checked my watch. It read twelve-thirty-nine. Wearing a dark jacket and dark pants, I would be hard to see and I remembered that there were no lights installed on the unpaved street by which I had entered the area. I sprinted for the inhabited neighborhood and quickly found my car. Ski mask had taken my gun, but had not bothered to throw away my keys. Inside the car, I recovered my cell phone and called DeNoli's home number.

He answered the phone with the slow speech of someone who had just been awakened from a sound sleep.

"Paul, it's Rick. I've found Vince Langlow! They have him in a half-completed house in a new development in Sherwood. They've got the place wired up with a bomb. They've taken the ransom money and ..."

"What the hell! You dealt with them? You paid them ransom money!"

"Yeah, I know. I can explain that to you. But right

now I need your help! They just left and we need a bomb squad to defuse this thing or to somehow get Vince out of there! He's tied up. They've rigged the bomb to be triggered by a motion sensor. They claimed they would disable it at one o'clock, but we can't trust them for that."

"Goddammit, Rick! If you and your sister had let us handle this, they wouldn't have gotten away. How much money?"

"A hundred grand."

"But Langlow's alive?"

"Yeah. I couldn't get close enough to see if he'd been hurt, but the bag man claimed they'd just drugged him to get him there and to stop him from triggering the bomb."

"So this bomb thing is to buy time for their getaway?"

"That's it."

I gave him the street intersection and said I'd be waiting there. He said he would alert the Sherwood police and the Washington County Sheriff's office to send their bomb squad. He himself would get there as soon as he could. I knew I had not heard the last of my effort to handle this on my own.

TWELVE

Friday, November 24th, 12:55 A.M.

The first officers, Sherwood police, got there within minutes. They arrived without using their sirens. They had been ordered to await the arrival of DeNoli and the bomb squad. Sherwood was out of the Portland Police Bureau's jurisdiction but, because the kidnapping had presumably occurred in Portland, DeNoli was a lead player. I fished my cell phone out of my car and called Debra.

"Debra, Vince seems to be okay. They'd sedated him so he was not able to speak to me, but he's alive and does not appear to be hurt. I say it that way, because they had rigged a God damned bomb triggered by a motion detector. The bomb is in an unfinished house and in the same room as where Vince is tied to a cot. They set it up that way, so I'd turn over the money and they would have time to get away. They claimed they would disarm ..."

"So Vince is still in there with a bomb!"

"Yes. But the bomb squad is just arriving now. They will defuse it and we'll soon have Vince."

"My God! How awful! Shall I call an ambulance?"

"Not yet. If they've just drugged him into unconsciousness, I'll take him to an ER and let you know where to meet us. But let's wait 'til we can communicate with him and check him over."

"Alright. But call me the second you know anything more."

I could tell that she was on the verge of tears … maybe from relief and maybe, too, from fear. Vince's life would still be on the line until we had the bomb safely deactivated.

By the time DeNoli was on the scene, it was after one o'clock. Right away, he took me aside.

"For Christ's sake, Rick! Are you nuts! You should have called us! There's a protocol for responding to kidnappers and it doesn't include free-lancing to give them the money. You put yourself in jeopardy and we lost our chance to surround the place!"

"Look, Paul. I figured you'd disapprove, but the demand said 'come alone and don't call the police'. Debra insist-"

"Of course the demand said that! They always do. They want the odds in their favor and you went right along."

"Like I was trying to say, Debra insisted. She *is* my client and the money wasn't really her concern. She wanted my brother-in-law back fast and with the fewest complications. She prevailed upon me to help. That's all I can say."

DeNoli threw his arm upward in disgust and turned away. We both rejoined the larger group and I repeated my story in much greater detail. It was decided that it was highly unlikely the gang was based anywhere in the neighborhood and that it was very probable any snipers had left by then. I led them toward the house where Vince lay tied to the cot. As we approached, I relived the moment of seeing Vince on the cot. Something about it had bothered me at the time, but I still could not quite put my finger on it. Of course it bothered me, I reminded myself … it was a lousy thing to see … my brother-in-law trussed up like a turkey beside a bomb and looking pale and disoriented. I thought harder about what it was that did not seem to fit. For one thing, it seemed strange that his expression had not changed even when I spoke to him. On the other hand, being heavily sedated would probably eliminate most facial expression and he may not even have recognized my voice.

Our group approached the house and it was agreed that the bomb guys would go in alone with their protective gear. It was also understood that the fewer persons moving around inside, the better, given the motion-detector trigger. They had been inside less than a minute when one of the squad came to the door.

"There's no one in there! The cot's empty! They must have taken Langlow with them."

"What the hell!" muttered DeNoli.

"That doesn't make sense," I said. "Unless … unless they felt they had to kill him once they had the money."

The technician in the doorway shifted his weight from foot to foot and shrugged his shoulders. "Just reporting what we found," he said. "I've got to get back to disable the bomb."

I watched him shuffle his feet in puzzlement when

it hit me. What I had been trying to bring out of my subconscious was that Vince had been wearing white trainers instead of his usual expensive loafers. True, he had just finished playing racquetball, but he had his own locker at the MAC and would never have left the club in athletic shoes. I stamped my foot in frustration and turned to DeNoli.

"I think I've been played! I don't think I *ever* saw Vince Langlow in that room! They had some double or someone wearing a mask or something. They knew we'd want proof that Vince was alive and they set me up!"

"Hold on! What makes you think that all of a sudden?" De Noli asked.

I told him about the shoes, about Vince's expression never changing, about the disappearance of the supposed victim … about how they wanted me picketed outside, away from the house and how I never saw any responsive signals from the snipers that were supposed to be out there.

"Shit! So Langlow could already be dead!"

That had been worrying me too. Then, a member of the bomb squad came back to the door to fill us in on their progress.

"We're going to send a man above the bomb in the attic space. We'll be able to rig some steel up there to give him some shielding from any explosion below. He'll carefully cut a small hole in the ceiling. Then he can very slowly lower some long-handled clippers down to that bomb assembly. We can't see all the circuitry, but we're pretty confident that once we cut the battery wires, it should be defused. Now all you guys need to move back another fifty, sixty feet."

Besides my constantly growing concern about Vince's well-being, I was now angry as hell that I had been so easily tricked. I wanted to find out all I could about the men who pulled this off. "Paul, I made a list of the make and plates of all the cars parked on the streets around this construction area. I'm going to leave for a while and inventory the cars that are still there. If any have left, we may have a fix on some of their vehicles."

"Smart! These bomb guys are going to go slow and careful. We'll probably be here a good hour. I'll have them crime-scene it, so forensics will be working after that."

"Good luck on your crime scene with the bomb squad tromping all over!"

"I know. They insisted that community safety trumped our need for an untouched scene. But I've told them to stay in those two rooms and to enter and leave only by that door. And, once they're satisfied it's disarmed, they won't touch the bomb assembly until after the criminalists make their first pass."

I stopped at the lamp post long enough to fish my gun out of the dumpster. I ran back to my car. I called my sister back.

"I've got some disappointing news, Deb. When the bomb squad entered the house, there was nobody there! I'm more and more convin-"

"Oh, Rick! I can't take much more of this! So they took Vince away with them?"

"Possibly, but that really doesn't make sense. I think they never *had* Vince in that room. I think they showed me a double ... probably someone wearing a mask to look like him. The light was dim and they'd really set me up for it. The police are gathering all the forensic evidence from the scene. We'll track these guys down! We can't be sure they have Vince but, if they do, we'll find him!"

I said that with more confidence than I truly felt, but I thought it was important to keep hope alive. I promised to call back whenever we learned anything new. I followed the same sequence I had driven earlier in the evening, making it easier to compare notes. Everything matched up until I got to the streets on the east side. The same side ski mask had run toward. There, I found two vehicles were missing: a Prius and a Ford pickup. The Prius had been on a street that bordered the construction zone and the pickup was half a block off, on a side street. When I got back to the house, the man in the attic had just cut the wires. For good measure, he had used an extension tool to place black tape over the motion-sensor lens. The rest of the men in the squad extracted him from the attic and joined us outside. The team of criminalists had arrived while I was away and they immediately went inside. Their jobs were to photograph, fingerprint, measure, diagram, vacuum for trace evidence, and bag all the physical evidence other than the cot and the bomb assembly.

I said to DeNoli. "I turned up one car and one truck that have left from street parking in the last hour-and-a-half. Can you have your people check the registrations and then call the owners on some pretext?"

"Yeah. I'll get that started right away."

I gave him the make and licenses of the two vehicles.

After a quarter of an hour, we got an early report from the criminalists:

"We found prints of two different sports shoes throughout the two rooms and some sticky threads from torn duct tape. And -- this is interesting – bicycle tire prints inside the house and outside. We'll track them as far as we can when we're done here. That should be another twenty or so minutes."

As the forensic crew was coming out, Paul DeNoli came up to me. "We ran down the ownership on those two vehicles. The Prius was owned by a couple here in Sherwood … in this neighborhood. Our people used the pretext of a possibly stolen car to contact the owners. The husband of this couple said his wife is a nurse and was working the graveyard shift at the hospital. We called and confirmed that she was there and that she had driven the Prius to work. The pickup is owned by a Howard Despaile with a Scapoose address. Mr. Despaile has no phone number. They'll check to see if he owns a cell phone. We may have something with this truck thing. In the meantime, I've ordered a radio alert on the plate."

The ordinance techs had gone back in as soon as the criminalists emerged. Fifteen minutes later, they came back out. "That thing's a piece of shit! It couldn't blow up a paper bag! It's cobbled together out of everyday items. We X-rayed the cylinder and we're almost positive that there is no explosive inside. The whole thing is a fucking sham!"

So it was another prop. Just as I was told, it was designed to buy time for their getaway, but it was harmless from the get-go. There never was a "disabling" phone call because there never was anything to disable! But that started me thinking. The snipers that may not have existed. The bomb that was not a bomb. The fact that ski mask never flashed a weapon, even when I held onto the briefcase. The fact that when he tossed the magazine to my gun, he never bothered to check if I had already chambered a round. The smooth-talking bag man who so skillfully shaped my expectations to make me ready to believe everything they showed me. The man who used a word like "soiree" and wore an ultra-upscale watch. I began to wonder if these guys *had* kidnapped Vince. It no longer sounded like the operation of a brutal kidnapping gang. What if they were just opportunists – con artists -- who saw a chance to stampede a frightened wife – and me, her stupid PI brother -- into turning over a fast hundred grand?

The criminalists had re-entered the house to unscrew the "bomb" assembly from the wall. They would take it and the cot and the rest of the evidence back to their lab where they would go over everything minutely.

DeNoli and I were hungry. Paul said he knew of a Shari's that stayed open twenty-four-seven. We agreed to meet there for a fast meal. As we ate a very early breakfast, Paul was setting up a team to visit Depaile. He had to go through local law enforcement in Scapoose, so it would take a little longer. He would not let me accompany his team, but promised to keep me in the loop. I finished off my last piece of bacon and headed home for a few hours of sleep.

THIRTEEN

Saturday, November 25th, 8:30 A.M.

My phone awakened me at eight-thirty the next morning. It was DeNoli.

"We talked to this Despaile guy about three this morning. Told him we had spotted his truck near a crime scene. He said he'd been home all evening, but we were welcome to have a look at his truck. My guys said, 'fine, where is it?' He says 'in the driveway, right out in front.' They humor him and they all go out in front. No pickup. He goes bananas and says my truck's been stolen! He insisted that they call it in. They do. He lives alone so no one can prove he's been home all night. Says he had a cell phone, but thinks he lost it in a shopping center about a week ago. Then we asked him if he owned a bike. He says 'no'. So we asked have you ridden one recently? This seems to shake him up for just an instant, but he says 'no, not for years.' "

"Sounds pretty convenient, doesn't it?"

"Yeah, but we didn't have PC to do a search and there was no bag of money laying around in plain view. We did check to see if he had a record, however, and guess what? Three arrests and one conviction for larceny by trick and fraud. He is, or at least has been, an impersonator and a grifter!"

"Once a con, always a con. Isn't that how it goes?"

"Yeah. So he's probably lying in his teeth, but right now we'll have to wait and see what else turns up. Your idea about keeping track of all those parked cars certainly gave us a person of interest, though."

I was still groggy from the let-down after the adrenaline rush of the night. I set the alarm for ten and pulled the covers back over my head. Walking around like a zombie would not do Vince or Debra any good. When I awoke the second time, I drank some strong coffee, and drove over to Debra's. I explained to her that I believed – especially now that we knew Despaile had a record of involvement in confidence schemes – that he was connected to the ransom demand. And he had to have had an accomplice. But, I told her, if the demand had been nothing but a scam, I was planning to let the police bunco squad work that case while I focused my efforts back where I started: on finding Vince. It was a little after eleven when DeNoli called.

"We just got a break," he said. "Last night the criminalists made a casting of the tread marks from the bike tire. Then they followed the marks in the dirt out to a paved street on the east side of the construction area. There was enough dust and dirt in the tread that they got a sense that the rider was heading in the general direction of Highway 99 once he got on the pavement. We figured they had stolen the bike, so we ran all the reports of recently stolen bikes. Nothing fit. Then about half an hour ago, the principal's office at a grade school not far from the highway called in that they had found an adult-sized bike in their rack. It obviously did not belong to any kid at the school and none of the teachers or staff rode in that day. A smart officer working property crimes remembered we were looking for a bike. We picked the bike up and saw a clear match on the tire tread. It was a brand new Huffy."

"Did they find any prints?"

"What I was about to tell you, Rick my boy. It looked clean at first. Then one of our techs thought to check under the curl of the seat at back. He's a bike rider and says that's the natural hand position when someone's walking their bike or parking it. And there he finds three nice prints that match up nicely with the ones we have on record for a certain Howard Despaile!"

"No shit!"

"That's right. So there are a couple of possibilities. Either he was the guy on the cot and used the bike to leave the house or he's the one that bought the bike and he handled it at the store."

It has been several years since I have ridden a bike, but I could easily visualize how someone might push a bike with the palm of their hand on the saddle and their fingers gripping it underneath. "Either way, he wipes the seat and the handle bars, but forgets about underneath."

"Yeah. Now the guys in bunco figure Huffy bikes usually aren't sold in fancy bike shops. More likely in Sears or Target, places like that. They've already started working the phones to see if any of those stores in the greater Portland area have sold a man's Huffy in the last two days. If they get any hits, they visit the stores and check credit card records, surveillance cameras, cashiers' memories … whatever. And they'll have a blow up of Despaile's driver's license photo in case they need to do a little in-the-field photo lineup."

"That's a good beginning, Paul. Who's handling it in bunco?"

"A dick named Morrie Lehman. I just recently met him, but they say he's good and he seems willing to get right on it. And I'm still involved. But there's something else I haven't told you yet. Some of my guys did a door-to-door with Despaile's neighbors this morning working the vehicle-theft angle. Seems the guy across the street is putting his cat out his front door around two in the morning. He notices Despaile's truck pull up. The garage door opens, in drives the truck and the garage door comes back down."

"And Despaile has told your guys that he left the truck out all night on the driveway!"

"Exactly! We caught him in a big fat lie!"

"Is the neighbor a stand-up wit? Was he awake enough to be sure? Did he stay at his front door the whole time?"

"Yeah, he's solid on that. We think he may be a little bit of a nosey Parker. Or, maybe he was just curious why his neighbor was getting home so late. Who knows? But he seems to be sure of what he saw."

"So Despaile is looking for an alibi for his truck

and comes up with this stolen ... but wait, if he ditches the pickup somewhere, how does he get back?" All of a sudden I'm seeing things more clearly. "So maybe his accomplice picks him up in the truck after he ditches the bike at the school."

DeNoli picked up on cue. "They ride back together to Scapoose where they split the money ..."

And I finish it. "And the accomplice ... takes the truck to leave the area. Maybe he doesn't have his own wheels and needs to get away or maybe he just dumps it somewhere and takes public transportation in the morning to wherever he calls home."

"That's pretty much the way we see it, too. We'd already put an alert out for the 'stolen' truck. Now we've changed that to an APB in Oregon, Washington and Idaho. If he's still driving it, we have a chance to nab him. If he's already dumped it, we still may be able to get forensic evidence from it."

I stayed with Debra for a while, both to calm her down and to ask her more questions about Vince. I wanted to hear every last thing she could tell me about his business and civic and social contacts ... things he was involved in, deals he might have been negotiating ... anything that might give me a lead. We had been over much of this already, but she was game to try again. Sadly, nothing I learned gave me any new ideas. Debra fixed us a late lunch and, afterward, I returned to the houseboat. I needed to get my brain off the bogus kidnapping and back into what could have caused Vince to disappear. I sat at my desk and started rereading all the notes I had taken. DeNoli called again a little before six.

"Rick, it's Paul. One of the bunco detectives hit pay dirt on the bike. Two stores had made sales in those two days. One was a sale to a family and it all checked out. The second was at a Target and the sale was to a couple of men. They paid cash and bought some other stuff too. That 'other stuff' was two pairs of cross trainers, latex gloves and a child's rubber stamp set!"

"That's got to be them!"

"We thought so too. They worked back from the sales slip to the cash register and time of day. That gave them the cashier. She was there working when they got to the store. She recognized Despaile's photo. Then they started checking the surveillance cameras. They're modern enough that they record digitally. Store security pulled up the images from the exit cameras on the date and time that matched the sales slip and bingo! We got two guys leaving ... Despaile with a bag, the other guy pushing the bike using the handlebars. We now have enlarged frames. The face on the other man is reasonably clear. We don't have photo match software yet in our statewide data system, so we can't tell if he's ever been convicted in Oregon, but at least we have a photo."

"Think it's enough for a search warrant?"

"Enough to arrest Despaile for sure and probably enough to search his place. My men met with an Assistant District Attorney and they've found a judge still at work. If she gives us the warrant, we'll be out at Despaile's house within the hour."

"Can I come a-"

"Along?" DeNoli interrupted. "No. Let us make the collar and do the search. We get him back to the Justice Center, you can have a crack at him. I'll keep you posted."

I was low on groceries so I went up to the Clinton neighborhood and had some tasty tandoori chicken at Vindalho. I spent the rest of the evening in my office rereading my notes yet again. It was almost eleven when DeNoli called.

"So here's where we are on the phony kidnapping. The judge gave us the search warrant. We got out there and Despaile's at home. He yells and screams about the warrant, but I can see he's shaken. Our guys go to work. They find nothing in the main part of the house or the garage. There's a little unfinished attic with one of those pull-down stairs for access. Up there, he's got suitcases, cartons, an old set of golf clubs, the usual crap. They go through everything, but no money. There's some plywood flooring where he got this junk. As the roof slopes lower, the flooring stops and there's that blown-in insulation covering the rafters. Our guys start poking a probe stick into the insulation along the edge of the plywood. Clunk, they hit something. Well it turns out to be a carton ... a carton full of hundred-dollar bills!"

"Fantastic, Paul! You got him and the money. How much was there?"

"A little under thirty thousand. And you told us how you'd marked some of the bills, so I called in one of the lab techs and they put various lights on them. Sure enough, we found your marks!"

"The other guy must have gotten the bigger share unless Despaile had another stash somewhere."

"Unlikely, our guys went over the entire property with a fine tooth comb."

"Was Despaile doing any talking?"

"About some things, yes. When we told him about the tire treads and his prints on the bike, the marks on the money, and the security camera pictures, he basically admitted his part in the scam."

"And Vince?"

"He swears they never took your brother-in-law. Says they've never even seen him. We gave him some incorrect descriptions of Langlow to see if he'd disagree or correct us. He never batted an eye. I thought he was telling the truth, but we decided to flutter him."

"Lie detector?"

"Right. I called in an examiner. He wasn't too happy about coming in late at night, but he came. Despaile passed the test on not taking Langlow."

"I see. Did he give up his accomplice?"

"No. I guess he thought he'd get a lighter sentence if he fessed up to his part of it, but he wouldn't tell us jack-shit about the other guy. So much for cooperation, huh? Seems he has this idea that cons don't rat each other out. That all may change as we get down the road a bit, but tonight he wouldn't talk about that."

"Anything else, Paul?"

"There's another piece of news on the forensic

front. The criminalists worked the crime scene in your sister's garden. They found indications in the soil that someone tripped or stumbled. A few feet further on, they found blood stains on some bricks in a lawn border."

"So, some DNA maybe?"

"They think they may be able to extract some. And your sister says she's never injured herself there."

"If it isn't Despaile's blood, it could be his accomplice!"

"That's our thinking, too."

"I'm glad you're involved, Paul. Will you keep working the case on Vince now that Despaile has passed the lie detector test?"

"I'm not sure. For one thing, a con is good at deception. Maybe this guy's good enough to fool the machine. It also depends on what my captain says. I'm guessing he'll let me keep working, but maybe only long enough to close out the Despaile angle"

I was afraid that might be the case. "I'm going to try to learn about Vince's past … see if that gives me any leads."

"Okay, and I'm going to argue that the circumstances are looking more and more like a crime occurred … a kidnapping or a homicide." DeNoli offered. "Maybe that will allow me to keep on it. Oh, here's another other thing on that scam. We had a criminalist along with the men doing the search at Depaile's. Out in the garage they found a freshly opened quart can of red paint. The criminalist had been examining the fake bomb earlier in the day and he noticed the paint was the same color. Back at the lab, it proved to be a perfect match. *And* they found a nice set of prints on the can. They weren't Despaile's so, maybe, they're prints of the accomplice."

"Terrific! Right now my one and only goal is to find Vince and, if he's alive, get him safely home. Once that's resolved, I'm going to be on Mr. Ski Mask like a cheap suit!"

"Still a little pissed about being taken in, I guess."

"Damn straight! And there's the little matter of seventy thousand dollars of Vince's good money, too."

FOURTEEN

Saturday, November 25th, 11:35 A.M.

Wy only two early leads had fizzled out. And the one series of events that seemed to have an immediate connection to Vince's vanishing turned out to be an expensive hoax. The phony ransom demand had cost me two whole days in my effort to locate him. It had been entirely believable at first and I knew we had been justified in putting all our energy into trying to affect Vince's safe return. But now that we saw it for what it was, I was furious that I had been deflected from my search.

Now I needed some deeper background on Vince to see if that would somehow suggest what was behind his disappearance. That meant the paper and Max Sobel. My friend and former editor at The Oregonian was due to retire on December fifteenth after a long and productive career in the newspaper business. Max had been my staunch defender when the publisher wanted to shove me out the door. He could not have denied that the Darmsfeld case had become a major preoccupation with me, but – like me – he believed I was just one step away from uncovering the smoking gun. I had learned a lot from Max. He could not save me in the end, but he remained a trusted friend.

I called Max at home and asked him if I could pick

his brain on a very important case I was working. I asked if he would mind meeting me at his office. He might have been tired from the crush of winding up his life at the paper, but – if he was – he never let on and he agreed to meet me at the paper in twenty-five minutes.

Traffic was manageable and I made it to The Oregonian building on Broadway in twenty minutes. In the lobby, I said Max was expecting me and, after confirming that, the security guard let me pass. Max's office was of a reasonable size for a senior editor, but it was all function and very little in the way of comfort. He cleared a chair of a carton half-filled with mementos and motioned me to sit. Max was wiry and energetic for all his sixty-seven years. He already seemed to have a five-o'clock-shadow on his Levantine face. His black eyes flashed behind his steel-rimmed glasses in a smile of welcome. In typical Max fashion, he wasted no words.

"You made it sound serious, Rick. What's going on?"

I said our talk had to be off the record, and proceeded to tell him about Vince's disappearance. "So I've probably eliminated a few scenarios, but I still don't have any insights into what has happened, let alone where Vince is… or even if he's still alive."

"So you're thinking maybe our archives could hold some useful information?"

"Exactly!"

Max keyboarded in some search parameters and

stared at his computer monitor.

"Well, we've done several pieces about Langlow Enterprises and a couple of smaller ones about your brother-in-law's charitable work and a Rotary Club award. And then there was the obit for his first wife and a spread on the society page when he married your sister. I'll print them out for you. Just glancing at the leads, all but the obit look like positive stories. I didn't see anything about lawsuits or ugly strikes or disillusioned former employees."

"Thanks, Max. I'll read them all anyway. The fact that his car is missing kind of confuses things. The police even implied that he might have used the car to voluntarily leave town. I don't buy that. The missing car suggests more than just a mugging on the street and if it were a carjacking, the owner is usually left on the sidewalk. I'm worried that this is a well-planned snatch of some kind: car and owner. And with no ransom demand, it gets even scarier."

"Did Mr. Langlow grow up in Portland?"

"Yes he did. Graduated from Franklin High."

Max thought for a second. "And he's in his late forties. There should be public school records, of course, but they probably won't tell you much even if they're still kept somewhere and supposing you could convince some administrator to show them to you. Was he Catholic by any chance?"

"No, they don't attend church, and I'm sure he's never been a Catholic."

"All right. So no priest or minister to talk to." He

stopped and absently scratched his stubble. "Something puzzled me a little, Rick, checking those archived articles. Everything we wrote about and know about this man begins about eighteen years ago. There seemed to be no connection to Portland before that time even though he was locally born and raised. And you have found nothing in his present life that suggests trouble." He shifted a paper weight from one side of his desk to the other before resuming. "I've always maintained that if the present is clean ... maybe too clean ... look to the past. Everybody has a skeleton in their closet."

"That makes sense, but can I afford the time? Even forgetting about his childhood and teenage years, that leaves me almost ten years to cover."

Max gave a sympathetic nod. "I would focus on family, old friends, and places more than on paper records. There may be more to be learned than you might think."

I took the printouts, thanked Max for the advice, and wished him a happy retirement. I had the recording device in my car and decided to stop by Debra's place to install it. I could read Max's printouts there.

FIFTEEN

Saturday, November 25th, 1:10 P.M..

Saturday, November 25th, 1:10 P.M..

Debra led me through their formal living room to a cozy TV room that projected a little way out from the rest of the colonial at the east end of the first floor. We sat on a velveteen couch. She was obviously very tired, but makeup and an elegant slacks-and-sweater outfit told me she had gotten past the frantic hours of believing kidnappers had her husband and were holding him in a room with a booby-trapped bomb . I showed her the device I would put on her phone.

"You didn't call me, so you must not have received any calls about Vince?" I did not quite have the heart to say "any ransom call".

"No. Only a few calls from women friends." She looked apprehensive, and I knew that she was not sure whether the absence of calls was good or bad news given our unstated fears that something even more serious had happened. I gripped her hand and tried a new tack.

In our haste and anxiety over dealing with the supposed kidnappers, I had never told her about my run-in with McPherson. "I thought I had a lead pointing to a disgruntled, mentally ill former employee of Vince's, but the police found out the man was in custody when Vince disappeared. And he wasn't the kind of person who would likely have had an accomplice. I think that's a dead end." I could see Debra's anxieties rising with a word like "accomplice", but she needed to continue to be prepared for the ugly scenarios that I still worried might be out there. "Max Sobel, my old editor at the paper, thinks we need to look into Vince's more distant past. Do you know anything about his life before he started his own business in Portland?"

"Not really, Rick. He never spoke of his past. I think he and Don Turley go back a long ways. I guess I just assumed he was always in Portland and was in the steel fabricating business one way or the other from the beginning of his career. He simply didn't bring up his early life and we had so much going on in the present I suppose it just was not something I felt the need to discuss."

I hooked up the recording device to Debra's phone and explained to her how it would work. Then, I slumped on her couch and began on the old Oregonian articles. She saw my weariness and brought me a cup of hot tea.

The articles were, as Max had surmised, positive stories about Vince's business and its growth and success. There were no suggestions of intra-corporate jealousy or discontent. Max's idea about contacting family was a good one, but Vince had no children or siblings and no living parents. I read the obituary for his first wife and saw that she was survived by her father who lived in Portland. His name was Peter Devereau. I opened Debra's phone book and saw only one listing with that name.

Peter Devereau answered almost immediately. I introduced myself and told him about Vince and that I was a private investigator working for Vince's current wife.

"The police have not really taken an interest yet, but the fact that he and his car suddenly vanished have us very worried."

Mr. Devereau sounded elderly, but I could tell he was clear as a bell mentally.

"That's terrible! He was a devoted husband to my Marilyn and very decent to me. He kept a close eye on business matters, but he seemed to be liked by everyone."

"Mr. Devereau, no one, including his present wife, seems to know much about his activities or business ventures or even where he was located prior to about eighteen years ago. If I could learn more about his past, I might find something there that would shed light on what happened. Can you help me with any of those questions?"

I heard a wracking cough and knew he was a smoker. I hoped that my having kicked the habit would save me from such a fate or worse. He gathered himself and said, "Well, I know he was in a partnership. I believe there were four of them. About a year after the partnership ended, he came back to Portland and met my daughter and they fell in love."

"What kind of business were the partners engaged in?"

"Oh, the mining business. They had a molybdenum mine."

"I see. Where was this mine?"

"Up in British Columbia somewhere. I can't re-member the name of the nearest town. It was kind of in the wilderness."

"How about their business name or the name of the mine? Can you remember that?"

"Let's see … it was a catchy name. The "Big …." He paused. "Molly! The Big Molly."

"Good! How about the partnership name?"

"I probably knew it once, but I can't remember that now. Sorry."

"That's alright. Did you know any of the other partners?"

"Oh, I think I met two of them once at a party, but I can't remember their names. In fact, I kind of remember hearing that one of them *changed* his name for some reason. He was the fellow who went to California. I'm pretty sure the rest of them settled in Portland."

"That's most helpful, Mr. Devereau. When you say the partnership ended, did that mean the mine shut down?"

"I'm not sure about this, but I think they had sold the mine a year or so earlier."

"Did Vince ever talk about the mine? Tell stories about those days?"

"No. Not in front of me. I remember once …" an-other fit of coughing, and he resumed. "…I remember once, when we were all together, Marilynn started asking about life at the mine and Vincent told her to drop it. He said it pretty sharply and in no uncertain terms. I was a little surprised."

"Did you ever hear him talk about his relationship with his partners?"

"Well one of them, Ben something, turned out to be a pretty good friend as I recall."

I thanked the old gentleman and closed the phone. So Vince had drawn a curtain over this mining business. I could not have explained it, but something told me to probe that chapter of his life. Maybe it was Max and his theory of skeletons. In any case, I decided to try to find this Big Molly mine. After a few minutes browsing the internet, I found a website on the history of molybdenum mining in Canada. That linked me to articles in geology journals. Ten minutes later, I found a reference to The Big Molly. It was not revealing for my purposes, but it did tell me that the mine was near Topley, B.C.

I had already cleared my calendar for the rest of the week. I told Debra that I was going to take a chance and make a fast trip to Canada.

SIXTEEN

Sunday, November 26th, 2:20 P.M.

It was mid-afternoon by the time my plane landed in Prince George. I found a couple of charter pilots' ads in the terminal. They told me at the Air Canada counter that those two operators worked out of a hangar about a hundred-and-fifty yards down the street. One of the pilots had a small Beechcraft and said he could fly me to Topley in about an hour. With Debra picking up my expenses, I figured it was worth it to get there quickly. Fifteen minutes later, we were taking off. The day was cold and raw, but visibility was clear. We more or less followed Highway 16 to the northwest. We cruised at three-thousand feet and I could see rugged evergreen-covered hills and narrow, glacially-carved lakes beneath us. There were also the scars of clear cuts and numerous sawmills. I even saw a sizable mining operation at a place the pilot told me was called Endako.

Looking down at terrain below, I remembered my first time in an airplane. I was twelve at the time and a crop duster who had come to spray fields for my father offered to take me up. I was afraid that my father would not let me go. I could see he was working several hundred yards away over by the silo. With a slightly guilty look over my shoulder, I said to the pilot, "Gee, sure!"

He helped me into the open cockpit and strapped me in. The flight was less than ten minutes with some tight banked turns and a bit of a bouncy landing, but the thrill lasted for years. My dad saw the plane land and watched me climb out. I got a stern lecture about checking with my parents before getting involved in such adventures, but I was pretty sure I saw a proud grin hiding behind his initial scowl. Several years later he told me, "if you don't try something new once in a while, you'll never know what you've been missing." I've tried to live by that advice ever since.

It was well after four when we landed in Topley. I took a business card from the pilot and told him I would call the next day to arrange my return flight. A middle-aged man in grease-stained coveralls walked out of the nearest hangar as the plane taxied away.

"What brings you to Topley?" he asked in a curious, but not unfriendly, way.

"I need to learn all I can about The Big Molly mine that used to operate around here. I don't know a soul in town. Any ideas who I should talk to?"

"The Big Molly! Now that was a while back." He stroked his beard and looked me over again. "Why're you interested in her?"

"I'm a private investigator. Not connected to the police. A client's husband has gone missing and it's possible there's some connection to the old mine."

"I'll be damned! Well, the best person – maybe the *only* person left around here who would know any-thing – would be Wally McNalley. He's retired now, of course, but he used to be the maintenance man at the mine. If you catch him sober, he'd probably be happy to fill you in."

"Great! Do you know where I might find him?"

"Yeah, he lives in a small house almost at the end of Dabney Street."

"Can I get a cab out here?"

The man laughed. "No cabs in this town, Mister. If you can wait about ten minutes, I'm driving into town myself. I'm going to quit for the day anyway and I might as well give you a lift to Wally's place. It's an American holiday weekend for you isn't it?"

"That's right," I said, "but looking for a missing person, I've no time for holidays. Anyway, I'm grateful for the lift."

The little air strip was not far from town. I asked my new acquaintance how many people lived in Topley. He said he did not know for sure, but everyone thought that the population was about eighteen hundred. He let me off in front of the McNally house.

Wally McNalley answered the door of his weathered, single-story, frame house with a cheerful, but baffled, look. I saw before me a lean, gray-haired man. I thought his clothes probably came from the Good Will and there were a couple of food stains on his shirt-front. His face was weathered and creased and he had probably been standing too far away from his razor that morning. I could see a fine web of purple capillaries spreading under his deep-set eyes. I introduced myself and said I had heard he was the local authority on the old mine.

"Yeah, I know old Molly. Come in. Said you're from Portland?"

"That's right. I'm a private investigator working on a missing person case. I'd be most grateful for anything you could tell me about the mine, its owners, and the history of its operation."

McNally sat in a well-used lounger and motioned me to an even older couch. I pulled a small recorder from my pocket along with a notebook. "I hope you don't mind if I record our conversation?"

"You're sure you're not writing a book or going to use it in some court trial?"

I chuckled. "No. I used to be a journalist, but this is strictly to help my own note taking and only then to help me find the missing man." McNalley nodded somewhat reluctantly and I took that as permission to turn on the recorder. "Did you know the owners of the mine?"

"Depends. It was prospected and claimed by a man I only met once. I wasn't working at the mine then. That guy sold his rights to some young men from the States and they are the ones who hired me. They also named the mine and got it producing. Eventually, they sold it to a corporation. I think that was somewheres around nineteen eighty-seven. The corporation kept me on and I worked for it until they closed the mine in nineteen ninety-four. I met the Vice President of that corporation, but he only came to Topley once every couple of months. Of course, I knew the mine manager very well."

McNally may have been a drinker, but he seemed quite sober as we conversed. "So these young men that started operations ... can you remember their names?"

"Well, first names at least. There was Ben... can't think of his last name. There was Vince .... Langdell, I think. He seemed to be the idea man. There was Richie B. That was how he was known. I can't remember what the B stood for ... that guy had a temper! The fourth fellow ... a nice young man, seemed a little out of place in mining and logging country... yeah, his name was Nick, Nick Matson."

"Do you know under what name these young guys were doing business?"

"Let's see..." he frowned and scratched the stubble on his chin. "Yeah. I think it was Northwest Molybdenum ... or maybe it was British Columbia Molybdenum. None of us ever called the play anything but The Big Molly."

"Okay. And your job at the mine, Mr. McNally?"

"I did all the equipment maintenance, ran the wiring, installed some pumps, serviced the vehicles ... you name it, I did it."

"You were obviously important to the operation. Any other names you remember from that period when the four young men owned the mine?"

"Well, they didn't have a manager because the four of them were here themselves most of the time. They had a geologist, Jerry something. Had a godawful Finnish last name. They were all young and things were pretty informal. We just used first names. I think

'Jerry" was really 'J-A-R-I', but he very quickly got called Jerry and he didn't seem to mind, poor kid."

"Why 'poor kid'?"

"Oh, he was killed in an accident."

"What happened?"

He sat up a little straighter in the lounger. "His pickup truck went off the road and over a cliff one night when he was leaving the mine. The Constable looked into it, sort of, and concluded that he just lost control on a curve. But the burns were really bad, they said."

"So his truck caught fire?"

"Yes, at the foot of the cliff. But it seems young Jerry—I call him that because he was still wet behind the ears. This was his first job out of college. Anyway, it seems young Jerry somehow got out of the wreck alive. They couldn't say whether he was thrown out or crawled out but, either way, the flames got him. They found him the next morning and it looked as though he'd climbed or crawled around the end of the cliff and then made it another sixty feet up the hill before he died."

"That's awful. But you sounded like you had some doubts that he lost control. Why was that?"

"Well, this Jerry was a straight-laced young pup in some ways. Pretty idealistic, I'd say. Anyway, there was talk that one night in a tavern back in Topley he'd had a few too many drinks and told people he was 'on to something' up at the mine. He never explained what he meant by that, but a week later he was dead."

"I see. Did you see him leave that night?"

"From a distance, yes. It was already dark and I was still mucking around inside one of the equipment sheds, but I saw him walk by with his lunch pail in hand. Then, a couple of minutes later, I saw his truck go through the gate."

"Could you see if he was alone in his truck?"

"No. Too dark to see anybody inside the truck. But I saw something else. I saw one of our big dualie pickups leave the yard, not thirty seconds after he did. They normally just left the keys in that truck until we shut down for the day. I couldn't tell who was driving, but Richie B. usually drove it around the mine area. Anyway, about ten or fifteen minutes later, I see the same truck come back into the yard. Maybe forty-five minutes after that, the last of us, including Richie B., cleared out. I locked the gate behind them and went home myself."

"Who was left in that last group?"

"Not sure I can remember. I know there was Richie and I think Nick and maybe a couple of the miners."

I turned off the recorder. Maybe there *was* a skeleton or two in Vince's closet. "But couldn't a truck have left and returned for any number of reasons?"

"Maybe during the light of day, but much less likely at that time of darkness. Besides, in fifteen minutes no one could get down the hill and through the valley to the town and back. That's a good twenty-five minutes each way."

"Did you see any flames along the road as you drove out that night?"

"No, I didn't, but the base of that cliff would've been a good ninety feet lower than the road. Even if the fire had still been burning, I might not have seen it."

"Did you service Jerry's truck?" I tried to ask the question matter-of-factly, but old Wally knew exactly what I was getting at.

"Hell, no, Mister! It was his private property. I only worked on mine stuff. You better not be thinking I had anything to do with his accident!"

"Sorry, I just thought you might have known if the truck was in good shape." That seemed to cool him down.

"No. I wouldn't know about that. Except that Jerry was a pretty careful guy. I don't see him neglecting his vehicle. Especially driving on those mountain roads."

"But you said you did service the mine's vehicles, like the dualie. Did you notice any damage to it?"

McNally waited a long time before answering and looked back at the table where I had first set the recorder to make sure I had put it back in my pocket. He scratched his whiskers and lit a cigarette. "Suppose I *did* look the front end over. In any case, the body was fine. The big, oversize bumper had lots of dents in it, but there was no way of telling if any of them were brand new. That truck was often pushing or bumping things around the mine area and dings and dents on the bumper were quite normal".

"You said the Constable 'sort of' investigated'. Did he question you?"

"No. I did not come forward. What could I say? A big pickup truck coming and going? So what? Of course everybody was sorry about the accident and we all went to the memorial service, but things at the mine didn't miss a beat. And I had a good job to think about."

I closed my eyes for a second and reflected on the fact that the rules of the game were maybe a little different in hard-scrabble mining towns.

"I sense that you had doubts about how thoroughly the Constable investigated. Why was that?" I could see Wally McNally was getting uneasy and I figured he soon might cut me off.

"The Constable's brother was one of the big suppliers to The Big Molly. We got diesel, lube oil, explosives, cement, some timber … all that sort of stuff from him. It was probably his biggest account in those days. I'm not saying the Constable was bought off or anything like that, but, through his brother, he knew the partners. I just don't think he had any interest in causing trouble at the mine … he simply wasn't going to waste much energy digging around in what clearly looked like an accident."

"Okay. Tell me why the mine finally closed."

McNally looked rather pointedly at his watch. I seriously doubted that he had any appointments other than maybe with a bottle, but I felt I probably already had as much as he was going to give me.

"Who did you say was the missing person?" he asked, avoiding my question.

"I didn't. It is Vincent Langlow."

"Vince Lang.... oh! The Vince who was one of the four young men! Interesting."

"Does that give you any ideas?" I asked.

"No. No it doesn't. Just wondered."

"So about why the mine closed?"

"The ore quality gradually got worse and worse. It finally wasn't economic to keep operating. By then, I was starting to get arthritis. I was ready to quit anyway when they closed and the company gave me a decent severance pay."

"Any chance you could show me the mine tomorrow morning?"

"There's nothing to see. The provincial government requires you to fence in the pits and take measures to stop any leaching when you shut down. The yard's overgrown and the buildings are near collapse. Besides, I don't own a car. If you really want to get up there, ask around at Dotty's Café at breakfast time. Maybe somebody will drive you up there in a four-wheel drive if you'll pay them."

I checked my notebook with a sense that there was something I had failed to follow up. Then I found it. "You said the young men sold out to a corporation and that corporation kept you on. What was the name of that company?"

"Crazy Creek Minerals."

"One more thing. Can you describe for me the curve where Jerry's truck left the road?"

He looked impatient, but managed to answer.

"Coming downhill from the mine, it would be … let's see … the sixth curve. It turns to the left as you go down. There's a steep, bare hill above it, almost a cliff itself. There should be a turnout on the outside."

With that he stood up and made it clear with body language that I had worn out my welcome. I thanked him for his time and then stopped on his threshold to ask him one more question. "Mr. McNally, is that Constable still living in Topley?"

"Jim Thornton? Yeah, he is. In fact, he's still the Constable. His office is on Main Street."

SEVENTEEN

Monday, November 27th, 7:55 A.M.

I spent the night at the Bagley Motel just off the highway at the north end of town. It was a cold walk from the local diner to the motel, but it gave me a little time to think. If the young geologist had been murdered, could my sister's husband have been involved? It might be a stone best left unturned but, if Vince's past up here in the British Columbia outback was somehow tied to his disappearance, I had to stay with it.

As soon as I got back to the motel, I called Angie who was back in Portland. I had called her the day before at her parents' home, and she told me she was having a wonderful time and had even gotten together with an old girl friend from high school days. At the end of the Portland call, she asked how my investigation was going. I did not volunteer that it had taken me far northward into Canada.

"I'm putting in very long days. I'm not sure I'm producing much for the client, but that's kind of typical at the beginning of these things. Once in a while you get lucky, but more often it's a lot of grunt work up front until you build up enough facts that you can start seeing patterns or angles."

"Rick, that's a basketful of generalities. You're sure playing this one close to the vest!"

I tried to laugh it off. "Right, Angie. That's why they call us *private* investigators! Did you take the Saturday afternoon flight?"

"Yes. You knew I was covering the Sunday news and, like we figured, that Sunday flight connection was too tight."

"Angie, I'm not sure where I'll be tomorrow. If I won't make it back by a reasonable hour, I'll give you a call."

"Works for me. Rick, as soon as I got back, I heard that your brother-in-law had vanished. There was a story in the papers. That's what is taking all your time, isn't it?"

"Yes. It was very delicate and uncertain at first. I really couldn't talk about it. My sister, Debra, has hired me to find Vince."

"I'm going to dig around myself. I'm sorry for your brother-in-law, but it is newsworthy when a prominent citizen goes missing."

"Yeah, that's true."

"Can you tell me what progress you're making?"

"Well, I can honestly say that I don't yet know what has happened to Vince. But, remember, I have to put my client's interests first. If it will help our cause, maybe there'll be a time when I could make a statement you could use, but right now that's not the case."

Angie seemed disappointed, but understanding. The next morning, after a restless sleep on an amazingly hard mattress, I was at Dotty's by seven. The windows were steamed to opaqueness and the smell of coffee and fried ham was enticing. Almost all the stools at the counter were occupied by men who obviously knew one another and were enjoying conversation over their breakfasts. The tired, yellow vinyl-upholstered booths against the windows were also filling up when I arrived. I now realized that I needed to add at least two more stops to my British Columbia itinerary so I wanted to get an early start on today's work in Topley. I took the last available stool at the counter and started a conversation with the men on either side. One of them was a bear of a man complete with a bushy beard and black watch cap. Lucky for me, he was a logger on his day off and he knew the road up to the old mine. His name was Harry and he was willing to drive me up there for gas and lunch money. He was a friendly guy, but I was sure that curiosity about my purpose in coming to Topley was also a factor in his agreeing to help me.

When Harry finished his second stack of flapjacks, we walked out to his Ford 450 pickup. Harry rested his mammoth fists on the steering wheel while he let the engine warm up. When he was satisfied that the engine was running smoothly, he put the truck in gear and we rumbled out of town. We reached the mine in about thirty minutes. The road had not been maintained and it was in bad shape in a few places, but Harry's truck with its oversized tires and raised suspension was able to navigate around a couple of shallow wash-outs, numerous deep ruts, and a few stray boulders. He even had to drive over a few saplings that had grown in the old road bed. McNally was right, there was not much to see at the mine and certainly nothing that would help me. I looked through the high cyclone fencing and saw a huge rock crusher leaning askew and two buildings with rusty corrugated iron walls and broken windows: forlorn specters of the past. But the real reason I wanted to make the trip was to check out the curve where Jerry's truck had left the road.

I was pretty sure I had spotted the place on the way in to the mine, but on the way out I counted the curves to be sure. As NcNally had described, there was a turnout on the outside of the curve. I asked Harry to pull over and stop. On the way out, Harry had finally asked what brought me all this way to see an abandoned mine. I had been a little vague in answering. I told him I was an investigator working on a case that involved mining in upper British Columbia. That seemed to more or less satisfy him, but he gave me a questioning look as we slowed to a stop in the turnout.

"Somebody told me there had been a fatal accident at this point," I said as I got out of his truck.

"Yeah. I think I heard that once, too. Before my time here."

I looked around. Here and there, amidst the weeds and rubble from the hillside above, I spotted some of the packed gravel that must have constituted the surface of the turnout back then. It was fairly long and reasonably wide. It would have allowed two or even three large trucks ample room to pull over. There were no guard rails of any kind. I walked over to the edge of the area and looked down. The hillside was very steep and rocky. There were only a few mature trees on its slope. I thought I could make out where a cliff began. It was not worth trying to get down there, especially in street shoes.

"Bad place to go over," said Harry.

"You got that right!"

I brought out my digital camera and took a couple of pictures from up the road a ways and another at the far edge. There was a heavy overcast, but plenty enough light to take photos. I had also taken a few pictures at the mine and I hoped Harry would just think I was photo-happy. We got back in the truck and I asked him if he knew anything about operations at The Big Molly.

"I knew it was in Topley and even thought about looking for a job there though I'm not much for using explosives. But they closed it down the year before I finally decided to come to Topley. So I don't really know anything about the days when it was a going concern. I have heard some people refer to it as a 'jinx mine', though."

"Why was that, do you know?"

Harry gave me a quizzical look. "Oh, you hear different stories. Some say because it played out early. Some say because of that accident back there. I've even heard that one of the miners got mauled by a bear that came into the yard. You know how it is. The name sticks even when nobody's sure how it got started."

When we got back to town I paid him as agreed plus

another fifty and asked him to let me off at Constable Thornton's office. It was housed in a relatively modern one-story brick building along with a communications center and a small jail. I explained to the deputy in the front office that I had come from Portland, Oregon and hoped that the Constable was in so that I could speak with him for a few minutes. The deputy said he was and I could. With a jerk of his thumb, he motioned me toward a partly open door behind him, at the same time yelling, "Jim! A man from the States to see you."

A stocky man, bald with a bushy white mustache, looked up from his desk. I told him who I was and that Vince was missing without a trace and that I was trying everything to come up with some leads including past events at the mine. I hoped that the implication of a kidnapping or worse would engender a spirit of cooperation in him, but he looked at me like I was on a colossal futility trip. Maybe he, as a cop, did not appreciate private investigators. Or, maybe he could not be bothered trying to remember long-past events. In any case, it looked as though I was going to have to work hard for whatever he was willing to tell me.

"So, right now, it's the death of this young geologist that I'm most interested in," I said.

"What's that accident got to do with Langlow going missing?"

"I'm not sure it has anything to do with it, but it's the only unusual event that is in any way connected to Mr. Langlow's past. Can you remember this 'Jerry's" full name?"

"I sure as hell can't pronounce it, but I think we could find the record." He yelled to the man in front, "Judd, pull the file from nineteen eighty-six on the road accident up by the old mine. The deceased was Jari Kirves-something. A couple of more syllables. A Finnish name."

The deputy returned with a file folder and handed it to Thornton. "Yeah, Kirvesniemi", and he spelled it out.

"Who found him? Or who first called in that he was missing?"

"One of the mine owners. I think it was Matson. Seems he didn't show up for work the next morning. Matson called his rooming house and the lady told him Jerry hadn't slept in his room the night before. So Matson called us. About two hours after that, someone in a cabin across the gorge was watching an eagle through his binoculars and caught a glimpse of the wreck. He called it in and we went out there and found him."

"What time was that?"

Thornton consulted the file. "Eleven-forty-five in the morning. We got the doctor out there and he said the poor bastard had only died a few hours before we found him."

"So he'd been ... alive...?"

"Yeah. Lots of broken bones and burned over a third of his body. Spent all those hours trying to climb back to the road. Poor sod! Imagine the pain he must've been in!"

"Did the doctor do an autopsy?"

"Naw. The cause of death was obvious. Trauma and burns."

"I mean to see why he went off the road."

"We found a good-sized boulder had rolled off the hill and across the road onto the turnout. There was some paint on it that matched the truck's paint. We figured he took the corner too fast, drifted over to the turnout, then careened off that boulder and lost control as he went over the edge. Or else the boulder came down right on top of him and diverted the car off the road and over the edge."

"Without an autopsy, I suppose we'll never know if he'd been drinking, but you didn't find any liquor bottles in the truck did you?"

I could see he did not like my harping on the lack of an autopsy. He scowled at me and said, "No. No liquor bottles."

"What about the truck? Any paint transfers on the truck?"

"What the hell are you getting at, Conwright?"

"Just wondering if he might have collided with another car, perhaps a hit-and-run," I answered ignoring his anger.

He sighed and looked again at the report in the folder. "No mention of paint transfers … except from his truck to the boulder."

"So your people looked for that?"

"Dammit, *I* don't know! We probably did, but the truck was smashed to hell."

"But you didn't leave it there? You had it pulled up and towed away."

"Yes, of course! And we *did* check the brakes and found they were in working order except for the fact that the wheels were all torqued from the wreck." Thorton rose behind the desk, his face flushed. "Look, I don't know what your angle is, Conwright, but you've got your nerve coming in here and questioning an investigation that was closed almost twenty-five years ago! You're as bad as the kid's father!"

"I apologize, Constable Thornton. I wasn't trying to be critical. I was just trying to see what facts had been established. If I'm going to be looking for some connection, I need to eliminate guess work as much as possible." He looked a little less defensive, so I pushed on. "You mentioned this Kirvesniemi's father. Did he come up here?"

"He sure did. I had no problem with his claiming the body of his son, but he was kind of a pain in the ass. He told me his son had written him a letter where the son said he thought things were "crooked" at the mine. The father had just received the letter when the accident happened, so he wondered if maybe there was foul play involved. He wanted us to keep investigating. And he poked around the Coroner's office and made a bit of a scene there."

"Did you ask any questions at the mine?

"Sure! We asked if anyone thought the young man was using drugs or was a heavy drinker. We also questioned people to see if anybody noticed what kind of a mood he was in that day. I even asked if there was any bad blood among the employees. It turned out he was well liked and wasn't using. They all said he was a little on the serious side, but nobody thought he was suicidal."

"This business about 'something crooked': were there any rumors or stories around the town to support that?"

"Well, shit, Conwright! I didn't have time to go polling the whole town! All I can say is my DC's and I never heard any such thing and we never received reports of any suspicious activity at the mine."

The man was clearly defensive, but he had answered my questions. I did not think he had lied to me, although I could see he was not about to elaborate on his answers or volunteer any personal opinions. I left feeling that he had probably done a cursory investigation, but was not knowingly part of any cover up ... if there even *was* a cover up. I called my pilot and made arrangements for him to pick me up right after a fast lunch. I wanted to get back to Prince George in time to visit the Fraser River Assay Laboratory.

EIGHTEEN

Monday, November 27 ͭ ͪ, 2:20 P.M.

The Fraser River Assay Laboratory was housed in a small two-story brick building with the public counter on the first floor and a laboratory area closed off behind. Upstairs were a few offices and more lab space. There was only one person behind the worn oak counter, a ruddy-faced individual who looked at the clock on the wall from time to time. The person in front of me seemed to be having a protracted conversation with the clock watcher so I sat down and flipped through back issues of the Canadian Mining Journal and Canadian Minerals.

After ten minutes my eyes were starting to bore a hole in the back of the miner at the counter. It must have worked because, a minute later, he left and I stepped to the counter. I told the clerk who and what I was and said, "I'm hoping your records go back about twenty-five or so years and would contain assays for the The Big Molly mine near Topley."

"Well, yes, our records do go back that far, but they would be proprietary unless the owner has relinquished the claim."

"I know the mine has long since closed. Would that indicate relinquishment?"

"No. Not in and of itself. In any case, records that

166

old would be in archives."

"Are your archives kept in a different location?"

His face got a little redder as he looked at his wristwatch before answering. "No, there're here, but I haven't got the time…"

"Look, I don't need a lot of detail. I wouldn't hold you very long and I'm not after any proprietary information. I just want to know generally how rich the ore was twenty-seven years ago and in the next four or five years after that."

"Well like I said, it would take me a while to dig that out…."

I doubted he was all that busy. In fact, I figured him as wanting to close up and get an early start on the evening's fun at his favorite pub. I laid a couple of twenties on the counter burnished to an auburn smoothness by decades of forearms. "I well understand the time issue. I've come all the way from the States and have to be in Vancouver tonight. It's really an important matter … possibly a matter of life or death. Even if I could arrange to come back, it can't wait that long. I'd be most appreciative if you could help me out here." I looked down at the bills as I finished.

He too looked at the bills and said, "Well, I suppose I *could* find the records, but without a formal relinquishment in the file…"

At that point, I knew he would help. I slid another two twenties onto the counter. "Like I said, just a few accurate facts. I may not even need numbers or specifics."

When I looked down, the bills had disappeared. He turned and headed for a flight of stairs. "Wait here. I'll see what I can find."

Less than ten minutes later, he returned with a file folder in hand. "So you're interested in assays done in nineteen-eighty-six, eighty-seven, right?"

"Yes. Unless there weren't any; then maybe a year or two earlier. And the following five years."

"Well, seems like there were two zones they were looking at. There *were* assays in late spring of eighty-seven. Both zones looked quite rich for molybdenum. I'd say they were pay zones... you know, profitable to be worked. In fact...." He paused as he seemed to compare a couple of the pages. "In fact, the two zones look to be damn near identical. Of course, that's not too surprising considering they are just different areas at the same general mining site." He turned a few more pages. "There were routine assays in Zone A with the same result all throughout the next years. Looks like A was the only Zone they were actively working. It seems Zone B was just over a low ridge, but still on the property. It wasn't until very early in nineteen-ninety-two that there was another assay for Zone B." He frowned, then continued, almost mumbling to himself, "Huh! Now Zone B looks weak, no longer a pay zone... even different trace elements." He looked up and his voice returned to normal volume, "And, about that same time, Zone A starts getting less rich." He flipped more pages. "Down the line a couple of years more and Zone A wouldn't pay either."

"I wonder… I think maybe…" I was stammering partly because my brain was working overtime trying out different scenarios and partly because I now realized that I needed a little more than the clock-watcher would be willing to give me. I decided to explain a little better why I needed his help. "I said I was working on a case. It's a lot more than that. My brother-in-law disappeared almost seven days ago. We're afraid he may have been taken… kidnapped… I believe there may be a link between his disappearance and his time of working at The Big Molly. I have absolutely no connections to or interest in the mining industry. I know you told me the details were proprietary, but I think I'll need to show the Zone B and Zone A assays from eighty-seven and from ninety-two to an expert. If the expert says there's nothing that can't be explained by variations in the samples, I promise to return any copies. If there is something there, I may have to keep them until we can figure out what's happened to my brother-in-law. But in any case, I'll never give or sell or loan them to any prospector or mining interest."

The clerk raised his hand as if to stop me. "I'd lose my job if anyone found out!"

I did not think his reluctance was a matter of money any more, at least not in any amount that I carried with me. It was fear of being fired and, at least some, loyalty to the rules of the system that were holding him back. I placed my hands on the counter and leaned toward him. "Look at it this way: the mine isn't commercial any more and likely won't be ever again. My client, assuming he's still alive, is in terrible jeopardy. Surely you can take a little risk with me on this!"

He stared at me for a long moment, then opened the file folder and shuffled through the papers inside. He selected four sheets and pushed them slightly above the edges of the manila cover. He checked his watch again. "I'm alone here today. I feel the need for a cup of coffee. I'll be across the street and I'll be back in ten minutes. Nothing can be missing from the file."

I watched him leave and then took the four sheets to the copy machine behind the counter. The copies were inside my jacket pocket and I had the file reassembled by the time he returned with a Styrofoam cup of steaming coffee.

"Thank you for your trouble," I said, shaking his hand.

I felt that I was making progress. I now had an idea about what had been "crooked" at the mine. But I certainly could not be sure what that led to back then, or if there was any connection to Vince in the present day. At the airport, I changed my return flight schedule so I could overnight in Vancouver. Then I got on the phone to an old newspaper buddy to ask a favor.

I had met my friend Tobias "Toby" Clark eight years ago when we collaborated on an investigative piece on Oregon's State Accident Insurance Fund. At that time, Toby worked at the Statesman Journal in Salem, the state capital. Toby is a Canadian citizen and, a couple of years after the SAIF story, he returned to Canada where he became a senior reporter for the BusinessBC section of the Vancouver Sun. We had remained friends and he was aware that I had become a private investigator. I needed information that I was quite sure would be found in the records of the British Columbia Securities Commission. The problem was that the BCSC records, assuming they could be found in some archive, might not to be open to the general public. It would be an unusual shortcut, but I was hoping that Toby had a contact in that office; a person who might be willing to help me and help me quickly.

Over the phone, I told Toby of the urgency of my inquiries. I explained that the police had only begun to take an interest and that I was following a lead on my own. He naturally was curious why I needed to check securities records while I was working on a missing person case. Toby was a trusted friend, but he was also a working business-news journalist. I did not want to get into The Big Molly details with him.

"It's nothing current at all. In fact, the information I'm looking for is about an operation that went out of business over twenty years ago. I'm quite possibly barking up the wrong tree, but it could be very important in figuring out what's happened to my brother-in-law."

"So you want to meet with someone tomorrow morning who can access old records about public offerings and stock sales. I do know one of the Commissioners. I'll call him and see if he'll cooperate. You sure this has nothing to do with any current investments?"

"Absolutely!"

"Good, because even if he were otherwise willing, he wouldn't give anyone access if it related to any possible trading. Can you stay at the phone you're using for ten minutes or so?"

I looked at my watch. "I have almost an hour before my flight." I gave him the number of my cell phone. "That should give me another forty-five minutes at least."

I thanked Toby and ended the call. I had not called Debra since early morning so I checked in with her. She had heard nothing. I told her I had visited the mine and talked with a former employee and had checked some mining records. She asked if I still thought there was any connection between Vince's time at the mine and his disappearance. I admitted that I was feeling that there was a connection, but did not elaborate. Ending the call, I started walking through the modest terminal toward a cybercafé I had noticed when I first arrived. I wanted to do some internet research and then follow that up with another phone call. There were more facts I needed to check before returning to the States.

NINETEEN

Toby had come through. Well before I boarded the plane in Prince George, he called me back. The Commissioner, Reginald Matthews, was going to be in his office the next morning and Toby had convinced him to meet with me. My taxi dropped me off in front of the building on West Georgia Street. There was a guard in the lobby and I gave him my name saying Mr. Matthews would be expecting me. The guard spoke softly over the telephone at the reception desk and then looked up at me.

"Mr. Matthews is on the fourth floor, room four-seventeen. He'll meet you in the upstairs elevator lobby. The elevators are secured for that floor so, if you'll follow me, I'll key it for you."

A minute later I was shaking hands with a tall, slim man in his early fifties. He wore a light brown cardigan sweater over a white shirt and perfectly-creased chestnut-brown slacks. His rather formal looking office and his impeccable attire belied his casual attitude.

"Call me Reggie. Toby says you're old mates from journalistic days in the States."

"That's right. We worked on an interesting story together down in Oregon."

"Well, Toby's a good stick and he says you're now

a private investigator and rather urgently need some information. He says you have assured him that your investigation has nothing to do with investments or litigation."

"That is exactly right."

"Good. How can I help?"

I told him that my brother-in-law had vanished and we were very worried about foul play. "My only lead so far seems to point to an abandoned mine here in B.C. It was owned by the missing man and his three partners. The time period I'm most interested in is twenty-seven to thirty-five years ago. I think the partners were doing business as Northwest Molybdenum or, possibly, British Columbia Molybdenum."

"So what exactly do you want to find out?"

"Well, to begin with, I need to know the identities of the partners and, if possible, who they bought the mining rights from."

"Our records won't necessarily reflect those facts. As you know, our main concern is in the public trading of securities. Did the partners ever incorporate?"

"Not that I know of. But they sold the mine to a corporation called Crazy Creek Minerals. I believe the sale was in nineteen-eighty-seven."

"We should have something on that." He motioned me to join him at a computer terminal to the left of his desk. He called up a database and entered the name I had given him. "Yes. Here it is. Crazy Creek Minerals dba CCM, Limited. We've only just recently finished digitizing some of the older records. I should be able to pull up the entire digital dossier on the company."

He clicked on the name in the index and the file appeared on his monitor. "Yes. Here are the records. Now," he continued, "if they had any stock offerings in that period, we should be able to see the prospectus and it might give you some information about CCM buying that mining property."

He scrolled through the file and a prospectus appeared. We saw that the corporation sold shares to the public just before its purchase of The Big Molly. An appendix to the prospectus showed the purchase agreements and there I saw the business name of the selling entity was Northwest Molybdenum. The names of the partners were listed. There was Vince, of course and three others: Nicholas W. Matson, Richard Bonaface, and Benjamin D. Turley. Now Matthews himself was getting interested.

"That's interesting," he said, pointing to some text on the screen. "This fellow Matson must have stayed on with CCM after they bought out the partners. Let me check the proxy information." He scrolled to other segments in the file and nodded. "Yes, he became an Assistant Vice President for Operations. Hmm. It appears he was granted stock options right from the beginning. Let's look ahead." He accessed the information for later years. "But it seems he left the company a little more than three years later, just about the time he was allowed to exercise the options." Matthews scrolled further and I saw that shortly thereafter, CCM, Ltd. had another public offering of its stock.

"I was new to the agency back then," Matthews said, "but I'm starting to remember some things about this company. That mine it owned, The Big Molly, was its principal asset and I think there was some controversy about the second stock sale when the mine's production slowed down."

He scrolled some more and we saw an article from a newspaper. The crux of the article was in the second paragraph:

> Fifteen months after the last public offering of this high-flying junior, its stock price has fallen steeply. Investors who had considered The Big Molly mine to have a bright future, were told that the main lode, "Zone A" was slowly but surely playing out. Zone A has been a highly profitable deposit for several years, but current assays indicate the production of quality ore is rapidly diminishing. The belief had been that there were qualtiy reserves in an area known as "Zone B", but this has not proven to be the case.

I asked Matthews if there had been any investigation triggered by the fall in the stock price.

"No. There was only one letter of concern, as I recall." He scrolled some more. "From this, it looks as though our staff reviewed the prospectus and found no overt misrepresentations or fraudulent non-disclosures on CCM's part. We took no further action."

"Can you tell the name of the person who sent in the complaint?"

"Well, it wasn't a formal complaint. But the letter writer was a Douglas Waterford," said Matthews and gave me the man's address.

"Thanks, Mr. Matthews. I'm very grateful for your taking the time to help on a busy morning!"

"I don't exactly see how it will lead to your brother-in-law, but you are welcome."

I used a telephone directory in the lobby to look for Douglas Waterford's number. It was not to be found. I called Directory Assistance asked for the number matching the address Matthews had provided. When I called that number and asked for Mr. Waterford, the woman who answered the phone said they had bought the house from Mr. Waterford two years ago and that they thought he had moved to the States, perhaps to Washington, six months ago.

I hung up the phone and considered what I had learned so far. Nick Matson had hooked up with the new owner of The Big Molly, but had left shortly before the mine's output had begun to taper off. I wondered if the other partners had known that. If there had been something fishy at the mine, Matson seemed to have positioned himself to suck even more profit out of the situation. Could there have been a scam? Could Matson have been behind it? And what did that suggest? Was Vince a threat to reveal damaging information about Matson or the mine? Did Matson need to clean up his resume by eliminating those with knowledge of his past activities? I reminded myself to not extrapolate too far beyond the known facts. Now it was time to try to nail down a few more of those facts.

My research the day before at the cybercafé in Prince George had turned up the name of a prominent mining engineer on the faculty of the University of British Columbia. I had immediately called and persuaded him to meet with me later on Tuesday morning. I had called a cab from the lobby of the BCSC building and, after a ten-minute wait on the windswept sidewalk, it finally arrived. I gave the driver the man's home address.

Philip Zuckerman had recently finished a stint as Head of the Earth Sciences Department. That told me he was a responsible academic and respected by his colleagues. But what grabbed my attention as I read faculty bios on the departmental website was Zuckerman's expertise in mine sampling and ore analysis. He had agreed to consult with me without mentioning fees, but I knew Debra would approve my retaining him regardless of the cost. He told me he would not be going to the campus until afternoon, but that I was welcome to visit him at his home. I climbed stone stairs up a low terraced bank to the front porch of his Dutch colonial home. He met me at the door and showed me to his living room. He appeared to be in his early sixties, but he moved like a person who could shoulder a pack and hike into the mountains at a moment's notice. We sat side by side on a leather couch so that I could spread out the copies of the assays on the coffee table before us. Zuckerman ran fingers through his thinning black hair and fiddled with filling the bowl of his pipe while I gave him some background. I started with Vince's disappearance and my suspicion that it could be some-how tied to The Big Molly.

"What it really comes down to, Professor, is I'm wondering if the two sets of Zone B samples – taken five years apart -- reflected in these assays were really from the same zone at this mine."

"Yes. I think I understand. And this zone had not been worked in the intervening years?"

"That's my understanding. They were working a different area, Zone A, and considered this zone sim-ply as a probable reserve based on the first assay."

Zuckerman put on some reading glasses and held the assay reports in hand as he studied them. After ten minutes or so, he cleared his throat and said, "Mr. Conwright, there are some similarities as is to be expected, but I find it very hard to believe that these assays are from the same zone. There are a few trace-element differences and, most importantly, the concentration of molybdenum is greatly different. There might be explanations for small differences: contamination of one sample, different technicians with unequal competencies, careless positioning of the sampling bores… things like that. But none of those factors could account for this large a difference. You said they were working the other zone at this mine? I seem to remember that The Big Molly was a producer in its day."

"Yes. Operations in Zone A were apparently quite profitable for several years."

"Is there any reason to believe the assays were

simply mislabeled? That the better, earlier, one purporting to be from Zone B was in fact from the zone where they were producing?" asked Zuckerman with a frown.

I remembered what the clock-watching clerk had mumbled as he looked through the file back at the assay office. "I can't be sure, but I think the first assays from both zones are very similar. Could you …?"

Zuckerman interrupted me. "I used the word 'mislabeled' because, in fact, they are identical. Looking at the later assay from Zone A, I would say the earlier two assay reports were both for zone A. But then what happened to the correct assay for the 'reserve' zone?"

"That's a good question, Professor. A very good question."

I offered to pay Professor Zuckerman for his services. He smiled and graciously declined. He said our meeting had only taken half-an-hour and he had not had to leave the comfort of his own home. He wished me success in finding my brother-in-law. I could sense that he wanted to question me about where I thought this was leading, but was professional enough not to ask. I was not sure of anything at this point, but the picture that was starting to come into focus was not a pretty one.

TWENTY

On the plane coming home from Vancouver, I mulled over something that had been bothering me. I finally remembered why the name Richard Bonaface had seemed so familiar. Earlier, in my days as an investigative reporter, I was digging into the local crime scene for a story about burglary rings. The name Richie Bonaface had come up. The word was that Mr. Bonaface might have served as a fence for a few, very valuable, items that had been liberated from their rightful Portland owners. My series was aimed more at home security measures, repeat-offender burglars, and law enforcement than at individual wholesalers of the stolen goods and I never was able to document a defensible link to 'Richie B.', as old McNally had called him. Now, I remembered that Bonaface owned a couple of exotic-dancer clubs on the East side of town.

Back in Portland, I dug up my old file and saw that he also was rumored to have a hand in a small-time numbers operation down the freeway in Woodburn. I needed to talk to every one of the original partners at The Big Molly and that meant an after-dinner visit to Richie B.

His office was at the Hunt Club – I'll spare you its nickname – and was located on southeast eighty-second

181

not far from Flavel Avenue. Eighty-second is a busy north-south street cutting through modest neighborhoods and some struggling commercial operations. The club was housed in a long, almost windowless, wooden-frame building with a low, barrel roof. The name was on a green neon sign over the entrance. In smaller letters, the sign added "live adult entertainment". I paid the cover charge and told the hulk of a man at the door that I would like to speak with Mr. Bonaface.

The hulk glowered at me and said. "Mr. Bonaface only sees people by appointment."

His voice was harsh, but startlingly high pitched. He could have been the tenor in a barbershop quartet, but I doubted that a suggestion like that would appeal to him.

"I understand, but I think he'll agree that my visit is important. Tell him it has to do with The Big Molly."

The hulk summoned another man to take his place and left me waiting. I could see booths against the west wall to the left of the door. Cocktail tables with chairs filled the center area. A gleaming bar ran most of the length of the east wall. The north wall featured the stage complete with a runway that pushed out into the room and a couple of gyrating topless dancers. Several doors ran along the wall to my right, presumably for offices. The goon at the door had entered one of them. After several minutes he returned and said, "Follow me."

Quite the conversationalist, I thought as he led me to an office at the end of the row. Well, maybe with a voice like his and the company he kept, one would not be a talker. "Here's the guy," he said to the man sitting behind a large, mahogany desk.

I saw a swarthy man of medium height and a generous head of black hair. A small scar showed under the man's right eye just above heavy jowls. Bonaface, if it was Bonaface, waved the other man away and he closed the door as he left. The man behind the desk made no move to rise and did not invite me to sit.

"You walk into my club and say you got to see me. You say it's about a big dolly or something. What's your game?"

"Are you Mister Bonaface?"

He scowled. "I'm Mister Bonaface. Now I asked *you* a question. What the fuck is this about?"

I did not feel like buying into his pretense that he did not understand the reference to The Big Molly. "It's about The Big Molly. The mine you used to own under the name Northwest Molybdenum."

He looked at me for many long seconds, then gestured toward a chair. His face was strangely unexpressive given his gruff tone. But his black eyes revealed a smoldering menace. "So I used to have an interest in a mine. That was a long time ago. What's that to you?"

"I'm looking for one of your partners from those days, Vince Langlow. He's gone missing. I'm working for the family trying to find out what's happened to him."

I could have sworn that Bonaface shuddered slightly when I said Vince was missing. "You're not the law?" he asked.

"No. I'm a private investigator. I'm only interested in Mr. Langlow's safety and his whereabouts. Here's my card."

Bonaface glanced at the card I handed him and the black eyes drilled into me. Whatever he saw, it must have convinced him that I was not an undercover cop because he looked fractionally more willing to continue our conversation. "So what do you want to know? I have no idea where Vince is!"

"When was the last time you saw him?"

"Hell, it's been years. Six years, at least. I guess I may have seen him a couple of other times at Blazers games ... places like that, but those weren't meetings. We just bumped into each other."

"Where did you get together the first time?"

"I'm not sure that's any of your business. It can't have anything to do with your finding him. "

"Have you spoken with him or communicated with him since that meeting six years ago? Other than at the Blazer games?"

"Look, I don't have any dealings with Vince these days. You might say we've gone our separate ways."

He obviously had avoided giving me a direct answer, but I let it pass at that point. "Tell me how things were between you two when you were operating the mine."

He seemed to me to almost flinch at the mention of The Big Molly.

"What do you mean? We were partners for Christ's sake!"

I waited him out. He finally continued, "We got along fine. We were young, single guys learning the mining business and working like dogs."

"So you four partners co-managed everything? Nobody had a veto power or had the right to make solo decisions?"

"It was informal. We all did our thing, but yeah, we talked things over all the time."

"What about getting the mine ready to sell? Appraising its potential?"

"Where're you going with this? God damn it, if I could help you with Vince, I would, but I'm not going to answer all these questions. You're time's up, Conwright."

He was plenty defensive about the mine and that reinforced my belief that somehow the mine was linked to Vince's disappearance, but Bonaface obviously was through being cooperative. I did not want him to call for his muscle to shove me out the door, but I needed to ask one more question.

"Can you tell me where you were Monday the twentieth from five pm onward?"

"You got a lot of balls, asking me questions like that! I told you I haven't had anything to do with Vince's disappearance! I didn't even know he was missing until I heard a couple of days ago on the TV." He stood up and leaned forward, his hands braced on his desk and his carotid artery visibly throbbing. "For your God damn information, I was with a realtor, Dan Sugarman, trying to close a deal. We were together from mid-afternoon 'til around eight in the evening. Now get out of my face!"

I walked out thinking his alibi was probably good since it depended upon a person not likely to be connected to the underworld. I would see if Sugarman could verify Bonaface's story as soon as I could reach the realtor. At a Seven Eleven down the street, I borrowed a phone book and looked up the home phone numbers for Sugarman and Vince's CFO, Dick Meadows. I called Meadows on my cell. I was not sure he would be home, but he answered on the fourth ring.

"Mister Meadows, it's Rick Conwright. Sorry to bother you at home, but there's a detail I need to check." He told me to go ahead. "Were there ever any business or financial links between Langlow Enterprises and a Richard Bonaface or a business called The Hunt Club?"

"Well, I'd have to carefully go over past records to be absolutely sure, but I very much doubt it. I would remember any significant transaction or loan or contract and neither of those names is remotely familiar."

"Is there any chance you could confirm that early tomorrow?"

"Yes, of course. I'll call you tomorrow as soon as I check. As I said, I'd be very surprised if there was any link."

My next call was to Dan Sugarman. I got an answering machine saying they were out. The machine's greeting said if I had a business need to reach Sugarman to call him on his cell phone and gave the number. This time, he picked up. I apologized for the evening call

186

and said I was one of Bonaface's "assistants" and one of my jobs was to keep track of his daily journal. I told him that Bonaface could not remember which day they had met and I was hoping he could straighten us out. It was a pretty lame line, but Sugarman was apparently at a social event and did not seem to want to take the time to question my reason for calling.

"It was Monday."

"A week ago?"

"Yes."

"And the time of day?"

"He can't remember that? Well, we got started pretty late, around half-past three and continued into dinner time. We must have broken up around seven or maybe a little later."

"Thanks. I got behind on this piss-ant little job, and now I'm trying to get the damn journal up to date."

I could tell he was already back into the flow of his party. "Okay. No problem."

I started my Acura and, twenty minutes later, turned off Tacoma Street just before the Sellwood Bridge and headed for my houseboat. Back at the marina parking lot, I punched in my sister's number. She picked up quickly.

"Debra, it's Rick. I got in a couple of hours ago. I have nothing new to report. I'm still working this angle about the old mine. But I need to ask you if you've ever met any of Vince's old partners at the mine."

"No. Not that I know of. I told you I didn't talk with him about his past."

"How about a man named Richard or Richie Bonaface? Ever meet him or hear Vince talk about him?"

"No. Never. Wait a minute. Did you say 'Richie' somebody?"

"Yes Richie Bonaface."

"I wouldn't know about the last name, but some-one who called himself Richie called on the phone for Vince the Sunday night before Vince disappeared."

"What did he say?"

"I told him Vince was out that evening – Vince was at a meeting with his fishing buddies planning a trip, but I didn't tell the caller that. Then he just said, 'tell him Richie wants to talk to him'. I meant to tell Vince about it at breakfast the next morning, but I forgot. In fact, I had forgotten all about it until you mentioned that name. It's a little unusual for a grown man to call himself Richie, so I guess that's why I thought of it just now. Does that call mean anything? Could he know where Vince is?"

I thought for a couple of seconds before I answered her. "One of Vince's partners at the mine was named Richie Bonaface. It could have been he who called. Do not *ever* agree to meet with him. If anyone using that name should call again, let me know right away, but don't let on that you are aware that he knew Vince."

"Is he dangerous?"

I could hear the anxiety in my sister's voice. I said, "I don't know but, now days, he's mixed up with the Portland underworld."

Minutes later, I parked the Acura and punched the

security code into the keypad on the gate at the pedestrian entrance to our boathouse community. I boarded my boat, unlocked the door, and disarmed the security system. To my right was a prized possession: a real brass enunciator that had once been on the bridge of a sea-going ship. The double levers moved indicators on the round dials on each face of the device. Enunciators were used to send engine-speed orders to a ship's engine room and to receive confirmation that the orders had been carried out. I had been checking marine antique shops for years before I found one. I paid plenty for it and it was undoubtedly one of the most expensive furnishings in my home.

I turned up the heat, shucked off my coat, and poured myself some Gentleman Jack in a rocks glass. Drink in hand, I entered my office and turned on the computer. I went to the website of a company that I had used once before in tracing a father who had skipped out on his child support and changed his name. Peter Devereau had said that Nick Matson had changed his name. I wanted to talk to Matson, wanted to hear his version of events at The Big Molly including his subsequent role with Crazy Creek Minerals, but that would be impossible until I learned the name he was now using. I logged in, gave my credit card information and put in the name. On my monitor, two names appeared. One Nicholas Matson had just changed his name six months ago. The second, more likely candidate, went through the process fifteen years ago. His new name was 'Nash Milliken'. Whether it is not having to buy new monogrammed shirts or is just a liking for the general rhythm of one's name, it is common that a name-changer will choose a new name with the same initials. Tomorrow I would have to figure out how to get in touch with "Nash". But now, my thoughts turned to Angie.

At the end of my call to Angie at her parent's home in Spokane, I had asked her if she could get a cab in from the airport because I wouldn't be there to pick her up. There was a pause and then, sounding a little cool, Angie said she guessed she could do that. I hated to disappoint her and hoped she had not called Bill-the-producer for a ride. But I liked it much better when I called this evening because she asked me if I wanted to come by her place for a nightcap around ten.

Angie had received her degree in communications from Whitman College in Walla Walla and had landed a job as a field reporter and non-meteorologist weather person at a Cincinnati television station. From there, she moved to a Boise station where she became a fixture on the evening news team. Now, at thirty-seven, she had moved up to big-city programming in the KOIN newsroom. She had the chops to fill an anchor position – that I knew she very much wanted – but as the junior member of the Portland team, she was back to field reporting and some weekend and late-evening news-desk slots.

As I understand it, she had been engaged to a young man at Whitman in her senior year. He had been killed in some kind of a car accident and, thereafter, she had never married. Ron, her brother, was a spiker on our volleyball team. Ron had been telling me about this sister of his who had just come to Portland to take a television news job. He seemed to think she and I would get along well together. I don't always watch the local news and, when I do, it's usually a different station. But after the second time Ron mentioned Angie to me, I switched to KOIN. When a segment by Angie about an overturned truck came on, the beautiful, blond reporter held my attention. My social life had been in the toilet. Maybe it was the twelve-hour days refurbishing the apartment building or maybe it was the struggle to get my new business up and running. Or, perhaps there was a faint, almost unacknowledged, hope that Justine would drop the divorce proceeding and come back. She did not and it's now official. In any case, I was as edgy as a teenager trying to get his first prom date when I called Angie. I guess Ron must have mentioned me to her because she seemed to know who I was and we agreed on a date for the last Portland Timbers soccer game of the season. The evening was warm, the hot dogs were good and the Timbers won. Despite the clamor of the fans, we spent more time talking to each other than watching the game. I can say that our date at Jeld-Wen Park was a big success. Ron had it pretty well figured out. We *have* gotten along well, and we've been seeing more and more of each other as the weeks have rolled by.

So there I was, using the intercom in the lobby of her apartment on a tree-lined block on Everett Street, a little before ten. The inner door buzzed to admit me and I headed for the elevator. When she opened her door, it was as though I had entered some kind of an irresistible magnetic field. Her hair gave off the fragrance of a scented shampoo. She had on white pants that hugged her trim hips and she wore a teal cable-knit sweater that offered a perfect outline of her breasts. She smiled and came into my arms. Our kiss was lingering and deep. When we came up for air, she closed the door and I said, "Welcome home, Angie."

"Thanks. I missed you, Rick."

"And you better believe I missed you, too!"

She turned and beckoned me to follow her into a small dining room. She opened a hutch and I saw liquor bottles inside. She gave me a small smile, "What'll you h-"

That magnetic field was surging around me now, overwhelming the fatigue and tension of the day. Before she completed her question, I touched her shoulders and spun her into another embrace. Her tongue probed my mouth sending a message that I was so ready to receive.

"To hell with the drink," I said huskily as her fingers unbuttoned the placket of my polo shirt.

She pulled the shirt out of my slacks and murmured, "Yeah. Superseded!"

I ripped my shirt over my head and lifted her sweater upwards. "Definitely! Other priorities." I slid the sweater over the fullness of her bra and felt the cresting of her nipples through the satiny material. We kissed again for a small eternity. Then she unhooked her bra and shrugged it to the floor. My hands explored every contour of her breasts. Her hands had discovered a contour of my own.

"Come with me," she said taking my hand and leading me down a short hallway to her bedroom.

"I can take precau …" I started.

"No need. I've wanted this to happen for weeks, Rick. I'm on the pill," she said as she guided me through the doorway.

In that room, we set a speed record for shedding the rest of our clothes. Angie pulled back the bed covers and we began a thorough, playful exploration of each other's bodies. She gave soft moans of anticipation and pleasure as our passion swept us into the ultimate ecstasy.

We had finally fallen asleep in the small hours of the morning. When I awoke around a quarter after eight, I found Angie nestled against my shoulder and her left arm across my chest. After a few minutes, she moved slightly and cracked open one eye.

"You awake?"

"Yeah. Just. Unless I've died and gone to heaven."

She pinched my ribs and said with an impish look, "No way. This is planet earth and you're right where you belong." Then she kissed me. I thought, this was one great way to wake up! As we kissed, I slid her over me. I felt the incredible smoothness of her skin along the whole of my body. When our kiss ended, we were wide awake and more than ready to repeat the pleasures of the night before.

Our lovemaking was followed by the quiet languor that lets lovers reenter the everyday world. We showered together a little after nine and Angie fixed a great omelet for our breakfast. We started reading The Orgonian over coffee, but I said I needed to get going. Angie took a sip of her coffee, looked at me over the rim of her mug and said, "Rick, I told you I would be looking into the Vince Langlow thing. Your sister is declining interviews which I can understand. I've learned that his car is also missing. Have you eliminated the possibility that he just took off?"

Right then, I knew what was coming.

I decided the best way to throw her off the scent was to admit the basics and downplay the rest. "That's true. My sister is concerned that he may've been in an accident … maybe even has amnesia. She's reported him as a missing-person. That may turn out to have been unnecessary, but she's worried and I guess it was a smart thing for her to do."

"But he hasn't turned up, has he?"

"No," I said as I reached for the coffee pot to top off my mug. I tried to shift the conversation to a different subject, but Angie cut that short.

"Rick, I spoke with a contact I have in the police department. He said they have just started an investigation and so far, there's been no sign of Mr. Langlow or his vehicle, but he implied there'd been a ransom demand."

"Angie, I'm sorry, but I really can't confirm or

deny anything like that right now. I'm working every angle I can think of, but we don't know anything about where he might be or what's happened to him."

What had happened to our romantic morning-after breakfast, I wondered. This was not my new lover, but a straining-at-the-leash newshound. "My sister's frantic," I continued. "Both for investigative reasons and for the sake of my confidential relationship with my sister, it just isn't something I can talk about."

"So is it a kidnapping? A possible homicide? Do you have any sense of why it happened?"

I took a sip of coffee and avoided her gaze. She was not getting my message. "Look, Angie, like I said, I couldn't discuss it with you even if I did have an idea. I'm working professionally for the family and you're a television newscaster."

"You're right, of course. I'm sorry to have come on like that, Rick. But Langlow's going to be front-page news from now on. Now that it's broken, other reporters are working the story too. Can't you just give me some background?"

"No. I won't give *anyone* background unless it would somehow help my own efforts. If that were to be the case, you would certainly be included."

"But not an exclusive?" she asked with a winsome smile.

"Possibly, Angie, but that would have to depend on how it would be most helpful to get the publicity. Anyway, I'm not at that point now."

That ended the subject, but I was more than a

little disappointed by the way she pressed me. We finished our coffee amiably enough, but there was an unmistakable strand of tension between us as I left the apartment.

TWENTY-ONE

I went straight to the Portland Justice Center after leaving Angie's apartment. I had called Paul DeNoli to prevail upon him to be there when I arrived. I took the elevator to the thirteenth floor and was cleared by the receptionist to enter the detectives' squad room. Paul saw me coming and motioned me back to his cubicle. The module's sound-absorbing wall above his desk was almost completely covered with family photos.

"Thanks, Paul, for making time for me."

DeNoli nodded with a smile. "No problem, Rick, but I don't have any good news for you. On the other hand, I don't have any bad news either."

"How active is PPB?"

"To be honest, I just got the green light last night. I checked with your sister and we'll get a tap-and-trace on her line. She said she has heard nothing. I told you I was able to jump the gun to get an APB out on Langlow's car. Nobody's seen it so far."

"Anything on his cards?"

"Not so far. We got his card numbers from his wife and we've alerted the clearing houses as well as his bank. There've been no ATM withdrawals and no charges incurred since he went missing. You said you were going to Canada. What was that all about?"

"It turns out my brother-in-law used to be in the mining business long before he married my sister. It was kind of a black hole in his personal history. I couldn't find any enemies or problems in his current life so I went up there to check out his past."

"Mining, huh? Find anything that shed any light on his vanishing?"

"I don't know. There were some vague rumors of skullduggery. A young guy who could have been a whistle blower met a nasty death in a car accident on an isolated mountain road. And there were some curious inconsistencies in assays on ore samples supposedly taken from one of the zones at the mine."

"Yeah. Well, we'll turn up the volume with our snitches and interview people at his business and check for witnesses around the Multnomah Athletic Club, but until the car turns up or ... well, a body ... we don't have much to work with. On the other hand, I don't have the staff to start probing a twenty-five-year-old mining scandal. If you think there's a connection, I'm afraid it's up to you to chase it down. Just let me know if you find a smoking gun or an honest-to-God direct link."

I could tell that Paul did not think much of The Big Molly thing. I had not articulated exactly what my theory was because it was still only a germ of an idea. But I was becoming more and more convinced that there was some form of blackmail going on that could be traced back to the phony assays at the mine. Had

Vince been eliminated because he was a blackmailer? Was he being held hostage as a threat to others to keep some secret? It was good that the police detectives had finally gotten involved, but I intended to continue to look for links leading out from the mine in the wilds of British Columbia.

"Fair enough, Paul. But do me a favor and run a criminal history on one of my mine investors."

"Sure. What's the name?"

"Actually, two names. This guy would be in his late forties by now. He changed his name. Originally, he was Nicholas Matson. Now, he's Nash Milliken. Can you use the federal data base as well as Oregon's?"

"Okay. It may take a while. You going to wait?"

"I'll look over your shoulder if you don't mind or, I can go find a morning paper."

Paul grinned and said, "No big deal. Pull up a chair!" He worked the computer and we had the information reasonably quickly. There were over a dozen Nicholas Matsons with federal criminal records, but only one with a birth date in our range. He transported a stolen car from Tennessee to Ohio at the time the four partners were working the mine in British Columbia. I felt sure he was not our man. Nash Milliken turned up nothing at all on either the federal data base or on Oregon's Law Enforcement Data System. Since there was no one but us using the computer at that time, I persuaded Paul to run credit checks on the name Nash Milliken. Without a social security number, we caught twenty-nine names. I recorded the addresses and phone numbers for all of them, even though only eight of them were in the probable age range.

I got out my phone card and asked Paul's permission to use one of the police phones. Four of the eight Millikens were not home on a late weekday morning. I was told by a spouse that one of them was terminally ill in hospice care. Another was a doctor who told me he had been attending a medical conference in Cincinnati on the Monday in question. I asked him for the name of the conference and the hotel. He sounded a little irritated, but gave me the information. My next calls eliminated a woman with the unusual first name of Nash and a man with a terrible stutter. Neither McNally nor Devereau had mentioned that one of the partners stuttered. I thought such a problem would have been unique enough to be included in their descriptions if the Nick Matson of The Big Molly had been a stutterer.

I knew Peter Devereau thought the partner who changed his name settled in California and my name-change search had shown one of the men with a Los Angeles address. Only one of the Millikens on whom I was now concentrating showed a California address. Devereau's information, even if correct at the time, was, by now, stale. The old Nick Matson could have gone to California and then moved to Maine for all I knew, but I had to start somewhere. The California Milliken's address from the credit check was in Mill Valley.

"Paul, I've been trying to reach the right Nash

Milliken. The one I need to reach moved to California fifteen or more years ago. Just one Milliken on my credit-check list shows a California address -- in Mill Valley -- and he didn't answer his phone. Would you be willing to contact your counterparts on the Mill Valley police force and see what they know, if anything, about this guy?"

"Sure, no problem."

Paul consulted a law enforcement directory and placed the call. He showed me how to join in from a nearby phone. Paul told the sergeant who answered the phone we were working on a missing person case and thought a Mill Valley resident named Nash Milliken might have some useful information.

"Did you say 'Nash Millken'?"

"Yes, why? Does he have a criminal record in California?"

"No, no. The man was murdered about four weeks ago! On October twenty-ninth!"

"Holy Shit!," said DeNoli. "Have you found the murderer?"

"No, we haven't. In fact we haven't made any progress at all. Can there be a connection to your case?"

"It's possible. How and where was he killed?" I asked.

"A sniper. He was out running on a trail on Mount Tamalpais. I'm not one of the guys working the case, but, as I understand it, there was a level place in the trail with a bench and a trail sign. Our homicide guys are guessing he may have used that as a turn-around place. It's almost exactly three-and-a-half miles from the trailhead where they found his car. He probably stopped to catch his breath before running back down and, for a few seconds, presented a stationary target. I heard that his wife said that's a run he makes at least a couple of times a week. I guess that suggests the killer knew his running pattern."

"Can you tell us if this guy ever changed his name?" asked DeNoli.

"Yes, I heard that he had! If you men know that, there must be some connection."

"Well, there is a connection all right, but whether it has anything to do with who killed your man and who may have abducted our man, we don't know at this point."

Paul asked him for the name of the detective heading up the case and left his phone number so the two of them could compare notes as things developed, if they did. Paul was now giving somewhat more credence to my hunch about ties to Vince's past. We agreed Paul would liaise with the Mill Valley detective and I would keep checking leads related to the mine.

I left the thirteenth floor and stopped to check a phone book at a booth in the Justice Center lobby. Richie Bonaface appeared to have an unlisted number. One member of my volleyball team, Doug Wilkerson, worked as a manager for the phone company. I called Doug and asked if he could get me Bonaface's address. He was a little uncomfortable with doing that, but I told him a life was at stake. I said I just needed to have a conversation with Mr. Bonaface. He agreed to call me back and I gave him the pay phone number. Two minutes later, I had Bonaface's address and phone number.

TWENTY-TWO

Wednesday, November 29th, 12:30 P.M.

Bonaface lived in a large mock Tudor in a well-kept, but older, neighborhood not far down the hill from the reservoirs on Mount Tabor in east Portland. I rang the bell, but no one answered. I went back to my car to wait. Given that he usually seemed to be present at The Hunt Club in the evenings, I thought there was a good chance I could catch him at home in the middle of the day. I was scanning the sports pages when Bonaface arrived. His Buick swung into the garage and the door came down. Two minutes later, I was on the porch again. A woman answered the door wearing a black dress. Behind her, Bonaface appeared wearing a dark coat and tie. I wondered if they had been to a funeral. I guess even minor hoods dress up for such occasions.

Bonaface swept his wife aside and glowered at me. "Conwright, I told you once to clear out. How'd you find out where I live?"

"I'm a detective, Mr. Bonaface." My humor did not seem to lighten his mood at seeing me on his doorstep. I started over. "I'm sorry to bother you, but I have some news I think you need to hear. Can we speak privately?"

"This better be good." Then, to his wife, "I'll handle this. We'll be in my office."

The house had a basement and his home office

was down there. I felt a little uneasy going down the basement stairs, given Bonaface's background and attitude. Maybe it was too soon after my experience with McPherson. I felt a little better knowing his wife was right upstairs, but, for all I knew, she was Bonnie to his Clyde.

Bonaface closed the office door behind us and lit a cigarette. We were in a knotty-pine-paneled room. I saw a flat-panel television mounted on one wall and a large, but somewhat scarred desk in front of a black leather office chair. We both remained standing. With his short fuse, I decided to get right down to business.

"One of your former partners was murdered a few weeks ago."

Some of the color left his face as he eyed me coolly. "One of my former partners?"

"In The Big Molly. Nick Matson."

"Nick! Do they know who did it?"

"They're working on it, but they have no leads yet."

"Where did this happen?"

"You don't know where he was living?"

"No! I told you, Conwright, I haven't kept up relationships with those guys."

"Do you know what name Matson has been going by lately?"

"What's that supposed to mean? You saying he changed his name?"

"Yes, quite a few years ago. Do you know the name?"

"No. Now that I think of it, I guess I *had* heard he

changed his name, but, if I ever knew it, I've forgotten it now."

"So you or Mister Turley would not have any reason to want Matson and Langlow out of the way?"

"Where did you graduate charm school, Conwright? You really have a touch! I don't know about Turley, but I haven't made any moves on Matson or Langlow. We got along ... no problems. I haven't seen them in years and I don't want them 'out of the way' as you put it."

Bonaface lit a new cigarette with the butt of his first one. I smelled the smoke as he exhaled. The familiar odor drove straight to the core of my nervous system. God, how I wanted one myself! I knew he would not offer me, an unwelcome guest in his home, a smoke. Even so, I was ready to ask. I finally got a grip on myself.

Bonaface took another draw on his Marlborough and said, "Look, I'm sorry about Vince and Nick," he said. "But leave me out of this! Got it?"

The scowl was returning along with a faint sheen of perspiration on Bonface's forehead. I knew trying to pin down Bonaface's actions on given days would piss him off, especially since not all of his activities were likely to be legal. Still, I wanted to see if he was in or out of the mix in the Milliken/Matson murder. "So, if you're completely disconnected with this thing, you wouldn't mind telling me where you were on the fourth of this month?" I asked.

"Shit. Why should I tell you things like that?"

"Because, there's a good chance your life may also

be in danger. If I like the answers I hear, we may be able to help each other."

That stopped him for a moment. Bonaface took a big draw on his cigarette and stared at me. Then, with a shrug of his shoulders, he moved to his desk and consulted an appointments book. "On the fourth, I had business here in town. I was at the club during the afternoon and evening."

That certainly did not constitute much of an alibi. I had no doubt that his staff at the club would cover for him no matter where he had been. But I had deliberately used a date after the murder and now I asked about the real date. "And how about on the twenty-ninth of October?"

"What are you going to do, write my biography day by day! Okay, that day I don't have to look up. I was at Good Samaritan Hospital passing a fucking kidney stone. Is that good enough for you?"

That answer sounded sincere, not to mention Bonaface probably figured there was some way I could check it and would not have chosen to lie about it. Of course, he might have arranged a contract killing or had one of his goons do it. But I figured him for a small-time crook and doubted his connections in the underworld would take him that far.

"Mr. Bonaface, there was a death at The Big Molly during the time you and your partners were operating it. A young geologist, Jari Kirvesniemi. Do you remember that?"

Bonaface lit a third cigarette with the butt of his

second and shifted his gaze to a framed poster on the wall publicizing a heavy-weight fight. "Yeah. I remember that," he said so softly that I could barely hear him.

"There was talk that this geologist had found some things that made him believe there was some fraud going on."

"Hah! You live in a mining community and half of what you hear is about claim jumping, fraud, unsafe practices. It's like people got nothing better to talk about on the long winter nights!"

"So you don't know anything about what was bothering the geologist?'

"Was *supposedly* bothering him, you mean. Hell, no!"

"How about the way he died? Any ideas about that?"

"Look, Conwright, twice I've let you come talk to me and twice you've stuck your nose in my business. I don't know why you think there's some connection from that time to Vince's disappearance. We're done here! And don't come around bothering me anymore."

He opened the door and we went upstairs. His responses to my other questions reinforced my growing certainty that, at best, the partners had somehow salted the assays for Zone B and that topic would continue to be out-of-bounds so far as Bonaface was concerned. As I started my car, I realized he had cut me off before I asked one last question. Where was the Big Molly's fourth partner? Not getting to ask the question did not matter a whole lot, because I was quite sure that I already knew the answer.

TWENTY-THREE

Wednesday, November 29ᵗʰ, 2:40 P.M.

It had come to me as I lifted a forkful of omelet at Angie's earlier that day. I was pissed at myself for not having seen it sooner. The fourth partner was identified in the records of Northwest Molybdenum as Benjamin D. Turley. I had *already* interviewed the fourth partner! He was Vince Langlow's long-time friend and his racquetball opponent on the day he vanished.

I called Don Turley' office and they said he had complained of a headache and had gone home early. I reached him at his residence and asked to meet with him right away. He mentioned his headache and hesitated for a good ten seconds before agreeing. I drove west on Belmont, crossed the Morrison Bridge and headed toward his home in northwest Portland. I crossed Burnside going north and passed by Portland's famous literary landmark, Powell's City of Books. This quirky, labyrinthine bookstore takes up an entire city block. The owner kept acquiring adjacent buildings as the business grew. Now, seemingly random stairways and access doors allow booklovers to roam from one genre to the next in the rambling complex.

Turley and his wife had a condo on the tenth floor of one of the new high-rises that were sprouting like tulips in April in the now upscale Pearl District.

I called him on the lobby phone and he gave me the elevator code. His wife was apparently out when I arrived. Their place was done in modern urban with blond maple floors, plenty of chrome, and a couple of nice pieces of art including lithographs of, I guessed, Klee and Miro. Turley met me at the door wearing slacks and a cashmere pullover. We walked through a broad entrance hall and past a spacious and richly appointed den to reach the living room. I saw the mounted head of a big-horn sheep on one of the den walls above a glass-faced teak gun cabinet as we passed. Turley showed me to a white leather couch in his living room and took a seat himself in a matching easy chair. I complimented him on a handsome home and then got right to the point.

"As I'm sure you know, we still have no idea what has happened to Vince. When I spoke with you on Wednesday, why didn't you tell me you and Vince were partners in a mining operation in Canada?"

Turley shrugged, "You did not ask about the distant past and I didn't imagine – still can't – how it could've been relevant."

"I told you I needed to know everything you could tell me about Vince…"

"I know, but I took that to mean everything in the present."

"Do you know that your former partner, Nick Matson, was murdered just a month ago?"

Turley's hands, for an instant, clenched the arms of his chair and he shuddered. "Murdered?"

"Yes. Not a random act of violence, but a premeditated murder. I don't think it's a coincidence that Vince has gone missing. The police are starting to work on the same linkage. Why don't you start by telling me where you were on the Sunday Matson was killed."

"When was it?"

"Sunday. October twenty-ninth."

"Sunday. Okay, let me think ... I was in Seattle. Two friends and I went up to watch the Seahawks game. We drove up and got into town about four o'clock on Saturday. Bill Hanford and Chris Deathridge, were the guys with me."

"All right. I'm assuming, at this time, that you were not involved in offing Matson. Incidentally, did you know he had changed his name?"

"Yeah, I did. I can't remember what he changed it to, though. We haven't been in touch for almost fifteen years."

If that was his story, I did not particularly want to tell him Matson's new name, just in case he later slipped up and indicated he did know how to reach him. "I need you to tell me about The Big Molly. What was going on up there with the assays of the ore?"

"Well, nothing. I mean you have assays done from time to time when you're working a mine."

"That dog won't hunt, Mr. Turley. I've seen the assays from Zone B. I've had an expert look at them. You guys were salting the mine; getting ready to sell it for more than it was worth."

"What are you talking about? If you want to make crazy accusations, you can leave right now! I thought you wanted to find Vince."

"Listen, I *do* want to find Vince. And that's *all* I'm interested in. My only interest in what was going on at the mine is to understand how it threatens Vince and possibly yourself."

Turley gathered himself. He got up and went to a wet bar in a corner of the room. He poured himself a Glenfiddich on the rocks and raised the bottle at me. "No thanks," I said. "So. The assays?"

Turley took a large swallow and looked me over for several seconds. "Yes, you might say that we jigged the assays. Samples from Zone A were submitted as being from Zone B. It started as an innocent mistake. The Zone B samples were somehow misplaced at the mine and someone thought the Zone A samples *were* the missing Zone B samples so they were sent to the assay lab. By the time we discovered the mix-up, the buyer had finished its due diligence. The deal looked good. Rather than redo the assays and possibly rock the boat on the closing, we just decided to keep quiet. It wasn't the honest thing to do, but we didn't plan it out *ahead of time* that way! Look, it didn't hurt anybody. The pit at Zone A produced far more quality ore than we had anticipated. The buyers had a more than decent return on their investment. The Zone B thing was wrong and I think we're all ashamed of it, but it's ancient history!"

"You say your scam didn't hurt anybody. What about Jari Kirvesniemi?"

"The geologist? He died in an accident!"

"He found out about the assay scam didn't he?"

"He… he claimed the assays were incorrect. He was young … idealistic. We tried to reason with him. We offered him a partnership. He wouldn't consider it. He tried to get us to withdraw that assay."

"That meant he was a big threat to you four. What were you going to do about that?"

"One of us said he would make him another, even better, offer."

"That would have been Bonaface?"

Turley took another pull on his drink and turned his back to me. "Yes. Richie."

"What if he still refused?"

"Richie said he would scare the hell out of him. Scare him away from the mine, away from Topley."

"What happened when he tried that tactic?"

"I don't know. The rest of us kind of kept out of it. Twenty-four hours later Jerry had the accident."

"What did Bonaface tell the rest of you?"

"He just said Jerry was considering our last offer. Are you implying….?"

"The young man's father came up there to bring his son's body back to the States. He thought his son was killed to keep him quiet."

"Look, Richie was a little aggressive. He liked to play the Alpha male role. But we never told him to actually *do* anything to Jerry. I suppose we figured he might rough him up a little, but…."

"Did you talk to the Constable?"

"Well, he came up to the mine after the accident and asked all of us some questions. So yeah, we talked to him."

"But not about the assays? Not about Jari's suspicions?"

Turley turned to face me with a tortured look. "No. I never lied to him, but I did not mention those things."

"And the rest of you never questioned Bonaface?"

"No. I very much wanted to believe it was an accident ... I really did believe that. I think the others did too. But we never questioned Richie in the way you mean."

"I think it's possible that one of you feels very threatened that the past up at the mine will come out ... come out in a way that could lead to a murder investigation. You must know that there is no statute of limitations on homicide. You all have left the mining industry and have been leading comfortable lives. If Vince and Matson wanted to get this episode off their chests, you or Bonaface might decide they had to be silenced."

"No! How can you think that! Vince is one of my oldest friends and, as for Matson, like I said, I haven't even heard from him for at least fifteen years. Besides, I think he changed his name to distance himself from that whole business. It doesn't make sense that he would try to rake it up after all these years!"

"But you're a respected citizen in the Portland area. You're at the top of your game in the business world. You could lose it all, if those days were scrutinized, if even just the assay scam became known."

"You may be right, but so many things have changed... I've changed. In those days, we'd get wild

hairs up our asses and just plunge ahead. Call it un-
checked ambition, or greed, or reckless disregard for
others ...whatever. I'm not that way anymore and
neither is Vince. We've both worked hard to become
different people. You could say we've tried to become
the best we knew how to be. That may sound corny,
but it's true! Vince and I rarely talk about the past, but
we both were driven to rise above it ...to be honest,
productive members of the community. Listen, even if
my business or my social standing were threatened, I
would never consider violence as a solution!"

"What if the threat were to be indicted as a co-
conspirator to murder?"

Turley again squeezed the arms of his chair and
took a pull on his drink before answering. "I don't
know anything about criminal law, but I know I never
planned a killing or even contemplated one! An investigation or indictment would be totally unnerving but,
still, I would *never* kill someone trying to expose me.
I would hire the best defense lawyer I could find and
prove my innocence."

"And Bonaface? What would his attitude be?"

"Richie was never the same after we left Canada.
He became quarrelsome, moody. Things did not go
well for him. He just kind of gradually slid into the
toilet. We stopped doing things together. I think Vince
was in touch with him a few times, but I just lost contact all together. I knew he was still around Portland
somewhere, but that's all I knew. I don't have any idea
where his head is these days. He used to be kind of

impetuous and he had a short fuse, but – even so – I can't see him trying to kill Vince or Nick."

"What if some of his activities over the years have been connected to the underworld?"

"Yes, I've heard those stories, but … I don't know …" he said, flapping his hands with an air of uncertainty and doubt.

I was starting to believe again that Turley was not responsible for Vince's disappearance even though he had not told me that their relationship went back to The Big Molly. I had been jotting down a few notes, but I laid my pen down and looked into Turley's eyes. "If we put aside blackmail or exposure of an embarrassing past, there is the possibility that someone has started a vendetta against all you partners, either over salting the mine, or over Jari Kirvesniemi's death. Given what you've told me about the assay and the sale of the mine, I think it's possible that what's happening now could be connected to the mine."

I could tell that Turley had also been thinking along those lines. He crossed his arms and sat pensively for a few seconds, then stood up and started pacing.

"All right. There's something else I haven't told you. About five weeks ago, I received a package delivered by United Parcel. Something very unique. It came without a valid return address. It was shipped from Sacramento. It was a small, rather heavy package. Inside, there was no message … just one thing. It was a small ingot of molybdenum. Stamped on it, was the logo of The Big Molly."

TWENTY-FOUR

Wednesday, November 29th, 5:10 P.M.

Turley had shown me the ingot. It was small, maybe three inches long, half as wide and no more than an inch thick. Its color was somewhere between the dull, darker gray of lead and the lighter look of unpolished aluminum. On its top surface, I saw an arched curve of letters that spelled "THE BIG MOLLY". I had asked him if the ingot was, in fact, refined molybdenum. He said he had taken it to be tested and, yes, it was molybdenum. I had asked him if it was refined and cast at the order of Northwest Molybdenum. Turley said they had never ordered any ingots that small from the smelter they used.

I had been hugely frustrated that Turley had already received the ingot, unambiguously referring to the mine, when I had first spoken with him about Vince and he had not told me about it. I had controlled my anger. He clearly had not wanted to talk about the ingot or the mine, so I had to at least give him credit for finding the courage to tell me during my second session with him. I doubted getting angry would have helped and I needed him to continue cooperating. I did wonder *why* he decided to tell me. Was it just that he had finally, after hearing the news of Matson's murder, realized a linkage of the past to the present? Had he coolly concluded that the advantages now outweighed the risks? Or had he been a little panicked ... fearful for his own safety and suddenly saw me as a personal defender? Or, was he playing me? Had he contrived to have this ingot and the story about its mysterious UPS delivery to throw me off the scent of his own involvement?

I mulled these questions over in my mind as I drove to my sister's house. Debra met me at the door. The dark half-circles were still beneath her eyes and she looked even more exhausted than the last time I had been to the house. I gave her a bear hug and held her for a long moment. To my great relief, Milliken's murder had erased the last tiny shred of my doubt about her and the insurance policy on Vince's life. Before, I had felt extremely guilty about even having such a passing thought, but the coldly objective, investigator-part of my brain had to recognize the rich-widow outcome as a conceivable motive.

I still entertained a faint hope that I could find Vince alive and that all this would somehow end well. For that reason, I did not want to tell my sister about the fraud with the assays or about the young would-be whistle blower. I was inclined to accept Turley's version that he and Vince and Matson had believed only that Bonaface would make one further effort to persuade the geologist and, failing that, would attempt to scare him away. That scenario was not very savory, but at least it was not deeply evil or homicidal. If Vince came through this alive, *he* would have to decide what to tell his wife. On the other hand, Debra was my 'client' and she was owed the truth to the extent that her decision-making depended upon it. I rationalized, for the time being, that she had asked me to find Vince and had not explicitly required me to inform her about details of his past. I ended up telling her that one of the mine partners had been murdered a few weeks ago and that I was looking for connections between Vince and other people related to the mining operation. She was so weary that she did not ask me hard questions about what Vince could have done back then that could have led to his disappearance.

Hearing of the Matson/Milliken murder made Debra even more anxious, but I wanted her to be realistic about what might have happened to Vince. I also wanted her to be extra vigilant for her own safety. Notwithstanding the recent intrusion on her property by the perpetrators of the ransom scam and the news about Matson, she steadfastly declined my offer to stay nights at her house. I told her there was something she could do to help.

"One of the other partners told me he had received a small molybdenum ingot by UPS." I did not mention Turley by name although Debra knew that I had been talking with him and with the former partner named Bonaface. "I believe that ingot has some significance in this whole business. Do you know if Vince got such a package in the last few months? Or ever?"

"No. At least he never mentioned it to me. How big was the package?"

I estimated the packing that would have been necessary to ship an ingot of the size and weight of the one received by Turley and showed her with my hands. "Well, I do seem to remember them delivering a couple of parcels for Vince in the last month. I think one of them was about that size. They were both addressed to him alone so, of course, I did not open them. I just put them on his desk and, each time, told him that a package had arrived."

"Will you help me search his belongings to see if one of those packages could have contained an ingot?"

"Of course. Let's start in his den and then we can try the shelves on his side of our closet and his workshop in the basement."

We found nothing in Vince's desk drawers or the cupboards beneath the built-in bookshelves. There was a small safe hidden behind some of the books and I asked Debra if she knew the combination. She did and, seconds later, she had the safe open. At the back of the top shelf inside, we found the ingot. It looked identical to the one Turley had shown me.

"Rick, what does it mean?" She looked at the imprint of The Big Molly logo. "Did this come from that mine?"

"Well, the metal may have been refined from ore taken from The Big Molly, but the partner who got the other one said they had never ordered any ingots this small. In any case, it certainly was intended to send some kind of a message about the mine to the partners. You're sure Vince never said anything about receiving this?"

"Absolutely."

"Can you remember if his mood changed in any way after those packages arrived?"

"No. Not really. There was one evening along about then when he stayed in his den all evening. I asked him what he was doing and he said he 'just had some business to take care of.' I didn't think anything more of it, at the time."

I had an idea and I called Turley on my cell.

"Mr. Turley, it's Rick Conwright again. I just thought of another question. Do you know if Jari Kirvesniemi ever owned an ingot, full size or otherwise?"

"Yes, I think he did. I remember he was real proud of our production and at one point he asked us if he could buy an ingot from the smelter. We had an exclusive contract to supply an alloy company so we had to get a waiver from them. We got it and gave him a copy, so I suppose he went ahead and bought one."

"Thanks."

"What are you thinking?"

"I'm wondering if that could have been the source of the little one you received."

"Jeez! So maybe a brother or the father... ?"

"I don't know. It's just an idea. I'm going to dig a little further and see what I can learn."

I ended the call to Turley and said good night to Debra. The rain that fell earlier in the day had stopped, but heavy clouds obscured the moon and stars. In minutes, I arrived at our little boathouse community in the Oaks Bottom district on the east bank of the

Willamette. I punched in the gate code and walked onto the floating pier that extended a few feet into the Willamette River. My houseboat is next to the last at the end of the poorly lighted pier which runs parallel to the shoreline. The last houseboat in line is owned by a retired couple who winter in Arizona so both of the last two boats were unlighted as I approached. I was about sixty feet from my gangway when a bullet whistled past my head. In the semi-darkness, I assumed the shooter was in the shrubbery just north of the parking lot on the shore. I sprinted for the relative safety of my houseboat and then heard the "ph-h-h-t" of a silenced automatic and another near miss. This one ricocheted off the pier behind me and I realized my mistake. I was running *toward* the gunman, not away from him. It was hard to see, running in the darkness, but I thought I saw a low shape on my roof. I figured that was the gunman, lying prone. Five more strides and I would be on the boat. Given his position above me, that seemed safer than turning around and running through his field of fire a second time. I jumped on board and crouched under the small eave of the roof.

A needle on my pulse-rate meter would sure as hell have been pegged! I bent double trying to regain my breath without gasping so loudly that the shooter could tell exactly where I was. I don't normally carry my gun when I'm out just interviewing people and, again, I did not have it with me. But I almost always carry a can of bear spray in my windbreaker pocket. I felt to be sure it was there. It was. I strained to hear the shooter moving on the roof, but could hear nothing. I considered using my cell phone to call nine-one-one, but ruled it out because I could not risk even whispering. I tried to sense whether the boat was listing slightly to tell me if he was on the same side as I. But houseboats are so heavy and stable that the weight of one or two persons would not cause enough of a tilt to be noticed. The ladder to the roof ran up the stern bulkhead at the far end, "the back porch", of the boat. I thought my chances of overpowering him were best if I could catch him descending that ladder.

I took off my shoes and moved in stocking feet toward the stern, keeping under the eves. On the stern, I had a large box-like storage locker where I kept some home-maintenance equipment and life preservers. I planned to hide by crouching on the narrow strip of deck that ran behind the storage box. I would be briefly exposed as I crossed the six feet of deck to the locker and another four feet to get to my hiding place. If I could make that crossing unnoticed, I could remain unseen from the roof. Before I left the starboard side and rounded the corner to the stern area, a better idea came to me. I had a small rhododendron trying to grow in a good-sized clay pot on my so-called back porch. There was a boathook resting on brackets right beside me. I silently took it in hand. I remembered stuffing a cap in my jacket pocket. I pulled the cap out and placed it over the end of the boathook. Still hugging the bulkhead, I eased around the corner. I stood at the base of the ladder and raised the boathook so that the cap just showed above the top of the ladder. It was a clumsy strategy, but I did not have a whole lot of choices.

The shooter must have been hoping I would check the roof and he went for my ruse. This time his aim was better. He let off two shots and one of them tore the cap off the boathook and it landed in the water. I instantly kicked the rhododendron pot off the boat. It made a loud splash and sank out of sight. I hoped that the splash, together with the cap floating nearby, would be enough to convince the shooter that he had nailed me. I ducked back around the corner to the starboard deck, squeezing the boathook with both hands.

A good minute went by before I heard very soft footsteps from above. That was followed by another minute of silence. The shooter surely realized he would be vulnerable coming down the ladder and probably was concerned not to see a floating body. I was counting on him wanting to verify his kill combined with his need to leave the area quickly before any neighbors took notice. At one point, he moved to the starboard side and must have been kneeling down to look more closely into the water. I pressed myself, motionless, against the bulkhead and hoped that my dark hair and dark clothing melded with the brown-stained siding on the boat.

Finally, I heard him start to descend the ladder. He came down quickly and had reached the deck just as I darted around the corner. I swung the boathook in a downward arc like a logger chopping a log at a timber festival. It caught his right arm and knocked the gun out of his grasp and into the water. The arm may or may not have been broken, but it hurt badly enough that he instinctively clutched it and stepped back. I launched myself at him and brought him down hard on the deck. He wore a ski mask, but even through the mask I could smell the alcohol on his breath. He swore some muffled, but prodigious, oaths as we wrestled. He was not much of a match for me with one disabled arm, but he was stocky and was thrashing with his legs. There was a chance we would both roll overboard and I did not want to contend with the man's bulk in the water. I snatched at the boathook that had fallen to the deck beside our bodies. On the second try, I grabbed it and, gripping it with both hands, I thrust it downward on his windpipe. That stopped the thrashing.

I yanked his mask off and looked into the sullen face of Richie Bonaface.

I eased the pressure on the boathook a little to let him breathe. He sucked in some air, then coughed and swore. "I couldn't even aim the fucking gun," he said bitterly. "I should've practiced with it. Now you've got my balls in a vice!" He paused and shuddered underneath me. When he continued, the anger had left his voice and he was almost wailing. "Get off me. I won't try to hurt you. I'm almost glad I messed it up."

I was wary of a trick on his part, so I gave him an awkward pat-down to be sure he had no second weapon. He was clean and I could not hold him down for ever, so I got off. I reached for the bear spray and held it in one hand and my cell phone in the other. I was ready to call nine-one-one, but something in the way he got to his feet made me hesitate. He was visibly trembling.

"You're a big, tough killer, Richie. You look ready to toss your cookies. Now tell me what you've done with Vince Langlow!"

"I told you. I didn't do nothin' to him! I'm not your man for that! I don't know a damn thing about it!"

"Right! So you just came over to my place for some target practice? Is that it?"

"I was scared shitless you were going to keep poking around in the mining stuff. I can't afford you to do that! I told you not to keep sticking your nose in the past. You wouldn't listen! I stayed in my office and finished off a bottle this afternoon. Then, as it got dark, I got this cockamamie idea that I had to take you out. I don't carry, but it wasn't hard to lay my hands on an untraceable gun. I cased your houseboat and knew you weren't at home. I figured after it got dark, I would climb the fence and wait up on your roof. When you finally showed up, my hand was shaking so bad, I couldn't shoot straight. What a pussy I am!"

The guy had just tried to off me and yet here he was blabbing about his weakness like I was his father confessor. Somehow, it had a ring of truth, but I kept my hands around the cell phone and the bear spray as we talked. "So convince me some more you had nothing to do with Vince disappearing."

Bonaface winced and held his right arm with his left hand. "I think you broke my fucking arm." He turned his face and looked away into the darkness of the river. "About Vince, what can I tell you? For the last ten years, Vince was the only one of my old partners who would even talk to me. We hardly ever saw each other, but if we ran into each other, he always said hello ... always asked if I was okay. I lied to you about that part. Hell, once I was desperate for cash. I was being squeezed by ... by a party that had loaned me some money. My operations had taken some losses and I could barely meet the vig. I called Vince and asked if he could help out that one time. He didn't ask what I needed it for. He just asked how much. I told him. He said it would be an unsecured loan at seven percent just from him to me. He brought me the cash two days later. He saved me with that dough. I paid him back, including the seven percent, over the next three years. I may not lead a model life, but you got to believe I'd never hurt an old friend who stood by me."

"Let me ask you something. Has anyone sent you a little ingot with 'The Big Molly' stamped on it?"

"Shit! How'd you know that?"

"So you have received one. How long ago?"

"About a month ago."

"Do you know who sent it?"

"No. It sure didn't feel right, but I couldn't figure out what it meant or who sent it."

"Why don't you want me looking into what happened at the mine?"

Bonaface slumped down to sit on the deck with his back to the bulkhead and kneaded his injured arm.

"I'm not going to talk about that."

"Listen, you son of a bitch! You just told me you tried to kill me so that I wouldn't poke my nose into the mine. Now I can call the cops right now and have you arrested for attempted murder, or you can answer my question!"

He was silent for many seconds before saying in a low, almost inaudible voice, slurred with alcohol, "Suppose a guy had to get another person to change his mind about something. To maybe even convince the person to leave town. Suppose the guy tried at first to talk the person into it, but the other person was a stubborn, self-righteous, young prick. So the guy has to make a show of force and give the person a real scare, to make him see the light."

Bonaface stopped speaking, but I kept quiet figuring my silence would eventually prompt him to continue. In the near darkness, I could see him shudder and snuffle before he spoke again. "So maybe they're on a deserted, winding road. Maybe the guy comes up behind the stubborn fellow at a place in the road where he knows there's a turnout. Suppose the guy bangs into the other's rear end and causes the kid's car to veer off the road into the turnout. So far, so good, huh? And the driver in front hits his brakes, okay? But then what if there's a boulder that's rolled down the hill and landed in the turnout? The kid hits the boulder kind of hard. Then suppose he stops braking for some reason. Suppose his truck bounces off the boulder and heads straight for the edge... it's not slowing down. It goes off the edge. It's steep there, almost a cliff. The first guy hears an explosion, sees a glare like there's a fire. Suppose the guy panics. This wasn't supposed to happen! The guy never tells anyone and the kid's death is called an accident. But the guy can't sleep at night, can't think straight during the day. He goes to confession. It's no help. He goes to a shrink. The shrink says he has a Raskolnikov problem, like putting a big name on it is going to help him. The shrink says the name comes from a Russian novel. What a dipshit! So maybe the guy goes back to his home town, tries to forget that night. Tries to make a life. But it's too late. Basically, he's already fucked up his whole life. He constantly worries that the truth will someday come out. He hates himself, hates what happened …"

Bonaface's voice was almost a whisper at the end. The man may have been drunk and he certainly had just finished trying to kill me, but his "hypothetical" tale told me volumes. He did not attack Vince. He was in the hospital when Milliken was killed. I now was sure that someone had made a list and names were slowly being crossed off that list. Bonaface's name was on that list and so was Vince's. I boosted myself up to sit on the storage locker and looked at the pathetic lump of a man across from me.

"Someone is out to revenge the death of Jari Kervisniemi," I told him. "Someone is coming after you and your three partners from the mining days. These ingots are sort of the killer's signature. They were sent to make each of you frightened and to underscore the connection to that death twenty-seven years ago. Dammit, Bonaface, you *have* to help me! If I can find Vince in time, if I can identify the person who is stalking you all, you'll be safe. The only smart thing you can do is give up any idea of rubbing me out and work with me to get to the bottom of this."

"If you catch this crazy son-of-a-bitch, everything about the mine will come out," Bonaface said dispiritedly.

"Think about it! What could anyone prove?" I was not going to tell him what McNally had seen. "Even if it came to a trial, this guy you talked about could take the Fifth. There might be some weak circumstantial evidence. That's all they could have against him. Some dubious hearsay from people who may not even be locatable or alive today. And there's the constable who looked into it and will want to defend his finding of accidental death. I'm no lawyer, but I'd guess the risk of the guy in your story being prosecuted is pretty damn small and the risk of a conviction, even for manslaughter, is even smaller."

"So what you're saying is I should watch my back and help you however I can?"

"That's it."

"What about tonight?"

"I'm making no promises until this business with Vince is over. But right now, I'm thinking you have shitty judgment and you had too much to drink. I don't think you're a killer and I'm not going to call the police. But if you ever so much as look sideways at me again, all bets are off. And remember, there's a gun with your prints on it down on the bottom of the river right alongside my houseboat."

I doubted the prints would survive emersion in the river, but I was not going to tell him that.

Bonaface rubbed the back of his hand across his nose and looked up at me. "I was all wrong about you, Conwright," said Bonaface. "You're a *buon uomo.* You've got a deal."

TWENTY-FIVE

Thursday, November 30ᵗʰ, 10:00 A.M.

I had more or less convinced myself that Bonaface was not going to make another attempt on my life but, to be on the safe side, I had used my cell to call a neighbor five boats down the line. I told him my circuit-breaker box was on the fritz and that I had lost power. He offered me a bed at his place and I accepted. If anyone were to come after me during the night, they certainly were not going to break into the other sixteen houseboats looking for me. Before I went to my neighbor's boat, I had used my laptop to write a narrative of the evening's events. I intended to print it out and place it in my safe deposit box in the morning. It was not exactly an insurance policy but, if anything *did* happen to me, it at least would put Bonaface on the list of suspects.

My neighbor and his wife worked downtown so, after we had breakfast together, I went back to my place. I was sitting down, ready to turn on my computer, when the phone chirped. It was my sister, Debra.

"Rick, you told me to go through our safe-deposit box and look for anything unusual that might relate to Vince's disappearance. It was a much larger box than I had remembered. It's taken me a lot of hours to read everything that was inside. I found pretty much what you'd expect, but this morning I came upon something different. There was an envelope with papers about a trust that was created years ago. It involved a mine and I saw Bonaface's name and a Benjamin D. Turley and a Nicholas Matson. Could Turley be Vince's friend, Don?"

"Yes. It almost certainly is Don Turley. Did you say it involved The Big Molly?"

"No. It refers to 'the Davidson Claim', but it does sound like a mining property. Anyway, I removed the documents from the box and brought them home if you want to look at them."

"I do," I told her. "I'll be right over."

When I arrived at Debra's house, she led me to the dining room table where I saw the papers laid out beside a fresh mug of coffee. The trust instrument itself was only four pages long. It was dated shortly after the sale of The Big Molly to Crazy Creek Minerals. I took a swallow of coffee and started reading. The essence of the arrangement was that the trustee was to contract with someone to operate the mine if it was economic to do so and he was to remit the net profits annually to the same four men who had been the partners owning The Big Molly. If the price of the ore was too low to justify operations, the trustee would leave the property dormant. The trustee could also sell the property with the consent of all the beneficiaries and then invest the proceeds. Then came provisions that were more unusual. The undivided quarter interests in the property or the proceeds of its sale could only be transferred to the other beneficiaries. A beneficiary could demand that he be cashed out at a specified price: essentially, his share of the appraised value or $30,000 whichever was less. And, if any beneficiary were to die before the trust terminated, his interest could not be bequeathed or pass by intestacy, but would revert in proportional shares to the then surviving beneficiaries. At the end of thirty years, the trust would terminate and each beneficiary then alive would take his proportionate share free of the restraints of the trust. The implication of those terms hit me like a bolt of lightning.

A few letters had been clipped to the trust instrument. The first letter was from the trustee, a Mr. Youngdahl. His letterhead indicated that he was a lawyer. The letter advised the beneficiaries that Richard Bonaface wanted out and would tender his interest to the others for a total of $30,000. Youngdahl's letter said that an appraisal had indicated a somewhat larger amount for a one-fourth interest so $30,000 would be the price. Subsequent correspondence indicated that Matson had declined to increase his share and that Turley and Vince had each put up $15,000 to increase their respective beneficial interests from 25% to 37 ½%.

I wrote down Youngdahl's address and phone number. He lived in Kamloops, British Columbia. The phone number by now belonged to someone else, but Directory Assistance finally found a number for Youngdahl in one of the suburbs of Kamloops. No one answered my call, so I left a message asking him to call me on my cell phone. I made copies of the documents and went back to the houseboat. I had been home about an hour when Youngdahl returned my call. He sounded like an older man. I explained about Vince's disappearance and said I hoped he could shed some light on the trust arrangement as we were trying hard to piece together what might have caused Vince to vanish. I told him Vince's wife had retained me and that she had shown me the trust documents.

"If you don't mind my asking, how did you happen to end up as a trustee on this matter?"

"Well," Youngdahl answered, "I'm retired now, but, in those days, my practice was rather specialized in mineral-rights law. I'd handled a matter for the young men previously. I guess you could say they felt that I knew a good deal about the mining industry and that they could rely upon me. I still serve as the trustee, by the way."

"Did the four of them own this property, the Davidson Claim?"

"Yes. It was actually more than just a claim. It had been an operating mine, but the previous owner shut it down as uneconomic to operate. The reserves were quite well proven, but the quality of the ore was not especially high. The young men bought it for a song, they got the whole thing, mineral rights, land, equipment, the facility, all for $120,000."

"Was that why Mr. Bonaface's buyout was set at $30,000?"

"Yes. Unless the appraised value was less than $120,000, the buyout price was the adjusted basis of the departing partner's interest. In the case of Mr. Bonaface, that meant $30,000."

"I see your letter said the appraised value was a little more."

"Yes,"Youngdahl said. "As you can imagine, the value of the mine varied with the price of the ore. At that time ore prices were rising somewhat, though they subsequently fell."

"What was the ore," I asked.

"An oxide of uranium. That's the ore from which uranium is refined."

"The terms of the trust look unusual to me."

"Yes, they are a little unusual. It's what a solicitor would call a modified Tontine trust: where the interests can't be transferred and only the beneficiaries who are living when the trust terminates divide the principal."

"What if a beneficiary were to die an unnatural death? Murdered for example?"

"Oh, I see what you are thinking! Well, if the unnatural death were accidental or if the person died, say, in a war, it would not change the outcome. But if he were murdered by one of the other beneficiaries and the murderer was convicted, under Canadian law, that survivor could not benefit from his own criminal act."

"Would the estate of the murdered beneficiary continue to have an interest under the trust in such a case?"

Youngdahl hesitated for several seconds before answering. "I could not say confidently without researching it. But, somehow I doubt it, because how could it be known if the deceased would otherwise have survived the termination of the trust?"

"Why did the four partners want to set it up in such an unusual way?"

"Well now you're asking me a question that would fall within the solicitor-client privilege. I wouldn't be comfortable answering that."

"Alright. You said the price of ore dictated whether the mine would be reopened and that in turn affected the value of the interests under the trust. Did you ever reopen the mine?"

"No. I came close once, but ore prices softened again, so it stayed closed."

"Would that appraised value have increased today?"

"Yes. With the price of oil much higher today and some renewed interest in nuclear power plants, the price of ore has increased substantially. I should think it will soon be economically sound to reopen the mine. Given that the trust will terminate in less than four years, that's a discussion I need to have with the three men who are still beneficiaries. In fact, I would not be surprised if I were soon to receive inquiries and offers from third parties to buy the entire mine."

"I see. I should tell you that Nicholas Matson has very recently been murdered."

"My Lord! I understand now why you were thinking along those lines! That's dreadful news. I did not know him nearly so well as I knew your Mr. Langlow or Mr. Bonaface, but it is still distressing to hear."

"Yes. If you did not know it, Matson had changed his name."

"I did know that. Rather strange, what? He informed me some years ago."

I thanked Youngdahl for talking to me and ended the call. I knew that I would have to question Turley again. But first, I needed more background on the man. I started browsing the internet to see what was out there. His credit was excellent and there were no indications that he was in any kind of financial straits. He had no criminal record and there was no record that his realtor's license had ever been suspended. A bio in "Who's Who in Oregon" told me he was a graduate of the University of Oregon, a member of a Portland Rotary club, and on the board of advisors of the local chapter of the Red Cross.

I called ahead to make sure Turley would be in his office. He was and, this time, he readily agreed to see me. I put my little narrative of the previous evening's confrontation in my safe-deposit box on the way to Turley's office. I pondered his background as I drove. Could a person with such an impeccable background-of-record be a calculating murderer? But knowing what I did about his complicity in salting The Big Molly, was his otherwise impeccable record that convincing in any case? Would becoming the sole owner of a potentially highly profitable uranium mine be worth enough to go on a killing spree? Or could I be wrong altogether in trying to link Vince's disappearance to past-events at The Big Molly?

I crossed the Willamette River on the Ross Island Bridge. For a brief moment, my thoughts went back to a relaxed day last summer when two friends and I did the Ten Bridges charity bike ride. Twenty thousand riders pedal twenty-some miles on a route that takes them across all ten of Portland's bridges spanning the river. Car and truck traffic on the bridges is diverted and the bicyclists get the rare treat of viewing the cityscape from the lofty perspective of the bridges. There is a Dixieland band on one bridge and a food fair at the finish line. It was a memorable experience for a good cause and I planned to include Angie in the fun next summer. My daydream ended as I left the bridge and entered the curving streets that would connect me to downtown. It was time to get some straight answers from Vince's "old friend".

When I arrived at Turley's office suite, the young woman behind the reception desk offered me a cup of coffee saying it would be just a few minutes. I declined the coffee and took a seat in a comfortable cigar chair. I found the day's Wall Street Journal on a chair-side table and had begun reading it when Turley appeared. We shook hands and he escorted me to his office. I was in no mood to indulge in conversational pleasantries.

"Mr. Turley we've spoken twice before. I want to know why you never told me about the trust for the Davidson claim?"

Turley looked down and his face reddened. "We … you … you were asking me about The Big Molly. It just didn't occur to me you would be interested in that property as well."

"Do you seriously expect me to buy that! One of the trust beneficiaries is missing and I'd just informed you that another beneficiary had been murdered and you didn't think I'd be interested!"

"So you know about the provisions of the trust?"

"I only found out about the trust this morning, thanks to your concealing it when we spoke before! If I can't find Vince soon or he doesn't turn up on his own, the police will surely deepen their investigation. The trust will be highly relevant evidence. Now I repeat my question. Why didn't you tell me about it?"

"Alright. Yes, I did consider telling you. But I changed my mind. You must understand why! The terms of the trust would seem to give me a motive for doing away with Vince and Nick. You said you were looking for Vince's kidnapper and that if you found that person in time, it would also protect me. *I* knew I was innocent and I had no reason to believe you had discovered the trust. Why should I have told you?" he asked defensively. "It would have diverted your attention to me and away from the real threat! Okay, that may have been self-serving on my part, but if you try to see it from my vantage point, I didn't keep it from you out of guilty fear. It was more like fear of being thought guilty when I wasn't!"

We were both still standing and Turley turned and walked over to the window, his face now quite red. Past him, I saw fog from the river still enveloping the buildings in the distance like a gauzy sheer on a theater stage. His defense was not implausible, but I was not totally convinced.

"Tell me why you four set up the trust. And why you chose those unusual terms."

"We bought the Davidson mine with some of our first profits from The Big Molly. We bought it when we were still excited about the mining industry and confident that we were going to get rich, developing mineral properties. We bought it at a bargain-basement price and knew it would not be profitable to operate at the prevailing prices for uranium ore. We were speculating that there would be higher prices in the future that would make it a great investment. But by the time we sold The Big Molly, most of that enthusiasm and confidence had left us. And the accident with Jerry sobered us as well. In fact, I think we really wanted to leave British Columbia and start our careers over."

"So why not sell the Davidson mine? Make a clean break?"

"In the first place there were no buyers. Not even speculators like ourselves. Since we were likely going our separate ways back in the States and the mine was not going to be worked in the near future, turning the property over to Youngdahl, whom we all trusted, seemed the best way to handle it."

"But why the survivors-take-all provision?"

"Well I guarantee you it wasn't because we all had plans on trying to eliminate each other! We were all still single at the time. We had been a pretty tight bunch of partners. We'd worked like dogs on The Big Molly and had taken a joint risk on the Davidson property. It just seemed appropriate in the spirit of our solidarity at the time. You know... one for all and all for one, if it came to that. Besides, we were in our late twenties and early thirties and I don't think any of us could imagine *not* being around in thirty years."

I thought that part of his explanation probably rang true. But circumstances and attitudes can change over twenty-five-some years. "So did you ever check on the value of the property?"

"Sure. Richie wanted out early on and we had Youngdahl check the value then. And I've followed the ore prices from time to time. I'm sure the others did too."

"When was the last time you checked those prices?"

Turley dabbed a handkerchief at his brow and his face reddened even more. "This morning," he said quietly.

"And before that?"

"I'm not sure. Probably three or four months ago."

"So even before Vince went missing you kept that trust property in mind? Were you aware of its increasing value?"

"Yes. But it wasn't the way you're implying! I'm a real estate man! It's perfectly normal for me to have that awareness. I never asked Youngdahl for a formal appraisal and never commissioned one myself. I just looked at the commodities section in financial newspapers a couple of times a year, that's all."

"Were you just being 'a real estate man' when you looked this morning?"

"Dammit, Conwright! Are you trying to humiliate

me? I'm not proud of that! I shouldn't have told you. Yesterday you presented me with the reality that there would be one less surviving beneficiary. I don't know whether it was greed or just curiosity, but – yes – that reality prompted me to check again."

I left a troubled Don Turley and drove east across the Willamette River. I thought that Turley's embarrassment at not having told me about the trust seemed genuine. His explanation for that omission was at least logical, but if he *were* murdering the other beneficiaries, he would do everything possible to stop me or the police from learning about the trust. And he was intelligent enough to have an explanation ready if someone called him on it. I had to move Turley out of the 'enigma' category and add him to my list of suspects.

It was now late afternoon, so I stopped at a Burgerville for a simple, early dinner.

Back on the houseboat, I paid couple of bills, then got on my computer and ran the last name Kirvesniemi through the national credit agencies. The name was unusual enough that I was banking on turning up a short list. It was short all right: just three names and all three were men. I started phoning. The first person I called was a young man, born only twenty-five years ago according to the credit records. He said he was a graduate student from Finland working on his doctorate at Vanderbilt. I asked if any of his family or relatives were in the States. He said 'no', they were all in Finland or elsewhere in Europe.

My second call was to a man living in Placerville,

California. He did not answer his phone. He was in his early sixties and could have already left for his job if he were still working. A man with a tremulous voice answered my third call. His credit record showed him to be eighty-one years old and he seemed a little confused by my call. He said he lived in a residential retirement home in Cleveland. He told me that he had never married and had no relatives in the States. I apologized for calling so late and took the name of the facility where he was living. A quick call to their office confirmed his infirmity and the fact that he had not left Cleveland since he moved in three years ago.

I tried one more time to reach the second Kirvesniemi. Again, there was no answer. Even with Turley in the picture, I still believed that Vince's situation was most likely linked to some kind of a family vendetta so I took a chance and booked a flight to Sacramento without making further attempts to reach Kirvesniemi.

TWENTY-SIX

Thursday, November 30th, 2:15 P.M.

Angie Richards knew that Vince Langlow's disappearance was destined to be an important story in the Portland metropolitan area. Even so, crime stories had brief shelf lives. Crime stories involving prominent persons held the public interest somewhat longer. They merited news time for a few days at the beginning and a few more days during the trial of the perpetrator. Yet Angie had an intuition that this particular story could support some investigative reporting and, depending where the story led, possibly a special documentary program. Due to some rebalancing of the newscasters' schedules, she had more uncommitted time than usual. She decided to spend it digging into the Langlow matter. Even with some extra time, she would have to be careful not to neglect her regular assignments. Her ambition to get a scoop while at the Boise station had almost gotten her into trouble. She had come up with a timely and useable story, but had to do some fast talking when her producer learned of her investigative efforts on top of her every-day schedule.

Like Max Sobel, Angie had begun her research on Vince Langlow in newspaper archives. Angie found nothing suggestive of motives for harming Langlow in the Oregonian, so she switched to Willamette Week, a respected weekly newspaper published in Portland. She had gone back twelve years before she found a pair of articles that caught her interest. They featured a rather public spat between Langlow and a prominent developer. She read that Langlow had recently bought the facility in which his company carried on its steel fabrication business. At the same time, he hoped to use some acreage he had bought to the south, across the street from his factory, to construct a more attractive office building for his managers and staff. The developer was planning a large housing community and had gambled by acquiring most of the rest of the land immediately south of the road. Angie read that all of the land south of the road was zoned for business. The developer needed a zone change to "residential" to proceed with his plans for a residential community. Angie understood what was at stake. If the change were made, the land was useless for Langlow's purposes.

The Willamette Week story explained that the Tualatin Planning Advisory Committee had recommended against the petition to change and Langlow was personally active in opposition to the change. The ultimate decision was to be made by the City Council. Three of the Council members were thought to be sympathetic to the petition and four seemed against making any change. But when the decision was finally made, the vote was four-to-three in favor of the change. A Council member, Gerry Fairbourne, who had historically resisted decreasing the amount of land set aside for business or industry, cast the surprise swing vote. Willamette Week followed the story as Langlow cried foul and claimed cronyism or worse. He went so far as to ask for an official investigation to look for irregularities in the decision-making process. His requests and complaints were denied. Langlow's appeal to the State's Land Conservation and Development Commission was not sustained and, several months later, he built a smaller office building north of the road a short distance from his factory. In the meantime, the developer broke ground for his housing development.

Something about the story seemed faintly familiar to Angie even though she was living in Cincinnati in those days. She snapped her fingers as the connection hit her. The developer's name was Clifford Darmsfeld. Darmsfeld, she remembered, was the man Rick had been investigating during his last year at The Oregonian. Rick had told her in confidence that he had suspected Darmsfeld had bribed public officials. He was unable to convincingly prove it and, when he left the paper, the story had quietly died. Angie wondered if Langlow, incensed by the manipulation that cost him his building site south of the road, had finally obtained proof that Darmsfeld had somehow corrupted the Tualatin City Council. If he had, would Darmsfeld have resorted to killing or abducting Langlow all these years later?

Angie left the archives and tried to make appointments with the seven persons who had been on the Tualatin City Council twelve years ago. The first thing she discovered was that Gerry Fairbourne had passed away the preceding March. Two of the former Council members had declined to meet with her and two others had moved to unknown locations out of the state. One former Council member had no meaningful information or opinions to share about the Langlow parcel rezoning.

The seventh former Council member, Leo Dalrose, had retired from politics and from his insurance brokerage. Dalrose had told Angie that he and his wife were snow birds and would be leaving for Tucson in two days, but he was willing to meet with her before they left. Dalrose met her at the front door of his stucco house nestled behind several overgrown rhododendrons. He showed her into a living room featuring chintz upholstery and a Thomas Kincaid reproduction.

"You say you're working on the Vince Langlow disappearance. I just heard about that in the evening news last night. How can I help you with a story like that?"

"Do you remember the zoning change on property that Langlow owned that came before the City Council twelve years ago?"

"Yes. I remember that. The developer, Darmsfeld, got his change. Langlow was disappointed to say the least. As I remember, he thought the decision was the result of undue influence."

"You voted to deny the rezoning petition?"

"That's right. I was in the minority."

"Were you surprised by the vote?"

"Yes, somewhat. It was Gerry Fairbourne's vote that was puzzling. A few weeks before the vote when the issue first arose, he made comments that suggested he was against a change. Are you thinking there's some connection between the disappearance and that fracas 'way back then?"

Angie was in the business of asking questions and preferred not to answer them. "Tell me about the late Mr. Fairbourne. Was he dirty?"

"I don't think so, but there were some things about him that didn't quite compute."

"What do you mean?"

"Well, as Council members we were virtually volunteers … we got token salaries and were reimbursed our expenses…, and the business Gerry owned was just a struggling little dry cleaning shop. Yet he drove a big, almost-new Mercedes. Okay, some people just like fancy cars and are willing to make big car payments, but it made me wonder."

"Anything else?"

"Not much, I guess. But one night Gerry and I went out for drinks after a long meeting. Jerry's tongue got a little loose and he started telling me the about how to protect my assets. Sounded kind of reactionary to me … 'don't let the federal government overtax us … keep our money safe' … that kind of stuff. Anyway, he said he had opened an offshore account in the Isle of Jersey. He wouldn't say why he needed such an account, but I thought that was pretty unusual for a guy with a business that was only marginally successful."

"Did you ever believe there was any out-of-the-public-eye contact between Darmfeld and Fairbourne?"

"No. I would have put something on the record if I

really knew about anything like that. But I had no solid basis for thinking Mr. Darmsfeld got to Gerry. All I knew was that Gerry's vote swung the decision the way Darmsfeld wanted it. And that really upset Langlow."

Angie thanked Dalrose and wished him a safe trip south. Minutes later, she carried her laptop into a Wendy's that had a wi-fi hotspot. She ordered a hamburger and started browsing the web. She found the names of Darmsfeld's various development, construction, and marketing companies. She saw that one company, CD Financial, had gone into receivership under the bankruptcy law. Angie was fishing, casting a broad net. She finished her late lunch and drove to the Mark Hatfield Federal Building. In the office of the Clerk of the Federal District Court, she examined the schedule of assets on file in the CD Financial bankruptcy proceeding. She was not sure what she expected to find. One asset caught her eye. CD Financial had held forty thousand non-voting shares of common stock in a United Kingdom company called Tamerlane Investments headquartered in St. Helier on the Isle of Jersey. The shares were valued in the bankruptcy at only a penny a share. The location in Jersey got Angie's attention. Was it merely a coincidence that Fairbourne had had an account there as well? Angie wondered what kind of development projects Darmsfeld might have been pursuing on an island in the middle of the English Channel. And why would such a savvy operator have made such a seemingly worthless investment? She jotted the information in her notebook and returned the file to the woman at the counter.

From her apartment, late that evening, Angie placed a call to the Commissioner of Corporations' office in St. Helier. She introduced herself and said she had some questions about Tamerlane Investments.

"Can you tell me who the incorporators and major shareholders are?"

"The incorporators are easy. They are a couple of local attorneys. You will find they are the incorporators for many, many Jersey corporations. The only other shareholder is one Samuel Hodgkins, but my guess would be that he was simply a nominee and probably assigned his shares soon after the incorporation to the true owner or owners."

"Can you give me his address and telephone number?"

"Yes." She read the information slowly so Angie could take notes. "He may very well be unwilling to reveal to you the identities you seek. Besides, that company was incorporated twelve years ago and he may not have retained the records."

"Does your office have those identities?"

"No. We *do* have a listing for the managing agent and I can give you that, but he, too, may not be willing to reveal the names of the shareholders."

"So this company has never gone public?"

"No. It has remained privately held." There was a pause and then she continued. "Oh. I see the corporation was dissolved a few months ago."

"May I have the name, address and phone number of that agent, please?"

Angie took down the information and placed her next call to the agent. He claimed to be almost ready to leave for a meeting, so Angie moved straight to her questions.

"Can you tell me who the shareholders of this company were? What the company's operations consisted of? What its net worth was?"

"Well, ordinarily, I wouldn't discuss those matters with regard to a privately held company. But I can tell you that it never carried on an active business. I don't know whether it was supposed to be a venture capital firm or what. It was pretty much dormant over the years. There were some private placements of non-voting stock from time to time but, except for money-market-type investments of their cash balances, no real activity. And now the company has been wound up. The liquidating distribution was in the middle three figures. Practically nothing."

"Can you tell me who bought the stock in the private placements?"

"Sorry, it would not be my place to do that."

"Why was it dissolved?"

"The owner died. The estate wound it up. Did you say you are representing creditors of the company?"

"No," said Angie. "I didn't exactly say that. I'm just working out the business affairs of a man who may have had dealings with the company. Can you tell me the name of the estate and where it was located?"

"I suppose there's no harm in that as it's a matter of public record here. It was the Estate of Gerald

Fairbourne and the Executor, Dorothy Fairbourne is based in Portland, Oregon. I remember that part because when the estate's lawyer initially contacted me, my first thought was Portland, Maine. I have a cousin who lives in Bangor. The lawyer straightened me out. Said it was a city in Oregon."

"Did the owner withdraw money from the corporation before he died?"

"I'm not comfortable answering questions like that over the phone, Ms. Richards. Perhaps that is the sort of question you should ask the estate."

Angie ended the call with a broad smile. She could well imagine that the company had been dormant. It was simply a vehicle to pass cash from Darmsfeld to Fairbourne. By broadly casting her net, she had landed a shark!

Angie was too energized to fall asleep. She had played the flute in a college combo that specialized in soft jazz in the styles of Stan Getz and early Dave Brubeck. Angie never played publicly or in a group after leaving college, but, in quiet moments by herself, she still liked to keep her touch on the instrument. She assembled her flute and played for half an hour, moving through a fluid medley of some of her favorite tunes. Finally, relaxed and centered, she called it a day. She would spend another day verifying details and then call Rick. If Vince Langlow had turned up the same information, he could have been ready to expose Darmsfeld. That, in turn, would provide a strong motive for Darmsfeld to want Langlow taken out of the picture.

TWENTY-SEVEN

Thursday, November 30th, 5:10 P.M.

Taylor opened the padlock and raised the roll-up door. He drove his pickup truck into the garage at the far end of the packing plant and closed the door. He left the truck lights on so he could see to start the generator. As he had with the broiler in the walk-in freezer, he had fitted an exhaust pipe for the generator through the roof. The broiler had been the hardest element to acquire. After searching the internet, he found that what he needed would be auctioned off in Texas at the liquidation sale of a bankrupt carnival food vendor. He towed the trailer-mounted broiler directly to the packing plant. There, he had disassembled it and rebuilt it to suit his present needs. Then he had made what he called the rotisserie out of scrap metal, a reduction gear, an old electric pump motor, and wheel bearings. Removing the floor planks in the small area at the one end of the plant where there was no cement floor and digging into the hard soil underneath had been his hardest physical labor. He examined the new calluses on his hands as he remembered that labor and thought ahead as to how he would extend the cement to permanently seal the area when his project was completed.

Disposing of Langlow's Lexus had presented a

problem when Taylor had finalized his plan. He was pleased with himself for finding such an efficient solution. It involved some bus travel on his part, but the car had effectively vanished forever twelve hours after he had taken Langlow.

Now, he carried his prisoner's supply of food and water for the next two days to the former freezer room. He set the rations down and pushed the plunger that released the heavy door. He pulled the Nixon mask over his head and flipped a light switch. He could hear a muffled scream as he pushed the door open and entered the room.

Vincent Langlow was lying on his stomach, his eyelids squeezed shut.

"Now we'll have some light!" yelled Taylor.

When Vince Langlow had first regained consciousness some days before, he found himself in total blackness. His ribs had been sore where the stun gun's darts had landed. His hands were still held in the quick-ties behind his back and that unnatural position sent daggers of pain to his shoulders. There was some additional play in the tie that joined his ankles, but his legs still cramped from time to time. His thirst was almost unbearable. He realized that fear would cripple him and make him more vulnerable than all his physical injuries and deprivations and he fought to control it. As the evening following the afternoon of his capture had begun, the ketamine kept him in a blurred delirium where he could not tell reality from nightmare. Later, the drug wore off, but fear and utter confusion overwhelmed him. Vince strained at his bonds and tested his freedom to move, but discovered he was virtually helpless. The tape had been removed from his mouth and he had yelled with all his strength, but the sound was brittle and contained. The darkness -- the absolute, impenetrable void -- added to his sense of isolation and terror. He had fallen asleep at five in the morning, exhausted and utterly depressed with the futility of his position.

He remembered that, many hours later, a blinding light had flooded the room. Vince had squeezed his eyes tightly shut and let out an anguished shriek at the sudden shock to his optic nerves. He had heard the muffled movement of a heavy-duty latch opening and the thick, insulated door swung open. He closed his eyes to slits until his pupils gradually contracted. When he could fully open his lids, he saw a man wearing a Richard Nixon mask. He had finally, during that first day of his captivity, been able to remember how he had been taken and he knew that he now faced his abductor. He remembered their first dialogue:

"Who are you? Why are you doing this to me?" he had asked, trying hard to control his voice and conceal his fear.

Cold eyes stared back at him from behind the mask. "You will soon enough understand who I am and why this is happening. You should look around and see the place where you will spend the rest of your days."

Vince had not wanted to show any servility to his captor. He had continued to look directly at his captor.

"So where have you taken me?"

"It's not important for you to know that. Let's just say it's an out-of-the-way place where you'll never be found, even if the authorities should decide you didn't just skip town on your own. Have you ever meditated?"

"Meditated?"

"Yes. Tried to gain insight to your own soul. Tried to understand, to evaluate your behavior, your actions on this earth. Tried to rate yourself on the big scorecard of a virtuous life."

"I suppose everyone does try, from time to time. Is this supposed to be a personal improvement exercise?"

"You're in no position to be sarcastic, Mr. Langlow."

"So you know my name."

"I know many things about you."

"What do you want? Money?"

His jailor had looked at Langlow for a long moment. "Money. You *would* think in terms of money wouldn't you? And everything, in your world, is a means to that end. Money, power. And if things aren't going the way you want, you spend money to set things more to your liking!"

Langlow remembered being desperate to keep the man talking long enough that there might be some clues as to what had driven his captor to single him out. There was also a chance that he might pick up some indication of how he could negotiate with this maniac. But he also did not want the other man to dominate the talk between them. "Why are you wearing a mask? Are you afraid to let me see you?"

There was a momentary silence. "You'll see me when I am ready. When your understanding has improved and your lifespan has shortened."

Langlow thought there was a slight inflection in the man's voice. He tried to place it. Was there a singsong lilt? Could his captor be an Asian speaking English as a second language? That did not seem exactly right and the intonation somehow seemed more personally familiar. Had he spoken with the man before? And why has this man so obviously focused on me, he wondered. Perhaps a disgruntled investor? No, too long ago. He would keep him talking and perhaps remembrance would come.

"What am I to call you? Are you also afraid to tell me your name?"

"You can call me Taylor. There is food on that platter on the floor and water in the ... oh, I see you have kicked the bowl and spilled some of your water. That's a shame. You should be more careful! You'll get some more water in the future, but for now, unless you lick the rest off the floor, well, that's all there is. Aren't you a little thirsty?"

At the mention of water, Langlow's eyes had dropped to the floor and he saw a few ounces of water in a dog's dish and splashes on the dirty, cement floor. His throat burned and, with Pavlovian suddenness, he wanted that water desperately. But he willed himself to continue the dialog with the fiend who called himself "Taylor".

"So Taylor, I obviously can't go anywhere. Why

bother to keep my hands and feet tied?"

Taylor scowled as he answered, "Makes you feel completely helpless, doesn't it? And probably not too comfortable either? Well, I guess you'll just have to learn to endure that while you do your meditating. Have you noticed the pail over there? That's your toilet. That's another thing you really should be careful not to tip over. Oh, and you probably have discovered that I have taken your watch. You won't need to know time in here, Mr. Langlow. Except, perhaps, to know that you are running short of it."

Langlow turned his head slightly and stole a look around. He wanted a survey of the room to see if he could deduce from his surroundings what the man in the mask had in store for him. To his left on the rear wall, he saw a strange piece of equipment. It looked to Vince like an open-faced heat exchanger or a giant gas barbecue tipped on end with several horizontal rows of burner pipes. Taylor followed Vince's eye and saw he had discovered the broiler.

"Ah, yes. A very significant addition to the room, don't you think? Can you imagine what it is used for? Well, all things in their time, Mr. Langlow… all things in their time."

This man who calls himself Taylor is obviously trying to keep me frightened and confused, Langlow had thought. Then Taylor had backed out of the room and the door clunked shut. The light had been extinguished and Langlow was left again to the inky despair of the false night.

That much Langlow remembered of his first conversation with Taylor. The next three times Taylor showed up were much the same. And now he faced him again. Langlow rolled over, staggered to his feet, and opened his eyelids a fraction of an inch. "I ask you again, why are you doing this?"

"I told you several days ago to ask yourself that question. I'm sure you'll be able to come up with the answer." Taylor sniffed the air. "Quite a stench isn't it? Well, I see you've learned to use the facilities," he said.

"You are going to kill me aren't you?"

"Now that's worth fretting about, isn't it? If I do, you won't die slowly, Mister Langlow."

"We've never done business. Whoever you are, I've done you no harm! You must be mistaking me for someone else!"

"Not a chance! And are you sure you have done me no harm?"

"I've never…"

"Don't deny your actions! I've told you to repent your sins, before you burn in hell. You have not been following my instructions. If I have to *tell* you, if I have to *recite* your crime, it won't be as meaningful … you won't have a chance to repent before you die. You owe me a debt, Langlow, an immeasurably large debt. And that debt is long past due!"

Langlow knew that the slightly accented voice he was hearing was his only clue. It had the same faintly familiar ring he had heard before, but he still could not place where or when he had spoken with the man in the mask.

Taylor replenished the water and the food and pushed the dish and platter forward so that Langlow could reach them. "And how did you like the darkness, hmmm? The deep, total darkness? Perhaps that is what death is like, eh?"

Langlow did not answer his captor's taunting question. He had nearly gone mad in the darkness. It fueled his fear and his sense of hopelessness. He fought that fear with all his will, but the darkness had pressed on him without end.

Taylor realized there would be no answer. "Well, I have a surprise for you: light from now on. But I'm afraid it may be a little intermittent!"

Taylor strode out and pulled the door shut behind him. Then he turned off the inside light and flicked a different switch: a switch that initiated the strobe light in the ceiling of the freezer room.

TWENTY-EIGHT

Friday, December 1st 11:15 A.M.

Fortunately, I was able to get an early flight to Sacramento and, by late morning, I had rented a car and was on Highway Fifty heading for Placerville. Once in town, I drove straight to Kirvesniemi's address, stopping only for a hamburger at an A & W Root Beer drive-through.

Kirvesniemi lived in a rather large bungalow with what looked like a sizable shop-garage in back. The grass needed mowing and the shake siding on the house was overdue for a painting but, otherwise, the place looked normal enough. I rang the doorbell multiple times, but no one answered. I walked back to the shop and knocked on the door. Again, I got no answer. I got back in the car and cruised slowly down the street a block to the west where there were some retail and commercial establishments. After a couple of blocks, I saw a tavern, "The Lucky Nugget", and pulled over. I waited a couple of seconds for my eyes to adjust to the dim interior light. Through the stale air, I could make out a pool table and unpadded wooden booths along one wall with a few neon beer signs above. The other wall featured a bar with a fiber-glassed top and an assortment of liquor bottles displayed on the shelves behind. I approached the man behind the bar.

"I'm trying to hook up with Miska Kirvesniemi. He wasn't at home. Does he ever hang out in here?"

The bartender gave me the once-over and asked, "Why do you want to see him?"

"A client of mine is into genealogy. She's creating a family tree and thinks they could be distant relatives. She's a wealthy invalid. If she wants me to do her leg-work, I'm happy to oblige."

My explanation was just far-out enough to be convincing. He rolled his eyes and gave me a knowing grin. "Yeah. Mike hangs here when he's in town. Seems like he's been away quite a lot in the last six months. He's left town again, and I got no idea when he might show up."

"Is he married? Have kids?"

"Was married. His wife died less than a year ago. Cancer. He told me they only had one kid and he was killed years ago in an accident."

This sounded like I had found Jari's father. "Gee, that's rough. I suppose the guy's pretty sad."

There was only one other customer in the place, so the bartender seemed willing to chat. "Well Mike's not a real cheerful guy under any circumstances. He's kind of a loner, sort of moody. Jesus, the man has a short fuse too. You know, some guys just keep stuff bottled up inside and things sort of ... sort of build up...."

"Any friends of his around? People who might be able to tell me if I can get together with him while I'm still in town?"

"Only friend I've seen him with is a guy named

Chuck. I don't really know Chuck's last name. I think he might be a retired veterinarian ... one time I heard him telling Mike about treating horses."

"So this Chuck comes in here, then?"

"Yeah. I guess you could say him and Mike are drinking buddies."

I dug a card out of my wallet and handed it to him. "I'll keep trying to get in touch with him, but if you see him in the next few days, will you call me at this number?"

The bartender eyed the card and said, "You didn't say you were a dick!"

"I'm not with the police, believe me. I'm just a private investigator taking what comes in the door. If that means an expenses-paid trip to California to run down blood lines, I do it."

The card had turned him a little sour. I realized I had made a mistake and that I should have simply scribbled down my phone number on a scrap of paper. Nevertheless, he took the card and slid it in among some others along the side of his cash register. I hoped that meant that he had bought my genealogical research story. I returned to the car and drove back to Kirvesniemi's house. What the bartender had said about him was not inconsistent with a parent obsessed over the death of a son, but that did not automatically define him as a serial killer.

Six months ago, a grizzled, veteran PI friend had taught me how to pick a lock. He had given me a set of picks and I had practiced on my own locks. Since

Kirvesniemi lived alone and was out of town, I pulled on some gloves and decided to test my newly learned lock-picking technique.

It went better than I had expected and I was inside the back door in under a minute. I walked through an enclosed porch, passed a washer and drier, and entered the kitchen. The milk in the refrigerator smelled very sour and two bananas in a bowl had turned black. In the living room, I saw the upholstery on the furniture was somewhat soiled. A TV table in front of an easy chair facing a television set suggested some meals were eaten there. A couple of issues of Popular Mechanics magazine lay on the floor between the chair and a faded couch. I saw two framed photos on an end table. One was of a young man in a cap and gown. The other showed a family trio with an older man and woman and the same young man. I used my digital camera to photograph the pictures. There was a desk in one of the bedrooms. I hurriedly looked through the drawers, trying not to misplace the papers after a quick scan showed me nothing connected to The Big Molly, to any of the partners, or to Portland. There was a low file cabinet with a combination lock, but my lock-picking skills did not extend to those kinds of locks. Above the desk, I saw a plaque with a photo mounted on it honoring a Verna Taylor as employee of the year at a local restaurant. The person depicted on the plaque was the same woman who was in the family photo in the living room. Either his spouse was a common-law wife or she had kept her own name to avoid having to constantly explain the pronunciation of her husband's name.

I looked at my watch. I had been inside for over fifteen minutes. That was already too long and it did not seem there was much more I could learn. I left by the back door because it had a simple in-knob lock that enabled me to lock the door and then close it behind me. I pocketed the gloves and cut through some shrubbery to gain the sidewalk, then walked casually down the street to where I had left the car. I stopped at a drugstore and asked to borrow a phone book. I looked to see if there was a foundry in Placerville. There was none. I asked the pharmacist if she had a Sacramento phone book. She nodded and passed it over the counter to me. I found four commercial foundries in the metropolitan Sacramento area. I jotted down the names and addresses and handed the book back to the woman in the white smock.

The first place I tried as I approached Sacramento was just a few blocks off the highway on Folsom Road. I digitally zoomed in on the man in the family picture and showed it to the seriously overweight man who came to the order counter. He said he handled all the orders and had never seen the man in the picture and had never taken an order for any small ingots. My second stop was a larger operation on the south side of town off of Fruitridge Road. A one-story framed office area projected out from the much higher corrugated steel walls of the foundry. A black-and-white sign over the door gave the company name and announced that this was the "customer entrance". The woman at the counter held my camera in her hand and stared at the viewer.

"Yes, he's been in here. Came in about seven or eight weeks ago. Are you the police?"

"No, ma'am. I'm a private investigator. I'm working on a missing person case. Did he by any chance order any ingots be cast?"

"Yes. I think he did! I remember now. I had to check with our manager to make sure we could process the metal. It was molybdenum and we aren't normally set up for that. The manager okayed it, but told the guy it might take a couple of weeks and would cost extra."

"Did the customer ask for any stamping or imprints?"

"Yes, he did, but I can't remember what it was to say. How will this help if he's missing?"

I did not bother to correct her misunderstanding about who was missing. "We think the disappearance may be related to a business situation and I'm trying to learn if that's the case." I fired my next question before she had time to become more skeptical. "Could you check your invoices to see what the imprint said?"

She did not look too thrilled. "I suppose so. What was his name?"

"Kirvesniemi." I spelled it for her.

She went to a file cabinet and started flicking through the tabs on the file folders. "There's nothing here by that name," she said.

"Well, it's a tough name to understand. Maybe he just used a first name. That would be Miska. Or perhaps you could find it by date. You said he came in about seven or eight weeks ago. We really want to find this person fast in case he's suffered amnesia or something."

She gave a sigh of resignation and kept looking. After five minutes, I thought she was ready to give up. Then she said, "Aha!" and waved a file at me. She looked inside. "No wonder we couldn't find it in the 'K's'. It was just ordered for 'Mike'. Miska sounds foreign, like his last name. Maybe he just goes by Mike." She studied the file for a few seconds. "The imprint was 'THE BIG MOLLY' with the words in sort of an arc. The ingots were just little babies... about three inches long ... he wanted four of them."

"Where did you get the molybdenum to melt into those little ingots?"

"It says 'customer supplies metal'. Oh, I remember that now too. He gave us a regular sized ingot and I think it had the same words on it, arranged the same way, only larger."

"Did he give an address?"

"Hmm, that's odd. He didn't. It just says 'customer will pick up'. And I know he paid cash in advance."

"Thanks, Miss. You've been very helpful."

"I hope you find this poor guy!"

"Yeah. Me too."

An hour later, I had turned in the car and booked my flight home. I was lucky again with the flight schedules. By eight o'clock I was boarding the plane. A wave of fatigue hit me as I buckled in and eased my seat back. My last thoughts before I drifted off to a fitful, airplane, sleep were that "Mike" Kirvesniemi was the killer stalking the partners and that I knew of a way that Richie Bonaface could help.

TWENTY-NINE

Saturday, December 2nd, 9:23 A.M.

Taylor was staying in an inexpensive motel in Milwaukie, a southeast suburb of Portland. He had returned to his room after breakfast at a Denny's. His eye fell on the cans of dog food on the faux-walnut-topped table beside the window. He had been spooning the contents of the cans onto the wooden platter that served as Langlow's 'feeding bowl'. He was already anticipating his trip to the meat packing plant that evening. He was interested to see how Langlow had held up under the strobe light. He wanted to crush his son's killers emotionally, but he had to be careful not to go too far. Taylor needed Langlow to be sane and rational when he entered the slow execution phase that Taylor had planned for him.

Taylor's cell chirped. He could not be bothered with the 'ring tones' that seemed so popular with cell-phone owners. He put the phone to his ear.

"Hello?"

"Mike, it's Chuck. I know you didn't want any calls while you were away, but something funny has come up."

Chuck Webster had been one of the few people in whose company Kirvesniemi had been able to relax. The retired veterinarian was also a widower and they

270

had spent more than a few evenings drinking together in The Lucky Nugget. Webster was a loyal and unquestioning friend. He had not even wanted to know why Kirvesniemi had asked him for some of the ketamine he had left over when he quit his practice.

"What do you mean, Chuck?"

"Well, I was over tipping a few at the Nugget last night. Jimmy comes over and says some guy was there yesterday afternoon looking for you. I said what was that all about and Jimmy says the guy claimed to be a private detective from Portland, Oregon. He told Jimmy he was working on somebody's family tree. The guy said he was hired by a rich invalid who couldn't visit people herself. Jimmy didn't buy it. He thought maybe the guy was an undercover cop."

Taylor – on the mission he was on, he was still thinking of himself as Taylor, rather than Mike Kirvesniemi – did not like that development. "Did Jimmy get his name?"

"I asked him that. He dug out a business card the man had left. He didn't hand it to me, but he read the name. It was Rick Conwright."

"Thanks, Chuck. It doesn't make any sense to me, but maybe I'll call him when I get back. Find out if I have a rich half-brother or something!"

"So when will you be back?"

"Not for a while yet, Chuck. This business matter I'm looking into? It's going to take a while longer."

The call ended and Taylor considered what to do. He opened the yellow pages of the phone book and found Conwright's name under "Investigators". He thought that made it much less likely that Conwright was a police detective. He saw the listing gave no business address and wondered if the man worked out of his home. Checking the white pages, he found a residence listing with a different number but, again, no address. Taylor thought it far too coincidental that this Conwright would be looking for him right after he had killed Matson-Milliken and Langlow had disappeared. He decided that Conwright was working for a rich woman all right, but it had to be Milliken's widow or Langlow's soon-to-be widow. Taylor leaped to his feet and kicked a waste basket across the room. He would not tolerate any interference with his plans! His preparations had been meticulous. His targets were too deserving of the fate he had in store for them! This Conwright could not be allowed to upset his schedule!

Taylor poured himself a shot of Old Granddad and sat down. He gulped the drink then balled his hands into fists as an involuntary shudder racked his body. He remembered again what his wife had said the day before she passed away: "if only we could've seen Jari along in his career, see him get married, maybe give us grandchildren!" Taylor's grief flashed anew and morphed into rage. The mine owners had taken their only child from them! And now, without his wife, he was totally alone. He lowered his head into his hands as the black bile of his hatred overwhelmed him. But he was not emasculated. With a roar, he gave voice to his anguish and determination. He rose to his feet. It was time to plan his next move.

While he was deciding how he would get rid of Langlow's car, he had explored vacant properties that might have served as disposal sites. There was that empty warehouse on Swan Island with the large open lot on two sides of the building. The grain elevators on the south seemed to operate with minimal personnel and the building to the north had no windows in the wall facing the warehouse. He concentrated as he tried to envision his line of fire. Finally, satisfied with the layout, Taylor walked over to the closet. There, he hefted the rifle he had used on Milliken. It was an HS Precision Pro-Series 2000 Takedown … a fine piece, he thought. The rifle broke down into three pieces that he could carry unseen in his backpack. He placed the rifle components in the pack, made sure he had enough ammunition, and strode out to his car.

THIRTY

Friday night, I was back sleeping on my own house-boat. I must have turned off the alarm clock, but I had no memory of that. It was a quarter to ten in the morning when I finally woke up. I made a pot of coffee and had just finished some pancakes and eggs when the phone rang. It was my sister.

"Rick! I justgotta call from a man who says he found Vince's car! Heezanightwatch…"

"Debra! Slow down! Who is he?"

"He's a night watchman for some security company. He's over at a warehouse on Swan Island. He said the property is vacant and he only comes through once an evening. He first saw the car there last night, but there was nobody around who might've been the owner. He said he came back there this morning and the car was still there. I guess he was going to call the property manager who's trying to sell the building, but he saw the car doors were unlocked so he looked inside. He said he found insurance papers in the glove compartment showing us to be the owners. He's through with his rounds and wants to go home. He said we can come and get it or else he'll call the property manager who will probably have it towed. I said we'd take care of it."

"Where did he say it was?"

274

Debra read me an address on Lagoon Way. "He said the car was around the corner on the water side of the building and out of sight from the street. It sounds like there's a fence up close to the building, but he says the car is outside the fence."

"Okay. I'll go over there. You stay at home. I'll call the police after I get there. Their forensics people should have a chance to go over the car where it stands, and I want to look carefully at it myself."

I risked a speeding ticket as I raced over to the peninsula jutting out into the Willamette River like a thumb that they call Swan Island. I glanced at my windshield-mounted GPS as I dropped off the bluff to the industrial flatlands of the "island". It confirmed that Lagoon Way was on the east side. Swan Island had once been a bee-hive of activity ranging from ship-building and ocean transportation terminals to heavy manufacturing. There was still a lot of industry and warehousing on the island, but a few operations had shut down and some other plants were starting to look a little dingy. As I drove down Lagoon Way, I reached for my cell phone to call DeNoli and tell him that this watchman had found Vince's car. At that moment, the GPS told me that I had reached the address the watch-man had given Debra so I turned into the driveway and never made the call.

The building looked like a three story warehouse and I saw a couple of "FOR SALE" signs. I did not see the Lexus next to the building so I parked my car and jogged toward the back of the property. A couple of rusty cargo containers sat beyond the black-top of the parking lot, but short of the pier. I saw the beginning of a gravel road that appeared to give access to the rear of the building. The watchman had told Debra that the car was "behind the building", so I figured if I kept going down that little road, I could check out the back of the property.

I rounded the corner and saw that the road I was on veered away from the building and toward the waterfront. There was a fenced-in area next to the building and a weed-covered dirt field leading to a mildew-darkened pier that looked as though it had not been in use for years. Other than a few pieces of old abandoned machinery at the far end, the field was empty. There was no Lexus. It was then, that it hit me that I had been set up. I turned and started to run back toward the parking lot. A bullet slammed into the gravel sixty feet ahead of me. This time, there was no mistaking the source of the fire. It came from behind me and I started running like hell for the shelter of those cargo containers.

Another shot was fired. I felt a jolting impact on my left side that almost knocked me off my feet. I only had another fifteen yards to go to reach the nearest container. There was no stabbing pain at that moment, just a sore, numb spot around my ribs. I dove behind the container and looked down at the left side of my chest. My jacket was shredded and there was some blood. I hoped it was only a flesh wound. I calculated that I would be too exposed trying to make it from the container to safety around the corner of the building. I had to hunker down right there. I punched DeNoli's number into my cell phone. They put me through to his partner.

"This is Sanchez."

"Sanchez, this is Rick Conwright! I'm working on the Langlow disappearance.

I was calling Paul. I know you're his partner. Listen, I'm under fire out at Swan Island. Someone set a trap – told me he'd found Langlow's car -- and I fell for it. I'm pinned down behind a cargo container. Some bastard is shooting at me with a rifle and I've been hit in the ribs." I reached into my pocket and found the piece of paper on which I had written the location. I read the address to him. "I'm behind the building, away from the street and toward the water. The shooter is probably behind some old machinery on the south end of the property. Get me some help out here as fast as you can."

"Christ Almighty!" He read the address back to me and I confirmed that he had it correctly. "I'm on it! Dispatch should have at least a couple of cars there in under five minutes. I'll round up Paul and we'll come too. Stay cool, Conwright. The cavalry is coming!"

Sanchez was as good as his word. I could hear distant sirens and the first car arrived six minutes after I ended the call. Two more black-and-whites showed up a minute later, followed by Sanchez and DeNoli in an unmarked car and an emergency wagon with a crew of EMTs. I had heard no more shots. The officers cautiously covered each other as they advanced to where I sat, slouched against the container. The medical techs looked me over, told me it was a relatively minor flesh wound, and bandaged me well enough to transport me to the emergency room. Once the area was declared safe, I wanted to walk to the wagon, but the techs made me get on their gurney. DeNoli said he would drive my car to the hospital and talk with me there. Before we left, I wanted to ask him some questions.

"It doesn't sound like your guys got the shooter."

"No. We found some squashed weeds behind that old compressor out in the field. We figure he was shooting from behind that, but he picked up his shell casings when he left. We'll hunt for the slugs he fired. The medical guys told me the one that creased you passed right on through."

"I'm glad to hear that! This being a peninsula, I suppose you cordoned off the roads leaving Swan Island?"

"Hell, yes! Give us that much credit, Rick! But, it probably took the rest of them at least ten minutes from the time of your call to set up a perimeter. The first cars came directly here to protect you in case he was still around. I'm guessing when he saw that you'd reached the container, he decided to call it quits. He probably figured it was better to get away than to stalk you in the daylight. And he probably knew there was the possibility that you'd been able to call for help."

At the emergency room, a doctor irrigated the wound, gave me antibiotics and re-bandaged me. He said the bullet had only creased my skin and maybe bruised my ribs. The nurse told me to take a pain-killer if it got uncomfortable and to take it easy for a few days. I was to come back in forty-eight hours so they could see how the wound was healing. As I lay there being ministered to, I thought back to my visit to Turley's condominium. I had seen the trophy head of a big horn sheep and at least two rifles in the gun cabinet. With the possible motive to be the surviving beneficiary of the Davidson Claim trust and with hunt-ing expertise, could it have been Turley who fired at me? He would have to have counted on killing me and on believing that I had left no paper trail leading back to the trust. That hope would not have been very re-alistic, given that I told him Vince's wife had shown me the trust documents. And, if I survived, he would surely be among the shooting suspects. I decided that, even if he were a murderer, those were probably not risks that he would be willing to take. I was not quite ready to take him off my 'suspects list', but I felt more and more confident that Kirvesniemi was the person we should be looking for.

When I walked gingerly back to the ER waiting area, DeNoli was there.

"You Okay?" he asked.

"The doc says I'll live. The bullet just nicked me. Another three inches though…."

"If you were a cat, Rick, you'd have used up one of your nine lives."

"You got that right!"

"Sanchez told me about the call you got. This has to be connected to the Langlow case."

"It does. The shooter lured me out there posing as a night watchman and saying he'd found Vince's car. Actually, he called Vince's wife, Debra, but I think that was just to throw me off guard. Somehow, he knows I'm working the case. He conceivably might have wanted to kill Debra, but I figure he has a telescopic sight and knew perfectly well he was aiming at a man and not a woman."

"So, any idea who the killer is?"

"I think I do." We sat in a pair of chairs covered in cheerful apricot vinyl at the far end of the waiting room. "There was that death at the mine up in British Columbia around twenty-seven years ago that I told you about. Vince and the man down in Mill Valley, Milliken, and two others were partners in the mining operation. The death was ruled an accident, but, like I said, there is some reason to believe that the deceased – a young geologist who worked for the mining company – had uncovered some fraud. One of the assays may have made the ore reserves look better than they actually were. The father of the young geologist came up to take his son's body home. He was very distraught and told the constable that he suspected foul play. Three of the partners – I don't know about Milliken – have recently received little ingots delivered by UPS. The name of the mine is stamped on the ingots. I found out just yesterday that identical ingots were made at the order of the father within the last two months. I think the father has obsessed over the death of his son all these years and that he has mounted a vendetta against the mine partners. I think he's coming after them one at a time!"

"Holy shit!"

"You should call your contact in the Mill Valley PD and have him find out if Milliken was sent one of these little ingots. They're about three inches long, made of molybdenum, and the name of the mine is 'The Big Molly'."

"If you're right and the pattern holds, that will give the Mill Valley police a big lead in the Milliken death. What's this guy's name?"

"His name is Miska Kirvesniemi, K-I-R-V-E-S-N-I-E-M-I, and he seems to be using Mike as a first name. I have a picture of him in my digital camera. Don't ask me how I got it. You can off-load a copy."

"Do you have any ideas where this Mike Kirve… where this Mike is?"

I shook my head. "I went to the man's house in Placerville, but he wasn't home and the bartender at his neighborhood tavern seemed to think he was out of town for a while. If he was the shooter just now, we damn well know he's in this vicinity."

"Right … You don't have any reason to think he *wasn't* the shooter, do you?"

"Well, no. I guess not. It's just that I never got a look at him."

"Your dig-into-Vince's-past strategy has really paid off, Rick!"

"Yeah, I guess you could say that. A logger up where the mine is told me it was called a 'jinx mine' by the locals. There's sure some truth to that. It looks as though it has produced a lot of tragedy ... a lot of craziness."

Paul offered to drive me home, but I told him that I would be fine to handle my car. As I drove, I wondered how Kirvesniemi had found out about me. Then I remembered my mistake of giving the barkeep in The Lucky Nugget my business card. Maybe he'd ratted me out and Kirvesniemi had put two-and-two together and decided I was a threat to his little vengeance project. On the other hand, I had not actually laid eyes on the sniper. And I had to consider that Bonaface had tried, however ineptly, to kill me less than seventy-two hours earlier. Could he have reneged on our deal and tried again? I did not really believe that and I suppose that is why I did not mention the little episode at my houseboat to DeNoli.

I pulled a beer from the refrigerator at home and plopped into a chair. My side was starting to throb and I thought this being shot at was starting to get old. I knew that if we had any chance of finding Vince alive, I had to keep pressing and following up on every possible lead. There was one avenue of investigation I had not yet had time to pursue. I needed to find out what had happened to Vince's car.

THIRTY-ONE

Saturday, December 2nd, 1:45 P.M.

On the car angle, the first call I made was to DeNoli. In the confusion of the morning's attack, I had forgotten to ask him if the police had turned up the Lexus. He said they still had no reports on the car. He told me they had broadened the alert to include security officers at commercial garages, the airport, and school and university campuses. I asked him if they had found the slugs that had been fired at me.

"They found one of 'em," he said. "The criminalists are going to take digital microscopic photos of the bore markings and transmit the pictures to their counterparts in Mill Valley. They'll also run it through IBIS. That should give us an idea if the same weapon was used in both shootings."

"What in hell's IBIS?" I asked.

"It stands for the Integrated Ballistics Identification System. It's a regional law enforcement data base we can use to look for matches."

We agreed to stay in close touch and ended our call. I checked my notebook for Richie Bonaface's number at The Hunt Club. I gave my name to the man who answered the phone and said it was important that I reach his boss. Bonaface was there and he must have cleared my name, because I was immediately put through.

His usual gruff voice was softer, almost contrite. Well, he damn well should be contrite, I thought. "Yeah, Conwright. Do you have anything new?"

That did not sound like the question of a man who had been drawing a bead on me through a sniper's scope a few hours ago. "Bonaface, I said you might be able to help me and help yourself at the same time. Now here's what I need. Vince Langlow's car has never turned up. He drove it into the garage at the Multnomah Athletic Club and when he left the club, he was taken. Whoever took him, also took his car. If we could locate the car, or at least trace where it went, we might learn something about this killer who's out there."

"So? You want my guys to help you hunt for the car?"

"No. The police are already hunting. That's the problem. They haven't found a thing. That makes me think of two other possibilities. The car might still be wherever he's holding Vince, assuming Vince is still alive. If they're both well hidden, that might work for a while. But the car itself is a source of evidence that could be used to convict this guy if we ever catch him. So I'm betting he's found some way to destroy it."

"You mean like a scrap yard?"

"Possibly, but that might take a while. Unless the fix is in with the yard, the car might sit around for months while customers stripped it. I'm thinking he sent it to a chop shop."

"Yeah, I see what you mean. Quick and quiet. The

VIN goes and the car just becomes a bunch of parts. Either that, or the whole thing goes overseas and turns up for sale in Bulgaria, no questions asked."

"Right. I don't know where to begin looking for those kinds of shops. I figure you maybe have some contacts? Could ask a few questions?"

"Yeah, I could ask around. What kind of a car?"

"A 2009 metallic-green Lexus 400. I looked at some maintenance records at Vince's home. The odometer showed forty-six thousand two hundred miles, two months ago. Every minute counts, Bonaface. Put the pressure on and let me know as soon as you can, even if you don't turn up anything."

"Cool your jets, Conwright. I'll handle this personally and I'll move it fast."

My side was hurting like hell, but I did not want to mellow myself out with a pain pill. I needed to keep my edge and, up to a point, the pain would help with that. Some history also entered into my thinking. My father nearly lost his forearm when a hydraulic line failed and a disc fell on him as he was under the equipment making an adjustment. He eventually healed and recovered most of the use of his arm, but weeks of needing morphine and codeine left him addicted. He was able to farm for a few more years, but he was never the same. Ever since, I have vowed to stay away from pain-killing drugs if at all possible.

I knew Debra would be tormented by not knowing what I had learned from the car. I called and she answered on the first ring.

"What took so long? I've been waiting for your call. Was it? Was the car Vince's?"

"No, Sis. There was no car. It was a trap and I was dumb enough to step into it. Somebody out there took a shot at me with a rifle."

"Oh, God! Rick, I'm so sorry! We should've just called the police. Are you all right?"

"Yes. One of the shots hit me, but it was just a nick around the ribs. They patched me up in the emergency room. I'm back at my place for a couple of hours of quiet. I'll be fine. Don't worry."

"So who called me?"

"I think it was probably the same person who took Vince. Listen, Debra, I think I was the target all along today, but we can't be sure of that. I want you to stay with a trusted friend for a few days. Take a cab to, say, Nordstroms and arrange for your friend to meet you there and take you to her house. Will you do that?"

"Yes. Okay. I'll ask Danielle Rawlings and I'll call you after I'm over at her place."

"Thanks, Sis. Take along a book of your Sudoku puzzles. They'll take your mind off the waiting"

"I doubt I could concentrate, Rick, but it's an idea. What if there's a ransom call? A real one?"

At this point, I no longer expected a ransom call, but I did not want my sister to become even more discouraged. "The police will leave the tap on your line and will have all your calls transferred to one of their phones with a policewoman doing the answering. That way, if a call about Vince comes in, they'll know about it and try for a trace. And, of course, they'll tell us."

We said goodbye. I made a sandwich and lay down on the sofa and thought about what else I could do. I really wanted to call Angie ... to see if we could repair our now strained relationship. But what would I say if she asked me how I was doing? "Oh, fine. Just nursing a little bullet wound, that's all." Yeah, she would be all revved up again with her reporter's nose twitching like a mouse's in a cheese factory. The alternative was more dissembling, and I did not have the stomach for that either. I thought better of the whole idea and finished my sandwich.

When my then wife, Justine, and I were in some marriage counseling, the psychologist asked me about my parents. I said my mother had walked out on my father and us kids when I was nine years old. I told her that I found out several years later that my mother had been seeing someone on the side. I said my father had not known. She had simply told him she could not take the farm life any longer and that we kids were old enough to cope without her. The psychologist looked at me and asked if I thought that had made me less willing to trust women, less willing to commit one-hundred percent to my wife and our marriage. I thought about it and told her that I did not believe it had had that affect on me. Now, I again thought about her question and my answer. I wondered if my reservations about fully trusting Angie could somehow be traced back to that event so heartbreaking for a youngster ...an event so layered with deceit and self-interest. I hoped my head was on straighter than that. I hoped that Angie and I could get past this professional conflict and heal our relationship. But, for the moment, I had to focus on Vince.

An hour later, Bonaface called.

"I think I got something for you," he said. "The first couple of places I called denied anything to do with a green Lexus. I had a couple more to go when I got a call from an employee of one of the places I'd already called. Seems he was out drinking with some of his buddies Wednesday night and another guy in the business was telling them this story about a 'gift car'."

"Gift car?"

"Seems the guy who runs the shop where the second guy works hears a message in his voice mail when he gets in Wednesday morning. The caller says there's a nice green Lexus parked right up the street from their shop. Says the VIN is taken care of and it's theirs for the taking! They start worrying that it's a police trap, but they scope out the car and determine no one's watching it. They can tell it isn't rigged with a GPS system or a homing device. They leave it sit a few more hours and then decide you don't look a gift horse in the mouth. The caller told them the keys were under a garbage can about twenty feet from the car. They find the keys and drive the car into their shop. Easy!"

"That's got to be it! Did the guy who called you get the name of the other man's shop?"

"He said his friend worked at Bunny's Body & Fender. It's on Highway 212 near the National Guard base, maybe a hundred-and-second. In there somewhere."

"Can you call this place and tell them I'm coming over? Otherwise they probably won't let me in the door. But will they be there on a Saturday?"

"I think they'll be there. And I can take care of getting you in. I know Bunny. He owes me. Anything else?"

"No. Not right now. I'll take it from there. Thanks, Bonaface."

I leaped off the couch, forgetting my condition. I gasped and shivered as a jolt of pain seared my left side. Significantly, Bunny's Body & Fender did not have a listing in the phone book. I guess they did not want legitimate customers coming to their shop and confusing things. I cruised down 212 close to the base. I did not see the shop on my first pass. Then I spotted a narrow, dead-end alley. I turned into it and, down a ways, I saw a fairly long, faded-beige, Butler building that fronted on the alley. There was no commercial sign saying "Bunny's". In fact, there was no sign of any kind. I did find a little three-by-five index card taped to the door that said "Bunny's". Next to a metal pedestrian door, I saw a roll-up industrial door large enough for a vehicle. I backed my Acura around in the stub of a driveway and returned to the street to find a parking place. I walked back to the door and found it was locked.

I pounded on the door until I heard a voice say, "Sorry, we're all booked up. We're not taking any more business today."

"It's Conwright!" I shouted. "Your boss knows I was coming."

I heard nothing for almost a minute, then the noise of a turning bolt. The door opened a crack and a slender guy with a bad case of acne eyed me. He patted me down to satisfy himself that I was not carrying and was not wearing a wire. Then he took my cell phone. "Okay. He's in the back."

I followed him through a real production shop. Production in reverse, that is. There were four cars, a Mercedes, two Pontiacs and a Jeep Cherokee, in various stages of disassembly and I counted seven men at work. There was a small office framed in against the rear wall. My pimpled guide knocked on the door and said, "He's here."

"Let him in, ass wipe!" came from behind the door.

A swarthy, balding man looked up from behind a desk when I entered. I had a lot of trouble trying to imagine how he got tagged with "Bunny". The slender fellow beat a hasty retreat. "Richie said weren't the heat. Said you had some questions. Said you could be depended upon to be dis-creet."

"That's right. I'm a private investigator, but all my client wants is to find her husband who we think has been kidnapped."

"Maybe she'll have to pay some ransom money," he said with a shrug.

"It's not like that. We think it's some kind of a loony that takes people and tortures them or kills them."

"Okay. So why come to me?"

"I've heard by the grapevine that somebody dropped a metallic green Lexus in your lap last week.

I'm ninety-nine percent sure that was the husband's car. Would I be correct in assuming that car is no longer available?"

"If there had been such a car, that would be a good assumption."

"The story goes that the donor of this car called your shop. Someone who knew how to reach you."

"I know all my suppliers' voices and this wasn't...," he cut himself off.

I could tell that I was getting close, but "Bunny" was not about to give any factual answers. "Would I be correct in thinking you use a cell phone for your business calls?"

"That's right."

"Listen, I've got to stop this psycho. Richie knows the man who's missing. He wants this guy stopped too. I don't have to share my leads with the cops and I can handle tracing the call without involving them. What I need you to do is tell me your cell number and the day and time the call came in."

"Giving that up would make my business number fucking useless."

"That may be true. Get yourself a different phone and give your contacts the new number! For crying out loud, I have a chance to save a life if I can find out who made that call!"

There was a Playboy calendar on the wall to his right. It seemed as though he were studying Miss December for an eternity before he turned back to face me. He heaved a great sigh and said, "Richie says this mug may be after him, too. Alright. I'll give you the number and the time. I don't have any more use for these crazy sons-of-bitches that go around killing people for kicks than you do. But if any DA ever tries to prosecute me and uses information about some green Lexus, I'll know where it came from, Conwright. I'll know where it came from."

He told me the number and said the call came in at seven-thirty in the morning on the preceding Tuesday. He did not look as though he wanted to shake my hand, so I simply thanked him. He yelled for the slender man who must have been waiting nearby because the door quickly opened. My escort returned my phone and practically marched me through the percussive sound of power wrenches in the shop and out the door. I punched a number into my cell as I hoofed it back to the car. I had another favor to ask of my volleyball teammate who worked at the phone company.

THIRTY-TWO

Saturday, December 2nd, 3:40 P.M.

Doug Wilkerson probably wasn't too thrilled to hear from me again so soon. And it did not help that I had missed one of our last volleyball practices when I was in Canada. But Doug is a great guy and when I told him that it was for the same critical case, he asked what I needed. I told him I had to know the originating number and location of a call to a certain cell phone made Tuesday morning the twenty-first of November at seven-thirty in the morning. I gave him the number of Bunny's phone.

"You know I just manage our landline business, Rick, so I'll have to involve the cellular division."

"But they can do it, can't they?"

"Oh, yes. Lucky for you the techs staff those computers twenty-four-seven. But depending on how busy they are and who's ahead of us on the main frame, it could take an hour or so."

I audibly groaned, and he continued, "Okay, I know it's urgent at your end. I'll ask them to put a top priority on it. They'll grumble, but we should get it fast. But please don't ever say I was your source. Disclosing this sort of stuff without a subpoena is against company policy."

Doug must have called in some favors, because he

called me back only forty minutes later. He started by reading me the number. "That's a pay phone in a bar near the corner of Roetke Road and McLaughlin in Milwaukie. I guess there's still a few of those phones around. It took a little longer than I'd hoped because a different carrier was involved. Will that do it?"

"Yes, thanks. I owe you and Marni a dinner out!"

I had been driving back toward my houseboat when Doug's return call came in. Now, instead of turning west through the Sellwood neighborhood to reach the river, I got on Milwaukie Avenue heading south. Milwaukie and its continuation, McLoughlin Boulevard, have too many stoplights and too much traffic to make time even on a weekend, so it took me a good fifteen minutes to reach the intersection in the Portland suburb of Milwaukie that Doug had identified.

I spotted the bar and slewed my car to a stop at the curb. I checked to be sure that the number on the phone matched the one Doug had given me. I was not too surprised that the call had been made from a pay phone. This killer obviously planned his actions carefully and would not use his own cell or a phone where he was staying. On the other hand, dumping the car on the street the morning after the kidnapping meant that he had to have moved quickly and efficiently. The man's home was in California. I reasoned that he had no brothers in the Portland area because, if he did, I would have found them in the phone book. He could have been staying with a married sister, but I doubted he wanted to be involved with family members while he carried out these kinds of plans. Judging by the lifestyle I observed in his home, I did not see him staying at a classy downtown hotel. That left inexpensive motels. I decided to walk a block in every direction away from the intersection with the pay phone casting my eye about for motels. I started to the south and intended to work my way around the compass clockwise.

I eventually reached a point a block north of the phone and saw the Rest-Well Motel a half-block further down the street. There were fourteen units arranged in an L-shape. Some climbing geraniums clung forlornly to cinder-block walls covered with gritty-looking cream paint. I entered the small office and saw a bell on the counter amidst a small rack of postcards and stack of brochures advertising helicopter flights over Mt. St. Helens. I pushed the bell and, almost immediately, a man of East-Indian extraction emerged from what I presumed were living quarters beyond the office.

"Would you like a room?" he asked.

"No thank you. I'm trying to locate a missing person." I pulled an enlargement of Kirvesniemi's photo from my notebook. "Have you by any chance seen this man? Could he have stayed here?"

"Oh, most certainly, sir. He came in two weeks ago. He still stays with us."

Bingo! Another helpful person had assumed that Kirvesniemi was the missing person. I was not going to correct that impression. "May I ask what name he is using?"

"Taylor, sir. Mike Taylor."

"Is he here now?"

The manager's caution light suddenly came on. "Who exactly are you representing?" he asked.

"I'm a private detective working for the wife of the missing person." I showed him my business card.

"I see. Well, he is here, I believe." He walked outside and looked into the parking area. "Yes, there is his truck." There were only four vehicles in the parking area and two were pickups.

"His is the Ford pickup truck?" I asked as casually as I could.

"Yes, that is it."

The manager was willing to confirm the man's presence, but did not divulge his room number.

I did not want to flush my bird before I knew where he had taken Vince. "We think he has been under considerable stress and I don't think it would be wise for me to contact him just yet. I'll report to my client first. Did he say when he was leaving?"

"No. He has paid for two weeks in advance and the second week will be up on Thursday. Of course, he may stay longer."

"Did he use his credit card?"

"No. He paid cash."

"Is he alone?"

"Oh, yes. Alone."

"Thank you for your cooperation. Because of his condition, I think it would be best if you did not mention my talk with you."

I hoped that I had not overdone it using words like 'stress' and 'condition'. I did not want the manager to think he was dangerous and try to evict him, but I had to be careful Kirvesniemi was not alerted to the fact that I had found him.

I sat in my car and tried to envision the best course of action. It was a good sign that "Mike Taylor" was still around more than a week after he had captured Vince. That gave me hope that Vince was still alive and I very much wanted to believe that. Calling DeNoli would have been the simplest course. I could have gracefully bowed out and left the police to question Kirvesniemi. But that was the problem. The man was seemingly obsessed and possibly even insane. I doubted very much that he would tell them anything when he was this deep into his vendetta. And if Vince were still alive in some hideout of Kirvesniemi's, he might die of thirst or starvation while the police wasted time in futile questioning. If this guy had kept Vince alive to torture him or to make him crazy with fear, I felt he would have to be with him from time to time. That made me think there was a chance he would lead me to Vince.

As I sat there thrashing out these possibilities, I wanted a cigarette so badly that I started rummaging around in my glove compartment. I finally remembered that I had long ago thrown out the pack I used to leave in there. I laughed at my own desperation and the need passed. The plan I finally chose was to stake out the motel to see if 'Mike' really would lead me to Vince. If he did not go to any place where he conceivably could be holding Vince by noon the next day, I would inform DeNoli and we would go from there. I shifted the car to a position from which I could see the entrance to the motel and the Ford pickup.

Between the adrenalin-laced events throughout the day and my painful ribs, I was completely zonked by eight-thirty in the evening. I had made a fast drive-through at a Burger King around seven, but the food had not helped much. It was time to call in a relief pitcher. I had Julio Mendez's home number on my speed dial.

Julio was a complicated human being, a trusted friend, and definitely one of the good guys. He's quite a story. In fact, that's how I first met him, research-ing a newspaper series about young Latino hoods and their chances of pulling away from a life of crime and violence. Julio Mendez had himself done time in ju-vie for petty theft and helping steal a car. He was still in high school and doing relatively well when he was arrested. The future he glimpsed from inside the ju-venile jail gave him the strength to cut ties with his delinquent friends. After his release, he stayed out of trouble and got his Associate of Arts degree from Chemeketa Community College. Then Julio started his messenger/delivery business. At first, he used just four teenagers on bicycles. From the beginning, he hired tough young men and women. But, before he would hire them, he had to be convinced that they had the desire to make a lawful living and rise above their troubled backgrounds. So far, every one of his employees had justified his faith in them.

His little company grew and developed steady customers. By the time I did the story, he had fourteen employees and used three Volkswagen vans and two motorcycles in addition to the bikes. He also had started a foundation to award college scholarships to deserving young adults, especially those who had overcome an earlier juvenile record. I found his dedication and social vision so inspiring that I featured his business and his foundation in one of the articles in that series. The second check I received from Wade McDaniels twelve days ago was a donation to Julio's foundation.

Julio and I soon became friends and, once I started in the detective business, I had actually used his people a few times. He always insisted – and I readily agreed – that they were not to be directly exposed to danger and that they would never be asked to do anything that might be construed to be illegal. His young men and women knew the city and the suburbs very well and were already street-wise, so they were naturals to help me. I used them for surveillance, the occasional tailing assignment, and sometimes for factual research. I am still a one-man operation, so being able to temporarily scale up my forces with reliable helpers from Julio's ranks is a great advantage. I only call on them when Julio can spare them and I pay them half-again as much as Julio can pay. They seem to thrive on the work and, I suspect, even take a little pride in helping out a professional investigator who is not a cop. When they help me on a job that ends successfully, I make a point of telling the client about Julio's foundation. That almost always leads to a donation from the client. In McDaniels case, it was a fairly hefty one.

Julio's wife, Maria, picked up on the third ring. She was a delightful woman and would have been a great mother, but she had suffered a dangerous miscarriage that seemed to have ended their plans for parenthood. Maria worked as an office manager at the local Habitat for Humanity headquarters and doubled as a bookkeeper for Julio's business. She called Julio to the phone.

"Julio, it's Rick. I'm working on a case. It's a case for my sister. Her husband's missing and we think it's possible that he's being held hostage. I'm down in Milwaukie staking out the person we think did it. I'm hoping he'll lead me to where he's holding my brother-in-law."

" Rick, that's terrible! Can we help?"

"Thanks for the offer, amigo. That's why I called. I'm a little beat up. In fact I took a bullet earlier today. I'm okay -- it just grazed me -- but I'm crapping out on this surveillance. Could you or some of your boys take over for a few hours right now?"

"This guy you're watching sounds dangerous."

"He surely is, but all we are going to do is watch him and tail him."

"Rick, I'll come myself and bring Ricardo Satello. You know him. He's my most senior guy. I don't want the younger men involved with a really dangerous person. My younger ones can be too eager sometimes …

and they might get too aggressive and get themselves in deep shit."

I gave Julio the address and told him my car was on the side street about a hundred feet to the east of the motel. Half an hour later, he pulled up and a couple of minutes after that, Ricardo arrived on his motorcycle. I showed them the picture of Kirvesniemi and told them about the Ford pickup. Our target might well be wary by now, since he knew I was on the case and I did not want him to spot Julio or Ricardo. My friends knew how to run a tail, but I coached them a little anyway. We exchanged cell phone numbers and they promised to keep me posted. I headed back to the houseboat where I crashed on the couch.

I had placed my cell right next to my head and awoke with a start an hour later when Julio called. "Hey, Rick. Your man went to a Seven-Eleven and came out with a package, probably food. Then he took off down the highway to Oregon City and then took two-thirteen toward Molalla. Ricardo and I were alternating so Ricardo's single headlight wouldn't be too obvious. But about ten minutes ago, Ricardo moved to the front and I dropped back. Problem is, they must have turned off onto a road I didn't see because they're no longer in front of me."

"Hell! Have you tried to call Ricardo?"

"Yeah, but he probably can't hear the phone while he's moving. He didn't answer."

I did not like the sound of that. "Can you tell me where you are right now?"

"I'm in Mulino. It's so small, it's basically just a crossroads."

"Wait there. I'll try to reach Ricardo, but in any case, I'll drive toward you. If I can't raise Ricardo, I'll meet up with you. If I do reach him, one of us will call you."

I had not been on the road five minutes when Ricardo called. "Sorry, Rick. This guy was moving fast and I couldn't stop to call you sooner. And I don't know where Julio is!"

"Don't worry about that, I just talked with him. What about our target?"

"We followed him down Highway two-thirteen eight or nine miles. I was in the lead when he turned east onto Spangler Road. That road jives around for about three-and-a-half miles and finally joins Beavercreek Road. That's when I noticed Julio wasn't behind us. The target turned south for almost two more miles then branched off to the east onto Upper Highland Road. There's a Lower Highland that you'll come to first, but don't take that. Upper Highland is the next turnoff after Lower. Your guy went a good mile down that road. Then he turned south onto a dirt road. I could make out an unlighted building at the end of that road. I went on by about half a mile, then turned off my headlight and came back to where he turned. I couldn't see his headlights, so I figured he parked and went into that building."

"And he hasn't come back out?"

"No. I would've seen him if he tried to leave while I was turning around. I walked up to the building and ..."

"Hey, Ricardo, I told you guys not to get too close to this guy. He's a killer!"

"It's cool, Rick. I was real stealthy. I didn't go inside. The windows are all boarded up and it looks like there's a garage at the back with a large door. I think that's where he put his truck. I didn't try to get inside, but I thought I could hear a motor of some kind. It was real quiet ... maybe a generator or something."

"You've done great, Ricardo. Now get back on the paved road and come maybe a quarter of a mile back the way you first came. I'm just now passing through Oregon City.

When you see me coming, flash your light twice. That way I'll know he hasn't left. Then you get out of there! If he tries to leave before I arrive, follow him again, but be careful! If I don't see you down the road, I'll know he's left. If you're tailing him again, call Julio or me as soon as you can."

I called Julio to bring him up to speed. He said he would move up to where Spangler Road crossed two-thirteen and rendezvous with me there. When we met, I told Julio that I wanted Ricardo and him to clear out once I was on the scene. He wanted them to back me up, but I insisted that as soon as I arrived and Ricardo was safely away from the place, they should go back to Portland. I said I would tell Ricardo to look for him at the intersection. Refusing their back-up was probably a mistake, but I make a distinction between asking my friends to help and putting them at great risk.

Why I did not call DeNoli at that point, I do not

know. Maybe I, like some of Julio's boys, was sometimes too macho for my own good. Maybe I was taking this too personally because the bastard had shot at me. Maybe I wanted to scout the situation in advance to give Vince the greatest chance of survival. Maybe all of the above. Whatever it was, I left the cell phone in my pocket and raced off to Upper Highland Road.

THIRTY-THREE

Saturday, December 2nd, 11:40 P.M.

I saw Ricardo's flashing light and pulled over to the shoulder opposite his bike. He jogged across the road as I rolled down my window. Ricardo was around nineteen years old and I guessed he weighed in at a solid hundred and eighty pounds. He had snapping black eyes, an infectious grin, and a trim, black mustache.

"Yo, Rick. No one's left the building. That's a spooky place ... looks as though your man really could be in there."

"I agree. Why else would our subject leave his motel and come out here in the middle of the night?"

"What are you going to do now?"

"I'm going to reconnoiter the grounds. I'll stay out of sight, but get close enough so that I can see, if he leaves, whether he's alone. If he leaves alone, I'll call the cops and go in. They should be able to catch him on the road or, worst case, back at his motel."

"I'll stay, man, and watch your back."

"No, Ricardo. I appreciate that, but I want you guys 'way gone from here. Julio's waiting at the intersection of Spangler Road and two-thirteen. Get together with him there and then you guys go to your homes. I owe you both for tonight."

Ricardo looked at me dubiously, but finally agreed.

He clipped his helmet strap and gave a farewell salute as he kicked the motorcycle to life.

A stand of young fir trees on the right blocked any line of sight from the building, so I pulled a few feet further onto the shoulder and left the car there. As an extra precaution, I placed my keys under a windfall branch a few feet away. If anything were to happen to me, Kirvesniemi would not be able to dispose of my car short of calling a tow truck. I wore jeans, a dark jacket, and dark gloves. I had my Beretta in a shoulder holster. I hoped my clothes would make me hard to see in the darkness. I made a mental note that, next time, I should add black greasepaint to my surveillance kit to complete the commando look. I turned onto the dirt road and loped along in a semi-crouch passing a riding lawn mower and a fifty-five gallon drum where the road widened out. As I approached the building, I saw that it was a single-story, monolithic, cinder-block structure. Basically, it was a utilitarian box about fifty feet by a hundred-twenty. As Ricardo said, it looked abandoned. The few windows I saw were boarded up. Around the far end of the long west side, I found the garage door Ricardo had described. I circled that end and saw low bushes close to the building walls that offered more cover on the east side. I was almost back to the north end when I saw a low window where the covering boards were partially detached.

I edged one of the boards to the side and tried to peer into the interior. I was looking into a dark bay of some kind. There seemed to be a faint, diffuse light showing from around a corner at the far side of the bay. I quietly pried two of the boards loose and laid them on the ground. This was the moment when I decided to call DeNoli. I knelt in the bushes and called up his home number on my cell phone. I pushed "send" and saw the display telling me "no service". It had not occurred to me that coverage would be spotty this close to Portland. My phone had worked back on two-thirteen and Ricardo had been able to reach me on his phone. I stayed there a couple of minutes cursing the vagaries of cell coverage and trying, futilely, two more times to reach DeNoli. I knew that I could not take my reconnoitering any further by entering the building. I would have to risk driving back toward Portland until my cell phone coverage resumed, all the while hoping Kirvesniemi would not leave while I was away. Once law enforcement personnel were on their way, I could return to continue surveillance.

Before I left, I wanted to have a better look through the window opening into the dark interior. I moved back to the wall and cupped my hand above the lens of my mini Maglight. I leaned into the opening and switched on the light. At that instant something with the feel of a white-hot poker drilled into my chest. I collapsed, folding double over the window sill. I was unable to yell, unable to move.

THIRTY-FOUR

Saturday, December 2nd, 11:15 P.M.

Taylor/Kirvesniemi was a person who normally needed little sleep so he was quite ready to make the trip out to the packing plant late in the evening. He had suffered one of his terrible headaches in the afternoon. The headaches had plagued him from time to time over the last ten months and he wondered if they were progressing toward full-blown migraines. He was enraged that he had missed Conwright that morning. He had had a perfect head shot in his sight when the man suddenly had spun about and broke into a run. Taylor thought his second shot was a hit, but his target had kept running so he obviously had failed to kill him. Once he saw Conwright reach the shipping container, Taylor had decided to cut his losses and get out of the area. He had parked his truck out of sight behind an adjacent building. He sprinted to the truck with the scoped rifle as an unwieldy burden. He managed to leave the peninsula just as he saw a black-and-white with lights flashing and siren screaming coming toward him. He had, by then, been absorbed in the general traffic heading south and the police car sped past. Taylor had no doubt that the anger and frustration of his failure to eliminate Conwright had produced the headache. It was well after ten before he had felt well enough to leave the motel.

Taylor knew that time was running out. He would have to accelerate his program with Langlow. The man would have to be killed that evening. He worried about how much this Rick Conwright had uncovered. He could not see how Conwright could know where he was staying in the Portland area or about the packing plant. Taylor had purchased the property in his wife's name while she was still alive. The cancer was, by then, ever more rapidly tapering her life toward its end. The disease had left her uninvolved in the transaction. She had signed the papers indifferently, without questioning his purpose. That was over a year ago and he had made several trips to Oregon since her death to make the necessary alterations to the building. It had once housed a small meat-packing plant and now stood desolate on some acreage off a little-used county road. The meat-packing business had failed and the building had been abandoned and boarded up for several years before his purchase. He had done nothing to change its outward appearance.

Taylor had worked as a mechanic specializing in servicing and repairing construction equipment. His inventiveness in devising work-arounds and in fashioning custom accessories for bulldozers and backhoes had made him valuable to his customers during his working days. He smiled as he thought how those same skills and his willingness to plan every detail in advance served him now. Taylor had wanted to avoid opening an account with the local power utility, so he rewired circuits in the building to accommodate a portable generator. Lack of funds had forced him to withdraw from college after his freshman year, but Taylor learned quickly and was not afraid to turn to library books or the internet for information. Electrical manuals had helped him become a competent electrician and on-line medical sites had given him an understanding of the ketamine he had used.

His thoughts returned from the building to this investigator, Conwright. Somehow Conwright must have learned about what had happened at the mine all those years ago. That had to be the only way anyone could have picked him out. His thoughts went back over every step he had taken to be sure he had left no clues, no physical evidence. The name of the ex-convict he had befriended with a temporary job in Placerville had never made it to his business records. The man had given him the phone number for Bunny's in Portland, but he had since moved on and would remain a nameless, faceless dead-end. No one at the chop shop had ever seen him. He had taken the pre-caution of procuring the Oregon license plates for his truck from a junkyard in Medford. Even then, he had paid cash and worn dark, aviator sunglasses and a cap. Since the transaction had been illegal, he had no fear that the junkyard employee would ever volunteer in-formation about the sale. His friend, Chuck Webster, might remember giving him the ketamine, but other-wise he knew nothing of Taylor's activities away from Placerville.

The only thing Taylor wished that he had done differently was to have detached the valuable scope and then thrown the rifle in a lake somewhere after he shot Matson. Then, he could have used a different rifle on Conwright. After Webster's call, he had decided it was necessary to kill Conwright immediately and he had not had time to obtain another weapon. He worried that if the police could find a spent bullet, they might be able to prove that the same gun was used to kill Matson.

Taylor was convinced that the loss of his son was due to the malevolent acts of the mine owners. This conviction had festered within Taylor's mind for over twenty-five years. By the time he had become fixated on the idea of avenging his son, he had lost track of the men he held responsible. It had taken Taylor over a year to track down the four partners. It was then the doctors discovered his wife had cancer. Two more years went by as his Verna battled her disease. Only after her passing, did he feel he could at last wreak vengeance for Jari's death. His planning had been careful and everything was designed to happen in an orderly sequence. Bonaface and Turley would slowly come to see that they were on someone's death list and would live in terror wondering when the other shoe would drop. Now, thanks to Conwright, Taylor realized that he also might have to go after those men much sooner than he had planned.

As he turned onto Upper Highland Road, he began speaking softly in the darkness of the truck cab.

"Jari, you were such a fine, young man. Your mother and I knew you were going to be a great geologist … a success in everything you did. They used you and then snuffed out your life like they were throwing away a broken tool! But I'm making them pay, son! One by one, I'm making them pay!"

Taylor eased his truck into the garage at the packing plant and locked the door shut behind him. He checked the fuel for the generator and added another few gallons. That taken care of, he entered the rest of the building and moved toward the walk-in freezer room. Before he entered, he again pulled on the Nixon mask. Then, Taylor switched off the strobe and flicked on the conventional light. He found Langlow on the floor, curled in the fetal position with his eyes tightly shut.

"So have you found the lighting stimulating, Mr. Langlow?"

An animal howl came from Langlow's mouth.

"Lost your tongue, have you? Well, when I last left you, I told you to have an answer to the question, why are you here? Time's up, Langlow!"

Langlow kept his eyes shut and said, "Your voice… it sounds like a man who worked for me a long time ago."

"Yes, yes! And…?"

"The man died. I think you must be his father. I had heard that you thought, back then, that your son's death wasn't an accident. That wasn't …"

Taylor kicked him in the ribs. "Don't tell me you

didn't kill him!" He shouted. "I know you did! He sent me a letter. He knew you were cheating and he was going to call you out on it!"

"I swear I never intended to harm your son... I, we..."

"Shut up, you pathetic sack of shit! Do you *know* how Jari died? *Do* you? After you people made his car run off that cliff, he crawled out of the car. He was horribly burned from the exploding gas tank. He had many broken bones. He *lived for fifteen more hours ...a living hell of unendurable pain ... praying to die. That's* how he died, Langlow! And now you're going to learn to appreciate what he went through. Do you see that piece of equipment over there?"Taylor pointed toward the oversize rotisserie he had fabricated. "That's how I'm going to roast *you*, Langlow. Only I didn't bring along a bunch of people to tell jokes!"

Taylor opened a small case and extracted a hypodermic needle. He inserted the needle in an ampule and drew the ketamine into the barrel of the syringe. Vince Langlow had opened his eyes enough to watch with horror. He tried to roll out of reach, but Taylor was instantly astride him and plunged the needle into his buttocks. "That will knock you out for half-an-hour and, by then, I'll have you all trussed up on my little rotisserie! That's when I'll start the broiler," said Taylor. "That's when your atonement will begin ... when you will achieve a full understanding of the righteousness of what I'm doing."

At that moment, a light started blinking on an

electronic console just outside the door to the freezer and Taylor heard a low buzzing sound. He leaped to his feet, dropped the syringe and left the freezer room. A glance at the display on the security system he had rigged around the building weeks earlier told him there was motion near the north-east end of the building. An intruder! Taylor grabbed the stun gun he had used on Langlow and had recently recharged. He ran silently to the old abattoir bay. His eyes adjusted to the darkness and he could see a less-dark rectangle on the wall that told him that someone had removed the boards covering a window. Taylor moved behind a bank of lockers and trained the taser on the gray rectangle. He heard a soft sound, perhaps clothing rubbing on the concrete wall. Then he could make out the silhouette of the upper half of a person in the opening. A dim light suddenly started sweeping the bay. Taylor steadied the stun gun and pulled the trigger.

THIRTY-FIVE

Sunday, December 3rd, 12:18 A.M.

A man wearing a mask pulled darts from my chest and grabbed me by the legs. He dragged me out of the bay and down a hallway to a lighted area. My head bumped on uneven places on the cement floor. I still could not move or speak. My brain seemed to be flickering in and out of consciousness. Then I saw him take some lengths of cord off a shelf. He took several turns around my ankles and knotted the cord. Then, he rolled me over, brought my arms behind my back and tied my wrists together. I thought I was regaining a little movement and I tried to say something when he pressed a length of duct tape over my mouth. The sense of feel was starting to return to my extremities, but I felt nauseous. If I were to vomit with the gag on, I feared I would choke to death so I fought with all my will to quiet my stomach.

The man in the mask rolled me over and took my wallet, the bear spray, my gun, and the cell phone. He patted me down to confirm that I was not carrying a second gun. He carried his booty out the door and returned a few seconds later empty handed except for my wallet. In the darkness of the bay when I had first been hit and was only semi-conscious, I had thought the mask looked familiar. Now, I saw Kirvesniemi was hiding behind the face of Richard Nixon. He opened my wallet and studied the cards inside.

"So, Mr. Rick Conwright, you have come to me again. Except this time, you won't run away. You will be staying here along with my other guests! I have a little area already excavated, you see. It might be a little crowded with four bodies instead of three but, when I finish pouring the concrete, you will have a little private mausoleum all to yourselves!"

I looked up at him from the floor and saw a well-muscled man, probably six feet tall. He had long fingers that flared, talon-like, from calloused palms as he punctuated his outbursts with wild gesticulations. My go-it-alone tactic had been a huge error. An error that I thought would probably cost me my life.

"Have you seen the man you have been searching for?" he asked.

He shoved my shoulders with his foot so that I had a view of the rest of the room. Vince lay, apparently comatose, on his back. There was a chain around his mid-section that led over to an eye-bolt in the wall. Vince was alive! That was the good news. The bad news was that there was not a damn thing I could do to help him and now we were both going to die.

"You must know," Kirvesniemi said with righteous certainty, "that this man and his criminal associates ran the mine up in Canada where my son was killed. Oh, yes! Killed! They disconnected the brakes on his truck. Or they drugged him so that he passed out at the wheel. Or they blinded him with spotlights as he approached that curve. I think Mr. Langlow will tell me the truth about how they did it before my little roast is over. Jari discovered what was going on at the mine. He would have exposed them, brought in the law. But they were too greedy, too craven, too ruthless! They decided to kill him before he could ruin their scheme. They were evil, evil men! And they still are! Masquerading as model citizens, living in fancy homes, attending charity banquets! That might fool people in Portland, but it hasn't fooled me. I found them. I tracked them down. That ignorant constable could not see that Jari's death was murder so I will avenge Jari myself. I will give these men fitting sentences ... death by burning just as my son suffered!"

He was screaming by the end of his diatribe. He yelled and charged back and forth inside the room, oblivious of me, his only conscious audience. He finally calmed down a little and pointed to a piece of equipment against the wall that looked like an oversize, vertically oriented barbeque.

"You see that? That's where Langlow and Bonaface and Turley will experience the last hour of their lives! That's where they will tell me the truth and beg their God for forgiveness ... where they will complete their understanding of what they have done!"

He stopped to gather himself for a moment and said in a quieter voice, "You, I will kill more mercifully. You had to enter into something that was none of your business. Now you have left me no choice. But first, I have to start the process of Mr. Vince Langlow's penance. He won't stay under much longer, so I must get him onto my very special rotisserie. I made it just for him and his associates," he finished with his voice rising again.

His "rotisserie" consisted of a heavy wire-mesh screen rising vertically from a circular base. The bottom of the plane of the screen formed a diameter of the circle. There were four cuffs attached to the screen: two at the bottom and two more at a height well above a man's head. The cuffs were adjustable and had strong buckles for closure. There was also a wide, buckled strap attached to the screen at waist height. An electric cord entered the base and I guessed that it powered an electric motor to rotate the device. Taylor tipped the rotisserie over onto its side next to Vince's prone body. He cut the quick ties on Vince's wrists and ankles and unlocked the chain around Vince's waist. Then he attached Vince's left leg to one of the lower cuffs. He worked in silence until both of us heard a soft buzzing sound. Kirvesniemi rose with an oath, then went through the heavy door.

I could see only his back as he stopped to check something in the next room. Then, for a second, he turned into my view and I saw an older man without a mask holding a rifle equipped with a night-vision scope. The next instant, he shut the door and the light was extinguished. Vince and I were left in total darkness. My heartbeat slowed a little as I realized Kirvesniemi was not coming back to kill me with the rifle. I tried to reason what could have happened. He had known to lay in wait for me when I pried the boards off the window. That must have meant that he had installed some kind of a perimeter security system. The buzzer that caused him to leave the room and grab his rifle could have been telling him that someone else had triggered the system. If I was right, he had gone to fend off the intruder. Could help have miraculously arrived? Could this psycho have had an accomplice that was just now joining him? Whatever the case, I knew I had only a very few minutes to try to save myself and Vince.

When Kirvesniemi had frisked me, he either did not find my cigarette lighter or did not think it worth removing. It was still in one of my back pockets. I could reach inside the pocket and feel the lighter. I very carefully extracted it. Clenching it tightly, I worked my body like an inch-worm to move over to a wall. I braced my shoulders against the wall and tested the play in the rope around my wrists. My knuckles were touching, but it seemed there was at least an inch between my wrists. I opened the lighter and pressed its igniter. I sensed the flame and tried to set the lighter on the floor as carefully as possible. If it tipped over, I would have to feel for it, pick it up and try again. I got lucky and it stood upright. I positioned my wrists as close to the flame as I could without burning myself or knocking the lighter over. This was a trial and error proposition. Kirvesniemi had not bothered to remove my gloves and they protected my skin to some degree. Even so, I twice burned myself and fought not to flinch. My muscles were starting to tremble, but

I smelled the polypropylene cord starting to burn. I willed myself to hold the position another minute. By then, flames from the cord itself were licking at my lower arm. Another thirty-seconds and I had to roll over and try to snuff out the small fire.

I rolled from side to side on the hard floor. The burning sensation eased and I found that I could move my arms slightly. I jerked both arms and the tension of the cord gave way. More pulling, and my hands came free. I ripped the tape from my mouth.

"Vince, can you hear me?" I whispered.

"Whoozat?" came a groggy reply.

"Vince, it's me, Rick. I'm going to get you out of here!"

As I tried to get him to understand our hope for survival, I was also working on the cord around my ankles with the lighter. It burned through quickly and I used the lighter to locate Vince and my wallet in the blackness. I undid the buckle that fastened his ankle to the "rotisserie". As I got Vince to his feet, I could see that he was too weak and confused to walk on his own. I half-supported, half-carried him to the heavy door. Kirvesniemi had closed it, but had not padlocked it. I pushed the plunger-type latch handle and we staggered into the next room like ungainly children in a three-legged race.

I held the lighter in my hand that was around his waist. In its faint light, I saw an electronic device with some green LED displays on a shelf. I guessed it was a component of Kirvesniemi's alarm system. I could not see where he had put my gun. We passed through that room and went down a hallway with doors to other rooms opening on the left side. I lowered Vince to a sitting position with his back to the wall inside one of those rooms. If Kirvesniemi were outside, I could not fight him holding onto Vince. If rescuers had arrived, I could lead them back to that room. If no one was outside the building, I could come back and get Vince out to safety.

I leaned over my mumbling brother-in-law and said in a hushed voice, "Vince. Keep quiet! I'll be back to get you. Stay here until I get back!"

I moved silently down the hall and found the large area where I had entered the building. My cigarette lighter was starting to flicker and was probably running out of fuel. In its last flicker, I saw my Mini Mag-light on the floor and picked it up. I must have dropped it when Kirvesniemi hit me with the taser. I could make out the outline of the window I had uncovered ahead of me. I climbed out the window and ran along the side of the building toward the road. A heavy cloud cover obscured the moon. But the darkness could not pro-tect me from a night-vision scope. Thirty feet into the open, I saw a red dot move across my body. That pscho had a laser sight and he again had me in his cross-hairs! The dot vanished as I cut hard-right like a tailback on a counter play. I sprinted into the meadow seeking cover before he found me again.

I was sure that I could outrun the killer, but that did not necessarily mean I could get out of the range of his rifle. Between volleyball and some occasional sculling on the river, my wind was pretty good, and I thought my chances were improving. That is when my foot caught on a length of barbed wire and I went sprawling. I lay there in the long, damp meadow grass for a few seconds to get my breath back. I felt for what had tripped me and touched the wire. I could tell it was no more than ten feet long so I picked it up as I started to sprint again. The meadow was falling away from me in a gentle slope. The red spot danced in front of me and I veered to the left. I knew that, by fanning the night-vision scope from side-to-side, he could eventually find me in that meadow.

There was a slight depression in the ground that threw me a little off balance. I was just regaining my stride when my left foot found a hole and pitched me forward. I was instantly engulfed in intense pain from my left ankle. My fall also caused a surge of pain from my wound. I touched my left side and felt a warm wetness through my shirt. My tumbles had started the wound bleeding again. The ankle felt like a bad sprain and I knew running further was out of the question. I hoped that I had covered enough ground to be out of range of Kirvesniemi's night-vision searching. In any case, I had to hug the ground and crawl my way to safety from here on.

The crawling was hard, especially since I still clung to the piece of barbed wire as my only defensive weapon. I had covered thirty or forty yards and had slid my body over at least three cow pies when I heard the sound of a light engine approaching. I looked back toward the building and saw a blinding set of headlights. The lights were close together and I figured he was coming after me with that riding lawnmower. I had less than a minute to settle on a game plan.

THIRTY-SIX

The low spot in the meadow where I had fallen resulted in a change of slope so the mower's headlights beamed into the distance, leaving the ground where I lay in darkness. Then the mower cleared the transition point and its lights again trained on the surface of the meadow. The plume of illumination crept toward me. I slid around to face uphill and then kept my head down trying to mold my body into the earth beneath me. The grass began to silver in the swath of light from the mower. I was determined to charge my pursuer despite the weakness of my ankle but, before I could rise, Kirvesniemi put the mower in neutral and turned off the headlights. For an instant, I was puzzled. Then I realized that his night-vision scope could not function in the drenching glare of the headlights. Instead of rising and attempting a charge, I rolled over and over to my right.

My rolling had taken me a good thirty feet to his left. I thought I saw the red dot of his laser sight sliding across the grass to his right of where I had been. I kept rolling and gained another twenty feet. Then the red dot reversed direction and came closer. He was scanning the terrain in front of him searching for the green cigar in his scope that would be me. I lost the dot for a few seconds, then saw it just feet away. I was preparing myself to charge when the dot stopped and moved back in the opposite direction.

I could hear voices in the distance back on the dirt road. I wondered if Turley had somehow convinced Kirvesniemi that he was in no way connected to Jari's death and had somehow formed an unholy alliance with the father. These crazy thoughts flashed through my brain in milliseconds as I watched for the red dot.

The headlights came on again and, through the glare, I could barely make out the shape of the man sitting on the mower. He had apparently given up trying to locate me through his scope. He put the mower in gear and veered slightly in my direction. Suddenly, I understood his new tactic. He must have suspected that I lay close by and was no longer able to run. He was going to find me using his headlights and then run me over. Being shredded to pieces by the spinning mower blade was not the way I wanted this to end.

It looked as though the mower would come abreast of me about thirty feet to my left. The edge of the cast of his headlights had drifted by without his seeing me. I waited until he was nearly alongside so that he could not turn the mower sharply enough to run over me. Then I lunged to my feet and galloped toward him. He saw me and started to crank the steering wheel in my direction. A second later, he must have realized his mistake because he tried to turn in his seat and bring his rifle to bear. I swung the length of barbed wire like a bullwhip. It made a sound like an angry wasp and raked his face.

Kirvesniemi gave a scream of agony and dropped the gun. He must have taken his foot off the gas at the same time because the mower stopped moving forward. Both his hands were covering his face and his shrieks rang out in the cold night air. From up the grade, I heard two men yelling as they ran toward us. They were calling my name. One of the voices sounded like the incongruous high tenor of the hulk that guarded the door at The Hunt Club. What could *he* be doing here, I wondered. I had no time to worry about it. The mower blades were still powered and I had to be careful as I closed in. I dropped the wire and wrestled Kirvesniemi off the mower and onto the ground. My pulling him off the mower seat must have killed the engine as, suddenly, it became quiet. My pain was completely forgotten as I tried to pin him to the earth. We fought and he continued to roar and snarl like a cornered badger. Now, I saw why. A barb on the wire had lacerated one of his eyeballs, turning it into a bloody gob.

The hulk and the other man piled on, helping in my efforts to restrain Kirvesniemi. Taking their appearance to mean reinforcements had arrived, I disengaged and limped a few feet away from the melee. It did not last long. The two of them soon had him motionless, face-down in the grass.

"Thanks! How did you guys get here?" I asked them between gasps for breath.

The hulk said, "Richie told us to follow you and keep him in the picture… baby sit you if we had to."

"How did you know I'd be to hell and gone out here?"

"We followed you from Richie's place the other day and saw where you lived. Today, we just watched your place and when you left, we followed you again."

"But I've been here for at least half an hour." I did not want to sound ungrateful, but there seemed to be a gap in their following-and-baby-sitting routine.

"When you stopped to talk to somebody at that junction, we had to stop too and lay back. When you finished talking, you started up fast. We didn't want to have your friend notice our tail, so we waited a minute before we got going. Then we came to a fork in the road and Tommytits here," the hulk nodded toward his partner, "said 'go left'. We did, and you must have gone right. By the time we came across your car on the other fork, you were gone. We saw the building and figured you had walked up the road and gone inside."

"So it was you who set off his security system."

"Must have been. We were right up next to the building when he comes charging out with a rifle. We took cover. He snuck around looking for us. A few minutes later, you came out and he began trying to shoot you."

"Are you guys armed?"

There was a pause as they looked at each other. Finally the hulk said, "Yeah. But you tore off the road and disappeared in the darkness. We weren't quite ready to show ourselves because we had also lost sight of the shooter. Then we hear this mower thing start up and we can see the headlights going across the meadow."

"Okay. I know the rest of the story," I said. "I've torn up my ankle and can't move fast. The guy this bastard kidnapped is inside that building. Can you keep him here until your friend and I get back?"

"No problem," said the hulk, who, I decided, was not so bad after all, now that we were on the same side.

His sidekick and I went back to the building. I showed him some more rope on the shelf so he and the hulk could tie up Kirvesniemi. While he was running back to the meadow, I went into the room where I had left Vince. I found him still sitting with his back to the wall when I aimed my flashlight into the room. He looked much better and actually tried to stand up when he saw it was me.

"Rick! Thank God! I've been to hell and back!"

He started to stagger and I told him to put his arm around my shoulder while I grabbed him around the waist. "I know. I know. It's over now, Vince. We found you and got the son-of-a-bitch who kidnapped you."

"I don't even know how long I've been here..."

"Over twelve days. Now we've got to get you out of here and get you to a hospital."

"No, Rick. Not a hospital. Maybe to my own doctor, but I don't want this whole thing in the public eye."

"I'm afraid that may be too late, Rick. Your kidnapping has made the news already."

"I see," he said dejectedly. Then, with more spirit, "I need to call Debra! Tell her I'm okay!"

"Sure, but there doesn't seem to be cell phone coverage out here. We'll call her when we get closer to town."

"Where are we?"

"Out in the country, south of Oregon City, not far from Mulino."

"I was kept in the dark, then the strobe light.... he drugged me too."

"Yes, you were on something when I found you. You were definitely in la-la land."

We careened out of the building, Vince unsteady and I limping badly. I could see Bonaface's two men emerging from the darkness as they led a hobbled Kirvesniemi toward us. Vince and I stopped our conversation while he sat down and gathered his strength. I thought I could hear the faint noise of sirens in the distance. The sirens sounded as though they were getting closer. The three men from the meadow reached the dirt road a few feet from us. Now the sirens were definitely growing louder.

"It sounds like police or sheriffs are coming. Even if they aren't coming here, we'll stop them if we can. They can either take him or radio for some others to get him if they're going someplace else. You told me you were carrying. If you aren't licensed, you better ditch the guns or at least hide them where you can get them later."

The hulk did not bat an eye, but his buddy nodded

and ran off toward the road. I guessed he had a little problem with the license business. "They'll want to know why we're all here. I'm going to tell them who I am and that I was hired to find Vince. If you want, I can tell them I hired you to back me up."

"That works for me," said the hulk.

"What are your names?"

"Walter Annison," he said somewhat sheepishly. "You can call me 'Crusher'. And the other guy's Fred Hagenbach.'

Two minutes later, Fred rejoined us. Thirty seconds after that, a pair of sheriff's cars wheeled onto the dirt road and skidded to a stop. Four deputies jumped out of the cars with guns drawn. We stood unmoving in the focus of their converging headlights.

"We're alright, although my friend here needs to get to a hospital and the man we captured definitely needs medical attention for his eye."

"Tell us who you are!" ordered one of the officers.

I gave him my name and started to explain what had happened. He interrupted me.

"Toss your ID over here."

I threw my wallet to him. He looked at it, squinted at my photos on the driver's license and the private investigator's license and came a little closer to study my face. Then he relaxed a little.

"Okay. Your friends called us and said you had tracked a kidnapper to this old packing plant and would be needing assistance. We told them to stay off the property 'til we got this sorted out, but they're right down the road apiece. They're in a car and on a motorcycle."

Good old Julio, I thought. He had more sense than I had!

"And who are the rest of you?"

"I brought Walt and Fred along in case things turned bad, which they did. This is the man I was hired to find," I added, jerking my thumb toward Vince who had, by then, regained his feet. "And the man with the hobbles is a murderer and damn near added two more of us to his count. His name is Miska Kirvesniemi."

"We'll get him cuffed and in a car and then you'll have to spell that for me."

Kirvesniemi yelled at the officers, "Don't believe them! They tried to break into my building. I'm entitled to protect my property! I came after them and they jumped me. They gouged my eye out!"

We looked at him in amazement. Did he really think the deputies would buy that story against our explanation, especially when I could show them his torture chamber inside? Before any of us could respond, Vince said, "That's a Goddamned lie! This man kidnapped and tortured me. These people came to rescue me!"

By then, I had found my voice. "That's absolutely right, officers. You can contact Paul DeNoli at the Portland PB's Detective Division. This is his case. And be sure to go down in that meadow. See that riding mower with the lights on? Close by it, you'll find a rifle. That's what he used to shoot at me and I'm betting it's the same weapon that he used to kill a man in California"

"Tad, get down there and bring the rifle back," one of the officers said to his colleague. "Treat it like evidence. Then get crime scene tape around the building." Then, to us, he said, "I'm ready to believe you on who did what to whom, but I'll have to call it in to Detective DeNoli, like you said."

Turning to Vince the deputy asked, "So what's your name, sir?"

Vince gave his name and told them his wallet could probably be found inside the building. Another of the deputies went to radio in their report and to query DeNoli. I told a third deputy that my cell phone, bear spray, and Beretta had been taken away from me when I was captured and were still somewhere inside. He said they would keep them for the time being to check for Kirvesniemi's fingerprints.

I thought it would save time if I drove Vince to the hospital rather than waiting for an EMT van to be called in. In a matter of minutes, the deputies had been patched through by their communications center and had succeeded in reaching DeNoli at home. He awakened quickly and confirmed our identities and told them that Kirvesniemi was a prime suspect for murder and for kidnapping Vince. I could foresee being called on the carpet again for my freelancing approach to finding Vince. But I felt that finding and capturing this psycho should earn me some gold stars in Paul's Captain's book. The deputies called the EMTs for their prisoner and agreed that the rest of us could leave.

"I've got a question before we go," I said. "What is an old packing plant doing way out here?"

One deputy shrugged his shoulders, but another deputy spoke up. "There used to be a lot more open pastures out this way. About twenty years ago, most of them were turned into Christmas tree farms and a few were made into vineyards. Guess that's when the packing plant started losing money."

Down the road, I picked out Julio's car and Ricardo's bike on the shoulder. I stopped, got out, and hugged them both.

"You guys, I owe you both, *big time*. This is Vince Langlow. Vince, this is Julio Mendez and Ricardo Satello."

Vince was still pretty wobbly, but he strode over and shook their hands and added his thanks to mine.

"Ricardo and Julio ran the tail that led us out here, Vince. And they called the sheriff to the scene."

Vince actually choked up and effusively thanked them again. I think the tension he had been under for the last week was starting to drop away and he was losing it emotionally. We got back in my car and as he buckled in, he started sobbing. I squeezed his shoulder and said, "Tomorrow's a new day, Vince. A damn fine new day!"

When we got to Oregon City, Vince called Debra. They both wept and expressed their love for each other. Debra thanked me repeatedly and said she would meet us at the hospital. Vince and I both needed to see a doctor. Despite my fatigue, and my pain and bleeding, I felt like a million bucks.

THIRTY-SEVEN

Sunday, December 3rd, 2:30 P.M.

We also had called the Langlows' family physi-
cian, Dr. Leonard Calspin, as we drove back to
Portland. Dr. Calspin had arranged for us both to be
admitted to the Oregon Health Sciences University
Hospital where he had medical privileges. I had been
doing fine with the driving when we started, but by
the time we reached the hospital, I was beginning to
feel light-headed. Calspin had taken one look at my
blood-stained shirt and had sent me to the Emergency
Room for an immediate transfusion. There, they also
irrigated the wound again and applied new bandages.
They x-rayed my ankle and told me that it was not
broken. A male nurse had taped my ankle, made me
sit in a wheelchair, and escorted me to a room that
Vince and Dr. Calspin had reserved. Vince had been
given a room nearby. Calspin had given him a sedative
and, by three-thirty in the morning, he was sleeping
soundly. Debra had seen him settled and then had gone
home, promising to be back when he awakened. I also
had received a sedative and was quickly asleep. It had
been nearly noon before Vince awoke. I had awakened
a little earlier, but I stayed in my room so Vince and my
sister could have some private time together.

I was to be discharged after my hospital lunch and a

final look-over by Dr. Calspin. Because of the taser attack, the good doctor even had them give me an EKG
that I was told I passed with flying colors. The doctor
wanted Vince to stay one more day for observation. He
was also arranging for a psychologist to see Vince who
still was not his usual upbeat, confident self. I had received a call from Paul DeNoli in late morning saying
he would come by to talk to both Vince and me after
lunch. By two-thirty, Dr. Calspin had cleared me to
go. I was carefully lacing a Nike trainer on my swollen
and taped left foot when Paul came through the door
of my room. He grabbed me by the shoulders – he was
careful not to give me a rib-crushing hug – and told
me how glad he was that I was alive. Then he began on
the lecture I knew was coming.

"Rick, you were a bloody fool to go out there
alone! Our deal was you were supposed to keep me
posted on every lead! When did you first find out
where Kirvesniemi was?"

"You're so right, Paul. I should have let you know
right when I found him. I tracked him to a motel in
Milwaukie in late afternoon. It's just that I had this
strong feeling that Vince was still alive and that, if we re-
frained from nabbing Kirvesniemi right away, he would
lead me to Vince. Things were moving pretty fast and I
thought Julio and Ricardo and I could do the tailing and
I could scout the place, if there were such a place."

"You didn't think *we* could make him talk?"

"Honestly, I didn't. I read him as completely obsessed, Paul. I thought if he had my brother-in-law

imprisoned somewhere, he would just clam up and let Vince starve to death."

"Okay. I guess maybe I can see your not wanting us to make an immediate arrest, but why the hell didn't you think we could follow him and carry out a raid?"

"I'm sorry. I guess you could have tailed him as well or better than we could."

I left unsaid my reservations about whether a police raid without any knowledge of the layout of the building would have been able to save Vince's life.

"It was Vince's safety you were thinking about, huh?" asked DeNoli in a little softer tone.

I nodded, "Yeah, I guess that was it."

"I think I understand, Rick. I'll stand up for you on this one, but I got to tell you some of the higher brass in the department are already calling you a maverick, sort of a rogue PI. You pretty much single-handedly got the perp and saved Langlow so they won't put on any pressure to pull your ticket, but in the future if you want to work with us, you damn well better *work* with us!"

"Message received, Paul!"

"Good. Now that I have that off my chest, I can tell you that the ballistics boys told me the weapon in that meadow was the same one that was fired at you out at Swan Island. And we have a preliminary report from Mill Valley that the rifling marks match up with the slug down there. The criminalists said the rifle had Kirvesniemi's prints on the stock and the scope. And they found more of his prints on that stun gun."

"How did the bastard get so well prepared up here if he lived in Placerville?"

"Well we checked into the title of that building. Apparently, the place was a meat-packing plant at one time. It belongs to a Verna Taylor with a P.O. Box in Sacramento for an address. He must have some connection to her."

"He did," I said. "She was his wife. She died of cancer. As we were driving to the hospital, Vince told me his captor said his name was Taylor. At the time, that jigged something in my memory … a connection to something, but I couldn't quite bring it up. The old memory banks don't work so well under stress, I guess. Have you seen that dungeon he rigged up out there?"

"Yes. I was out there last night. He's one sick fuck! Oh, yeah. I forgot to mention that the criminalists also found a couple of his prints on that broiler thing he'd made."

I shuddered at the mention of that evil machine. "He actually planned to roast Vince alive!"

"Man, that's out of the Dark Ages!"

"Was he traveling around in that old pickup?" I asked.

"Looks that way. The truck had Oregon plates, but those plates belonged to a car that had been totaled. When we traced the VIN on the pickup this morning, it was a California registry and he was the owner. How he got in to the Multnomah Athletic Club from the motel, we don't exactly know, but there are lots of ways he could have handled it. And we still haven't figured out what he did with Mr. Langlow's car."

I knew sooner or later Paul would ask me how I found out where Kirvesniemi was staying so I probably had to say something about the car. "The D.A. isn't going to charge him with car theft, is she?"

"I doubt it. Especially if she has the nice tight case for aggravated assault and kidnapping that I think she has."

"Then let's just say I found out what happened to the car and that gave me a phone call to trace and that led to the Rest-Well Motel. Did your people find any drugs? Vince can't remember anything about how Kirvesniemi took him from the MAC. I know he used a taser-type gun on me, but Vince was definitely under the influence of something while we were being held."

"We found hypodermic syringes and some ampules of ketamine at the packing plant. The hospital is analyzing Vince's blood and they should be able to tell us if that's what he used on Vince."

"This was a close call for both of us. I sure as hell hope Vince pulls out of it okay."

"Yeah," DeNoli agreed. "An experience like that can really mess with your mind. I'm sure he'll get the best of attention."

"Yes he will. His doctor has already arranged for some counseling."

DeNoli slowly shook his head. "I've seen some brutal homicides, Rick, but I'm still trying to wrap my mind around the fact that a death all those years ago could turn this guy into a twisted killer trying to take the law into his own hands."

"I guess the death of a child, even an adult child, would have an emotional impact that we can't even imagine."

This was the part of the conversation that I had been dreading. Many of the details about events at The Big Molly would almost certainly come out at Kirvesniemi's trial, so there was no point in refusing to discuss it. But for Vince's sake – and his family *was* my employer – I did not feel any need to offer conjecture or to go beyond the little I had told DeNoli earlier. Vince had asked me as we drove to the hospital whether he should consult an attorney. I had told him that the prosecutor or her investigators always interview the crime victim. Then I had advised him to at least discuss matters with a good criminal lawyer and to do that before he was interviewed. I finished tying my shoes and was able to switch the topic of my conversation with Paul to the University of Oregon football team's chances in the upcoming bowl games.

Vince had insisted on covering my hospital bills, so I walked right past the business office and out the door. In my car, I opened my cell phone. I had a couple of phone calls to make.

THIRTY-EIGHT

Sunday, December 3rd, 4:00 P.M.

The switchboard at The Oregonian had put me through to Max Sobel. When I had asked if I could monopolize the last hour of his day, he said to come ahead. Inside his office, I could not see that Max had not made much progress in his packing. He gave me his usual strong handshake and merry-eyed smile.

"Sit down, Rick. Sit down," he said gesturing to the only chair not stacked with papers or memorabilia of his long career on the paper.

"Max, we found Vince Langlow."

"Excellent, Rick! Was it foul play? The stories lately, including a piece in our paper, have suggested some kind of a kidnapping."

"That's what it was, Max. And thank God, we found him in time."

"So he's alive? He's okay?"

"Alive, yes. And he has no serious physical injuries. But, off the record, you can imagine that being held captive by a madman for almost two weeks is incredibly hard emotionally. He's a resilient person and I'm pretty sure he'll be fine in a couple of weeks, but right now it must seem like a terrible nightmare."

"Did it turn out to have something to do with his past?"

I countered his question with one of my own. "Have you got time for one more scoop before you hang up your spurs?"

"Hell yes! Whatever you can tell me."

"Thanks. I appreciate your putting it that way because there may be some things that must remain confidential. You're the one who told me to look into the past when the present offered no clues and, yes, it did have something to do with the past. Many years ago, a young employee of Vince's died on the job. This had nothing to do with Langlow Enterprises. It was before then. The guy's truck ran off a winding road and down a steep embankment. The burned wreck was not discovered until the following morning. Tragically, the young man lived through the night down in this ravine before succumbing. It gave the appearance of being an accident. But the man's father had always blamed Vince for the death. It looks as though, over the years, the father became more and more obsessed with his son's death and more and more convinced that Vince's company was responsible."

"Was there any basis for the father's belief?" Max asked.

"Nothing at all concrete. He was going home in the winter darkness after work when it happened. One could think of any number of explanations why a truck would leave the road. Apparently, due to one inference in a letter from his son, the father thought the young man had discovered something compromising about the company's operations. But let me tell you the real story: how this man waylaid Vince and where he took him and what fate his twisted mind had devised for Vince."

I wanted Max, for his past loyalty to me and for offering me his good advice, to have a shot at the first newspaper coverage. The story was going to break regardless and I owed him that much. Perhaps I had put a slight spin on the long-past events, but Max was a responsible journalist. He might decide to delve into what had transpired at The Big Molly, but he would not sensationalize ancient history. I went on to fill Max in on how Kirvesniemi had pulled off the kidnapping, how he transformed the packing plant into a grisly torture dungeon, and how I too was caught, subsequently escaped and, finally, overpowered this would-be killer. Julio had asked me to leave Ricardo and him out of it and I did. I also left out the parts about Turley and Bonaface. It did not seem too likely that the prosecution would need to use them as witnesses, though it would not have surprised me if their names were to come up somehow during the trial. By my lights, Bonaface had been living in his own private hell for almost three decades. That certainly did not make what he did right, but it did seem to go some good way toward penance.

Max took notes as I spoke and asked me about my own fears and decisions. I told him I was plenty scared and, at times incredibly angry with myself for a couple of unwise choices. I said, in the end, I deserved no credit for being a hero: I was simply in a fight for survival against a maniacal villain. As I left, he was already at work dispatching reporters and hammering on his keyboard.

My second call was to Angie Richards. She was through work for the day and I reached her at her apartment. I told her that Vince Langlow had been rescued and that there were some things I now could share with her. She invited me to come straight over to her place. Fifteen minutes later, I was knocking at her door. Our kiss was somewhere in between a polite peck and a thermostat-raising, passionate clinch. Soon after, we were sitting together on her burgundy-velvet couch and I had a tumbler of Bushmills-on-the-rocks in my hand.

"You're not trying to loosen my tongue, are you?" I gibed.

"Afraid not. I might even cut you off after this one!"

"I've already talked to Max Sobel, my friend and boss from my newspaper days. The Oregonian will have some kind of a story in tomorrow's morning edition. If you can use what I have to say in your ten o'clock evening news, you're welcome to it as a semi-exclusive, Angie."

"I think we already have some bare-bones stuff from a runner who picked up a few details from the Clackamas County Sheriff's Office, but whatever you can tell, Rick, I'm excited to have."

I told her basically the same version I had given Max. She listened attentively and scribbled notes as I talked.

"So is this Kirvesniemi guy insane?" she asked.

"If the defense takes that tack, I'm sure both sides will have their expert psychiatrists on the stand. Anyone who planned and carried out an attack like that might seem demented to some, but I'm not the one to judge that."

"Rick, I know you didn't want me meddling, but what happened to you is so scary. I wish there had been something I could've done to help!"

"Thanks, Angie. But you know, it really happened so fast, there wasn't much anyone could've done."

"I want you to know that I tried to call you this morning, but I couldn't reach you at your houseboat or on your cell. Now I know it was because you were in the hospital!"

"Yeah. And the perp took my cell away from me. Why were you calling? Social or professional?"

"Both, really. On the professional side, I had a theory about Vince. With hindsight, I see that it did not solve the kidnapping, but I want to tell you about it anyway. I dug up some old Willamette Week stories and saw that Langlow and Clifford Darmsfeld had fought over a zoning issue years ago. Langlow virtually accused Darmsfeld of corrupting a city council on a rezoning petition. I followed the thread and I think I may have turned up evidence that Darmsfeld bought off one of the council members!"

"I'll be damned!"

"I had it wrong," she said. "I thought Langlow had found the same evidence and Darmsfeld had tried to get rid of him to keep it quiet. But, in any case, if this holds up, your old suspicions about Darmsfeld will be completely vindicated!"

I thought about that for a few seconds. Eighteen months ago, I would have jumped right back on the story and, with or without Angie, turned over every last rock until I had Darmsfeld ready for drawing and quartering. But today I felt differently. I had let go of that crusade and I had no desire to pick it up again. I was excited that Angie had a great story in the making and that a real scumbag was likely to get his comeuppance, but I liked my new life and the way things had worked out. A private investigator I had become and a private investigator I was going to stay.

"That's great, Angie. Congratulations on some damn good work! I still have a box full of research about that guy in a closet on the houseboat. You're welcome to the stuff. I waggled my nearly empty glass at her. I felt like a little celebration. "How about a touch more?"

"Okay. Talked me into it." She went to her cupboard bar and refreshed my Bushmills.

"You were limping when you came in and you sat down like an old man who aches all over. Did this madman injure you?"

"A little. I said he set a trap for me earlier in the day. He tried to get me with a rifle. One of his shots grazed my ribs. It'll heal, but it's plenty tender in the meantime. And, when I was running across that meadow dodging his laser-sighted rifle, I sprained my ankle pretty good."

"Oh, Rick!" She gave me a hug and another kiss, one that we both put a little more oomph into. Then she was back to business. "One of our runners got a look at the incident report in the Sheriff's Office and there were two other persons mentioned as being on the scene working with you. Who were they?"

"Just a couple of guys I used for back up. They have regular jobs and won't want to be mentioned in any media stories."

"Well, I still might try for an interview. Anyone on the scene would have exciting things to describe and talk about. Were they held by this creep also?"

"No. Thank God, they stayed outside the building. But when I was fighting with Kirvesniemi, they helped subdue him. They earned their keep right there because, like I said, I had sprained my ankle and was not at my fighting best."

"Hah, Hah. And who were these people who called the Sheriff?"

"More extra help. I occasionally call them in to assist with surveillance. They weren't on the scene when things went down, although they tailed the villain to this place he had out in the country. But they too have day jobs and really don't want to be connected to a crime story. You know I'm kind of a low-budget operation. I just call on these guys for help when I'm in a pinch."

"Even that sounds like an interesting angle. You're a hero, Rick. People are going to be interested in how you pulled this off."

"Nice of you to say so, Angie, but go easy on these other guys. It's understandable they may not want the limelight. Let 'em have their privacy."

"I'll bear that in mind, Rick. I really will. But even after you figured out who this kidnapper was, how did you know *where* he was?"

I gave her the simplified traced-the-car-and-phone-call story as casually as possible, as if the only interesting parts began when we tailed Kirvesniemi from the motel. That seemed to placate her for the time being.

"I would ask you to stay and have dinner and ... whatever, but with this story breaking, I'm not even stopping for dinner myself. And Rick ... I really appreciate your giving me the first television crack at the story. I may want to talk with you about these things again in the next few days, but that will be entirely up to you. And, the other kind of talks? Well ... call me soon, okay? I don't want to lose what we've had!"

I looked at this enigmatic beauty with conflicting emotions in my head and heart. I nodded and stood up. "Yeah.... I know."

THIRTY-NINE

Vince was released from the hospital late Tuesday morning with assurances from Dr. Calspin that he would suffer no lasting physical effects. No one could say, at that early time, about his psychological health, but Debra and I were betting on his having a healthy resilience. I spent Tuesday in my office paying bills, finishing a preliminary report on a pending case, and phoning a new client to explain why I had not yet begun work on his assignment. Fortunately, his problem was not urgent and I had gained some nice cover from the stories – Angie's included – about my rescuing Vince.

As soon as those necessary details were out of the way, I was driven to get back on the trail of the con artist who had masterminded the phony ransom demand. Not only did I feel responsible for Vince being out the remaining sixty-seven thousand, but I also had a score to settle with the shitbird who had set me up. Dr. Calspin wanted me to let the bullet wound heal at least another couple of days, but I argued for a compromise of one more day. They had taped up my ankle at the hospital and told me use a cane until I could put full weight on that leg. I figured a couple of days using the cane would not kill me and it *did* make it easier to walk. I loafed around the houseboat reading an Eliot Pattison mystery novel the next day and decided I could drive and foot it enough to pick up the trail the next morning. If there *was* any trail to pick up.

Angie called and asked if she could come over in the early afternoon before her shift. I thought about it for about a second-and-a-half and said 'sure'. She helped me ice and rewrap my ankle and we talked around the edges of where our relationship would go from here. It was a more comfortable conversation than I would have guessed and we parted with a lingering kiss.

I had DeNoli's permission to talk to Morrie Lehman, the detective on the PPB bunco squad whose team had arrested Despaile. I made an appointment to meet him at the Justice Center Wednesday morning. It was a little after eight as Lehman shook my hand and led me to his cubicle.

"Damn good job with Langlow! I hear you caught some flak for working alone – again – but you got your guy and nabbed that crazy fucker from California at the same time."

"Thanks. Yeah, it all worked out okay in the end. Tell me whatever you can about the second guy in the con."

"Are you back in play with him?"

"Yeah. My client is still out most of the money. There's no way to insure a risk like that. So I'm still working that aspect of the case. But I'm just focusing on identifying and locating the guy who has the money. Maybe I can get some stronger evidence if there's any to be found. I intend to work as closely with you as you'll allow. I'll share any leads I get once they look solid enough to be of interest."

"You won't approach him directly if you pick up his trail?"

"No. No percentage in that. He's seen my face and heard my voice. I'll work with you if we get that close. And any collar … that's your department."

"Alright. If you can stick to those rules, we'll try working with you. Unfortunately, I can't tell you we've made much progress in actually finding the perp. Despaile still won't give us his pal."

"So you still don't have a name?"

"Maybe yes, maybe no. In our search, we got Despaile's cell phone and he hadn't gotten around to erasing his 'last ten calls received' list. So in the forty-some hours between the first newspaper story about Langlow and their getting the money from you, we find one number that comes up three times: a phone belonging to a Nathan Berriman. We ran that name through our data base and the fed's. No hits."

"Did you run the other callers?"

"Sure. There were only three. A cousin of his in Toledo, a guy trying to sell aluminum siding, and the manager at a bar where he works part time calling about a schedule change."

I wrote Berriman's name in my notebook. "Well, the odds may be that the first guy is the accomplice given those repeated calls."

"Correcto! We're going to keep working that name

and hope something comes up. I got some more good news. We *did* turn up the old pickup truck. In a supermarket parking lot in Kelso."

"Washington, huh. Your APB worked?"

"Well, not a first. We only heard about the truck yesterday and got it back from the Kelso police last night."

"Any prints?"

"No. Wiped clean. Our criminalists found a couple of hairs on the driver's seat and headrest, but we don't think the Kelso people were too careful about isolating it. At first they thought it was simply abandoned so it was back in the impound yard before they rechecked the stolen vehicles list and later yet when they finally tied the truck to our APB. So you've got a tow truck driver, the yard man and maybe a cop or two sitting in that seat. Still, the hairs could belong to our guy, so the criminalists have saved them."

"I don't suppose anybody saw the person who left the truck?"

"Not too likely if it was very early in the morning, but we did ask the early shift clerks in the supermarket and the gal at a nearby espresso stand that opens early. Nada. We have shown the security camera photo to the detective who handles fraud and property crimes for the Kelso police, but he didn't recognize the guy's face."

"Any chance I could have a copy of that photo?"

Lehman lowered his voice. "I guess that would be okay. I have some extras," he said as he slid one of the pictures across his desk to me.

"I appreciate that. And thanks for filling me in. I think I'll head up to Kelso myself and nose around. I'll let you know if I turn up anything."

Kelso is a straight shot up I-5 and I made it there in forty minutes. Kelso is a pleasant enough little town close to Longview, Washington. Longview is a somewhat gritty mill town on the bank of the Columbia River and is the site of the closest bridge downstream from Portland crossing into Oregon. Just a few miles north on the Oregon bank was the site of the now-demolished Trojan nuclear power plant, its huge cooling tower once a salient landmark for travelers on I-5.

Morrie Lehman had given me the address of the supermarket and that was my first stop. I saw a standard-issue Safeway with a blacktop parking lot in front. It was a mall security officer who called the Kelso police when she realized the truck had not moved for several days. I tracked her down, but she was merely a roving patrol who covered three mini-malls in the same general area. She knew nothing about when or by whose hand the truck had arrived.

It was true that Despaile lived in the small town of Scapoose, but somehow I did not see Ski Mask in the same light. I saw him as a little more sophisticated operator ... one who would probably hunt for his marks in the more affluent big cities. If Ski Mask had in fact driven the truck to Kelso, my guess was that he was heading for Seattle. Of course, he might have been cautious enough that he just paid some stranger to drive the truck and leave it in Kelso to create a false trail. But would he have been that careful? Especially if he and Despaile thought the stolen vehicle gambit would succeed? More likely, I figured, he was a little concerned that someone might have noticed the truck in Sherwood and that that could lead to an all-points-bulletin. By dumping it and switching to some other means of transport, he would break the link from him to the truck and be extra safe. And, even without an APB, leaving it in Kelso shored up Despaile's stolen-truck story if it needed shoring up.

In the same mini-mall, I found a bookstore where I bought a Kelso city map. I saw that the downtown was about three-quarters of a mile from where I stood. I planned to drive downtown to look for a train station or a bus station or even a rental car agency. Before I started the car, I queried the portable GPS cantilevered off my windshield. I punched in "bus depot" on the points of interest and had it calculate the route to the Greyhound station. I reasoned that a bus for Seattle would leave earlier than the Amtrak and that Ski Mask would want to move north as soon as possible. I left the car in a passenger-loading zone in front of the station. Inside, I saw that only one ticket window was manned. There were two people in front of me but, when I finally reached the head of the line, I was alone. A surprisingly cheerful older man with mutton-chop sideburns asked me where I wanted to go.

"Actually, I don't need a ticket. I'd like to ask you a question, if I may."

He looked at me quizzically above the half-lenses of his reading glasses. "Yes?"

"Were you working here the morning of Friday the twenty-fourth?" He nodded. "What time did you start?"

"Six forty-five"

"Was yours the only ticket window open that morning?"

"Yes. What's this all about?"

"I'm trying to trace the movements of a certain individual. I don't know what name he may have been using. I have a picture. I'd like to ask you to look at it and tell me if you remember selling him a ticket that morning."

"Are you with the police?"

"No. I'm a private investigator. We think this man swindled my client out of a large sum of money. We believe we've traced him from Portland to Kelso. We do not think he had his own vehicle, but have some reason to believe he was attempting to reach Seattle."

The agent stroked his sideburn and gave me a serious, but not altogether unfriendly look. "You say you're a PI. How do I know you're not a hit man for the Mafia?"

I passed him my license. "The Portland police are involved, but I'm working to recover the money. Believe me, this is not part of any underworld war."

He gave the slightest nod, as if he had been persuaded to cooperate. He held the photo at an angle and peered through the half glasses. "Actually, I think I *have* seen this person. I remember that he paid with a hundred-dollar bill. You don't see too many of those. He bought a ticket for Seattle."

Bingo! "Did he have luggage?" I asked.

"Hm. Well, yeah, I think I checked a bag for him. And he had quite a large briefcase. I told him that it wasn't likely to fit in the overhead rack, but he didn't want to check it … said he'd put it on the floor between his feet."

"Do you have a record of his name?"

"I don't remember it. It would be in Greyhound's data base somewhere, but the best I could do would be to get a list of all the Kelso customers who purchased Seattle tickets for that morning's bus. And, in any case, it's against company policy to give out that information."

"How about if the Portland or Kelso police asked for the list?"

"I don't know. It might have to be reviewed at the regional office in Seattle. They might want their lawyer to look at it."

I thought it wasn't worth going to the mat over this right that minute. I would tell Lehman we had a positive ID on the bus passenger and let him get the names. Besides, Ski Mask probably did not give his real name anyway. But, somewhere on that list might be an identity he would keep using for a while if he were lying low. It was worth a try.

"Can you tell me the name of the driver on that bus?"

"I imagine it was Ted Brewster, but that's easy enough to check." He keyboarded in a query on his terminal. "Yes. Brewster. I suppose you want his address or home phone. I can't give those out, but he carries a cell phone and I can give you that number."

"Excellent!"

"He's on the road right now. It's against company regulations for him to use the phone while he's driving, but you can leave a voice-mail message and he might return your call."

"Good idea." I wrote down the number. "Do you have a surveillance camera in the station?"

"Well, we do have one focused on the ticket windows, but it's been down for the last ten days and the repair people haven't gotten to it yet."

I thanked him and walked outside where I called Brewster's cell. He picked up. I told him who I was and, in a general way, why I was calling. He said he was at a stop and had only a couple of minutes to talk with me, but he sounded willing to help. I described Ski Mask as best I could using the photo pulled from Target's security camera.

"Do you have any memory of such a passenger who got on at Kelso on Friday, November twenty-fourth?"

"The Friday after Thanksgiving? Oh, wait a minute! Maybe I do. Our buses often make a quick roadside stop at Federal Way. It's not a real bus depot ... just a coffee shop. There was one lady waiting to board and then this guy – a guy who I think looked pretty much like you just described – came up and said he wanted off and could I open the luggage compartment so he could get his suitcase. I kind of look over the tickets of any new passengers when they board and I didn't remember anyone scheduled to get off in Federal Way. I asked him if he was sure and told him that we were still almost twenty-five miles from downtown Seattle. He said 'no problem, I just decided to look up an old friend'. It didn't seem like a big deal, but it was a little unusual so I guess it made an impression on me."

"Thanks, that's very helpful. How about his luggage? Anything besides the suitcase?"

"Hmm. I think maybe he was lugging a large briefcase … he must have had it with him in his seat."

"And what time of day would that have been?"

"If we stop in Federal Way and if we left Portland on time – which I'm pretty sure we did that day -- it's almost always around twelve twenty-five."

I was wondering if maybe our guy had gone to ground in Federal Way and bought the ticket all the way to Seattle just as a smoke screen. But I still liked my big-city operator theory. As long as Brewster was in a helpful mood, I thought I might as well cover all the bases. "So is there another northbound bus later in the day?"

"Yes, there is. It would be at Federal Way by five in the afternoon. There's also an express around eight, but it doesn't stop in Federal Way." He was starting to talk faster and faster. "Listen, I got to go. Good luck with finding this guy."

I went back into the station and went back to the

ticket clerk. "I just talked to Ted Brewster. Nice guy. He said there is an afternoon bus that stops in Federal Way and continues on to Seattle. Could you check your data base and tell me who the driver was on that bus on that Friday? The twenty-fourth?"

"Well, they won't let me into the human resources data base, but I can tell you, unless he was sick or taking a day off, it would've been Al Bailiff."

"Good. I don't suppose you know his cell phone number also?"

"No. But if you want to hang around, he should be hauling in here a few minutes before two. You could catch him then."

I thanked him again for his help and said I did not think I would wait around. I had already decided to drive up to Federal Way myself.

FORTY

Wednesday, December 6th, 11:00 A.M.

I wanted to poke around Federal Way and I could interview Mr. Bailiff up there. Brewster had told me
the name of the coffee shop and I located it as soon as
I arrived. It was just a block beyond the off-ramp. I
had a couple of hours to spare and I wanted to check
out motels and banks in the town. I did not believe
for one minute that Ski Mask was suddenly inspired to
"visit an old friend." I fairly quickly learned that there
were five motels in town. Luckily, they were all within
four blocks of each other. Three of them were owner-
operated and no one recognized the photo. In one of
the other two, I was able to talk to the desk man who
had been on that Friday night. He too did not react to
the photo. In the fifth motel, the person who had been
on the desk that day was not available, but the clerk
checked the records and said all their customers were
couples with cars. That gave me some confidence that
Ski Mask – or Berriman if that was who he was -- had
not stayed overnight in Federal Way. So he either called
a friend for a bunk or a ride or took that five o'clock
bus.

My next idea was to check the banks. There were
five. I figured if he had hopped off the bus in Federal
Way to stash the money, he would have been looking to

rent a large safe deposit box. I doubted I would be able to get a name or box number, but I was hoping someone in the bank might be willing to look at the photo. The first bank I entered was a small local operation. The manager was pretty curious about my inquiry, but seemed comfortable telling me that no one had rented or tried to rent a box in the last two weeks. The second bank was also local and the manager was, at first, reluctant to answer my questions. I showed her my card and said I was working with the Portland police and just wanted bare bones information. She led me back to a windowless conference room where we sat across a walnut table.

"Am I correct that someone wanting to open an account or rent a safe deposit box would have to deal with you?" I asked.

"Well, my assistant manager would handle it if I was away, but I'm here most of the time and, yes, such a person would deal with me."

I showed her the photo and asked, "Ten or eleven days ago, did this man come into your bank and do any business?"

She studied the photo for a moment and then nodded. "Yes, he came in. I think it might've been the Friday after Thanksgiving. I remember it was a pretty slow day."

"Would I be correct in thinking that he wanted to rent one of your largest safe deposit boxes?"

A frown crossed her brow and then melted into the slightest smile. "You might be."

"Would he be required to have or to open an account in order to have the box?"

"Yes, you need an account to have a box, but you can activate an account with as little as a fifty dollar deposit."

"So such a person would show you identification, sign a signature card, and open an account if he did not already have one."

"Correct."

"Would you or any of your staff know what went into such a box?"

"No, of course not. Our customers are given privacy once we use our key to start the unlocking process. We do not know what goes in or what comes out."

"We're almost positive this person has very recently defrauded my client out of a sizable amount of money, in currency. The police are searching for the person in that photo. Is there any way you can tell me the identity he used and the address he gave?"

"No. I can understand your wanting to know, but surely you understand that banks don't divulge that kind of information without a subpoena or at least a search warrant."

"How about the name Nathan Berriman or Nate Berriman?"

"Who's he?" she answered with a slight grin. "But, in any case, I told you I can't give out our customer's names."

So it seemed that he had not used that name.

"I understand your situation. I'll have Detective

Morrie Lehman of the Portland Police Bureau contact you. By then, he may well be working with or through the King County Sheriff or the Federal Way police. They will very likely ask a judge for that search warrant." I handed her my card. "May I at least ask you to contact me if this customer revisits your bank? My cell number is on the card. No need to tell me anything confidential … just that he's back at the bank."

"I think I could do that," she answered as she took the card with a warm smile.

I made it back to the coffee shop where the bus stopped with five minutes to spare. The driver, Al Bailiff, was willing to help, but he could not make a positive ID from the photo. He told me two people did board the bus that day in Federal Way. He was fairly sure one was a woman and the other a man. He thought the man might have been Ski Mask, but he was far from certain and he had not paid attention to the names on the tickets. I decided to follow my hunch that the man I was after had continued on to Seattle and I headed north.

I called Detective Lehman on my cell as I drove and filled him in on finding the bank in Federal Way and the need for a search warrant. He was not at all sure that the Target photo and the fact that a man who looked much like the photo boarded the bus in Kelso and rented a safe-deposit box in Federal Way was enough to get a warrant. He did say he would contact the bank and Federal Way and Seattle police and the King County Sheriff's office to try to initiate a cooperative investigation. Meanwhile, I had to find a man whose name we were only guessing at in a metro area of nearly a million people and then get evidence to tie him more closely to the crime.

FORTY-ONE

I wondered if Ski Mask was staying in touch with Despaile. If they were a team or were old friends in the game, he might be. If they had merely been opportunistic partners, they might not be in contact. Regardless of their ongoing relationship, they might have decided it was safest not to communicate with each other so the apprehension of one could not lead to the other. If they had not been in touch since Ski Mask-Berriman drove the truck away from Despaile's home, there was one gambit I could try.

I had worked with a detective agency in Seattle about a year ago on a fraudulent- insurance-claim case. My counterpart there was Janice DeVoore, a sharp operative and a fine looking woman. I met with DeVoore as soon as I arrived in Seattle. The agency's office was on the second floor of a nondescript brick building between Seattle Center and Lake Union. She gave me a little guff about lurching around with a cane and I told a short version of my escape on the meadow. Then we got down to business. I filled her in on the fake kidnap victim and the ransom demand. I have to admit that I kind of soft-pedaled the fact that I brought the money and how completely I was taken in. I reviewed the things I knew about my target: the initials NAB

364

on his watchband, his approximate height and weight, his cigarette breath, the name from the phone records, the arrest of his helper, Despaile, and the fingerprint on the can of paint.

"What I'd like to try is to place a message in the paper under 'personals'," I told her. "We use the message to set up a rendezvous. Except--if he comes-- he meets with you instead of his buddy."

"What do I do if and when he shows up?" she asked.

"We need to pick a place where he can meet you alone … a neutral place, but with privacy. A place where he actually enters the room you're in before he realizes it's not his accomplice that he's meeting."

"Our agency's done some work for a restaurant-bar in town. I think I can arrange to have the use of a private dining room late at night for an hour or so. We can clue the bartender in and make him the gatekeeper."

"That could work. After the target sees you, he'll know it wasn't a message from his partner. You need to distract him – calm him down -- at that point, get him stay for a drink. I want to know what name he'll use with you. You need to get his prints on the drink glass. See if he's wearing the watchband with those initials. I'll be watching from outside, but he knows my face so he can't see me. Give him a little encouragement, but not too much. When he leaves, call me on my cell and I'll tail him to where he is staying."

"So you want me to dress for sex appeal and give him a few seductive looks, basically."

"Yeah. Just enough so he doesn't turn tail and cut

out as soon as he sees you. We'll have to give you a story that makes it all seem like a plausible mix-up."

"What do we put in the paper?"

"I'm thinking some like 'Nate. Big problem with what happened in Portland. Urgent we talk. Meet me at --- this restaurant you mentioned --- at 2300 hrs. Thursday 7th. Ask bartender for H.D. If you cannot make Thursday, same time and place on Friday 8th. No phones. H.D.'"

"So I'm Holly DuMont or some such and my boy-friend is Nate? And maybe I've discovered that I'm pregnant after our fling in Portland?"

"That's the general idea. You'll have to tell me how to find the restaurant. I'll scout the area and figure out where to be so I can see him leave and be able to fol-low in my car."

"Sounds like a bit of a long shot, but I can handle my end. The meter runs on my hours and any expens-es with the restaurant, but the expenses shouldn't be much. If he shows up and if I can stop him from bolt-ing, you ought to get what you need."

We phoned in the personals ad and I left to check out the restaurant. It looked well suited for our pur-poses: not top dollar and not in a great location, but not sleazy either. The next morning, I verified that the ad appeared in the Seattle Times. I called Morrie Lehman who told me that they had been watching for credit card activity on the Nathan Berriman name, but had seen no activity. He said that they had not been successful in getting a search warrant for the Federal

Way bank. Thursday night Janice DeVoore and I waited in vain for "Nate" to show up. The next day, I busied myself with obtaining some Seattle-based information for a client on a different case. That night was a different story.

From my darkened car across the street, I saw a man with the right build and walk to be Ski Mask arrive at the restaurant twenty minutes early. My pulse was pounding as I walked by the place close enough to see him sitting at the bar having a drink. I figured he was moxie enough to look the place over before asking for "H.D.". At five after eleven, he had a short conversation with the bar tender, then got up and walked toward the rear of the restaurant. If someone responded to the ad, we had instructed the bartender to say only that "the person who wants to see you is in a private room. It's at the back on the right."

Janice DeVoore told me later that as soon as he entered, she recognized him from the photo. She said something like "you're not my Nate!" He stopped in his tracks, but took a few seconds to check out the sexy looking woman in front of him. She said he apologized and muttered something about a mistake. He told her that he thought the message was from his estranged wife, Heather, and that it referred to their failed attempt to reconcile at a recent get-together in Portland.

Janice said that was when she gave him the come on. She claimed she had been stood up, and said he might as well stay and have a drink with her so their evening was not a total loss. He bit, and she got an introduction where he used the name Kevin Turell. After a couple of drinks, she declined his invitation to continue the evening at his place, but asked him the time. She told me that she saw the initials "N A B" on the band of his expensive watch and could tell by his breath that he was a smoker.

Seconds after DeVoore alerted me on my cell, I saw our target emerge from the restaurant. It was not hard to tail him to a decent residential hotel on Eighth Street. The next morning, I gave Lehman the details. He told me to deliver DeVoore's affidavit and the glass with Ski Mask's fingerprints to the fraud unit of the Seattle PD who were happy to cooperate. He called me back that afternoon to say they had a positive match with the prints on the paint can in Despaile's garage. Then he told me that they had found a credit card charge in the name of Kevin Turell in Federal Way on the same day that someone with his face rented a safe deposit box there. Two hours later, Lehman called again to say they had asked a King County judge for a search warrant and were turned down. The judge reportedly said they needed a stronger connection to the safe deposit box.

I had been worrying that this might happen and my worries led me to a new plan. I called my friend and sometimes associate, Julio Mendez. The same Julio who had helped me track Misha Kirversniemi to the packing plant.

"Julio, it's Rick. I'm up in Seattle working on a case. It involves a con artist who has swindled Vince

Langlow out of a hundred grand ransom by posing as the real kidnapper. I need someone to play the part of a drug lord's henchman as the key part in the con of a con. If it succeeds, we get Vince's money back and the sleaze bag goes to the slammer. Would you be willing to do it? Can you take a couple of days away from your business?"

"Yeah, maybe. Do you think this guy's dangerous?"

"I can't absolutely guarantee that he's not, but I very much doubt it. He deals in non-violent scams. He's clever, but I don't think he resorts to weapons or muscle. I'll be very close by and we can put me on your speed dial. I'll watch your back."

"Alright, I'll help you. Where do I find you in Seattle?"

I told him where I was staying and he said he would be there by ten the next morning. When he arrived, we spent two hours in my hotel room rehearsing his role for a critical five-minute performance. We treated ourselves to a fine lunch at Ivar's Acres of Clams on the Eliot Bay waterfront. After that we found a toy store and I bought Julio a very authentic-looking toy gun. Then we began our stakeout at Berriman/Turell's residential hotel. He left the hotel at a quarter to five on foot. There was a small pocket park a block-and-a-half from the hotel in the direction Berriman was walking. I dropped Julio at the park, cruised around the block, and parked in a loading zone across the street so I could watch from the car.

FORTY-TWO

Nate wanted a before-dinner drink and was heading for a cocktail lounge he had noticed the previous day just a few blocks from his hotel. He had
found the Friday night meeting with "Holly" unset-
tling. Part of his morning paper ritual was to check
the personals. Over the years he had found more
than one promising mark that way. He and Despaile
had agreed not to communicate by phone or e-mail
for at least a month. Even so, what surprised him was
how easily he had assumed the personals ad was from
Howie and how readily he had gone to the meet. At
least he had had the good sense to arrive early in order to spot anyone who did not seem to fit in and he
had used the name that matched his new identity. But,
still, he kicked himself for being too unquestioning
… particularly in his line of work! It seemed to have
been just a strange coincidence, though he was not
a big believer in coincidences. And why had Holly's
ad said "no phones?" He had casually asked her about
that and she had explained that she was staying with
a nosey aunt who had been known to listen in on an
extension phone. He thought that was plausible, but
not altogether convincing. And why did she not even
know where in Seattle her so-called new boyfriend

370

lived? Had it been such a sudden, impulsive affair that she never found out?

But spending an hour with an attractive woman was not the worst thing in the world. If her boyfriend had run out on her, she might even be more available and worth pursuing. But she had inferred she was knocked up and he did not need that kind of complication.

Nate took a short cut on a path across a pocket park. His musings about his interlude with Holly were cut short when a Latino man blocked his way.

"We need to talk Mr. Berriman or Turell … whatever," said the man in a quiet, but firm voice.

"Who are you? I'm not Mr. Berri —"

"There's a bench over there," the man interrupted, pointing to a cement bench beside a bird bath. "Don't give me no bullshit about the name! Maybe you're Turell today. Doesn't matter to us. Now just walk over there and listen."

The twilight had not yet turned to full darkness and there were still plenty of passers by, but Nate was off-balance as a result of this stranger accosting him. He was also deeply curious. He decided not to try to escape and turned toward the bench.

The man, perhaps Mexican, had a solid build and smoldering dark eyes. He sat at the opposite end of the bench. His windbreaker was partly unzipped and Nate could glimpse the handle of a pistol in a shoulder holster. What the hell was this about, Nate wondered, feeling beads of sweat on his forehead at the same time his hands felt clammy cold. And how did this guy know his real name? His pulse rate had risen and he willed himself to be calm.

"This is about the money. You got a hundred large from Vince Langlow. That showed some style, but you see there's a little problem. The money wasn't Langlow's. He was … uh … kinda like a banker for us with that money. It was *our* money. Somehow his wife got a hold of it. Now he's back home and he will have to pay the vig until we get it all back. But you've got more problems. The cops picked up your pal. We hear they got thirty thousand of it when they arrested him. Langlow probably got the thirty back, but he's too hot for us to deal with him right now."

"I don't know what you're talking abou—"

"Drop the act, motherfucker! We had a little talk with your pal, Howard, when he made bail. He may not have talked to the cops, but he gave us you in a heartbeat. Now here's the deal. You have forty-eight hours to get us the hundred grand. I'll call you Monday at two o'clock and tell you where you make delivery. You can't get all of it, you get us the seventy and then you're going to be our guest until we get the rest."

"Even if I had your money, I couldn't deliver it in forty-eight hours!"

"Don't make excuses. My boss, he don't like excuses! We already cut you a little slack here. Kind of a professional courtesy, you might say. Just a nice quiet talk in the park instead of picking you up in a car for a trip to nowhere. But that's over Monday when I call. We get the money or the game changes. We don't have at least the seventy by Monday, you life isn't worth yesterday's fart. If you're so fucking clever, you gotta see the smart move here. We get the money, we forget you stuck your dick in our Margarita. No money, and you can forget your dick and everything else!"

With that, the man with the smoldering eyes stood up and walked away. Nate Berriman sat rooted to the bench for another five minutes. He cursed his luck. In working an inspired con, he had stumbled into some drug lord's money-laundering operation. Despaile had been caught and had dropped the dime on him to this drug cartel enforcer. Berriman forced himself to think rationally. His booty was surely not worth gambling his life. The drug gang had somehow found him and probably had him under surveillance. He knew these gangs had a "take no prisoners" mentality. They always made an example of someone who crossed them in order to defend their turf and protect their assets. And that someone almost always ended up dead. Nate was in "the con game" and would probably always be a player, but he also wanted to live to a comfortable old age. He decided it was time to fold his hand.

FORTY-THREE

Monday, December 11ᵗʰ, 10:00 A.M.

After a nearly sleepless two nights, Nate rented a car and drove to Federal Way. He had disposed of Langlow's briefcase as soon as he had put the money in the safe deposit box. He stopped at a luggage shop to buy a new briefcase and reached the bank at eleven o'clock. By pre-arrangement with Lehman, the bank employee managing the vault claimed not to find "Kevin Turell's" signature card. Nate had to go through a second authentication-of-identity process, using his new driver's license and social security card. To Nate, it seemed that this took an unusually long time. In the meantime, the bank manager had alerted the Sheriff's office and two plain-clothes detectives and Morrie Lehman had arrived and were pretending to do transactions at the tellers' windows. Nate finally was led into the vault and the bank clerk turned her key to his box. Once alone, Nate scooped the bills into the briefcase and left a rhinestone ring and two old-looking books he had purchased at a flea market in their place.

He left the vault area and was heading for the sidewalk when the two detectives materialized on each side of him. "Nate Berriman, you are under arrest," said the man on his right.

Nate looked aghast at the man who then took a firm grip on his arm.

"Lie down on the floor! Now!" the detective shouted.

Nate did as he was ordered and even before he was handcuffed and searched, the briefcase had been taken from his grip. Two real customers in the bank shrank back from the action unfolding before them. Lehman joined the King County detectives as they read Nate his rights. Outside in the parking lot, Rick Conwight and Julio Mendez waited for the group to emerge. When the handcuffed Nate was led to the Sheriff's cruiser, Rick and Julio strolled over.

Morrie Lehman had been working with the King County deputies and assistant district attorney to stay in close touch with the judge who had previously denied the search warrant. Janice's and Julio's affidavits, the fingerprint evidence, and the sworn telephonic testimony of the detectives that Berriman/Turell appeared to be emptying his box were now added to the evidence presented previously. That was enough for the judge to issue both an arrest warrant and a search warrant. She faxed the warrants to the deputies in care of the bank and they had closed in for the arrest.

As Julio and I approached, they were getting ready to insert Berriman into the patrol car. I heard him say, "This drug gang enforcer threatened me. He said they'd kill me if I didn't give them money. It's my money …

it's not stolen from anybody. But, Jesus, you'd do the same thing if they threatened you!"

I asked the deputies to hold up stuffing him into the back seat for a moment. "So you're the tough guy in the ski mask," I said. "You might remember me from that night in Sherwood. Well, guess what? Those bills you claim are yours have been marked by yours truly. You're toast, you limp dick! But what I think you really need to understand is that the lady you met in the restaurant and the 'enforcer' you felt so threatened by? Well, they were both working for me."

I think Berriman had probably figured most of that out by the time they cuffed him, but it still did me good to tell him to his face.

FORTY-FOUR

Thursday, December 14th, 8:00 P.M.

The three of us, Vince, Debra, and I, sat around the gleaming rosewood table in their dining room. Vince had been out of the hospital for almost two weeks. His color and strength had returned. Outwardly, his spirits had greatly improved, although he was still jumpy and nervous. What was going on inside, I had no real idea, but I thought I saw signs of healing and strengthening there as well. My sister was doing a great job of being supportive and loving without making him feel like an emotional cripple.

Vince already had been visited at home by Dick Meadows and by his Chief of Operations. Vince told me he planned to drop by the office the next day. I knew him well enough to think it wise that he not go back full-time too soon. He was a full-speed-ahead guy and once he got back in the saddle, he would need his full confidence and energy.

Debra was so relieved that Vince had been found and brought home safely that she had not really questioned me in depth. I told her generally how I had come up with Kirvesniemi's identity. I told her how I checked on his casting the ingots and how I had warned the other partners. I told her that she and Vince would never see their Lexus again and how that

377

had led to tracing the phone call and finding the motel. The rest of the story had been pretty much covered by the media.

I was not sure how much of the back-story Vince had told Debra. She was my sister and my client, but I figured that part was really up to Vince. I very much doubted those details would in any way diminish her love for Vince. I felt that Vince had led an exemplary life since those days in British Columbia and I was truly convinced that he had never ordered or expected anything serious to happen to Jari Kirvesniemi. That reasoning might or might not have cut it within the strictures of the criminal law, but it was good enough for me.

After dessert, Debra excused herself and Vince offered me an Upmann Monarch cigar. I nearly weakened. I even started rationalizing about not inhaling and all that.

"No thanks. But go ahead and enjoy one yourself. What ever happened with the Broadway Repertory Company? When I was looking for you, one of my leads was a man named Ralston. I eliminated him as a suspect, but I learned that you were worried that he'd been dipping into BRC's till."

Vince looked a little uncomfortable. "Sorry, didn't mean to pry into BRC's business," I said.

"No. It's not that. I know you would be discreet. It's just an unhappy subject. Ralston hasn't shown up at the BRC office for over a week. When the president of the board tried to contact him, Ralston's wife said he had left her suddenly. When the treasurer wanted to check something a few days ago, he discovered that the books have vanished and computer records were deleted."

"Ouch! That sounds like you were right."

"I'm afraid so. We had fidelity insurance which should cover it, unless the insurer tries to claim that Ralston was not really a salaried employee. But, any way you size it up, it isn't good news for BRC. It seems that his little auto-parts business was having cash-flow problems and that was probably what started him skimming."

Vince sighed and snipped the end of his cigar. He lit it and looked intently at me as he changed the subject. "Rick, Debra says she hired you to hunt for me. I know I've thanked you already from my heart. You saved my life... it's as simple as that! But I want to settle your fee. Whatever you normally charge, we'll triple it. No arguments."

"Vince, I was never planning on charging you. Debra's my sister. This was a family thing!"

"I understand what you're saying, but you spent three weeks of your time, twelve hours a day. You were shot at! You put your own life in jeopardy to locate me inside that building. You got the ransom money back! You're a professional and a damn good one at that! You deserve to be paid and I want to reward your skill ... your courage. I really insist. Debra agrees with me."

A fat fee sounds great to every PI and my own cash flow situation was not all that spectacular, but I was not about to accept pay for this job.

"Tell you what, Vince. You can certainly cover my expenses. I did some traveling, hotels, long-distance calls, extra personnel, that sort of thing. That's fine. As for the fee part, here's my proposal. I have this friend, Julio Mendez. He and his friend are the ones who tailed Kirvesniemi out to the packing plant. And he helped me again to close in on the con artist who had your money. You met him that night at the packing plant, but you were still a little drugged up and you may not remember."

"No, I *do* remember," he protested. "He helped save my life too!"

"Good. Anyway, Julio has started a foundation. It's a charity to provide college and vocational school scholarships for underprivileged young Latinos and Latinas. Why don't you make a donation to Julio's foundation instead of paying a fee to me?"

"That's a great idea. I'd like to do that *and* pay your fee though."

"I know, but that's the way I'd like it."

"Alright. I'll honor your wishes. By the way, Ben Turley called right after I got out of the hospital to ask how I was doing. He told me you were aware of the Davidson mine trust. I gather things became a little tense between you two on that subject."

I waved my hand dismissively. "I'm happy to say I was dead wrong. He thought he did the right thing by not mentioning the trust to me, but his hiding it made me suspicious. At that point, I was ready to pursue any lead. I hope he understands."

"I think he does. In any case, he and I talked about the trust for the first time in years. We decided to ask Youngdahl to restructure it so that Nick's widow can retain Nick's 25% interest. It seemed the least we could do!"

"Bravo! Will you be reopening the mine?"

"Only if it would facilitate a sale. Ben and I plan to sell it as soon as feasible and close that chapter of our lives for good."

Vince finished his cigar and Debra rejoined us for a game of scrabble. Vince cleaned up on us and I took that as a good sign. He was definitely going to get his life back. As for me, I went back to the houseboat thinking things have a way of working out for the best.

The techies in the forensic lab had been able to coax a little DNA off the brick from Debra's yard. Five days later they told us that the specimen taken from Berriman was a perfect match. The serial numbers on the marked bills were also a match to the list I made when Debra gathered the money. With more and more conclusive evidence piling up against them, Berriman and Despaile cut the best deal they could with the DA and pled guilty. Soon after their sentencing, Vince finally got his money back. My pal Julio received a hefty donation from Vince and Debra for his charitable foundation and got a healthy bonus from me to share with Ricardo. Vince's balance sheet was returned to normal and I had the satisfaction of getting even. And getting even in this case was as sweet as it comes.

Vince, Debra and I enjoyed a dinner at Higgins to celebrate the wrap-up of the whole affair. It had been one hell of a time for all of us. But it was over now and it had ended well. It was nearly eleven when I returned to my houseboat. I flipped on the interior lights and my eye fell on the brass enunciator. With a contented grin, I moved the handle on the enunciator from "full ahead" to "finished with engines" and headed for bed.

Acknowledgements

I wish to thank the following persons: Joyce Swan for her patience and support; Bob Miller and Del Thomas for their meticulous reading of early drafts and most helpful comments; Peter Mellini, Kathy Brault, Don Lefler, Bill Benedetto and the late Barbara Benedetto, Jerry Diethelm, and Pierre Vanrysselberghe for thoughtful critiques of the manuscript and sound suggestions to improve it; and Dr. Jerry Vergamini for information about disturbed personalities.

CPSIA information can be obtained at www.ICGtesting.com
Printed in the USA
BVOW07s0258300714

360919BV00001B/6/P